Praise for
MIRACLE BEACH

"*Miracle Beach* gives the reader a vivid sense of the Pacific North-west and the world of show jumping, but most important, it shows how characters shattered by grief can put the pieces back together in an entirely new way. Erin Celello writes of loss and resilience with a sure, honest hand."

—Heidi Jon Schmidt, author of *The House on Oyster Creek*

"*Miracle Beach* ripples with surprising twists and turns. Erin Celello has a knack for writing characters that jolt the reader with the risks they take while also creating a satisfying sense of rightness. Love is here, grief, the beauty of place, suspense, and an ending that fits just right. Erin Celello has given us a fulfilling novel in *Miracle Beach*."

—Tina Welling, author of *Cowboys Never Cry* and *Fairy Tale Blues*

"*Miracle Beach* is a lyrical, surprising novel, set in a landscape as wild as memory. Erin Celello understands that the past is always present, and she takes that age-old truth and spins it into a story of secrets, sorrow, and second chances. A marvelous debut."

—Dean Bakopoulos, author of *My American Unhappiness*

MIRACLE BEACH

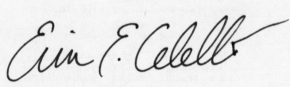

· ERIN CELELLO ·

NAL
ACCENT

NAL ACCENT
Published by New American Library,
a division of Penguin Group (USA) Inc.,
375 Hudson Street, New York, New York 10014, USA
Penguin Group (Canada), 90 Eglinton Avenue East, Suite 700, Toronto,
Ontario M4P 2Y3, Canada (a division of Pearson Penguin Canada Inc.)
Penguin Books Ltd., 80 Strand, London WC2R 0RL, England
Penguin Ireland, 25 St. Stephen's Green, Dublin 2,
Ireland (a division of Penguin Books Ltd.)
Penguin Group (Australia), 250 Camberwell Road, Camberwell,
Victoria 3124, Australia (a division of Pearson Australia Group Pty. Ltd.)
Penguin Books India Pvt. Ltd., 11 Community Centre,
Panchsheel Park, New Delhi - 110 017, India
Penguin Group (NZ), 67 Apollo Drive, Rosedale, Auckland 0632,
New Zealand (a division of Pearson New Zealand Ltd.)
Penguin Books (South Africa) (Pty.) Ltd., 24 Sturdee Avenue,
Rosebank, Johannesburg 2196, South Africa

Penguin Books Ltd., Registered Offices:
80 Strand, London WC2R 0RL, England

First published by NAL Accent, an imprint of New American Library,
a division of Penguin Group (USA) Inc.

First Printing, August 2011
3   5   7   9   10   8   6   4

 REGISTERED TRADEMARK—MARCA REGISTRADA

LIBRARY OF CONGRESS CATALOGING-IN-PUBLICATION DATA:

Celello, Erin.
Miracle Beach /Erin Celello.
p. cm.
ISBN 978-0-451-23382-0
1. Loss (Psychology)—Fiction. 2. Family secrets—Fiction.
3. Vancouver Island (B.C.)—Fiction. 4. Domestic fiction. I. Title.
PS3603.E4M57 2011
813'.6—dc22   2011005354

Set in Minion Pro • Designed by Elke Sigal

Printed in the United States of America

*For Dorothy and Marge, without whom this book
would not be, for so many reasons.*

MIRACLE BEACH

Chapter One

THE MARE'S BREATH HAD STOPPED RATTLING IN THE STALL BE-hind her. Nash lay slumped on the other side of the aisle. And all Macy could see was that damned ugly baby.

That baby, with its pimples and purple blotchy face and slightly coned head. That baby, whose mother thrust it toward Macy every time she and Nash ran into her and her doting husband, usually at Tim Hortons on Saturday mornings, as if it were a perfectly natural thing to want to hold someone else's child. As if that were what the baby would have wanted. As if Macy were even fit for such a thing.

"Go on," Nash would say. "He's not going to bite." Then he'd chuckle and shake his head, as if Macy herself were an unruly child acting out in public.

Usually she would hem and haw long enough so that Nash would hold it. But every once in a while, the baby's mother would be extra persistent and lunge at Macy. "Here," she would say. "It's easy. Easy does it."

Macy would barely get her arms out before the mother dumped the baby into them, and then she'd hold it stiffly—far out from her body, the way one would a pot of boiling water—before making an excuse as to why she and Nash had to get going.

"I'm dropping him the next time she does that," Macy told Nash once.

"It's not that baby's fault that the parents passed on the worst of both of them," Nash said. "If only he would've gotten her nose and his chin instead of the other way around." He slung an arm around Macy's shoulders and started in on how they should spend their day, but Macy didn't hear him. The words *passed on the worst of both of them* rang too loudly in her ears.

Macy didn't often give much thought to the ugly baby, save for those occasional Saturday run-ins. But here it was, its face floating in front of her, superimposed over everything: the dying mare, the folded body of her husband, the blood, the deafening quiet. And the ugly baby shook its head scornfully and clucked its teeth (this newborn had teeth) as if to say, "Look at what you've done. Look at the mess you've gone and made."

Macy thought of the bed, still unmade. Days-old glasses of Coke sitting on the kitchen table. The Pyrex pan last used to cook burritos soaking in the sink. Nash's watch placed neatly inside his Brewers cap on the dresser, just like always.

She hobbled slowly up the steps, dragging one leg up and then the other as if the signal from her brain to her limbs were working at half speed, like a newborn foal figuring out the mechanics of its body for the first time.

She missed the screen door handle on first reach, fumbling for the keys in her pocket with the other hand and then dropping them. How many times had she gone through this same routine? For how many years? It was an action she performed mindlessly before. But she was having to think her way through each step now, through each twitch of every muscle, coercing them to move so she wouldn't collapse. Her hands shook. She used one to try to steady the other.

Macy knew she had to go in eventually. But she didn't have to do it right this minute.

She dropped the keys back into her pocket and headed back down the front steps. She followed a cobblestone walkway around the back of the house through the struggling vegetable garden and out the back gate, where the bricks beneath her feet gave way to fine gravel. Light drizzle lacquered strands of hair against her face. She could smell the mix of fresh sawdust and manure that always hung heavy and sweet in the spring air. Tall grass, long overdue for mowing, licked her feet and ankles as she neared the barn. Its big old door slid aside with ease.

Gounda nickered at her, soft and low. It was his customary welcome whenever he heard her footsteps on the cement walkway. Most of the other horses "talked" only around feeding time, but not Gounda. At horse shows, people walked up and down the barn aisles throughout the day and night—but Gounda could pick out her footfall from all the others, his greeting unfailing every time.

Macy could see Gounda straining to catch a glimpse of her at the corner of his stall. He nickered again. The other horses' noses were buried in their feed. Muzzles banged inside buckets, and buckets banged against walls. Macy loved those sounds: horses being well cared for. Fed. Happy. She didn't quite know who had taken over chores at the barn, just that someone had, and for that she offered a silent thanks. There had been so many doctors to talk to, so many arrangements to make.

The mare's stall stood empty. Someone had stripped the used

bedding and replaced it with fresh, sweet-smelling shavings. The barn had been cleaned—it smelled faintly of bleach—and straightened. Pitchforks and brooms hung on their proper hooks. Nothing seemed amiss.

Too small, grimy windows distorted the lighting into hazy waves of gray, so that the stains common to any barn floor blended together—neat's-foot oil, glycerine soap, thrush ointment. But because she knew what to look for, and where, Macy could still see the faint splatter of red on the stall across from where she stood. She could still follow a spotted trail winding down the walkway.

It surprised Macy that she could look at the stains. And not only look, but examine them so closely: That was where Nash must have been standing when he surprised the mare. (Or perhaps she had surprised him.) That was where he landed after the mare had thrown him with the strength of her head and neck against a wooden support, solid as steel. That was where he slumped over on the ground, a tiny stream of impossibly red blood coming from his ear.

Macy looked for another stain, this one across the aisle from Nash, where she had crawled after catching one of the mare's flailing hooves in her stomach; where she had sat, waiting, every breath a knife, cramps rolling through her abdomen like waves. Compared to the bright trickle that ran from her husband, the blood that had spread beneath Macy was wine dark.

She had known what she was risking that night. She had known that going to the barn to help the writhing mare, her own unborn foal sitting up inside of her like an obedient dog, could be the undoing of the tiny bundle of expanding cells within Macy's own belly. The fertility specialist had warned her: strict bed rest for two weeks, no riding, no strenuous activity. Yet she had gone anyway. She had gone willingly. And by the time Macy had come to, the mare lay on her side, stone still, while Macy's mistake pooled wet and dark between her legs and onto the cement where she sat.

And then there was the imagined baby—hanging in the air and staring down at her. Tsk-tsking her. That goddamned ugly baby.

Macy marked each stain with her eyes, matter-of-factly. A detective without a case, examining the evidence only to assure herself that something had happened there, but not what or why—questions she couldn't bring herself to ask. Not yet. They skirted around her thoughts, animals stalking a perimeter.

Nash never did wake up. Doctors had disconnected tubes and wires, and she sat with him until they couldn't wait any longer. She wasn't going to be the first to leave. Not then. She had been leaving him in the tiniest of ways, over and again, since they had first met. Not because she wanted to, but because she had known, even if he hadn't, that he deserved better. And so, this one time—maybe the only time she ever had—Macy was going to stick.

Eventually, they wheeled him from the room, a sheet pulled over his face. Macy held his hand, then his fingers, and finally just the tip of one, until the motion of the rolling bed separated her skin from his. She had asked them not to do that with the sheet. She asked them to pull it up to Nash's chin if necessary, but not over his head. She explained how her husband would have hated having a sheet over his face like that, thinking of how, when he dressed, Nash would bunch the bottom of the shirt as close to the collar as possible, the way women gather their panty hose in a bunch at the toe before unfolding them up the leg.

Nash would pull a shirt on and let it hang around his neck before struggling his arms through their respective sleeves, never lingering with his head inside while the arms poked through, like so many other people did. And even though she knew it couldn't matter to him then, it made Macy feel better when the attendants stopped to peel the gauzy fabric down to his shoulders.

After that she went about the business of gathering his things. Most of his stuff had been placed together in a small cupboard. Nash's jeans, henley, and red fleece were in a plastic bag, though Macy didn't know why anyone had saved them for her. They were unusable now, in awkward, scissored pieces and crusty with blood. She had wanted to pull the shirt to her face, to smell him, make him real for just a moment longer. But not there. Not then.

Someone had folded his socks, rolled one inside the other with sharp, neat corners. She unfolded them, balled each one separately, and stuck a sock into each shoe, just as Nash liked to do. That habit of his had always driven her crazy. She chalked it up to laziness; he claimed it helped his shoes hold their form. She thought of them, then—rows of shoes stacked in cubbies at the back of Nash's closet that his feet would never slip into again. That thought, the stupid shoes, almost crushed her.

Almost. What actually did was stepping through the hospital's sliding doors. Macy sucked in the fresh, bright air and choked on it. She felt her legs give way, like the bones in them had disintegrated right then and there. Because, she realized, Nash remained inside. Because he wouldn't ever step through that front entrance designed only for the living. Because she would have to drive away from this place without him. Because she no longer had a reason to come back.

In the end, she didn't drive away from there. She couldn't. And so her sister, Regan, did. And when Macy told Regan that she couldn't go home, Regan took Macy back to the hotel where they had been staying, across from the hospital, and tucked her into bed, still fully clothed. Macy couldn't bear the thought of climbing into the bed she had shared with Nash for nine years, alone forevermore, yet she couldn't stop herself from imagining how she would have to do just that. Soon.

Macy willed the crying to start. She wanted to sob the body-racking moans that a good widow should. She thought that maybe that was the thing to help the hurt ebb even a little, the salve to apply to the gaping wound her life had become. But she couldn't eke out a single drop. Instead, she lay in bed, tracing the neat beige lines of the hotel wallpaper with her eyes. Up and down, and down and up.

Now Macy ducked into Gounda's stall and situated herself in the far front corner. He stood against the back wall, resting a massive hind foot. He craned his neck to look over at her. Then he took a step toward her and lowered his head.

He stared at her with big tar-pit eyes, cast soft and low, and Macy swore just then that he would have wept if able to. There seemed a sorrow reflected so deep in those eyes that it panged her. He snorted and sniffed. She wondered whether he made the connection that his own mother had died, too, that they had both lost someone. If nothing else, he had to know the agony the mare had gone through, screaming and bleeding to death in the next stall with a struggling-to-be-born foal inside of her.

Even if Gounda knew, Macy decided, he would likely have forgotten it all by now. Horses were supposed to have tiny little brains not designed for things like long-term memory. She felt both sorry for and jealous of him. What she wouldn't give to be able to forget that night, yet Nash was the only thing she let herself think of. Standing around with a small group after the burial, she had found herself smiling—almost laughing—at a story one of Nash's friends told, but it didn't feel right. Like outgrowing a favorite pair of blue jeans, it seemed Macy had outgrown happiness in one short chain of events. Her. The mare. Nash. She had only to think back to the cacophony of thrashing and moaning and screaming to remind herself.

Other times, she tried to remember Nash as he had been, but in a cruel twist, those memories never came back as vividly as the ones of that night. Mere days after Nash died, there were times when it seemed the picture of him in Macy's mind was quickly following suit. She would try to conjure him, but only his lips, or the color of his hair, or a certain splattering of freckles on his forearm would jell together. A portrait of disjointed parts. The rest of the picture lagged behind, faded or altogether blank. And she'd feel as if she were failing him all over again.

Times like those, panic set in. If she was forgetting parts of him already, when would her mind empty itself of his image completely? In a couple of years? One year? A few months? Just the other day, while walking across the hotel room en route to the bathroom, it had happened again. She got only his dimples, but no eyes. No smile. She stopped herself then, midstride, and flipped through old memories until she found one where his features were whole and intact. Only then did she let herself step forward.

But really, there was nothing the matter with her memory. She knew full well that her favorite mare—Gounda's dam—was gone, that the tiny bundle of multiplying cells inside her was gone. Nash was gone.

"Just the two of us, bud," she said to Gounda. She dragged a knuckle softly against his muzzle. He wasn't the only horse in the barn, but he was the only one who had given himself wholly to her. And he was the only one to whom she had ever fully belonged.

Sitting on a pile of hay at the back of Gounda's stall, her knees pulled up to her chin, Macy shook. She stuffed her hands deep inside the cuffs of her sweatshirt and raised one to either side of her neck, now slick with tears. Gounda edged closer to her, one cautious step at a time, until his boxy muzzle rested on one of her fists. He blew his breath across her ear in a slow, breezy lullaby. A sweet musk of molasses and grain.

Macy breathed with him.

In and out.

In and out.

Chapter Two

MAGDA TURNED HER RING OVER AND OVER ON HER FINGER, staring at it instead of her husband.

"You need to pick up that phone and call her, Magda Allen," Jack said. "Right now. Or today, at least. You need to call her today."

It was a modest ring—a thin gold band with a tiny chip of princess-cut diamond fastened to it. For a while, after he had built up a successful business, Jack had insisted on getting her a bigger, flashier ring that would stand up against those of her friends, but Magda wanted to keep the original. She liked to say that it reminded her of where they had come from.

"Just check in, see how she's doing. This is as hard for her as it is for us, you know," Jack added.

Magda raised her eyes to him slowly, deliberately, and spoke to him in the same way. "What did you just say?" She pictured the words leaving her mouth like needle-sharp icicles.

"I'm not trying to make comparisons," Jack said. "I'm just saying that Macy's going through a lot, too. Nash was her husband."

Magda felt a familiar rage start to boil deep within her, bitter and heavy. She had kept it in check since the incident at the funeral.

"But *I* was his *mother*," she wanted to scream at Jack. She stood and walked to the other side of the kitchen table, where Jack stood with arms held open, waiting for Magda to fall into them so he could console and hold her. Instead, Magda lifted her right hand and struck him across the cheek. She didn't see whether he held a hand to his face, or know whether he crumpled onto one of the chairs. She was already out the door.

The stench hit Magda as she walked toward the river. Green Bay stank in the months that stretched from spring to early summer. No matter which way the wind blew it assaulted the senses— from one direction, thawing cow manure; from the other, the acrid tang of surrounding paper mills.

Each time Magda drove or flew into Green Bay, the city's ugliness struck her. Jack loved it, called it "charming." But she saw only the sprawling factories spewing slow plumes of smoke, nestled in among warehouses and strip malls and the dingy gray smog that seemed to envelop it all. When Magda pictured whichever Egg—she could never remember if it was East or West—in *The Great Gatsby*, it looked a lot like Green Bay.

She and Jack had made their home outside of the city, in a suburb filled with old, historic homes—streets of miniature mansions with rows of massive oak trees that formed thick canopies over the neighborhoods. There was a river over which a private college and most of the houses, including theirs, stood watch, and though it had been designated a Superfund project, thanks to the carcinogens that local paper companies had dumped into the water, the river still made for a pretty picture.

That was where she headed now. Their house was only about a half mile from the college, from Magda's favorite spot—a grassy, parklike area in front of the student union close to the Fox River. She liked that it was private, despite being part of campus, yet there was still plenty to watch—the crew team practicing, students running along the Main Street Bridge. Magda usually liked to sit with her back against one of the large oaks and slide her bare toes through the grass, but a picnic table nearby provided a good alternative option on days when the ground was wet.

Today she climbed onto the tabletop and brought her knees to her chin, wrapping her arms around her legs. Carvings scarred the picnic table's surface. Jagged hearts, oversimplified beer mugs, and roughed-out pornographic carvings among an alphabet of initials. She labeled each carving in her mind: Lovesick. Drunk. Perverted. All of the above.

Magda let a finger trace the grooves like diminutive canyons, the serrated edges worn smooth with time. She remembered Jack carving their initials, framed by a heart, into a tree at the top of a mountain he had dragged her up during a trip to Michigan's Upper Peninsula back when they were first dating. Jack's carved heart had looked just like a cliché come to life. She made the mistake of saying that, only to watch Jack's face harden, then fall after he thought she had looked away. She had vowed to be more careful with him then, to watch her tongue. And she had, for the most part. Except for today. Though, if she were being honest, her words weren't the problem. It was that she was fresh out of words, and had used her hand instead.

Magda's eye caught something to the right of her foot. Initials. NA+MA. She reached down and let her fingers follow the grooved letters, Nash's and Macy's initials. Or maybe not. Macy always signed her name Macy Armstrong Allen, or Macy A. Allen. She said it was a safety check, that if anyone ever stole her checkbook or credit card she could prove it wasn't her signature, because most people wouldn't include the middle initial or name. Magda thought it was because she was a snob.

Almost one year before, Nash and Macy had visited Jack and Magda over the Fourth of July, which coincided with Nash's thirty-second birthday and Macy's thirty-fifth. To celebrate, Jack and Magda had thrown them a real bash. They were so excited to have their son home for a holiday for once. Macy always seemed to have other plans at Christmas or Thanksgiving, which she didn't even celebrate. There was always a horse show she just couldn't miss, and Nash never wanted her to spend the holidays alone, so along he went, leaving Magda and Jack with only each other. It was a far cry from the holiday visions of family that Magda had conjured while pregnant with their only son.

Magda, determined to make their visit memorable, invited all of Nash's old friends from high school, college, and the bank where he had worked in Milwaukee. They put up a white tent in the backyard, had Pierre's do the catering, and even hired entertainment—a small jazz band with a lead singer who was just the most darling little blonde Magda had ever seen. They rented a small dance floor, and Magda hung strings of white lights inside the tent and on the bushes around the backyard. She bought tiki lights for along the patio and the walkway leading to the back gate. She floated candles in the pool. Everything looked positively enchanting.

Only one year ago.

Magda remembered standing off to one side, near the bushes at the edge of the yard, watching Nash sway Macy awkwardly around the dance floor. At one point Nash stepped on Macy's toes and Macy chucked him on the arm, holding her own arms stiff to keep him away from her. They had laughed at each other, and then Nash took Macy's face between his hands and kissed her lips, and then her forehead, lingering there and closing his eyes. Macy fell into the circle Nash's arms had made around her.

As much as Magda hated to admit it, as much as she had suspected it wouldn't last, she had to admit one thing: Love looked a lot like that.

It was what she had always wanted; it was what she didn't think she had ever quite gotten right.

She had walked over to Jack then, thinking that if you couldn't have that feeling on a night like tonight—a night that felt and looked like romance incarnate—when could you? She pictured twirling with him under strings of soft white lights and the even softer stars above, the rough skin of his hand gentle on her cheek, his arms solid and strong around her. She wondered how long it had been since they had danced. How long it had been since they had even embraced for more than the cursory good-bye or hello. They weren't unusual, she and Jack. Magda knew that. They had worked hard building a life together and raising a son. Theirs had never been a relationship like in the movies, but if there was ever a time for a little magic, surely this was it.

Jack had been standing with two members of his regular golf foursome, slapping backs and downing beers while debating the Packers' pickups in that spring's draft. The band had just struck the first notes of Van Morrison's "Moondance." Magda placed a hand on Jack's arm and smiled up at him. "I'd love this dance, Mr. Allen. May I?"

"You know I don't dance, Magda," he said, laughing as if she had told a joke. "Never have, prolly never will." Then he turned his back to her and inserted himself right back into the conversation, which had moved on to debating whether Brett Favre would or wouldn't stay retired.

"The man just didn't want to dance," Magda's best friend, Ginny Fischer, had said to her later that night. "It's not like he said he was leaving you."

But Magda couldn't help but wonder—then and now—whether that wasn't exactly what he had been doing.

Magda tried to get comfortable on that picnic table, sitting on the top and leaning back on her elbows, but they dug into the wood. Then she moved to the bench, only to find the same problem with her derriere, which she would have thought had more than enough padding.

Now a handful of college students had started to make their way down the hill toward her. They were about to commence a cookout, by the looks of it, and surely didn't need a sad old woman ruining their party. So Magda stood up and brushed the tabletop debris from her back cheeks, straightened her jeans and blouse, and grabbed her flip-flops. They weren't the most practical things to walk in, but as soon as the weather inched anywhere near sixty degrees, Magda couldn't stand to have anything else on her feet. Her favorite thing about summer was that her toes were finally freed from their sock prisons.

In her head, the scene from Nash's funeral played on repeat as she walked the familiar route back to the house. She couldn't believe that Macy had insisted on having the funeral on the island, anyway, when Nash's home had always been Wisconsin. Where his parents—his parents!—still lived. It was where Jack had taught Nash to swim. Where Nash and his friends spent summers riding their bikes to the Dairy Queen down the street, sitting on the pier behind it all afternoon, daring one another to jump into the Fox River to see if the water would melt their skin like urban legend said it would.

It was where Nash, after hockey practice one night close to Christmas, had convinced his entire Squirt team to go caroling with him on their way home. By the time he showed up, almost two hours late, Magda had been beside herself with fright and sent him straight to his room. Days later, she found out from one of the other mothers what had happened. When Magda had asked Nash why he hadn't just told her why he had been late, he shrugged and said, "I broke the rules."

That was her Nash. And who could blame Magda, really, for being upset that he was now, forever, thousands of miles away? Her heartache and anger had mixed and calcified into a sort of organ inside her. She should have been able to drive a short distance and sit by his grave site. Instead, she was relegated to the banks of the Fox River, watching a group of college students unpack a haphazard-looking picnic and attempt to light a grill. If Magda had wanted to place flowers at his grave site, say on his birthday, or on any day she felt the need to tether her grief to his final resting place, she'd have to pay hundreds of dollars for an airline ticket and fly more than four hours each way. Macy had insisted they move back to British Columbia after the wedding because her barn was there, her trainer, her horses. It was all her, her, her. And now, because of Macy and her stupid horses, Nash was dead.

She had only whispered it, at the wake, to Macy's sister. She knew she shouldn't have, but not because it was untrue. She had caused a scene, and that was one thing a lady never did. But all these people hugging Macy, touching her cheek tenderly, offering to help in any way they could. *What about me?* Magda had wanted to scream. He was *my son*! But the people kept on coming. Wrapping their arms around Macy, helping her play the victim when it was her own damn fault. And all day they kept on coming, repeating only generic consolations to Jack and Magda—"I'm so sorry for your loss" or "Nash was such a wonderful young man; I'm sure you're proud of him"—because hardly anyone there knew them.

And then there was Macy's sister, Regan. Sitting in the alcove near the bathroom after it was all over, on a stupidly bright paisley love seat with a gob of tissues in her hand, eyes puffy red, cheeks slick. She caught Magda's eye.

"Oh, Magda. Are you holding up okay?"

Magda had nodded.

"Will you look at me!" Macy's sister said. "Here you are, makeup intact, and I'm a mess. I'm so sorry, Magda. Can I do anything? Get you anything?" She reached out and touched Magda's shoulder. Magda knew the gesture was out of kindness, but it still made her feel sick.

"Your sister did this." The words had tumbled out before Magda even knew what she was saying. But she couldn't have stopped them regardless.

Macy's sister stared at her, mouth agape. "Magda, you know that's not true," she finally said. "It was an accident."

"And now this time . . ." Magda continued on as if Regan hadn't said a word. Her voice faltered, just for a second. "This time, it's for good." Magda looked hard at Macy's sister, opening her eyes wide and cocking her chin, as if to ask Regan if she understood. She could feel the blood vessels in her face and neck straining to explode. She could feel herself redden.

Macy's sister had stood up then, one of her hands working the tissue in it into a firm little Ping-Pong ball. Magda could tell that Regan didn't know what to say to her—a woman who was technically family, but whom she had met only once before. This woman who had lost her only child, her only son. Regan looked as if she couldn't decide whether to take Magda into her arms or lash back at her. Before any decisions had been made, or acted upon, Regan had caught sight of Macy, looking as if she would crumple right in on herself, like she might melt from the grief. She had somehow heard the whole exchange.

"How could you say that, Magda? How?" Each time Macy repeated the word *how*, it sounded more and more pleading, and grating, to Magda's ears.

Magda didn't answer her. She had simply turned and walked out.

That was two months ago. It was the last time she had seen Macy, the last time they had spoken.

In those two months, Magda had replayed that scene in her head, willing herself to regret what she said. Was she overly harsh? Perhaps. But wasn't she also right? And shouldn't—couldn't—someone cut her just a little tiny shred of slack? She was his mother, after all. He was her son.

Was. That one word, three tiny letters, had become a cannonball capable of bringing Magda to her knees.

She plodded along North Broadway toward home, remembering by rote the places in the sidewalk that rose unexpectedly like mini seismic faults, and the places where it suddenly dropped off. She never had to look down to check the topography of her path. If she had, Magda likely would have missed the tiny, wilted, and nearly obscured Estate Sale sign at the corner of Fulton Street.

There were only three things that made Magda more instantly sad than those two words: semi trailers full of cattle, their noses jutting out all pink and wet and hopeful in spite of the EAT MORE MEAT sticker on the back; elderly people eating alone; and bloated animals left on the sides of roads. Because estate sales meant only one thing: the person who owned that house died, and their things that they loved and valued in life were sitting somewhere unwanted, waiting to be scavenged.

Just those two words—*estate sale*—in a newspaper or on a sign would cause Magda's chest to constrict, her lip to quiver, her hands to shake. She weathered those two words much the same way others did news stories of child or animal abuse or war. Regardless, she always went. She always went in.

The house could not have been more nondescript: white vinyl siding and two stories tall. It had precast cement front steps and a wrought-iron railing spotted with rust. Faded green-and-white-striped fiberglass awnings capped each of the two front windows, which looked out onto Franklin Street like a pair of sad, lidded eyes. Magda drew a deep breath and stepped through the front door, greeted by a musty haze and a perky young woman with long brown ringlets.

"Take a look around and be sure to let me know if you have any questions," she said to Magda. "There are some great finds to be had!" Then she winked.

Magda wanted to slap her. *Great finds. Show some respect*, Magda thought. But she just nodded.

Magda wandered the first floor—sitting room, dining room, kitchen. She brushed her fingertips along the backs of two Queen Anne chairs, an end table, a Zenith floor radio that looked like it had been purchased only the day before. And although she knew it was silly, Magda apologized to each: *It's not that you weren't wanted. I'm sure they didn't mean to abandon you.* Either this person hadn't had children or the children hadn't taken a single item from the home. Silverware, cups and saucers, even a vase on the dining room table, created the impression that the former occupant had run to the store for a carton of milk in the middle of cleaning out their cupboards and would return at any minute.

Eventually she made her way upstairs. That was where they always were, after all. The pictures. Time spent on the lower floors of estate sales was never about browsing. It simply allowed Magda to work up the gumption to tackle the upper levels.

Once upstairs, Magda headed to the very end of the hallway, guessing that to be the direction of the master bedroom. She was correct. A handmade quilt, priced at fifty dollars, covered the bed. One could buy the entire bedroom set—a brass double bed, bedside table, and dresser with attached mirror, for only three hundred dollars. Magda wasn't browsing, though. She was after one thing: the pictures that sat atop the dresser, as they almost always did.

There were three picture frames of various sizes: one with a man and woman posed stiffly in wedding garb, wearing thin, nervous smiles; another with the same man and woman in a rowboat, now much older, wearing life vests and each holding an oar, laughing; and the last a faded, reddish-tinted portrait of a serious toddler posed behind a giggling baby, the baby's arms waving wildly above its head.

"These are beautiful frames, aren't they?" the perky sales agent gushed to Magda.

Magda could feel her eyes growing wet. Frames? These were someone's children once. Someone's photographs. They should be wanted. Remembered.

"How much?" Magda croaked, picking up the picture of the

two babies and holding it in one hand outstretched toward the agent.

"Oh, for that one? Are you sure? The other two are much nicer. But for that one, five dollars."

Five dollars. For an antique frame. For someone's memories. For a snapshot of their life, left behind.

Magda fished a handful of dollars from her pocket and handed them to the woman.

"Anything else?" the agent asked her. "There's an absolutely fabulous floor lamp in the next room over. Not to be missed!"

Magda shook her head, holding the frame tight against her. "No," she said. "Just this."

Magda, still clutching the five-dollar picture frame, peered into the garage window to make sure Jack's truck was gone. She would do this—this thing he was insisting she do. But she wanted to do it on her own terms. Alone.

In the kitchen, Magda stared at the phone. It hung on the long wall near the kitchen table. That table had always seemed too large with its four chairs, and now it looked more so, even if that third chair with its back to the wall hadn't been occupied regularly for years.

Maybe Macy wouldn't be home, Magda thought. It was the middle of the afternoon, after all. She'd be out with her horses or grocery shopping or doing any number of things people did, not sitting at home waiting for the phone to ring. Magda could just leave a message on the answering machine. She could say she tried, she'd apologize for her behavior earlier, and then Jack would be happy.

But what would she say? "Macy? Magda calling. I would like to straighten things out"? No. She didn't really want to straighten anything out. Jack wanted that. Maybe someday she'd be ready to. Maybe, but not now. Plus, she didn't want to lie. Ladies didn't lie—they might tell a little fib now and then, but never blatant lies. How about, "Macy? Magda. Please call. If I don't hear from you I will try you later on tonight." That would work, she thought. Nice and businesslike, not too gushy or personal. She could always be busy later tonight.

She dialed the phone number, willing an automated voice to answer and instruct her to leave a message.

"Hello?"

Magda froze. Her answering-machine speech teetered uselessly on the tip of her tongue.

"Hello—o? Anyone there?"

"Macy?"

"Yes."

"It's Magda."

"Oh, Christ."

"Macy, please. Language?"

Macy let out a loud sigh. "So you rang me up to give me a lecture, is that it, Magda? That's fantastic. Just the thing I was hoping for, actually."

"I just don't, well, I don't really appreciate when people take the Lord's name . . ." Magda's mind went blank and she trailed off. She twirled the phone cord around her finger. The cord made her feel hemmed in. She needed a cordless to pace the kitchen properly in situations like this.

"What?"

"Excuse me, dear?"

"What, Magda? What do you want?"

Magda knew this call was a bad idea. Darn that Jack. "I . . . I . . . I just wanted to talk."

"I'm not sure now is a good time," Macy said.

"Oh, well—okay. I just thought we might . . . But perhaps another time would be better, then."

"I doubt there's going to be a good time."

"Well, I just thought I might see how you're . . ." Magda coughed, finding the words had lodged themselves in her throat. "How you're hanging in—"

"I'm fine, Magda."

There was a long pause. Then Macy added, "So?"

"So?" Magda parroted, confused.

"You called me," Macy said. "Why? What's going on?"

Magda's thoughts reeled. Why had she called? Why had she let Jack talk her into this?

"Was this Jack's idea?" Macy asked. She was laughing, then. Cackling. "It was, wasn't it?"

Magda sputtered like a car that had run out of gas. Her mind had gone blank. There wasn't one word in it for her mouth to serve up.

"Oh, Magda," Macy said, still chuckling. "Well, I actually should get going. You take care."

After a spell, the dial tone jolted Magda from the trance of staring at the sparkling white tile under her feet. She was surprised to find the picture of two nameless, smiling babies still clutched tight against her breast.

Upstairs, in her sewing room, Magda surveyed the shelf that ran along three walls and held framed pictures of every shape and size that had only two common threads: each was of a baby Magda had never met and would never know, and each had been left behind. Discarded. Unwanted.

She placed the picture of the two smiling babies she had bought that afternoon at the estate sale between one of an

African-American toddler with wispy pigtails in her curly hair secured by purple bows, and another black-and-white photo from the early 1900s of a wide-eyed, wide-smiling androgynous baby in a lacy smock and posed on a chair. Jack had once called the collection of photographs "creepy," so Magda tended to keep the door to her sewing room closed. But it comforted her to see them, to sit surrounded by them as she worked to the steady hum of her sewing machine. It gave her a sense of pride and satisfaction to give them each a place of honor. Some of the babies in the pictures had long ago passed on. Others might still be very much alive. Regardless, there in Magda Allen's little sewing room, they would have a place. They would be remembered.

Magda stared at the cluster of moles on Jack's back, illuminated by a faint light that filtered in from the street lamps. A small spattering just under his right shoulder blade looked, to her, like the constellation of Ursa Major. She had taken an astronomy course a few years back at the college, just for fun—something to take up a little free time. It turned out to be anything but fun. All the math and formulas and scientific figuring were way more than she had bargained for, but she stuck it out because she would have received only a seventy percent refund by the time she was in over her head. In the end, though, the only thing she took away from the course was the odd ability to pick out the Ursas—and only the Ursas—from a canopy of stars. The Dippers, Big and Little, Orion's Belt—all the easy ones were lost on her.

Jack's mini Ursa comforted her, though. It made her feel secure. She knew that if he were ever burned beyond recognition or maimed, and she had to identify his body, they wouldn't even need to match his dental records. "Just flip him over," she would tell the coroner, and she'd look for the unique little cluster of brown dots on his upper midback, a little right of center. Her knowledge of them was intimacy that went beyond sex or the twining of psyches. It was primitive, basic, true. The fact that she knew his back so well meant that she had spent years studying Jack as he slept, always turned away from her.

Magda had slowly learned that Jack's feelings toward her had absolutely nothing to do with his sleeping position, and everything to do with the simple, thoughtful things he did: buying Weidner Center tickets when she had mentioned only in passing a show she wanted to see, even though he would rather sit through an entire evening of infomercials; coming home after a long day at work and mowing the lawn in the growing dark because he knew they were having guests that weekend and Magda wanted things to look nice for them; or making her favorite dinner—rib eye with butter-soaked mushrooms and twice-baked potatoes—at even the inkling of a bad day, and sometimes for no apparent reason at all.

He was a good husband. Great, even. Definitely the best husband out of any of their friends. He had never stayed out all night, had never been a big drinker. And Magda could say with absolute certainty that he never seriously considered taking up with another woman. Once in a while she'd catch him gawking, but that was fine. She'd give him a look, and he'd smile and laugh and say, "I can still look at the menu, Magda." And she'd wink and say to him, "Just don't order anything."

He was solid, practical, dedicated. But even on the best days, it felt to Magda as if she merely had a great roommate, not a husband. Other days, it felt like they hardly knew each other.

Like tonight. Tonight she was obviously upset, and Jack hadn't said anything even mildly comforting to her. He hadn't said anything at all, actually, even after she had apologized. He had nodded and kissed her on the cheek before heading to the back deck with a Miller Lite in one hand and a cigar in the other.

Magda ran her fingers back and forth over his shoulder, light enough so she could say she just wanted to touch him, but hard enough so he'd definitely wake up. He brushed her hand off his shoulder. She stopped for a second, and then started up again.

"Magda, knock it off."

"Are you sleeping?" she whispered.

"Was."

"Oh." She started rubbing his shoulder again, harder this time.

"Magda, enough. Go to sleep."

"I can't sleep. I'm all wound up, Jack. I need to talk." Although she was trying to whisper, Magda knew she wasn't. It was one of those womanly traits God had for some inexplicable reason denied her. It never failed: At brunch after Mass, in the church's basement, Magda would try to contribute something to the group's gossip—about how Sally Pierce had once again signed up to bring a dish and failed to do so, or why the Van Antwerps and their six children couldn't once—just once—be on time for services instead of marching up the aisle right behind the priest—and she'd be promptly shushed by all the other women. Magda had eventually learned to hold her tongue and stay silent, since she sure as Pete couldn't manage to be quiet about things.

Jack rolled over, sighing. "And *I* need to be up in four hours. Come on, can't we just do this tomorrow?"

He was patronizing her now. More than anything, Magda hated when Jack talked to her like this, as if she were a child. "Fine," she said. She rolled away from him and glared at the wall.

"Listen, Magda, you need to knock this shit off." He rarely ever swore around her. At least she knew she was getting to him.

"Knock what off? I just want to talk."

"About what? Let me guess. About how you're having a tough time? About how no one is being supportive enough of you? It's always about *you*, Magda."

"That's not fair."

"Oh, no? Then tell me, just what is it you so desperately need to talk about at one thirty in the goddamn morning?"

Magda kept staring at the wall. She wasn't going to help him mock her.

"For Christ's sake, Magda. You woke me up—now you're going to lie there and sulk. Tell me what's wrong."

"Lord's name, Jack."

"Oh, for crying out loud. Good night, Magda."

Magda breathed as loudly as she could, and when that didn't get Jack's attention, she started sniffling.

Still no response.

"Jack?"

"What?"

"It's this thing with Macy."

She was greeted only by silence from Jack's side of the bed, but she could feel him listening.

"It didn't go well this afternoon," she admitted.

"I know it didn't, Magda."

"Well, then, why didn't you ask me about it?"

"Because I knew."

Magda felt Jack's hand on her shoulder, rolling her toward him. He made Magda look him in the eye. "Magda, there's something that you've somehow gotten through life without knowing that you need to learn pretty quickly."

"What?"

"How to say, 'I'm sorry.'"

"I said I was sorry to you," she said.

"Any other time, Magda? To anyone else?"

"All the time. What, you want me to list them off for you? Tick them off on my fingers like this?" She held up one hand and flicked the tips of each finger with the other. One of her nails felt like the edge of a saw, and she realized with a start that she hadn't resumed her regular manicure schedule.

"He was my son, Jack."

"He was mine, too," Jack said. "But that's what you can't seem to get. He was my son; he was Macy's husband. And no matter what you think of her, she loved him. They shared a life." He rolled onto his back and sighed. "Did you even come close to apologizing to her?"

Magda rolled onto her back as well. She and Jack stared upward at the ceiling, its water stain a murky eye above their bed.

"I didn't have a chance," Magda said after a span of silence, during which she tried, and failed, to match her breathing to Jack's. His breaths were too deep, too far apart. "She hung up on me."

Magda nearly added, "But I don't think I could have," but she stopped herself.

As if Jack had heard the words rattling around inside her head, he took a long inhale, as if he were going to say something else. Instead, he exhaled, blowing air out through his nose. They turned onto their sides, then, almost in unison, backs to each other and facing opposite walls.

Magda watched the moon's light dance over the tree branches outside their window, plating each leaf with a shadowy silver. She couldn't see the moon, but she knew it hung somewhere in that night sky. Kind of like Nash, she thought. She could sense him sometimes. Even though she knew he wasn't there with her, really, he was somewhere. Somewhere out there.

And then came the vapor-thin dreams of Nash that she conjured every night on the border of sleep: nursing him in the wee hours of the night, his little eyes focused on her and his tiny hands impossibly soft and warm against the skin of her breast. His first day of school, when he ran back to her from the bus stop, placed a hand on either side of her face, and said, "Don't cry, Mommy. I'm going to have a great day!" Watching him shoot free throws in their driveway. Coming downstairs late at night to find a high-school-age Nash, head capped with thick waves of orange hair, hunched over his homework, lips moving silently. His senior state debate performance—how handsome he looked that night in the navy blue suit they had bought him from JoS. A. Bank especially for that occasion. His graduation from college, and how Magda had been struck for the very first time, seeing him in his cap and gown, by how much like a full-grown man he looked, and how surprised she was, all of a sudden, that he barely resembled the freckled, glasses-wearing little boy of only a few years before.

Somewhere, on the outer edges of those memories, Jack's voice floated in and said, "I'm flying out to visit Macy next week," and Magda settled deeper into Nash, not much caring any longer what the hell Jack did.

Chapter Three

"ANOTHER DRINK, SIR?"

Jack consulted his Beam and Coke and waved the flight attendant off with a half smile, so as not to seem rude. He had finished more than half of the drink, but had sipped it so slowly that the melted ice kept the glass nearly full.

He had never been a big drinker, not even in college. But Magda still had a thing against Jim, Jack, Jose, or any of their kin. Not because she had a problem, or because she was the wife or daughter of someone with a problem. No, it was purely on principle. As long as he had known her, Magda had maintained complete control over every aspect of her life. Her sobriety was no different.

Another flight attendant was already standing over him with latex gloves and a garbage bag, motioning at his drink. *Jesus*, Jack thought, *they sure don't give you any time to leisurely enjoy a drink anymore.* Then he realized it was probably just another moneymaking ploy by the airlines. It wasn't enough that they sold you a box lunch for the price of a fancy restaurant dinner these days; they rushed you through a drink just to get you to buy another one.

But Jack aimed to please, so he held up one finger to the lingering flight attendant and nodded. She smiled at him. Magda wouldn't have been happy, but Magda wasn't there.

He figured that the occasional pile of vomit on the sidewalk or in the yard or in the bushes in front of their house, left there by the college students stumbling home from the bars, only helped to reaffirm Magda's attitude toward alcohol. One Sunday, Mikey, their old chocolate Lab, trucked through a pile of puke and tracked it all through the house. Magda was pissed. But not as pissed as when one of those students stumbled to his Jeep at two a.m. and drove it right into their front porch, demolishing the latticework, the front steps, and Magda's prized rosebushes.

Jack suspected she mostly abstained to prove that she could, to look the part of being just a little above everyone else. That was Magda—stubborn as a mule in heat. One night not too long after their wedding, Jack joked about her bad driving skills on the way out to dinner and Magda downright refused to drive for the next two years. Renewed her license when it came time, but never set one ass cheek in the driver's seat. Made him sorry for mocking her. If she wanted, she could sure drive a point home. Drive a nail into his head, he liked to say. He handled Magda with kid gloves from there on in. She mistook it for respect, but it made her happy regardless. And that was easier for both of them.

Right about then, though, Jack would have taken hours of scolding from Magda over the constant yapping of the lady in seat 7D. He had been at the office at four that morning and put in a solid four hours of work on a new deal his concrete company was negotiating before his flight left Austin Straubel at nine thirty a.m. All he wanted was to grab a little shut-eye before they touched down.

At the same time Jack's eyelids slid closed, he heard the woman in 7D say, "So that's why I'm going. And you? Are you on business or pleasure this trip?" The words sounded like they were doing loop-de-loops from her mouth, as if she were trying to sound uplifting and urbane. Jack thought she sounded like a fruitcake.

He turned his head toward her, opened his eyes, and gave her a wide, thin smile before closing them again.

He didn't want to be rude. He just didn't know what to answer.

Really, if he was to be completely honest, Jack had booked this flight because when he tried to fall asleep at night, all he could manage to picture was Nash. Not Nash's lopsided smile or the way he called him "Pops," but Nash laid out in the hospital, the right side of his face blotched in the painful hues of black, purple-blue, and yellow, scales of old blood crusted in his hair and in patches over his face. Nash with tubes running in and out of him. Nash lying cold and clammy and stiff in the morgue, his eyes fixed on nothing, no longer able to see at all. The thought of morticians cutting him open, no blood rising up to meet the knife. The blood that should be bubbling up, that should be bright, neon red, resting in black puddles under Nash's shoulder blades, his buttocks. Jack knew it was beyond morbid to think like this, but the images scuttled around like insects through a crack. He would try to clear his mind, to pray even, but nothing worked. There was no stopping them.

But how to explain that to the woman in 7D? How was he supposed to fit that into a quip of small talk that didn't stray outside the bounds of normal, decent conversation? It was easier to let the woman think he was an asshole.

He thought back to the week before, to the phone call with

Macy, when he had let her know he was coming. That was right after Magda had slapped him and walked out, right about when he figured that he couldn't keep on like he had been. Macy had seemed appreciative and receptive—as soon as she learned that Magda wasn't coming and wasn't even aware of Jack's plans—but her voice never registered anything approaching excitement.

"If it's too weird, or if it gets to be too much for either of us, I'll be on the first flight back to Wisconsin," he had promised Macy. "I miss him in a way I can't quite put my finger on. I need to try to be close to him."

"Jack, it's only been a couple months," Macy said. "I'm still getting my bearings. We all are."

"Nine weeks," Jack said.

"Nine weeks," Macy repeated. "And you really think this is a good idea? That it'll help?"

"I can't think of anything else to try," he said.

"It's hard to know what to do," Macy said. Her voice had been steady and much more distant than the thousand-plus miles that separated them. It wasn't the warm response he had hoped for. Although with everything that had happened, he could hardly have blamed her. "Okay, then," she had said. "Okay."

But what he couldn't come close to telling the nosy woman next to him, what he hadn't told Macy—what he hadn't told anyone—was that he had started to think that maybe Nash wasn't really dead after all. That he was simply still in British Columbia. Jack would walk through his living room and past Nash's Little League team portraits and pictures of Nash as he grew, looking so impossibly alive that Jack had a hard time believing that he wasn't.

And so, even though he knew it wasn't rational, Jack still couldn't help hoping that Nash would be there, waiting as always, when he walked off the plane.

A cool Vancouver breeze flapped through Jack's button-down shirt as he stepped through the terminal doors and walked to the general passenger pickup curb. After hours of stale airplane air, and after weeks and weeks of relentlessly hot weather back home, it felt refreshing. Lately, in Wisconsin, the humidity made it feel as though a thin sheet of rubber had settled down over everything. Cool and brisk was a welcome change.

It wasn't long before Jack heard the low rumble of Macy's truck approaching. It was one hell of a truck, one he wished he could justify owning—a one-ton diesel dually, black, with an extended cab, a long box, leather interior, and a GPS system. It was a man's truck, but Macy handled it with ease, and her demure frame even gave it a touch of elegance.

She whipped into a curb space Jack would never have thought to try, reached over, and freed the door handle.

"Jump in!" Macy said, throwing the door open. "They get pissy around here if you stop for long." She hadn't even shifted into park.

"Just push that shit aside, or throw your stuff on top of it. Nothing breakable," she added, adjusting her rearview mirror.

Jack barely had time to throw his suitcase in the backseat and haul himself up into the front seat before she took her foot off the brake.

Macy looked younger than he remembered, which wasn't what he expected. He had this memory etched into his mind of his four aunts sitting around his mother's kitchen table one

Christmas a year after his father had died. "This last year has carved caverns into her face," his aunt Joyce had said, talking about Jack's mother.

But Macy didn't have any caverns. Not even furrows. Her cheeks glowed ruddy from the summer sun. She had her sandpaper-colored hair pulled back in a low, loose ponytail— her usual style—and it, too, seemed to have its own sheen from within.

Her body looked smaller, too—not a drastic change, but slightly more toned, more streamlined than Jack remembered. Her arms poked long and lean from the sleeves of her red T-shirt, the rest of it clinging close to her torso, the slight bulges she had always carried below her bra line and just above her waist now gone. She looked good, he thought to himself, really good. And then he scolded himself for thinking of his former daughter-in-law—or was she still his daughter-in-law?—in even close to that way.

The thought sneaked past his lips anyway, though. "You look great, Macy," he said.

"It's amazing what a tragedy or two will do for your waist-line," Macy said, realizing too late the change in her usual audience. She shook her head and slapped one hand against her forehead. "God, Jack, I'm sorry. That was stupid. I'm not used to being—"

"No sweat," Jack assured her, hoping to sound equally flip, hoping to keep all the apologies and seriousness at bay for a bit longer.

"—around people lately. Shit. I'm sorry."

She steered with her right hand. Her left elbow rested on the window ledge and she had pressed the fingers of her left hand hard against her temple. Jack reached over and squeezed her elbow. "It's okay. No problem," he said.

She nodded at him and smiled a sad smile.

"You really didn't have to drive all this way to get me," Jack offered, changing the subject.

"Jack, 'all this way' is a whopping couple of hours. And if nothing else, it gave me a break from the same old tired conversations every time someone drops off a casserole."

"Lots of food?"

"My place could pass for the Hamburger Helper test kitchen," Macy said. "I'm only one person. My freezer is overflowing and I've had to throw a lot of it away, which made me feel bad. And some days I needed to not talk about how hard my life was or how I was doing, so I wouldn't answer the door. And this really nice gesture on the part of a lot of people ends up racking me with guilt," Macy said. She shook her head, then pointed a finger at Jack. "So you're my new line of defense."

Jack laughed. "I can do that. You'll tell me, though, if I'm inconveniencing you at all."

"Oh, I'll tell you. But during this little visit of yours, I think we need to say what we want and do what we want without worrying about making each other happy or angry."

"Honesty," Jack said matter-of-factly.

"Honestly?" Macy asked.

"What you're talking about is honesty. Being honest with each other."

"Absolutely," Macy said.

That was, perhaps, his favorite thing about Macy—her directness. He admired that in a woman. So many—too many—were wishy-washy or passive-aggressive. They'd tell you they didn't care or that everything was fine, and then brood secretly and fervently. But not Macy. No one ever had to wonder where she stood on an issue or what she was thinking. Jack remembered asking Nash what made him give up his search for a banking job and instead pursue his love of photography. "Macy told me to do what I loved," he said. And each passing day over the last decade or so of getting to know Macy, and watching Nash flourish in his new career, Jack had felt pride in his son, and gratitude for his daughter-in-law, that had grown. She made his son happy, and as Magda always said, "You're only as happy as your unhappiest child." He smiled.

"What's so funny?" Macy asked him.

"Just remembering something from a long time ago," Jack answered.

"Nash?"

He nodded his head, still smiling.

"It's always at the weirdest times," Macy said.

"It's all the time," Jack said.

As they drove south toward the ferry terminal, Jack noticed the looming shape of a solitary mountain in the distance. It looked like a jagged piece of the moon that had fallen and planted itself right there in the lower mainland of British Columbia. It had a fantastic translucent glow, as if it were lit from within.

"Wow," Jack murmured under his breath.

"Pretty cool, eh?" Macy said, her eyebrows arching to accentuate the question.

"Whistler?" Jack asked. It was the only mountain he could think of in these parts.

Macy shook her head. "Mount Baker," she said. "In Washington. Whistler is actually a couple hours east of here."

Jack nodded in acknowledgment, but without looking in Macy's direction. He couldn't take his eyes off that mountain. *That*, Jack thought, *is God right here on Earth—God saying, "Hi—'member me?"* Jack had always had an affinity for this area, and moments like this—with Mount Baker lit up like a Japanese lantern in the late-day summer sun right when he needed a little reminder that there was something bigger than him out there—moments like this were why.

Given the views and climate of British Columbia's coast, he couldn't understand why people would choose to live anywhere else. Wisconsin, with its fields and trees and cows, had always suited him just fine. He had felt at home there, a true part of it, until he saw this place for the first time. This place with the mountains and the ocean and the gentle drizzle now starting to coat it all. It made a person feel whole and humble all at once, like a person should feel. If it wasn't for his business and Magda and the house, and the post–September 11 tightening of the INS rules, he would have moved out here in a second. *But you didn't*, he reminded himself, thinking of how different his relationship with Nash might have been if he and Magda had bucked inertia and routine and taken that leap. How different he would have felt just then. There still would have been grief to stumble through, but there wouldn't have been regret, heavy and stinging, heaped atop it all.

They made the rest of the trip in silence, punctuated only by Macy's sporadic singing to a Canadian band that she said was called the Tragically Hip. It was as if neither of them wanted to start the business of bringing up all that had happened, even with it all looming so large over them.

On the ferry ride to the island they split up. Macy planted herself at a table with a Diet Coke and a magazine, while Jack wandered around the decks, stretching his legs. Magda didn't much care for this corner of the world; she often wondered, out loud, why Macy would choose to live on Vancouver Island, of all places—why not somewhere a little more civilized, like Vancouver or Calgary at least? But looking out over the dark, roiling water, watching the island emerge from the horizon all lush green and peaceful, Jack understood perfectly. In Vancouver, you could smell the ocean a little bit; but on the island, it was all you could smell. It was the sharp, salty fragrance of hard work and perseverance and Mother Nature waiting right out there at your doorstep. It was a smell that percolated in your blood, so that it became more than a smell, more than a pretty view. For islanders, it became a way of life. And once it got into you, Jack could see how someone would have one hell of a time getting it out.

Once off the ferry, Jack settled back into the motion of the truck and stared out of the passenger-side window, the trees and houses and restaurants and gas stations blending together in a late-afternoon light as if they were caught between the pages of a flip book. If he looked out the window a certain way, everything was in plain view. But when he turned his head just a touch, the edges of the buildings and landscape blurred into one another and back out again, a hazy amalgamation that seemed to pass them by, instead of the other way around.

Jack wondered if Nash used to sit in the passenger seat like he was now, letting Macy pilot the beast of a truck down the asphalt, admiring her quiet ease in doing so. Had Nash hummed along with her singing, or had he joined his wife in a duet? Jack wondered what kind of music Nash listened to, what his favorite movies were, what television shows he and Macy watched. He wondered if Nash was content, or happy even. He wondered what would be on tap for Nash's perfect day, what he really wished for in life, what he still really ached to do, what he hadn't yet accomplished. Sure, they had talked at least weekly since Nash had moved away, but it was always about how the Pack was doing, how Nash's job or Jack's business was going, about how busy they both were. But never about the important things. Never about all that he so desperately wanted to know now.

Jack thought back, trying hard to remember why he hadn't come out here more often. There were whole months, whole years, when he had convinced himself that they were too busy to get away, but now he couldn't remember one single thing that was so important it should have kept him tethered to Green Bay.

He thought back to Ms. 7D's question, "Business or pleasure?"

Why did everything always have to be either/or? *Both*, he decided, before reconsidering. Because there was also *neither*, and that was just as good an option.

Chapter Four

EVERY DAMN YEAR MACY FORGOT WHAT HARD WORK THIS WAS.

By the end of a week of tamping dirt and pulling wires taut and hammering nails into errant boards, her muscles would start to get used to the foreign motions. Then fence-mending would be done for another year, during which time Macy's muscles would go back to their old familiar patterns, and next year this time, they'd hurt like hell all over again.

"You don't use barbed wire?" Jack asked. He tipped at the waist, resting an elbow on a bent knee, a hammer dangling from one hand. His face glistened strawberry red, and rivulets of sweat ran from his brow line downward, dripping off the cliff of his chin.

Macy shook her head and turned briefly away from Jack to wipe her face with the bottom part of her T-shirt. "No barbed wire," she said. "Not for horses. People who use that are either too cheap or lazy to do it right. Usually both."

Jack raised an eyebrow at her.

"Cows and other animals only need a couple strands of barbed wire or a single rail to keep them from wandering. But not horses," Macy explained. "They're stupid enough and they don't see well enough to not tangle themselves up in it. And God forbid they do." Macy paused to line up a nail against the post she was working on. With three deft strikes, it slid firmly into place. "You don't want to see what happens when a horse goes through barbed wire. A leg or windpipe ripped straight open by that stuff is not something you want to happen to a horse that's worth more than your car, or your house, if you can help it."

Macy saw Jack suck in a gulp of air. "House?" he asked, wide-eyed.

"Well, maybe cottage or cabin," Macy compromised. "At least, most of the horses here," she said, waving her arm to indicate the span of her farm. "You'll get to see a few that are worth a lot more than that if you come to the show with me."

Macy had designed her pastures carefully. Even though she was still a teenager when her grandfather bought this place to pass along to her when she turned eighteen, she'd had clear ideas of what she wanted it to look like. Both for aesthetic and safety reasons, her fences consisted of four board "rails" tacked at even, one-foot intervals to posts secured with cement footings, with two strands of electric wire on the the pasture side to help the horses respect their boundaries. Yet somehow, every year, posts leaned and electric wire came unfastened and boards fell or were kicked down by horses arguing across pasture lines.

They had started that morning with the small paddocks nearest the barn intended for individual turnout, mostly for Macy's show horses that could handle only a few hours outside because of the bugs or sun—enough to stretch their legs and "get the boogies out." Most of the horses spent the remainder of their day in their stalls or in the indoor riding arena if it wasn't in use, so as to protect their sleek coats from fading and changing color.

Jack and Macy had moved through those smaller paddocks quickly, mostly pounding nails into boards that had been loosened by chewing, kicking, or leaning. Once in a while they'd tighten the electric wire in places. Only a few of the boards actually needed replacing this year.

But Macy rarely got out to walk the fence lines of the back pastures, which, luckily, was where most of her more docile horses spent their days. And that was where she and Jack had focused all their efforts and energy. Now she and Jack stood far from and slightly above the barn and the paddocks in the rearmost pasture, which was shaped like a lopsided "L" that ran from the barn alongside all the other pastures in a long corridor, opening up into square acreage of treeless, rolling hills. They were currently standing at the back edge of that square, looking across the expanse with her matchbox of a barn at the opposite end. She could hear the metronomic waves crashing onto the beach just beyond the tree line to her right. This was Macy's favorite pasture, the one that Gounda's dam had called home, the first pasture that Gounda had bucked and played in alongside his mama. It was the pasture that the mare would be grazing in right now, a little sister or brother to Gounda cantering stiff-legged beside her, or nestling in to nurse from the mare while she chomped lazily along, if only— Macy couldn't finish the thought, though she could see the mare and that foal in front of her like a mirage, like a pair of ghosts come to life. Her breath caught. Pressure built behind her eyes. She turned her energy to the board Jack held, waiting for her.

Like a bald angry man, the sun had climbed high into the pale blue sky and, without cover of clouds to deflect its rays, beat down hard on Macy's back, neck, and arms. Gone was the island's typical refreshing sea breezes. Macy could feel heat stinging her forearms—thousands of tiny electrical pricks, flirting with that thin line between discomfort and pain. She could feel her back working itself into tightly strung cords of muscles with each swing of the hammer, with each bend and each straightening. She could feel the strength steadily draining from her shoulders. And it all felt so painfully good.

Once in a while, a glimmer of wind would stir, replacing the sweet, wheaty smell of manure with whiffs of the ocean. Down near the rocky beach, the ocean's scent sat heavy in the air, almost intrusive. But up here, in the back pastures, the aroma was lighter, refreshing—like that of a just-ended thunderstorm. Macy breathed in deeply. The Oceanus bath salts and lotions, of which her mother-in-law was so fond, smelled nothing at all like the real thing, and in Macy's opinion, they were the worse for it.

"Ready for a break?" Macy asked Jack. She could feel sweat beading in tiny clusters across her forehead and even on her upper arms—a place she always forgot could sweat until days like today.

"Lunch?" he asked.

"Yeah," she said. "Let's."

She waved Jack toward her, and he made one last check of the wire fencing, pulling at it to test the tightness, before following Macy across the field to the battered old farm truck she used precisely for tasks like this—mending fences, hauling feed and hay out to the broodmares who lived in the back pastures, bringing shavings into the barn. The truck, once red but now a nice shade of rust, waited under a cluster of trees with its tailgate already down. Macy hoisted herself onto it and dug into the cooler, pulling out a bottle of water she had frozen to help keep their food cool. It had melted almost completely, but still felt cold to the touch. Macy offered the bottle to Jack, who snapped it up like a hungry dog offered a piece of meat.

"Whoo-ee. Needed that," Jack said, finishing off a long gulp. "The Sahara has nothing on my innards right now. I thought this place was supposed to have nice, mild summers?"

"It does—most times. But every single year since I can remember we have two unbearably hot weeks here."

"When is that, usually?"

"Whenever I put up hay or fix the fence."

Jack laughed.

"Honestly. It never fails. I could do it in May or August, and it's always like this." Macy jabbed a finger at the still-cloudless sky. "Perverse sense of humor those weather gods have, I tell you. I don't know what I ever did to them."

"Well, if you could make amends by tomorrow, I'd really appreciate it." Jack laughed again, accepting a tinfoil-wrapped sandwich from her. "Or this afternoon, even."

"I'll see what I can do, Jackie."

Macy looked up from unwrapping her sandwich to see someone walking across the field toward them. Dirty overalls, knee-high rubber boots, strands of gray hair escaping at crazy angles. Macy recognized these telltale characteristics long before she could make out the woman's face.

Macy waved an arm high above her head. The figure waved back.

"Who is that?" Jack asked.

"That," Macy said, "is Mama Sophie. She lives just down the road."

"You tryin' to kill yourself out here in this bloody heat, girl?" the woman yelled.

"You're the one wearing swampers, you crazy ol' coot," Macy yelled back.

Mama Sophie walked up to Macy and forced her into a half

hug, shoulder-to-shoulder. "It's good to see you out and about," she whispered to Macy.

"Good to be out," Macy whispered back. Then she turned to Jack. "Jack, meet the infamous Sophie McLean. Mama Sophie, Jack Allen."

"Infamous, huh? I'm up to infamous now?" she said to Macy. Jack held out his hand. "It's a pleasure, ma'am."

Mama Sophie grabbed Jack's hand and pulled him in for a hug. Macy knew that the Allens weren't a hugging family, which had always fit her just fine. Discomfort showed on Jack's face. He looked like the cartoon characters who were squeezed until their eyes started to bulge.

"Welcome to Campbell River, Jack. Or back to Campbell River, I guess. I know you've been here before, but it's nice to finally get the chance to meet you. But don't you dare go ma'aming me. It's Sophie—just Sophie." She patted him on the back, then took her arm from his shoulder and placed it on top of his hand, sandwiching it between hers. "I'm sorry I couldn't have been here for the funeral. I'm so sorry for your loss," she said.

"Thank you, Ms. McLean," said Jack.

"Is he a little slow on the uptake, darling?" Mama Sophie asked Macy, who smiled and shrugged.

"How long you been here, Jack? How long you planning to stay?" Sophie asked.

"Been here about a week," Jack said, raising one finger, "and no real idea," he said, raising a second finger.

Sophie nodded. "I've been out guiding all week. Sorry I've missed you." Then, turning to Macy, she said, "Caught some really nice sockeye this mornin'; you want some?"

"Oh, is that the reason for the fabulous footwear?" Macy kidded her.

"You want the fish or not, you little smart-ass?"

"How about this," Macy said. "You bring your catch of the day over about seven tonight and we'll throw it on the barbecue."

"You like salmon, Jack?" Mama Sophie asked.

"Love salmon," Jack said.

"Good." Turning to Macy, she said, "He can stay awhile. Mends fence, eats salmon. We can work on the rest."

Jack chuckled.

"I'll see you at seven thirty, then," Mama Sophie said, already walking away from them.

Jack mouthed to Macy, *I thought it was seven?*

She waved him off and whispered, "Mama Sophie does what Mama Sophie wants.

"You going to change for dinner?" Macy yelled after her.

"You going to have anything to eat if I decide not to come?" she called back over her shoulder.

"Bye," yelled Macy, feigning exasperation.

Mama Sophie waved back at them without turning around.

"Quite a character, that one," Jack said. He and Macy watched the old woman tromp through the grass and weave herself limberly through the fence rails.

"Just wait till she gets a drink or two in her," Macy said. "You'll be wanting a little stronger word than *character*."

Jack looked at Macy with his head cocked, seemingly surprised, though at what was hard to tell. That the old woman who had just trounced over here and back—probably a kilometer either way as the crow flew—would drink, maybe? Or that she had appeared at all? Macy caught a fleeting glimpse of a much younger Jack Allen as he looked back over his shoulder and his gaze lingered in the direction Mama Sophie had gone.

"Bourbon," Macy said. Jack turned his attention back to her, his eyes keen, focused, and dancing all at once. "Straight. Three cubes. Serve her up one of those without her having to ask and you'll have her eating right outta your hand in no time."

Macy raised her water bottle in the air in front of her as if making a toast. Jack raised his. They clicked the lips of their bottles together.

Jack and Macy finished up the second-to-last row of fence line as wispy clouds crawled over the sun. They decided that the last section of fence—an extraordinarily long one—would take them the better part of the next morning, or the day even, and this was as good a place as any to stop.

Driving back toward the barn, Jack suggested they maybe start around this time tomorrow and work until dark. "We'd get four or five good hours in," he lobbied.

The thought had never occurred to Macy. Probably because she wasn't much for innovation. And also because it felt good to punish herself in the heat. Even before everything that had happened, she had felt that way. Like every hammer swung and every pound of wire lifted and every step trudged through back pastures equaled some sort of mercy that she owed. To whom, she couldn't be sure, but it felt good to store it all up. For safekeeping, to pay later.

Having Jack here was much in the same vein. When he called to say he wanted to come, her first concern was that his worse half would be making the trip alongside him. But even when he assured Macy that Magda didn't know about his plans, she couldn't muster the cheer she figured others in her same situation surely would. The thing was, what had happened still stewed raw in her mind, like a soup that hadn't yet come together. She couldn't make sense of it all, but she didn't want someone else making sense of it for her, and didn't want Jack or anyone else to make sense out of any of it before she was able to. Macy wanted to get this grieving right, but it was tricky. And if Jack came in and had all the answers, it might only add to the long list of things she hadn't been able to do well enough, or at all.

More than any of it, though, she wanted—no, needed—to have Nash to herself for a little longer yet. She knew what Jack was after long before his Allen Edmonds–loafer-clad feet touched down on Vancouver soil, and she just couldn't do for him what needed doing in his mind—answer countless questions about Nash: Where was his favorite place to have a beer? What was his favorite kind of beer? Where did they go on Friday nights? How did he spend his days? Where did he get his hair cut, his car serviced? Where did he work out? Did he work out? How did he take his coffee? What did they do about breakfast— were they brunch people or did they skip it altogether and delve right into lunch?

She knew these questions were coming. She could hear them in his voice when he had called a couple of weeks back. She could see everything he wanted, gathering like a far-off storm. And at the moment, she didn't have a shelter built for two. Hell, right about then she didn't even own a goddamned umbrella.

In the moments that had stretched between Jack's saying he was going to come and now, Macy would get angry at Jack for asking this of her: that she share all she had of Nash—the island and their life here—with him. Then she would reprimand and remind herself that Nash was his *son*. What must it feel like, she would scold herself, to spend your whole life protecting this little being, a little baby that grew up to be a man but was still always a little bit that baby, only to outlive him? She was certain that no matter the pain she felt, it paled next to Jack's—this man sitting and staring pensively out the half-lowered passenger window of a beat-up truck owned by a stranger-woman his son had thrust on him by taking a vow that wasn't even made in a church. Who was *she*, after all? Nash was this man's flesh and blood. Nash was Jack's heart, walking around outside of his body. Macy wasn't a mother to Nash's children. Her life had barely begun to intertwine with his; theirs wasn't a history that spanned decades. She was barely his wife—little more than a woman Jack's son had lived with for a time.

Really, how could she have said no?

Chapter Five

JACK WATCHED MACY SLICE THE RED, GREEN, AND YELLOW PEP-
pers into thin slivers from where he sat at the kitchen table. Her
hands were scrubbed clean, nails trimmed short but painted a
soft, almost translucent pink—a physical oxymoron to the rough
brown skin stretched taut over protruding veins and knuckles,
so much larger than the bones they joined together that her
wedding ring floated freely along her finger between the joint
and hand.

They were a woman's hands. Not a lady's hands, like
Magda's—lotion-soft and cushiony, always adorned with the
"sophisticated look" of the fake nails that she preferred. No, Macy's were callused and ruddy and looked like they belonged to
someone ten or twenty years her senior.

Those are the hands that touched Nash, thought Jack.

They knew Nash better than anyone else's in the world. Better, even, than Magda's—the very hands responsible for diaper-
ing his downy bottom or smoothing his feverish forehead for so
many years. Because Macy's were the hands that could trace by
rote, like Braille, the gradual curve of Nash's neck to his collar-

bone or the slow, shallow dip below the inside of each hip bone. And Jack was slightly jealous of this—jealous that this woman in front of him, deftly slicing a red pepper, knew Nash in ways that he or Magda never, ever could have.

"You okay?" Macy asked, pausing midchop.

Jack looked up at her, thought a moment, and said, "Yeah. It's that . . . being here, I don't know . . . it's—"

"Weird?"

He nodded. "I mean, it's nice—to be here, but I didn't really think this through a whole lot before I got on that plane. I don't exactly know what I'm doing here, you know?"

Macy grabbed handfuls of chopped peppers and dropped them into a bowl where cucumbers and tomatoes were waiting to be tossed together. Jack had seen her make this same version of a Greek salad several times on previous visits. When he had remarked on the frequency with which the salad showed up at meals, Macy admitted it composed approximately one-fifth of her cooking repertoire.

Macy made a few tiny nodding movements with her chin, and then looked up at him. "You know what Magda always says: 'A reason for everything.'"

"Yes, that is what Magda always says," Jack agreed. The smell of salmon wafted from the grill. Sophie had wrapped it in newspaper and dropped it on the porch with a note, begging off dinner for a last-minute early-morning guiding trip.

"You know," Macy said, "sometimes I think Magda's full of shit."

"Only *some*times?"

Macy laughed.

"But you never know," Jack said, smiling.

"No," Macy said a little quieter, "you never do."

They sat there a moment, smiling at each other, minds and thoughts clearly drifting elsewhere. Jack snapped himself back to the present and made an abrupt move to get up. "Can I help with anything?" he asked.

"Yes, you can," Macy said. "You can get me a beer, get yourself a beer, and then sit right back down on that chair and entertain me while I finish up."

"That I can do. One beer and some riveting conversation, coming right up."

And for a flash of a moment, Jack didn't feel like bolting to anywhere other than where he was, or like crawling straight out of his own skin. It didn't even bother him that he didn't know why, or that a minute later he could feel the familiar way his son's memory cut his stomach like shrapnel. The fleeting moment of feeling okay—that moment was enough.

Jack had expected the show grounds at Windmist Farms to look more crowded. According to Macy, this was a major event, but there seemed to be only a smattering of motor homes and trailers, most of which looked like mansions on wheels, around the show grounds. All had "slide-outs"—whole sections of the motor home's side that popped out on hydraulics to give the residents more living space. Through windows he could see lighted display cabinets, leather couches, and more square footage than he and Magda had had in their first apartment together. More than one had a group of Mexicans diligently washing and polishing the exterior. They chattered as they worked, their quick back-and-forths in Spanish sounding like a song.

Macy caught him gawking.

"Not too shabby, huh?"

Jack shook his head and let a low whistle escape his lips. He made a decent living with his concrete company, and he and Magda ran in a social circle made up of prominent local doctors, lawyers, and Packers front-office executives, but this was a whole different level of success. He knew that most of these rigs had to cost more than his and Magda's house, and just by reading the ads in magazines stashed throughout Macy's truck, he knew that the horses did, too.

"How do they do this?" Jack asked.

Macy shrugged. "That one there . . ." She pointed to a massive black-white-and-chrome bus with slide-outs on both sides. "That one belongs to this amateur lady. She buys a new one every single year. Her family's old money; her dad was a railroad tycoon or something like that. Just for tax purposes she has to spend a million or so a year. That's how the chatter goes, at least," she said. They walked by motor homes, gleaming semi trucks pulling giant horse vans, and cars that should have been in a showroom somewhere, or at least under protective covers—not parked haphazardly along gravel driveways and grass embankments. "Family jewelry store, insurance company, hotel chain, oil," she explained, pointing at each rig or car of note as they passed.

Jack wondered what it would be like to have that kind of money. He figured that, at the very least, he'd have a pretty stellar golf game.

"Oil. Wasn't that how your grandfather made his money?" Jack asked.

Macy offered an affirmative nod only, nothing else. But Jack had heard enough of the story through Nash. Her grandfather had had more money than he could have spent in his lifetime. He ensured that his wife—Macy's grandmother, who was now in some sort of home—had been fully taken care of, and after Macy's father had died, ten or fifteen years ago, he set both Macy and her sister up financially for life. Instead of handing each of the girls a chunk of cash, though, Macy's grandfather sat down with them separately and discussed with them what they most wanted to do with their lives. Then he set up a fund for each of them that would pay any and all expenses, but only those that had to do with their designated career paths. Regan, who wanted to someday act on Broadway, was given an apartment in Manhattan, a full ride to New York University, and any and all acting, singing, or dancing classes she could take. For Macy, their grandfather bought a farm on Vancouver Island, imported from Europe one ready-made show jumper and several additional mares that were in foal, and ensured she had the best possible truck and trailer that she could need. The horses' feed, her show entry and trainer's fees, and vet and farrier bills were all covered. As long as either granddaughter could tie an expense to her chosen field, it would be paid. Before he had passed away, their grandfather had solidified the arrangement with a raft of legal documents to be executed by the accounting firm to which he had been loyal his whole life.

They were on their way back to Macy's truck and trailer, parked and waiting to be unloaded, near her assigned stalls.

"I hate this part," Macy said.

"What's that?" Jack asked.

"All the setup work. Hauling tack trunks in, bedding stalls, hanging buckets. There's no better feeling than walking into an arena, with every eye on you, but I loathe the unloading and loading."

"You could hire someone," Jack suggested. They both knew Macy could afford it.

Macy shook her head. "You're right—people do," she said. "But as much as I dread all the work, the braiding and bathing, there's something you lose when you don't spend that kind of time with your horse. They get to know you better, bond better with you. And when you get into the ring, that's key."

Macy snapped Gounda's lead rope onto his halter and backed him out of the trailer while Jack held the door open. He helped her unload the other two horses as well—young "projects" that Macy was showing to sell—and helped her cut open and spread the bags of sawdust that had been delivered to each of her stalls. They put up water and feed buckets and hung extension cords and fans outside the stalls. Then Jack held each of the three horses while Macy bathed them, amazed at how they would simply stand and let someone hose them off. He noted that Macy was the only non-Hispanic—and, he assumed, the only rider—bathing a horse in the wash stalls.

By the time each horse had been tucked back into its stall, matching sheets on each of them that bore Macy's initials across the barrel area, it was nearly ten o'clock, the show grounds had filled to capacity, and Jack was exhausted.

"Almost done?" he asked Macy, planting himself on an overturned bucket in the middle of the aisle. She was puttering around in her tack stall, organizing and arranging saddles, bridles, and grooming equipment.

"Still have to braid," she called out.

Jack's spirits sank; he hadn't eaten since they had stopped for lunch, and his stomach felt like it was about to eat itself. "I'm going to run and pick us up some food then," he said to Macy. "Any requests?"

"Tim Hortons?" Macy said. "There's one just outside of town—take a right out of the grounds. Turkey on white bread, a low-fat iced cap, and a few Timbits, please." She rummaged through her tack trunk for the keys to her truck and tossed them to Jack. "Be careful with her," she joked.

"Always," he said.

He thought, driving to Tim Hortons, how strong Macy seemed. He didn't know quite what he had expected, exactly. And, granted, he didn't know what it was like for Macy in those moments before sleep came, when loneliness seemed magnified a million times over, or the shock of it immediately upon waking. But he knew what those moments were like for him, and truth be told, he wasn't managing all that well as it was. Since his arrival on the island, though, Macy's stoicism, her resolve to keep moving forward, had inspired him.

But upon returning from his food run, Jack walked down the last row of stalls in barn C with the sandwich and iced coffee Macy had ordered and saw her standing on her braiding stool, slumped over Gounda, her face buried against his neck and only half his mane braided. She didn't look up.

He set the food on one of Macy's shiny wood tack trunks rimmed with brass and entered Gounda's stall, so that he faced her over the horse's thick arch of a neck, which tapered into an equally thick head that was bobbing in and out of sleep.

"Macy?"

She still didn't look up.

"I can't do this," she said, her face still buried in the horse's neck.

"What was that?" he asked, not quite hearing her.

"I can't. I can't."

"Can't what?" Jack asked quietly. He brushed her hair, which had fallen on Jack's side of the horse's neck, away from her head.

"I shouldn't have come here."

He put his hand on hers. She raised her head, and then her eyes, to meet his. "Aww, Macy girl? Come on now. This is your thing," he said, patting her hand. It felt like a child's under his. Small and delicate.

"It's not the same without him. Nothing's the same. I can't do this. I don't want to."

"You can—and you will," Jack said. He ducked under Gounda's neck and tugged on Macy's sleeve to get her to step down off the stool. Like a drugged puppy, she let Jack guide her down, and he put an arm around her, leading her to the tack trunk just outside Gounda's stall.

He knew these bouts. Oh, how he knew them. He knew how fast they hit, how they seemed so deep and impossible to crawl out of. They could be brought on by a song, or a smell, or, as he had experienced at Festival Foods only a few weeks before, seeing Nash's favorite childhood cereal—Count Chocula—on a walk down aisle five. He had left that day with Magda's shopping list in shreds, and his dignity in a similar way after a concerned fellow patron, and then a stock boy, were unable to rouse him from where he had crumpled, unable to catch his breath or cease his sobbing. After that, he and Magda had arranged to have their groceries delivered.

It was an impossible feeling to deal with, that kind of loss. It was impossible to predict what might trigger the flood of memories. And it was equally impossible to understand—the finality of someone who always was, suddenly being nothing. Nowhere.

One early morning, not long ago, he had woken suddenly from a dream about Nash. He and Nash had been in a white room with no decorations and no furniture except for the orange, molded-plastic chairs they were sitting on. There was one slim door in the far wall.

"What took you so long, Pops?" Nash asked.

"What took me so long for what?" Jack asked back.

"To get here. I've been waiting for you."

"I should've called," Jack said. "Sorry to make you wait, Nashville."

Nash laughed lightly at the mention of this long-forgotten nickname.

"Did I ever tell you why we named you that?" Jack asked. Nash shook his head, still smiling. "Your mom and I went there—to Nashville—on our honeymoon. Drove down there. We didn't have a penny to our names then. We were opening up envelopes and cards people gave us for the wedding every time we had to get gas or eat. And there was something about that place—the lushness of it and the energy of it—that was just like fairy dust. And when you were born, almost nine months later exactly, and you were lying there all purple in your mother's arms, and we still didn't have a name picked out for you, she looked up at me, radiating joy, and told me that the only time she had ever felt as happy was with me on our honeymoon. There were three of us, now, she said, and we should include this little guy in all our happy times, even the ones he wasn't quite present for. I smiled down at her and she looked up at me and said, 'Nash.' And I agreed. Nash it was." Jack looked up to see Nash tying his shoes. "Where are you going?"

Nash turned to face him. "I have to leave now, Pops."

Jack could feel the light in the room getting brighter and brighter. "No, not yet. Please don't go, Nash. Just a little longer. We could talk, like before."

"Sorry, Pops," Nash said. He was smiling as he walked toward the skinny door. Like he used to do when Jack asked him to go one more round in cribbage and Nash had had somewhere else to be. "It's time for me to go. Have to. I love you, Pops. And I'll be around; don't worry."

Jack found himself in the room alone suddenly, and he woke with a start to see the red digits on the alarm clock glaring at him: 4:11. The empty darkness had startled him, pressed hard into him with its nothingness. He so desperately wanted to stay in that light-filled room with Nash.

He had gotten up then, wandering frantically from room to room in their house, hearing Nash's words, *I'll be around. I'll be around*, and taking them for gospel.

"Where?" he had cried out.

In the opaque darkness, he stumbled against the buffet table in the front entranceway, knocking pictures and knickknacks to the floor. He picked one up—a silver-framed photograph of him and Nash salmon fishing north of Campbell River a few years ago. Glass shards jutted across their windblown faces, one just in front of the other, each half-hidden by the hoods on their yellow rain slickers. "Where, Nash?" he had whispered desperately, looking into the blackness of the foyer. "Where?"

That morning, when Magda came downstairs to start the coffee, she had found Jack clutching the photograph tight to him, curled up amid a mosaic of glass shards, and fast asleep.

He told Macy then, with Gounda's breath moist on his outstretched hand, about how these feelings would pass. About how every time she wallowed through one of the bouts they would get easier and easier, until one day—maybe one year or ten years down the road—without her even knowing it, they would cease altogether, and she would be left with only happy memories of Nash that didn't sear and tear when they came bubbling up.

"How do you know?" she asked.

The truth was, he didn't. That was only what he told himself. Because if all the hurt and gut-gnawing emptiness didn't ebb away over time, he didn't think he could bear it either.

Chapter Six

It wasn't even seven o'clock, and Magda was already tipsy. She was sitting at a cocktail table with Ginny Fischer, one of her oldest and dearest friends, finishing a glass of white zinfandel and waiting to be seated for dinner. They were at Poultry in Motion, a hot new restaurant on De Pere's main drag that was receiving rave reviews, but it was so busy that the restaurant had instituted a no-reservation policy. So Magda and Ginny had arrived at six o'clock sharp, expecting to beat out the seven-o'clock crowd, and had been waiting ever since. Magda had been drinking seltzer water up to a point, and then somewhere around six thirty decided to have a glass of wine, anticipating that they'd be eating soon. But here she was, no sign of a table opening up and not even a whole glass in, her toes and fingers had already starting to tingle.

"Why, you don't drink, Magda. What's going on?"

"I don't *usually* drink, Ginny. That doesn't mean that I can't *ever* drink."

"Are we celebrating something?" asked Ginny.

"Goodness gracious, Ginny. What do you think I have to celebrate?" Magda said.

Ginny's face crumpled so horribly that Magda changed her tone and added, "Well, I suppose I am celebrating a bit, with Jack gone and all. I mean, not that I don't adore him, but I was thinking the other day—we've been married almost thirty-four years and haven't ever spent much time apart. I'm enjoying this new-found freedom a little. It's nice."

"I wish I had a little freedom like that," Ginny said. "I just read this book about a woman who left her husband and family for a year and took a kayaking trip around all the Great Lakes—or maybe it was only one of the lakes—well, anyway, it was all about her spending this year on her own, and the self-discoveries she made, and then, at the end, she was more than happy to come home to her husband and such. Totally content to be back, because she had this great adventure. It left me feeling a little jealous. I'd like to do something like that. Put the spark back into things with me and Frank."

"You've lost your spark?"

Leaning toward Magda, she asked, "Haven't you and Jack?"

"Well," said Magda, "not really, no." It wasn't technically a lie. Truth be told, there hadn't been a whole lot to lose.

Magda raised her glass to take a sip of wine. The cocktail napkin stuck to the bottom. She peeled the napkin off and put it back on the table. Then she reached for the saltshaker and spilled a bit onto the napkin. Jack had taught her that trick.

Ginny looked as though she wanted to ask Magda about the salt on her napkin, but instead marched on. "Yes, I suppose," she said, lowering her voice, "but do you and Jack still—you know—"

"Why, Ginny Fischer!"

"I'm just asking," Ginny said. "Friends can ask that sort of thing."

"They can, but they shouldn't," said Magda.

"Well, Frank and I don't. Haven't for years. *Years*," hissed Ginny, shaking her head. She took a long swig of her own zinfandel.

Magda was intrigued. Talking about someone else's sex life—or even her own—always made her uncomfortable. It just wasn't right. But this—Ginny's *situation*—this warranted a little talking about.

"*Years*," Ginny repeated.

"Ginny, keep your voice down. I heard you the first time," Magda said. "It's just hard to know what to say to that." She took a sip of her wine. Its sugary sweetness coated her insides like liquid velvet. She wondered why she didn't drink more often, or why she had mostly given it up in the first place. It felt positively wonderful.

"Have you tried—"

"Talking, counseling. *Lingerie*." Ginny said *lingerie* in a whispered hiss, as if it were a swear said by someone who never swore. "You name it, we've tried it. Everything. We've tried everything. But *nothing*."

Magda shook her head slowly, racking her brain for something to tell her oldest friend. Just when she thought she had the answer, Ginny started in again.

"And then I found the Viagra in his drawer."

"Oh, wonderful!" said Magda. "So he's taken matters into his own hands. That's perfect. A man with a little initiative. You sure don't find those very often."

"The bottle was half-empty," said Ginny.

Magda looked at Ginny quizzically, her head tilting to one side. She inhaled sharply. "Oh, my," she said. *This* was turning into an awkward conversation.

"He denies it, of course," said Ginny.

"And you believe him?" Magda asked.

"Should I? I don't know. I want to; I do. But I don't know if I should."

"And you haven't—you know—at all? Since he got the prescription filled?" asked Magda.

"Not once."

"You're sure? Positively sure?"

"I'm pretty sure I'd know, Magda."

"Oh, my," Magda said again. "My, oh, my. Yes, yes. You likely would then, wouldn't you?" She inhaled another jagged breath.

"I wish someone would tell me what to do." Ginny shook her head back and forth and kept her eyes downcast. "Because I don't know. I really don't."

Magda nodded. She remembered back in high school, on career day, when a classmate's father, a writer for the local newspaper, said that the most important quality in a journalist was an unyielding curiosity about people, and that everyone—everyone—had a story to tell; you just had to excavate it. And Magda remembered thinking that maybe she could do that eventually; maybe that curiosity about people was something that grew over time. But she knew now, as a middle-aged woman, that she just didn't have it in her, and she worried sometimes that it made her a bad person. So, now and then, she'd make stabs at it. She'd try to see whether, just maybe, curiosity had grown in her, secretly, down in her inner reaches, like those beautiful flowers she saw on the Discovery Channel that divers had found hundreds of feet underwater.

But if she were really, truly honest with herself, she'd much rather talk about what was going on with her. She also figured that if anyone else were being really, truly honest, they'd come to the exact same conclusion about themselves.

Tonight felt different, though. Magda actually felt for Ginny. Or maybe she just agreed with her. As a young woman, Magda had had all sorts of ideas about what it meant to be an adult. She had been wildly off the mark as to how fun and fulfilling some of those ideas would turn out to be.

"You need to turn it over," Magda finally said.

"What do you mean?" asked Ginny.

"Turn it over to your higher power," Magda stated. "To God. None of this is in your hands anyway."

The hostess approached them with menus. "We'll be able to seat you in a few minutes," she said, "but here are some menus to look over while you wait."

"I'm not feeling much like dinner anymore," Ginny whispered to Magda. "What do you think?"

"That's fine with me. Maybe another drink and then head home?" asked Magda.

Ginny nodded. The hostess sighed loudly. In fact, she did just about everything in her power to signal annoyance short of rolling her eyes: She tapped her foot, put a hand on her hip, and then snatched the menus from their hands before Magda could even get out, "We're not going to be dining tonight, after all, but thank you."

The hostess left without so much as a nod in their direction.

"Maybe we should order some appetizers, at least," Ginny suggested. "This wine has gone right to my head."

"Good idea," said Magda, not because she wanted to stay any longer, but more because she felt like she should. That was, after all, what friends did. So she waved down another, friendlier-looking waitress and ordered bruschetta and two more glasses of white zin.

"So, what were you saying?" asked Ginny.

"Sorry?"

"You were talking about turning things over—that I need to turn this over," said Ginny.

"Oh, right," Magda said. She was suddenly tired, and couldn't really remember her previous train of thought.

Ginny waited, looking expectantly at her, but Magda couldn't bring it back, whatever it was she was going to say.

"I don't really know, Ginny. You have to believe that things will turn out for the best, whether it's with Frank or not. Things will be okay." She felt like a walking, talking greeting card—*Your strength will get you through this difficult time. Thinking of you in your time of need. Thank you for being my friend.* Blah, blah, blah. After all, thought Magda, it wasn't like the man was dead; he was just having an affair. What did that really matter in the grand scheme of things? Ginny could still talk to him, could still see him. Hell, she was still living with him. And he probably still loved her just the same.

"Plus, that's the way it is with men, Ginny. Sex isn't about love and love isn't about sex with them. It's that whole mother-whore complex, you know."

If Frank were dead, or dying even, then none of this would even matter. Ginny would be begging for just one more day with him, one more hour. No matter whom else he had been with the day or week or month before.

She was losing her patience. Not just now, but in general. Magda couldn't even watch Oprah or Dr. Phil anymore, when she had for years reported to the couch each day from exactly three until five p.m. as if it were her job. All those people who thought their lives were in shambles just because their spouse had an affair or their child lied to them. Big deal. "Wait till one of them dies!" she wanted to yell at them sometimes. Or maybe she actually had. "Wait till that happens and people stop asking how you're doing, stop being concerned about you, only a matter of months later, when you're not really doing all that much better than the moment you found out."

"You're so lucky, Magda," Ginny said.

Just that morning at the Luna Cafe, Magda had sat next to an older woman with a very active young child. The boy was coloring "pictures," which were really just scribbled lines on a paper, but he was so proud and kept running from the kids' play table over to the woman saying, "Look, 'Amma. Look."

"He's precious," Magda had said to her.

The woman beamed. "My very first grandbaby. They're just so wonderful. Do you have any yet?"

And that was when it hit her like a freight train. Hit her and ran her over and backed up to do it again.

She had been so busy grieving for the son no longer here that she'd clean forgotten about the kids he'd never have. She'd never be able to celebrate Grandparents' Day, never get one of those cheesy "World's Greatest Grandma" mugs. And after seeing the woman with her grandbaby in the coffee shop—a woman she'd never be—that had become the only thing she could think about. There had been only one other time in her life when she had felt unluckier than she felt today.

When Ginny added, "To have someone like Jack," Magda stopped and thought about it a second. Jack. She did still have him. He'd never pull a Frank. He'd always be there for her. Her rock. She was lucky in that, at least—lucky to have him. She really was. And every last part of her missed him just then.

"Magda, are you drunk?"

Jack's voice floated over the phone lines. Across thousands

and thousands of miles of phone lines. To her. Just for her. Her Jack.

"What do you mean?" she asked coyly, and then hiccuped.

"Lit. Blitzed. Bombed. Crocked. Are you, Magda?"

"I'm allowed to have one little glass of wine now and then."

"I didn't say you weren't allowed," Jack said, laughing. "I just asked if you were drunk."

"I'm not *drunk*, Jack," said Magda. "I'm a little tipsy, but I'm not *drunk*." She hiccuped again and sat down at the kitchen table. She wished she could lie down on the couch at the moment. *Must look into getting one of those cordless phones*, she thought.

"So what's going on there?" Jack asked.

"What do you mean, 'What's going on here'?" Magda shot back at him. "What's that supposed to mean?" She was feeling less lucky to have him by the minute, even though, rationally, Magda knew Jack hadn't said one thing that should have made her feel that way.

Jack exhaled audibly. "I didn't *mean* anything by it, Magda. I was just wondering what you've been doing. I haven't talked to you in a while."

"This phone rings, too, you know. Why didn't you call this weekend?"

Magda hated herself for the way she was acting, but couldn't seem to do a thing about it. She felt possessed—of loneliness and heartache and too much white zinfandel.

Jack told her about the horse show—about the trailers and motor homes and the horses, about how well Macy did, and about how well she rode.

"You should see it, Magda. These horses—we could sell everything we own and still not afford one. It's another world."

Magda fought the urge to remind Jack that she had seen it.

With him. They had flown to Las Vegas years back to watch Macy. She wrapped the phone cord around her hand and then let it unwind. "So, when are you coming home?"

"I don't know," Jack said.

"You don't *know*?"

"No. I don't know," Jack said more firmly.

"I want you to come home."

"I will, Magda."

"When?"

"I don't know yet, Magda. Not yet."

"No."

"No?"

"No. How about now instead? Or tomorrow. I miss you," she said, and she really did.

"I miss you, too."

"So why don't you just come back, then? There's a scramble we could golf in this coming weekend at the country club. I could call and sign us up. It's a little last-minute, but I'm sure Jerry could—"

"Magda, I can't come home this week."

"—get us in. Yes, you can," said Magda. "You have an open-ended ticket. It's not like you're not going to be able to get a flight back, middle of the week and all."

"I know I can, Magda," Jack said. "But I'm not quite ready. Not yet. Being here feels so good for me."

"And being here with me isn't good for you?" Magda asked.

"Magda, that's not fair. You know it's not. You're comparing completely different things. Apples and oranges."

Hot tears smarted at the corners of her eyes. When she was hurt or angry, or in this case both, she cried. "You'd rather be there with *her* than here with me."

She knew she sounded juvenile and whiny. And yet, she had long ago stopped asking anything extra of Jack. In the early years of their marriage he had been up to his ears in the stress of starting a business. There had been debts to pay and long hours to work without so much as a dime of it going back into their pockets at first. Magda knew how hard he worked, and admired so much his drive and dedication. She had made it her mission to make the rest of his life as seamless as possible: potty training their son, then carting him to a never-ending series of events as he grew, managing the always-there mountain of laundry, making sure groceries were bought and dinner made. She had even dampened the desire to have another baby because of the financial pressure it would have placed on Jack and the need she would have had to involve him in the domestic front of his life.

She hadn't ever asked a thing of him before. Just this one time.

"Magda, this isn't about her or you. This is about me. What's good for me."

Magda paced around the kitchen table, tethered to a course of half circles by the phone cord. "It's about us, Jack. And you're choosing her right now. I need you. I need you, and you're choosing her over me."

"You can act like such a toddler sometimes, Magda. I don't know how else to explain this to you. This is about *me*. Me and Nash. No one else. I've taken care of everyone else my whole damn life, and right now I just need a little time to take care of me. That's all."

"Whatever," said Magda.

"Don't do that, Magda," said Jack. "Why don't you give me a call tomorrow and we can talk this over when we're both a little more rested?"

She sat back down at the table, remembering the image that hadn't really left her all day. The Luna Cafe grandmother. The way she smiled at her little grandson. The way he went to her, arms open, ready to be scooped up into hers.

"Magda, this is going to be fine. We'll talk tomorrow."

She didn't answer. She just sat at the table, thinking of that woman and the boy. And then she started to sob. Big, loud, hiccuping sobs.

"Magda?"

"It's not going to be fine tomorrow."

"I promise it is. Have some water and go to bed, and we'll talk tomorrow, okay?"

"You're not *hearing* me, Jack." That was one of her favorite Dr. Phil–isms. That people could be talking to you, but not hearing you. And that people needed to be *heard* to feel *validated*. "I'm never going to be a grandmother."

"Oh, Magda," Jack said.

But there was nothing more than that to say. He couldn't say that it wasn't so. He couldn't tell her that she might be someday.

So she hung up the phone. Then she laid herself down on the fresh, cool tiles of their kitchen floor and willed her world to stop spinning.

Chapter Seven

"I'll see you next week, madame!" Martine called to Macy.

Macy waved to him, unusually relieved to see him go. Normally Macy looked forward to her biweekly lessons with Martine, this year especially, since they were working on qualifying Macy for Jump Canada's Talent Squad, a precursor to World Cup competition and getting onto the Canadian Equestrian Team. But today, Macy couldn't bring herself to partake in Martine's joviality, which always seemed to be turned up a notch or two whenever he got to "horse around," as he called it, with Macy.

Martine had been a godsend for Macy. An accomplished show jumper in Paris, he had suffered a bad fall and permanently injured his back. Unable to continue riding, he followed his Canadian wife to Victoria and threw himself into earning a living teaching his native tongue. But he felt, as he would later tell Macy, like a "beached whale"—which Macy later learned was his way of saying "a fish out of water." Right around that time, he had pulled up behind her truck and trailer at the Horseshoe Bay ferry. He had been hungry to talk horses with anyone, and couldn't believe his good fortune when he found that Macy was a fellow hunter/jumper rider, and an aspiring Grand Prix rider at that. Martine desperately needed to find a niche, and Macy had desperately needed a trainer.

That was more than a decade ago, and in the years that followed, they had formed an unlikely team. Macy had found that she couldn't—didn't want to—ride for anyone but Martine. And she liked to think that he felt the same about her.

Today, though, she wanted all to herself.

She had sent Jack off with Sophie, assuring them both that she had no interest in showing Jack around town and couldn't possibly cancel on Martine on such short notice. This was true. But so was not wanting to be stuck in the backseat of Sophie's jalopy station wagon like a teenager on a road trip with her parents.

She checked the time on her cell phone. Twelve twenty-two.

Macy dismounted and rubbed Gounda's wide forehead, planting a quick kiss on his velvety muzzle.

"You were a very good boy," she told him. And he was. He always, always was.

She loosened his girth and slipped the reins over his head, and he plodded along behind her toward the barn. Once inside, she unfastened the girth on the right and then on the left, set it on top of the saddle, and stripped the saddle off, heaving it onto a standing rack with one hand. She swapped Gounda's bridle for his halter, taking care not to bump his teeth with the bit as she eased it out of his mouth. Then she led him to the wash stall. She let the water from the hose run over her hand first, testing the temperature. Even though Gounda had worked up a good sweat, Macy was careful to use only lukewarm water on him so as not to startle his muscles into spasming. If he stood patiently as she ran the water over him, she knew she had gotten the temperature right. Too cold, and Gounda would tap-dance around the wash stall. But with a bit of heat to it, he would stand patiently, like now. He almost seemed to enjoy it as Macy sprayed his front feet first before moving slowly up his legs to his chest, and then letting the water cascade over his neck, back, and haunches. The salt ran off of him in white rivulets.

Macy grabbed a squeegee and took care to get as much excess water off of Gounda as she could, not only to help him dry, but to keep his fur from trapping a blanket of water that would actually make him hotter, not cooler.

She checked the time again: twelve thirty-seven.

She repeated the process of hosing and scraping Gounda once more and then put a hand on his chest, almost between his front legs, to gauge his temperature. He had cooled down enough, but Macy hand-grazed him before turning him out, just to be sure. Gounda, like any horse, would binge on water after a workout and make himself sick in the process. Hand-grazing took care of that problem. He was clean, dry, and cool by the time Macy led him to his paddock. Once he was inside, Macy turned him so that he faced her before removing his halter, and clucked to him, encouraging him to run off. In true Gounda form, he simply ambled away.

Twelve forty-six

Inside the barn, she hung Gounda's halter back on his stall. She unzipped her gaiters and unlaced her paddock boots, removing both in one motion. Then she peeled off each sock and slipped on a pair of flip-flops. After pulling a backpack out of her tack trunk, she was finally ready.

She started toward the back pasture—the one with a slight

rise that overlooked parts of the water, Saratoga Beach and Oyster River up-island to the left and Miracle Beach to the right, where Gounda's mare used to frolic with her babies and the other broodmares. Used to.

A gangly, dark brown foal with a blaze and four white socks teetered over to her, following her at a safe distance as she walked. Then something rustled in the woods beyond and the foal bucked and ran back to the safety of its mother and the rest of the herd. It stared accusingly at Macy. Its feather duster of a tail twitched, and it snorted a foolish little snort. Macy chuckled. "Tough guy Tuesday," she said to him, then thought that might not be a bad name for the little guy, and made a mental note to check and see whether it was available.

She hopped the fence line at the very back corner of the pasture and followed a wooded path that gradually gave way to sand. Eventually, the trees fell away and Macy found herself on a wide, flat expanse of sandy beach.

Far to her right, a swarm of people dotted the scene like ants. Macy could make out beach umbrellas and chairs. She imagined a crude sand castle or two was under construction. An inlet of water had made its way up the beach and now ran parallel to it, in her general direction. She guessed the water in it was far warmer than that of the ocean just beyond, judging from the number of young kids splashing and playing in it. She imagined they were shrieking and laughing, but she was far enough away and the breeze off the water was just heavy enough that on her own plot of sand, she heard only what was supposed to be there: wind, trees, water, and the cry of an occasional bird.

Macy walked halfway to the water and set down her backpack. She removed a blanket, which she spread with the help of the wind, two wineglasses, a corkscrew, and a bottle of Bordeaux that Martine had brought back for her and Nash from Paris.

Twelve fifty-eight.

It had been a wedding present. Nash, guessing it was a good, expensive bottle, insisted they save it for a special occasion.

Macy opened it and poured wine into each glass, filling them equally, halfway.

This was their special occasion.

Nine years before, at three o'clock in the afternoon Green Bay time, in a gazebo on the banks of the Fox River, Macy had worn white. She had said, "I will," to a number of questions, and finally, "I do." She had married Nash Allen.

"Happy anniversary, baby," she said. Her voice startled her.

She had wanted to wear slacks—a nice, presentable pantsuit—but Magda had shamed her into a dress, and Macy spent most of the afternoon and night silently cursing Magda. The straps of the dress kept falling off her shoulders, the boning poked her ribs, and there was no fabric to stem the streams of sweat that ran down her legs.

To have and to hold . . .

Macy remembered picking out this piece of land with her grandfather. She remembered loving it, even then. Even before a single building went up on it. She could see its promise. She remembered towing a U-Haul trailer packed with Nash's belongings up the driveway days after their wedding. And she remembered the days that followed, filled with unpacking—merging utensils, CDs, closet space, ideas about how things should be organized. She remembered looking at him as he confidently took a glass out of the cupboard and a Coke out of the fridge, and thinking, *He lives here now.* The space seemed more full with him there. Not only his things, but his presence. The promise of a whole life to be lived in tandem with hers.

In joy and in sorrow . . .

She had taken Nash riding for the first time not long after he had moved there, only a week or two after they had married. It had been impossibly hot, and Martine had rescheduled her lesson for later that week. She remembered how out of place Nash looked on top of Gounda, sitting too far back and nearly overhanging the back of her old saddle, his jeans having ridden up above his ankles, his runners pushed straight through the stirrups and toes down, instead of the balls of his feet resting on them with his toes pointed up. His body rocked with each step Gounda took, and it seemed as though Nash thought that he might be able to push the horse forward if he simply bobbed his shoulders harder. Macy could sense Gounda's irritation with his new passenger, and she barked at Nash on Gounda's behalf. "You've got to sit up straight," she told Nash. "Hold your core tighter. You're jackhammering his spine." Sometimes she wondered what her life might have been like had she married another show jumper—if she'd enjoy it more, being able to fully share what she most loved with the person she most loved—or hadn't gotten married at all. She wondered if she'd be a better rider. She wondered if she would be more dedicated, more focused, more willing to go from show to show instead of always coming home in between. Sometimes she found herself frustrated that her real life didn't more closely line up with that alternate reality in her head. Sometimes she took that frustration out on Nash.

They had ridden down to this very spot. Gounda, knowing exactly where he was and what the excursion meant, plodded purposefully toward the water. "Whoa," Nash said, pulling on the reins. "Whoa," he said, louder and with more authority. But Gounda paid him no heed. Nash might as well have been a sack of flour fixed to the horse's back.

"Just go with it!" Macy called to Nash. He looked back at her for affirmation just as Gounda waded into the water. She was about to yell to him to hang on to Gounda's mane, and wondered if perhaps this hadn't been the best idea, when she saw Gounda give a push and begin to swim. Nash instinctively reached for a handful of mane. He hovered above Gounda's neck in the water. He whooped as the horse motored through.

Eventually, of his own accord, Gounda turned toward shore, and the two of them, dripping wet, walked up to where Macy's own mount stood knee-deep and splashing the water with one front leg. Nash shook his head, smiling at her. "What an amazing life," he said.

Macy loved him, in that instant, perhaps more than she ever had before. She remembered thinking that they would do this when they were old and gray. By then, the pastures would be chock-full of horses who simply needed a home. They would have built another barn or two. She would make them all bran mash when nights got cold and treat them to ice in their water buckets during the occasional summer swelter. Then she'd come in from the barns and find Nash grilling something or other. He'd hand her a glass of wine, and from the back porch they'd look out over the fencing and green grass and happy, happy horses, and remember what they had built. Together.

Macy took a sip of the wine. It coated her tongue, sweet and hinting of spice and then a little bitter. It evaporated in her mouth after she swallowed it, like an apparition, as if it had never been there at all.

Until death do us part.

This wasn't how it was supposed to go. Not yet. And if sheer will was what it took, Macy could have conjured Nash out of thin air. She ached for him. In ten short years, she had forgotten how to be her without him. She hadn't the faintest idea of how to go about untangling her life from his, from theirs. She also didn't want to. If she held him close enough, if she thought about him often enough, if she didn't forget to mark things like his birthday, Christmas, the first day they met, days like today, maybe she could keep him there with her. Maybe she could somehow prevent him from being relegated to a part of her life that was now over. Her own personal past tense. How ridiculous she had been to have wanted a man who could jump a horse over a bunch of painted wood rails like she could. Instead she had stumbled into a life with a man who could do everything else. Who had become everything else to her.

On their first wedding anniversary, Nash had started a tradition she had grown to secretly relish. Each year on their anniversary he would bring home two splits of champagne. Macy would come in from the barn to find the mini bottles chilling in a bowl of ice (they had never registered for a champagne bucket, never anticipated that they would need one) on the back porch, flanked on either side by a glass flute, paper tablet, pen, and a sandwich baggie. They sipped the sweet bubbly in a silence broken only by the scratching of their pens moving over the paper. That first year, Macy wrote the vows she would have written for their wedding, had Magda not insisted on tradition and had Nash not been so quick to appease his mom. She had continued her vow writing each year after, changing what she wrote to reflect what had happened that year. Last year, her note had said, "I promise to love you when you run out of gas at two a.m. on the way home from the Quinnie when you surprise me by showing up in Langley with chocolate cake and roses for my birthday as I exit the ring from a perfect round, for the way my name sounds when you say it and the way my hand feels in yours. I promise to love you in the morning when I'm crabby and at night when you snore. I promise to always love you, even when I might not feel like it, and I promise to try to be a person who's always easy to love. I love you, and I love our life, more than I ever thought I could. —M."

She never knew what Nash wrote. After they had each finished their notes, they would slip the folded paper into a baggie and stuff it into their respective bottles. Then, using leftover wine corks and candle wax, Nash would seal each bottle. The wax dried and hardened as they walked to the beach, near where Macy sat. They would stop at the water's edge and roll their pants to their knees, and then walk into the ocean on a sandbar that stretched hundreds of meters out. Sometimes they would stop with the water at their knees. Sometimes it reached midthigh. They would count together, "One, two, three," and toss their bottles into the air, toward the setting sun.

Standing there—the waves tugging at her legs, the sun dipping lower and lower in the sky, Nash's arm around her shoulders and his lips whispering against her hair, "To us. To another year"—had become Macy's favorite moment of every year. If she had known she'd have such a finite number of them, she'd have talked Nash into doing it more often. She'd have made him linger there, long after the sun had gone down. She'd have noted exactly how his breath felt against her forehead, exactly where his hand rested on her shoulder.

God, she wanted him back. She would take a minute. She'd settle for a second. Just a glimpse of his smile. Just a flutter of his skin on hers.

She hadn't ever believed in ghosts or psychics or religion or afterlife. Yet how she wanted to just then. She scanned the beach, and then the horizon.

A breeze picked up. A branch cracked somewhere in the distance. A foal nickered to his mom.

It wasn't fair that Nash could be parted from her by death, while she sat on a windswept beach on their anniversary, alone. Still tied to him. Maybe forever tied to him. And what about her? What was she supposed to do now?

The other glass of wine remained at her feet, untouched.

She remembered the jolt of electricity as Nash kissed her after the officiant gave him permission; the softness of Nash's hand on hers as the two of them stood at the edge of the reception, marveling at having all of their favorite people in one place; missing her parents terribly at that very moment, and Nash, as if he read her thoughts, pulling her to him and telling her that she was now his to take care of, officially.

So take care of me, then, she challenged him. *If there was ever a time I needed taking care of . . .*

Macy leaned back on the sand. She closed her eyes. When she opened them, she half expected—or maybe she just wanted—Nash to be leaning over her, stroking her cheek with the backs of his fingers, a concerned expression on his face.

Macy's phone rang. She cursed herself for not leaving it back at the barn. She silenced it, but it rang again only a minute later. She looked at the caller ID. It was her sister, Regan. She knew that Regan would keep calling back. Her sister had an aversion to voice mail that Macy had never deciphered—leaving them or picking her own up—and if Regan deemed something urgent she would press "redial" until the person on the receiving end relented. It was a metaphor for how Regan ran the rest of her life. Macy pressed the green telephone icon to take the call.

"Hi," Macy answered.

A din of noise greeted her on the other end. Garbled snippets of talk radio competed with shrieks of kids. Regan was always either trying to simultaneously conduct her three kids in an art project and make dinner, or she was rushing one of them to or from a lesson, game, or playdate. Regan was essentially a single mother, with a workaholic ghost of a husband. Except Craig worked for Goldman Sachs. He was an incredibly rich ghost.

"Jacquie, sit *down* now! Sorry, Mace. I'm up to my eyeballs in sugar-crazed kids." Before Macy could tell her not to worry about it, Regan continued on, talking right over Macy as she had been doing their whole lives. "Anyway, the girls are starting riding lessons—aren't you proud? They need helmets, and there are just so many choices that I don't know which one to get for them. I figured I'd check with you to see which ones would be best."

"I don't know," Macy said. "I'd—"

"I mean, do I go for the most expensive one? Does a pricey helmet really offer that much more protection than a cheap one?"

"I'd have to check," Macy said. Regan had lived in Manhattan for six years and New Jersey for another thirteen. The region's fast pace and brash directness that Macy found so charming in others, her brother-in-law included, took on a judgmental air in Regan.

"How can you not know? Seriously, Kevin—get that out of your nose!"

Macy liked to think that this—the parallel conversation Regan constantly had with her kids and anyone on the other end of her phone call—was the reason they didn't talk often. In reality, when Regan gave birth to Kevin, nine years ago, it had simply become a convenient excuse for them both not to have to try so hard anymore.

"I mean, isn't this what you *do* for a living?"

Macy explained that she hadn't bought a new helmet in a few years, and pointed out that it had been much longer than that since she'd been in the market for a kid's helmet.

"I'll check and get back to you," Macy said. She didn't want to start an argument with Regan. Not today.

"Okay, but their first lesson is a week from Monday, and I'll need some lead time to order them or pick some up, though I don't know where you get riding helmets in New Jersey."

"You can order them from—"

Macy fell quiet, sure that the squabbling of her two nieces and nephew in the background and Regan's yelling at them to stop had drowned her out. Macy compared the chaos of Regan's house with the relative silence of her own. If only she had been as brave as her sister. Macy found herself stifling a sob that had risen out of nowhere, hot and thick at the back of her throat.

"Something wrong, Mace?" Regan asked.

She doesn't remember, Macy thought. It was inconceivable to her how this day that had loomed so large and threatening on her own horizon could be just another twenty-four hours to everyone else. This day that Macy had feared and steeled herself against and planned down to the minute was, for her sister, another in a long string of days in which dinner and e-mail and refereeing kids and researching riding helmets took top billing.

"No," Macy said. She took a sip of wine. A tiny bug had landed in the red liquid, fluttering hopelessly. Macy dipped a finger in and lifted it out, though it was probably already a goner. "Can I say hi to them?"

Macy had met her nieces and nephew only a handful of times, and long ago, when they were much younger. She sent birthday presents and holiday cards. She tried to call them regularly. But those gestures were a cheap substitute for actual visits. Regan wouldn't take them to British Columbia. She said it was too expensive to fly the whole family west, and Macy would bite her tongue as Regan switched subjects to their Hamptons share or Craig's promotion or how they were thinking of moving back into the city but just couldn't afford a place with space enough for all of them. The last time Macy had seen the kids, four years ago, she had discovered the real reason. After a late-night talk over strong gin and tonics that Craig had mixed for them before going to bed, Regan looked at Macy and said, "You remind me so much of her." Then she added, "Too much," quietly and with her head turned away from Macy. Even at a whisper, those two words were an accusation leveled at Macy like a pair of arrows. The next year, when Martine suggested going east for the Hampton Classic, Macy begged off. "It's just another horse show," she told him. "Nothing worth going all that way for."

"The kids? Oh, maybe later, okay? I wanted to call quickly, while I was thinking about the helmets, but I'm just getting dinner on the table, and you know how hard it is to get them all to sit down and eat at the same time."

Macy didn't, actually. "Regan, can't I say hi to them while you're finishing up? Maybe put them on speakerphone."

"It's really not the best time. When you have kids you'll understand," Regan said. It was one of her go-to phrases. Macy had no doubt her sister loved being a mom and that she was good at it. But she couldn't help suspect that part of what Regan loved about motherhood was pointing out how busy, demanding, and full her life was in comparison to everyone else's, Macy's in particular. She had assumed, clearly in error, that her status as a newly minted widow might exempt her from Regan's barbs for the time being.

"Fine," Macy said. She rested an elbow on one knee and her forehead in her hand. She noticed that the bug she had rescued from her wine was still perched on her jeans leg, trying to get its wings working.

"Macy, don't sulk. It doesn't become you. Oh, shit, Claudia just smeared hoisin sauce in Jacquie's hair; I've gotta go. Talk soon!"

And then she was gone.

Macy shut her phone and tossed it on the blanket beside her. She watched the bug on her leg flutter and struggle. It did a quick spin, and suddenly lifted up, up, up, until it blended into thin air and she could no longer see it.

Macy scanned the water, left to right, straining her eyes for the glint of light off a bottle. But the sun hung low in the sky, and it bounced rays off the water so that even if a giant vanity mirror were floating out there, much less an empty champagne split, it would be nearly impossible to tell from her perch.

She picked up her glass of wine, and then, thinking that her walk might take a while, poured herself a little extra. Macy walked toward the water and stopped where it met the sand, suddenly aware that she was bringing glass into the water and feeling like maybe she shouldn't. But whole ships went down in these waters, she reasoned with herself; a little broken glass wasn't going to hurt the ocean any.

Once Macy located the sandbar she walked out onto it, her direction steady and unhurried.

You're a madwoman, she said to herself.

But what if? she answered.

Each year, on their walk down to this spot and out into the water, champagne splits in hand, Nash would tell Macy one message-in-a-bottle story. Macy never gave them much thought, instead chalking them up to his encyclopedic memory for totally useless information.

There was the Swedish sailor who, tired of the unchanging views of water and his shipmates, wrote a note "to someone beautiful and far away," threw it overboard, and married the daughter of the Sicilian fisherman who found it.

There was the Japanese sailor who was shipwrecked on an island with forty-three others and no freshwater, and realized, as he watched them each die from starvation and dehydration, that none of them would never see their families again. So he carved the story of what had happened to them on thin pieces of coconut tree bark, found a bottle in the ship's wreckage, and set his rough, knife-hewn notes adrift before he himself passed away. More than a century later, the bottle turned up—on the shore of his tiny Japanese village.

Then there was the story about two friends walking around a lake in Wisconsin. They had just buried their friend Josh, who had completed a tour of duty in Iraq only to return home and die in a car accident. They asked each other why. They railed against the senselessness of it all. And then one of them spotted a bottle bobbing on the water's surface. A vanilla bottle. Inside the bottle was a note that read, "My name is Josh Baker. I'm ten. If you find this, put it on the news." It was from the boy version of their friend, recently put to rest. Josh's mom had confirmed it to them, and then to the media outlets. She remembered him dumping her whole bottle of vanilla out when he was a kid, said her house smelled like it for weeks.

Nash would pepper the stories with interesting facts—that bottles are the most seaworthy vessels, capable of sailing unfettered through hurricanes and storms that would capsize anything else. That you couldn't predict the direction a bottle would travel, even if two were dropped together: like the two bottles sent off the Brazilian coast, one drifting east and washing up on a beach in Africa, and the other heading northwest to Nicaragua. That the United States Navy used floating bottles to conjure detailed charts of the oceans' currents. Or that Queen Elizabeth I's fleet of ships had used them to send ashore information about enemy positions and that "Uncorker of Ocean Bottles" was an official post in her court.

But it was the stories that Macy clung to now: A shipwrecked Japanese sailor's bottle reaching his native village a hundred and fifty years after he set it afloat. A vanilla bottle finding its way to the very people who needed it most, at just the right moment. Was it really so much for Macy to ask that just one of the notes Nash wrote to her wash back up here on Miracle Beach? Things like that clearly happened throughout the world. Was it too much to ask that it happen to her, just once?

But as far as she could see, there was nothing but water. And Macy reminded herself that the only thing that had washed ashore there lately was a severed right foot, still wearing its shoe.

Still, she walked. Until the sun sank and the water rose higher and Macy grew dizzy from the constant scanning. Looking over her right shoulder, she could see that the thick stretch of Miracle Beach where people tended to congregate had emptied. The water, as clean and clear as the air, had turned opaque below her without the sun shining on it. Three fires flickered on the sand in the almost-night. The mountains that stood dark and tall across the strait now nearly blended with a deepening sky. Soon, in a matter of minutes, not hours, they would look less like shadows and become almost invisible as night closed in around them. And her.

Macy had run out of time. Her day—their day—had ended.

She gulped the last of the wine from her glass and tossed it as hard as she could. She thought she heard it break, the sound like a wind chime. *Take that*, she thought. She wished she had another to whip at the water.

She did, she realized. She had another glass, and a bottle. And then she felt foolish. The glasses, the corkscrew, the wine. Hauling it all out here in a bag at exactly three p.m. central time. For what? So that her dead husband could conspire with the universe and send her a message in a bottle? And what if he had? What difference would it make?

Because Nash wasn't there. He wasn't anywhere. He was just gone. And he wasn't coming back.

Chapter Eight

THE BLACKNESS OF THAT NOWHERE TIME BETWEEN MIDNIGHT and dawn settled on Jack like a stifling blanket. He had never been big on sleep, had never needed much, although as a much younger man, he had always been able to will it to him if he wished. But the older he got the less often it came. It seemed to know he wanted it, needed it—if for no other reason than to fill a few more hours in the day—but it taunted him from just beyond the footboard; it forbade him to fall into it.

So, on those mornings—or late nights, as the young folks and those who believed they were still that young swayed their way home from the bars liked to think of them—Jack would walk.

Despite it being summer, Jack could feel the bite of the night air coming through his window. He swaddled himself in layers of outerwear and, after gingerly closing the door behind him, headed behind the barn and down toward the beach.

Too many times to count, Jack had trudged through Wisconsin's thick northern woods in the November dark, his way lit by the moon on snow layered like powdered sugar. He was always the first one out of camp, hoping to arrive at his hunting post before the deer. A little snow on the ground now and he might've been right back there. But before long, the canopy of trees and pitch-blackness gave way to a wide expanse of beach lit like a stage by the moon.

The rocky beach growled beneath Jack's feet as he made his way toward a giant driftwood log that looked to be the perfect place to camp out and watch the ocean.

The water was Jack's favorite thing about Vancouver Island. Wherever you went, it was there, always in motion. The sound that sang to him like a lullaby—the lap-lull-lap-lull-lap beat of it flirting with the beach. Kiss and retreat, kiss and retreat. In no other place did water make that kind of sound or keep that particular rhythm. Even the ocean in Mexico seemed to speak differently, Jack thought. There, the water whispered over sand beaches. Here, it moved sternly over rocks, stating its case. He stripped off his jacket to put underneath him before settling back against the log.

Jack must've slipped off to sleep, because he woke to someone calling, "Hey, there! Everything okay?"

He waved to the figure, lit by a beam of moonlight, and gave a thumbs-up in the general direction from where the voice was shouting, a rowboat about a hundred feet offshore. Then he took a second, closer look.

"Ms. McLean? Sophie? That you?"

"Jack?" the voice called back. "You wait there. I'll row in."

"Well, I'm sure as hell not going wading," Jack muttered.

As Sophie pulled her rowboat onto the beach, it struck Jack how small she seemed—like a kid playing dress-up. She had on yellow waterproof pants that seemed fit for someone three times her size, held up only by built-in suspenders. Even her black fleece sweatshirt draped from her shoulders as if on a waifish storefront mannequin.

"What are you doing out here?" Jack asked Sophie. "It's the middle of the night."

"Actually, it's around three in the morning. And I should ask you the same thing," she said. They looked at each other, neither of them speaking. After a time, Sophie asked, "Well, are you getting in?"

"Uhh, I don't know," Jack stammered. "What are you—I mean, how long do you think—"

"How about I make this easier for you? Get in."

Jack did as he was told.

He climbed into the middle, thinking that he could row—although where to, he wasn't quite sure. But when Sophie pushed the little boat from shore and hopped in, she settled at the stern. With a couple of quick pulls, a motor so tiny that Jack hadn't even noticed it murmured and came to life, and Sophie guided the boat out into the ocean. Jack had turned himself around so he now faced rearward. He fixed his gaze on the boat's tiny wake cutting through the water's opaque surface, a paper cut bleeding silver.

Jack remembered Nash telling him that no matter what time of year it was on the island, in the mornings and late evenings, fall always felt just seconds away. Maybe this was why Nash had liked it so much here—twinges of his favorite season all year round.

They were headed straight across toward Quadra Island when Sophie cut the motor unexpectedly.

"Problem?" asked Jack.

"Only if you don't like catching fish," Sophie said. She pointed, drawing his attention to bursts of splashing he could now hear all around them. First at three o'clock to their boat, then at seven, and another at one, all originating from under the water and jumping straight up.

"Are those *fish*?" Jack asked.

"Not just fish, Jackie. Salmon."

Their little boat bobbed on a quiet ocean as Sophie got to work. Two poles seemed to materialize, and onto both she threaded a transparent line. Then she rummaged in a tackle box at her feet and produced two spoons that flashed intermittently in the moonlight.

"Lucky dog," she looked up and said, as if finally remembering Jack was there.

"Huh?"

"We're going to use Lucky Dogs for lures. They'll work fine."

"Is there something that works better?"

Sophie thought for a moment. "Nah, not really. Not for this time of day. I'm partial to my other Luckys"—she held up a red-and-white shovel-nosed wooden lure that resembled a small fish—"Lucky Louies. But they're sort of a collector's item, if you will, and the tide is still out, so the dogfish are probably out in force right now, and I don't want to risk losing any of these guys."

Jack had no idea what the hell she was talking about. He was a hunter: deer, duck, and pheasant. He'd never been much of a fisherman, for no reason he could pinpoint at the moment. He nodded, if only to acknowledge that Sophie had been speaking to him.

She handed Jack a pole, which upon examination he was surprised to find was missing two things he thought were imperative to catching fish: a barbed hook and live bait.

"Uh, I think you forgot something here, ma'am," he said. And he knew as soon as he said it what was coming.

"There you go ma'aming me again. Gal darn, Jack. I'm not *that* old, you know!" Sophie shook her head at him. "Anyways, you're all set there. Go ahead."

"But there's no bait."

"Don't use bait, Jack."

"What about this hook?"

"What about it?"

"There's no barb," Jack pointed out, though he wondered why he needed to.

"Nope, there isn't," Sophie said. "I like to fish Tyee Club rules. That means no jigs, no bait, and barbless hooks only. Oh, and no motors. Usually. Though it would take these old arms eons to row all the way out here, so tonight we cheated a wee bit."

"But why?" Jack couldn't understand for the life of him why, with fish all around them nearly jumping into the boat, Sophie wouldn't want to nab one and get home.

"It levels the playing field," she said. "Makes things fairer for the fish. Gives them a bit of a fighting chance. And then I don't feel as guilty—like when I get one, I don't feel as though I've tricked it. So even when I'm way outside the Tyee Pool—that's a particular area the club fishes—I still fish by as many of those rules as I can. Plus, I can only eat so much salmon, and my clients tend to take more than their fair share. The rules even it all out."

Sophie cast out and nodded for Jack to do the same.

"Plus," she added, "I promise you've never seen a sadder thing than a fish starved to death because of a barb stuck in its gullet. They don't ask for that. We shouldn't give it to 'em."

Jack nodded. There wasn't much argument he could think to muster against that point. And so he watched Sophie, who watched the span of water in front of her with a mix of reverence and intensity. Sophie's rod seemed to be an extension of her body, the line an extra set of fingers with which to sense the motion beneath the water's surface.

"How did you start doing this?" Jack asked. "How did you learn it all?" He thought of Nash then, living here on an island focused on fishing like Green Bay was on the Packers. He wondered if anyone had ever asked Nash how it was that he didn't know how to tie a lure or even cast. He wondered what Nash might have said. Jack felt a sick stab in his gut that he'd never made time to take his son fishing. He'd done other things for Nash, he reasoned—coached his hockey team, helped him with geometry, grilled steaks and potatoes for a small group of Nash and his friends before his senior prom. But he'd never set out onto the Fox River or one of the nearby lakes with his son, just the two of them alone in a boat for a good stretch of the morning.

"My dad," she said.

Jack nodded. Of course it had been her dad. Those were the sorts of things dads were supposed to do.

"It took me almost fifteen years to catch my first certifiable Tyee," she said. "And my pap rowed me to it the day before he died."

Sophie dug inside the pants of her survival suit, and Jack, unsure as to what exactly was going on, looked away. But he heard her say, "Here," and when he looked back she was holding a worn photograph inside a plastic sleeve.

Sophie was standing near the weigh scales, her fifty-one-pound fish nearly as long as and looking heavier than she was. The fish, hanging by its tail, mouth agape, seemed surprised to find itself in that position. Sophie had one sun-browned and scrawny arm slung casually around the fish, the way most young girls posed with their best friends. The camera had caught her stealing a glance at her father, who stood off to the side, beaming, with both arms extended out toward Sophie as if to say, "Look at this girl—my girl!"

"It was a good moment. It was a good day," she said.

And then she told him about the day that followed. How, before dawn the next morning, her father boarded a friend's commercial fishing boat to fill in for a sick deckhand. They'd headed north through the Seymour Narrows—a spot Captain George Vancouver described in the late 1700s as "one of the vilest stretches of water in the world" because of the twin peaks of Ripple Rock that lurked just beneath the narrows' surface and the spontaneous whirlpools they produced.

That was the last time Sophie McLean had seen her father. "They just vanished," she said. "And there was no searching for people who went down in the narrows." Sophie told him how, years later, when engineers attempted to soften Ripple Rock's peaks with the biggest nonnuclear explosion on record, she was sitting at her family's kitchen table—that picture in hand—remembering that day she caught the Tyee with her pap, as the salt and pepper shakers rattled against the seashell napkin holder, all the while hoping that her dad's final resting place was elsewhere.

Jack didn't have any idea what Nash had done the day before he died, or whom he had spent it with. And how expensive would it have been to call his son at the end of every day, just to check in? Jack scoffed. Money wasn't the thing. Still, if someone had told him to do just that, Jack would have dismissed the idea out of hand. His son had his life to live, after all. There wouldn't have been all that much to talk about every single day. But having something to talk about seemed absolutely ludicrous now.

Simply hearing Nash's voice, his deep belly laugh, would have been more than plenty.

Jack leaned over the side of the boat and tried to peer down into the water, but the sky was still black and the surface shone back up at him as a mirrored sheet of sequins, prohibiting any real depth of vision. He would do this whenever he was out in large expanses of water, trying to see what was down there, underneath. And it scared the bejesus out of him every single time. Jack had seen Shark Week and programs like it, and none of those underwater scenes looked anything like the ones found on bedspreads or made into poster-size prints—all colorful and idyllic.

He imagined that hundreds, even thousands of feet of water stretched out below, straight down. Their measly little boat resting precariously above it all, above all the strange and beautiful and sometimes vicious creatures that water held so gently.

"Fish on!" Sophie called out, and Jack wheeled around to see the nose of her rod tipped sharply toward the water. Sophie waited a quick second before setting the hook. The line whirled as the fish zigged across the water, and she let it run for a little while before checking it back to her. The fish rallied hard against the line, the rod, and Sophie's sinewy arms, and so she let it run a bit again. "It's a salmon," she said. "We're in for it now, Jackie!"

Jack arched an eyebrow.

"Salmon fishing isn't much like other kinds of fishing. It's not all hook and reel and muscle. You can't will these guys into the boat," she said. "Oh, no. You've gotta negotiate with the fish, strike a deal. Or just wait until one of us gets too tired to wrangle."

Jack could imagine the burn simmering in Sophie's arms and neck. They had been tensed for what seemed like hours. The line would strain and then whirl, strain and whirl—the water roiling and falling still, and roiling and falling still.

"Jackie, can you reach in my pants for me?"

Jack's head snapped up. "Excuse me?"

"Don't get all excited," Sophie said. "There's a flask in my right pocket."

"Why don't I just hold the pole for you?" Jack asked.

"Because I don't trust you not to lose this fish, and because I'd really love a sip of bourbon at the moment," she said. "Now, are you going to help a girl out or not?"

Jack slipped an arm inside the rubbery pants, careful not to hit any improper areas. Would that really be so bad, though? The thought came out of nowhere and he dismissed it just as suddenly.

"This is the part I love—bantering with the fish, Jack. This is the sport of it," Sophie said, taking a pull from the flask that Jack offered. She explained that she never much cared to see the fish lying in the bottom of her boat afterward, its huge tail poking like a fan of night sky out of the basin, its gills winking at their unnatural habitat, at the brutal air. That sight, she said, always made her chest tighten, made her sad. "Honestly, I'd much rather the fish argue for a while and then split. Deep down, every time, that's really what I hope for."

And as if she had wished it, that was precisely what happened. After a countless number of under and backs beneath the boat, the fish had started to tire. And just like that, the line went slack.

Sophie reeled in to find only a piece of the fish's head dangling from the hook.

"What happened?" Jack asked. His mind immediately went to scenes from Shark Week of rows and rows of teeth lining jaws that could swallow their tiny rowboat whole.

Before Sophie could answer, there came a sort of honking noise from in back of them. Both Sophie and Jack turned to see a seal, illuminated by a ribbon of moonlight, floating on its back, the salmon between its flippers and teeth. It seemed to be laughing at them, which amused Jack. He laughed with the seal. Sophie did not. "There's a reason your kind get clubbed to death!" she hollered at it. "You asshole!"

This made Jack laugh even harder. Sophie glowered at him.

"Does that mean we're done?" he asked.

"Nope," she answered.

Veins of red were already draped across a murky sky before Sophie got another fish on the line and got it in close enough to the boat to gaff it. Jack watched as the fish looked up at her from the water, as if it were conceding, right before the point of the gaff shot into its gills and up through its head with a crunch. Sophie netted the fish and dropped it into the basin. Jack looked away, staring toward shore.

"Miracle Beach," she said, tossing her chin in the direction Jack was looking and taking a swig from her flask.

Jack looked at her with eyebrows arched. "Odd name," he said.

"Legend has it that the Cape Mudge Indians were always being attacked by other tribes. They weren't so much for fighting, you know. Then one day a starving stranger stumbles in and the Indians feed him and give him clothes and this stranger tells them that it's their lucky day: He's a messenger of the Great Spirit, and because of their generosity, they'll be protected and rich. But the messenger warns them not to get too full of themselves, which, of course, they do, and another tribe attacks them. The messenger makes the Cape Mudgies sweat it out, but he eventually saves them, only to turn one of their princesses into that little island over yonder, Mittlenach." Sophie nodded north-east over her shoulder. She offered her flask to Jack and, when he refused, capped it and reached an arm back inside her survival pants to put it away.

"So what's the miracle?" Jack asked. "I don't get it."

"Well, Mittlenach looks like it's moving away from you when you boat over to it." Sophie shrugged. "But that's more of an op-tical illusion than a miracle, I'd say. Your guess is as good as mine."

She started the minimotor and it sputtered to life, slowly picking up speed and propelling them toward shore, Miracle Beach growing ever larger in front of them as their boat cut through the liquid black.

Chapter Nine

"HEADS UP . . . *HEADS UP!*" A VOICE YELLED AT HER. A MAN'S
voice, not Martine's and not friendly.

Like a spawning salmon, Macy was headed in the opposite
direction of the river of horses and riders in the warm-up pen,
which would have been acceptable protocol had she actually
been paying any attention. She pulled her right rein hard, forc-
ing Gounda to switch leads and directions a split second after
landing. He took the change of plans in stride, relaxing back
into her hands and collecting himself as if preparing for the next
jump. Although she knew *smart horse* was probably an oxymoron, at times like this she had to wonder. It couldn't be all in-
stinct, after all.

"My God. Pay attention! You're going to hurt someone out
here."

The other rider shook his head at her, scowling as though she
had actually run into him, instead of just almost. Ian Painter. She
knew him. Everyone did. He had imp black hair. Eyes to match.
A jawline that could cut granite. He and his regular mount, Rosetta, had won more Grand Prix rounds than any other team in

Canada's history, and he was currently looking at Macy as if she were gum stuck to the bottom of his very expensive field boots.

There were hundreds of ways this situation could have been avoided.

First of all, she could've looked ahead, out of the corner and through to the landing of the jump, before nearly colliding with one of the country's premier jumper riders.

Also, she should never have come here in the first place.

The last show in Victoria had gone beyond poorly, though at the time, Macy had convinced herself that it hadn't been her fault. Even when the young filly she had taken to that show had tried to jump a box oxer too early, even when Macy had checked the filly back hard and held her there to get one more stride in before she took off instead of going with the filly's forward motion like she should have, and even when the filly argued and jumped anyway, as any horse that green would have, dropping her front legs between the one-meter span of the two jumps and tumbling like an Olympic gymnast with Macy still fixed to her back, Macy had pinned it on Jack.

Still blowing brown snot into a tissue days after her initial fall, Macy decided that her dismal performance could be squarely attributed to Jack's need for constant hand-holding, his constant need for entertainment. She couldn't concentrate. None of it, of course, had had anything to do with her. And that was how, on a whim, Macy came to drop off Jack and her young project filly at home, load up Gounda and some more hay, grain, and bales of bedding, and make the almost two-day drive to the July Classic at Calgary's Spruce Meadows, where she currently had no business riding.

And then there was the matter of the hole inside of her. The one that felt as though someone had come along and scooped out all of her insides, leaving her feeling like a papery shell of someone she used to know.

That could've all been pretty easily avoided, too. She would've needed only to have told Nash no back in the very beginning. Right at the very start.

He had missed a connecting flight in Calgary and, stuck there until the following morning, saw an advertisement for the horse show in the airport, rented a car, and decided to go exploring. Months later, when Nash would turn what should have been a two-hour drive into a seven-hour expedition of roadside histori-cal markers, Macy would decide that this was classically Nash.

Though if she had a chance to turn back the clock, Macy still wasn't sure she'd be able to resist him. His earnest way and aw-shucks charm. Because even at that very moment she was bank-ing on the off chance that death didn't actually work the way everyone thought it did. Her eyes scanned the sea of jodhpurs and polo tops, saddle leather and dusty sweat, half hoping Nash would saunter out of the crowd in a navy blue suit, just as he had years ago, and not far from the practice ring where she now stood.

She could have walked away from him that day, but she would have missed so much: the way he would reach across and brush his thumb back and forth over the nape of her neck on car rides; the little disjointed dance he'd do on any happy occasion—whether he had just finished the dishes or landed a huge ac-count; how he taught her to snap her fingers, throw a Frisbee, and skip rocks—all required skills that she had somehow left childhood without learning—and the pure pleasure he took whenever she actually got the hang of them. She would've missed the way he looked at her when she shot her first deer back in Wisconsin, beaming, with his breath escaping from his parted lips in wispy tendrils. The way he fumed when he was mad at her, shaking his head and biting his bottom lip to keep from smiling, even then. The way he'd mumble, "Morning, munchkin," when she woke him up with a small peck on his cheek—groggy but content—then wrapping his arm around her neck and pulling her into the crook of his to keep her close for just a few more minutes while she'd struggle to escape, anxious to start the day.

Now it was as if their first conversation were happening fresh in front of her, all over again.

"I'm not quite sure what I'm doing here," he had said to her.

They were in line at the concession stand. She wasn't even sure that he had been talking to her.

"Excuse me?" she said.

"I've never been to one of these things before. Where do you go? Where are the performances?"

"Competitions. Not performances," she had corrected him.

"Oh," he said, mopping at his brow with a handkerchief. Macy had never seen anyone younger than her grandfather use a handkerchief. "Like I said, I've never been. But my motto is that a lot of great things can happen if you don't always insist on a plan. Pretty exciting stuff here, from the looks of it. Anyway, you involved in all this?"

She remembered how sweat beaded his forehead and ran in streams down his hairline, how sweat had started to seep through his suit coat, and that he asked for a "brat" before settling on a plain hot dog when the woman behind the counter had no idea what he was talking about. Almost before she realized it, Macy had said to him, "I am, but I don't ride for a while. I can show you around if you want."

And so, for the next couple of hours, she kept him company. They walked through the barns and Macy pointed out to him the elaborate stall decorations each farm or trainer put up—some complete with living rooms and full bars. After that, she had sat in the stands with him, providing a play-by-play during each rider's go: what the point of each class was, what the rider did well, what he or she did poorly, and what the judges were looking for.

Macy loved to talk horses—especially to people who didn't know them. People like Nash, newcomers, didn't care about the gossip: who paid how much for which horse and what trainer was involved and what trainer had been caught with what client by that client's wife (or husband). No, people like Nash, they were just like her back when she was still a horse-crazy little girl—in awe of their sleek coats, their spindly legs, their raw power. In awe that something so beautiful would agree to be ridden at all. She had been feeling burned-out lately on all of the politics and posturing, and seeing it all again through fresh eyes had been just what she'd needed.

Macy looked around her now at all the intensity in the practice ring. At the concentration and will to win that drew lips into hard, straight lines. And then, more than feeling out of sorts and out of place, she found herself longing, lonely. For Nash.

For Nash, who that day eleven years ago, right on these grounds, had asked all the right questions, like wondering, when one horse refused a jump, whether the horse had been stubborn or the rider had done something wrong.

And for the Nash who had said all the right things in the most genuine, heartfelt way.

Throughout that afternoon she had found herself entranced by the cuts of muscle on his beefy, freckled arms, his crooked smile, the way he put his hand on her knee without thinking and without any reservation, as if he had been doing that his whole life. But when Nash sat down on a hay bale in front of Gounda's stall, patting the space next to him and saying that he was really into her handsome horse—not pretty, but *handsome*, which fit Gounda like no other word—Macy forgot all about her reasons and rules and reservations. Because right about then, she couldn't seem to catch her breath.

"Madame Armstrong! *What* is the matter?" Martine, who had never made the switch to Macy's married name, stood in front of Gounda, hands on hips.

He looked perplexed, not angry. Even so, without warning, Macy started to cry. The whole thing felt wrong. Just like in Victoria. Only this time she had played chicken with Ian Painter and Rosetta and had made a complete heel out of herself in front of a whole long list of premier riders.

Macy shook her head. She didn't know how to explain it to Martine. She couldn't see a distance to save her life. Riding up to the practice jumps she would count down, three-two-one, and Gounda would take off on two or zero, leaving her behind, her hands catching him in the mouth midair. Each time they landed he wrung his tail and kicked out just a little. It was the most subtle of protests, but Macy was used to the two of them operating as a single unit, her thoughts melding seamlessly with Gounda's actions. The disconnect between them panged her. And it was solely her fault. Macy was sure it would be only a matter of time before she crashed them through a fence.

"I don't know what I'm doing here," she finally said. "I shouldn't have come."

Martine shook his head. His perplexed look had morphed to

disappointment. "Just because of that little thing that happened in there?" He said *zing* instead of *thing*.

"That was not a 'little thing.' And yes. But no. I mean, I'm just not up to this right now."

"Sure you are," Martine said.

"What I am," Macy responded, "is a danger to myself and—clearly—to others."

Martine shook his head again. Then he turned and walked toward the ring, calling over his shoulder, "Come with me."

"No," Macy said. "I can't. I can't do this."

Martine changed course and walked back toward Macy and Gounda.

"Madame Armstrong, I do not say this to be angry, but it needs saying. It is not 'cannot'; it is 'will not.' If you want to be a professional, you must start acting like it." He gave her boot two quick pats, said, "Now, come," and walked off again.

Macy followed. Her hands shook.

"We will take a step in reverse and do preliminary work, yes?" Martine said. He stood in the middle of the sand exercise ring, next to the oxer of her and Ian Painter's fateful initial meeting. Another jump stood adjacent to the oxer, a plain and simple vertical. Martine lowered both to standard "hunter"—which, along with "jumper," formed the two parts of any over-fences division—height. At about two to three and a half feet, the hunter courses were meant to simulate the types and heights of jumps one might find on a foxhunt, while the obstacles in the jumper classes trended toward bright and high: every color of the rainbow and five to six feet in height.

Riding jumpers was harder, yet simpler. Larger and more difficult jumps required horses who threw their entire being into getting over them, and as such, those same horses tended to be both more fun to ride and a bit tougher to control. They weren't willful, just athletic and talented, with only two main modes in the jumping ring: standing still and full speed ahead. Macy found that riding jumpers required a delicate partnership of constant communication: asking and telling that went both ways. The larger and more difficult jumps—along with tighter and more technical angles, and a timed jump-off to crown the winners— also tended to weed out anyone who couldn't really, truly ride.

Today, that happened to be Macy.

The practice ring had mostly cleared, and she no longer had to worry about running into other riders and dodging traffic. Those who were jumping that evening were at the tail end of their warm-ups, needing to finish up and walk the course before it closed. Martine instructed Macy to take the two jumps in a nice, easy circle.

Macy cued Gounda into a canter, but on the approach to the first jump, she couldn't find a pace she liked. She legged him on, then judged the distance they had yet to cover to the base of the jump; then she checked him back. Then, estimating that there were either two strides or four before takeoff, she legged him forward again, but too hard. The poor horse got in two strides and a quick stutter step before lurching over and taking a rail down with his front legs in the process.

The next approach replicated the first, only this time Gounda somehow—through his own sheer will and skill—avoided knocking a rail, though the result was not significantly more attractive, nor any less tenuous.

Already Martine was calling, "'Top! 'Top!" Macy pulled Gounda to a stop. *Please, God, just let him admit I was right and we'll both be done with this*, she hoped, now that Martine had seen for himself what a total and consistent mess she was.

He walked over to Macy, stopping even with Gounda's neck. His chest faced the front of her boot. He placed his left hand on the crease where Gounda's neck met his shoulder, and placed the other on Macy's calf. Tears had started to stream down Macy's cheeks again. She hated herself for the weakness they represented, and pretended they weren't there.

"This horse, right here," he said, shaking Macy's calf. "This horse is *très* talented. And you . . ." Martine shook his head.

"Are riding like a moron?" Macy finished.

"No," Martine said. Then, cocking his head, he reconsidered: "Well, actually, yes. Yes, you are."

"I'm so embarrassed," Macy said.

"There is no need for embarrassment, madame."

"No need? Come on. You're probably right now regretting that you ever even talked to me on the ferry."

"Madame Armstrong, you are a spectacular rider. And you have a spectacular mount."

Now it was Macy's turn to shake her head.

"You won the Young Riders competition. You've been on the short lists for the Talent Squad. These are not levels just any rider can reach. I don't need to tell you that you harbor immense talent. Or perhaps I do. Because today it is like someone has borrowed your body. Things are not quite right—this I know. You must focus," he said.

Only focus came out *fuckus*. Unfortunately, it was Martine's favorite word, his favorite thing to yell out to Macy across the warm-up ring at shows—"Fuckus, fuckus, fuckus! You must fuckus as hard as you can. You cannot stop!"—much to the amusement or, if children were in range, occasional embarrassment of onlookers. "This is the very best preparation you will get before qualifiers next month," he added.

He was right. The qualifying show for Jump Canada's Talent Squad was only a handful of weeks away. Last year, when she didn't make the cut, she had promised herself that this would be the year. No excuses, no holds barred. But that had been before. Long, long before.

"So is that a yes, then? You want to try once again?"

Every fiber of her being wanted to say no. But she nodded.

"All right, madame. You listen: Gounda would jump a bus on fire if this is what you ask of him. But you are squeezing him too tight between your fists and legs, like a vise. You are leaving him without options. And you know better. You cannot force him to do what you wish, and you must quit overthinking. Get out of your own way and start feeling. That is all. Okay?"

Macy nodded a third time.

"Okay. We go."

Martine instructed Macy to canter along the rail, following it counterclockwise. 'Round and 'round they went, lap after lap. "Now clear your head, loosen your reins, and just breathe," Martine told her. "Inhale, one-two. Exhale, one-two. Feel that rhythm. One-two, one-two, one-two." Martine's voice was like a metronome, and Macy matched her breaths to Gounda's footfalls, concentrating on nothing else. Gounda's four legs found a steady beat and kept it, all flow and rhythm. It seemed as though Gounda could have gone on like that all day, and, after the first lap, Macy along with him.

"Now, on the next corner, you're going to turn left and take this *petit* oxer, and you will not change a thing. You will not squeeze your legs. You will not pick up your reins. You will breathe and count and count and breathe, and you will trust your horse. Understand?"

At the corner, Macy did as she was told. The worst that could happen, she figured, was that Gounda would slam on the brakes and send her flying—and if that happened, perhaps she'd break something, which would allow her to put this whole charade to an end. Macy cleared her mind of everything except that one-two beat. She didn't move her hands. She kept her legs steady. And then, as if after an eternity, she felt Gounda lift up through the shoulders, preparing to carry them safely over the jump. Macy leaned forward, closing the angle between her torso and her hips, and ran her hands up either side of Gounda's neck, the reins slack beneath it.

As soon as Gounda's front feet touched down, Martine said, "Reins loose. Breathe! One-two," launching Macy right back into the familiar pattern.

Again they did this. And again. Occasionally Martine would raise the height of one jump, then the other. Again and again.

"That is it, madame! Yes, this I like very much. Very much!" Martine, standing in the middle of the arena, made a grand sweep of his arms. Even though he hadn't ridden in years, he still wore a button-down or polo shirt, jodhpurs, argyle socks, and paddock boots. So proper. Macy always thought that he flat-out *looked* French, far before he ever opened his mouth to speak.

"Please let Monsieur Gounda walk now," he said. "That is enough."

Macy nodded, lowered herself into the saddle, scootched her seat underneath her, lowered her heels deep into the stirrups, and closed her fingers loosely, yet with purpose, around the reins, like someone might around a pen. And when Macy sat, Gounda slowed gently and came to a walk. They were so in sync, her movements so subtle, that an onlooker might have thought she had communicated to him through ESP.

Finally, Macy released the reins completely, holding them on the buckle with one hand to let him stretch his neck out and down. Macy rolled her own neck from side to side and let her body sway with Gounda's sure-strided march.

"How do you feel?" asked Martine.

"Better," answered Macy.

She always forgot how good this felt—the catharsis that came from placing herself in the care of her horses. Even being near them helped. Straddling an overturned bucket in the tack room, dipping a moist sponge into the saddle butter, working it until she felt the leather grow soft and supple between her fingers. Even those times when she wasn't on horseback, the mindless circles soothed her in ways that not much else ever could.

She didn't need a shrink or pills. Saddle oil and sweet hay. The feel of dusty sweat on her skin. The rhythmic thud of hoof-beats in her ears. These were enough.

Macy heard the call for her class, which meant it was time to change into her show clothes and put the finishing touches on Gounda.

In the tack stall she swapped jeans, ankle-high paddock boots, and leather half chaps for white breeches and knee-high boots that she pulled on with the help of a generous dusting of baby powder and two large-handled hooks that fed into notches located inside each boot. She pulled a sweaty polo shirt off over her head and replaced it with a crisp white hunt shirt, fumbling with the buttons on each cuff and, at the end, fastening the matching choker embroidered in light blue cursive with her initials in its center. Over that she layered a black hunt coat and buttoned it. She put her helmet on, but left the chin strap unfastened for now, and secured a few wayward wisps of hair with extra bobby pins from her jacket pocket, ignoring her still-shaky hands.

She was, if not ready, at least dressed properly.

Macy ran through the course in her head. She thought through each of the thirteen jumps, the distance between them, what she'd have to do to prepare for each—leg Gounda on through the corner for a strong approach to one, balance him back onto his haunches to round out his frame over another, try to add a stride onto one line, and see if she couldn't get by with a straighter line and dropping a stride going to another jump.

This was the part of the game that had always intrigued her, excited her: the strategy of it all. It was, she often thought, like a moving game of chess. You not only had to think about the strengths and weaknesses of your competitors—the line and jump choices they might make—but you had to honestly evaluate your own and come up with a workable game plan. And after the second jump, you might have more horse under you than expected, or it might start raining and slick the footing, and you'd have to recalculate on the fly. You just never knew. And the not knowing never failed to send little sizzles of excitement through Macy. What tests would the riding gods throw at her during each go-round? Would she and Gounda pass them?

Macy edged Gounda's stall door aside and entered. She patted him on the neck and scratched a knuckle across his muzzle. She inspected his mane braids, which she had plaited that morning—forty-two of them—twisting one errant nub that had gone horizontal back to its proper vertical position. Then she brushed out his tail, picked his feet, and ran a soft brush over his whole coat. Next she fastened leather splint boots to each of Gounda's four legs to support his tendons, protect the splint bones, and guard against debris like rocks being kicked up, or his striking himself with a hind leg. Only then did she saddle him, slipping the breastplate over his neck like a yoke and running the loose end through the girth on the saddle, which she tightened enough to hold it in place but not too much, so that Gounda could still relax. Right before mounting outside of the show ring, she'd tighten it fully.

Moving back toward his head, Macy again patted the horse's neck. Gounda responded with a deep exhale, licking his lips. She liked to think Gounda liked this time as much as she did—just the two of them, preparing for battle together. Their own little team. Every other rider she had ever met had their own groom, sometimes several, and she always felt like the oddball for doing it all herself. But Macy wouldn't trade those stolen moments with Gounda for all of the convenience in the world. She couldn't imagine someone handing her the reins as she walked into the ring, not knowing what kind of mood her horse was in until she got on his back.

Macy held the bridle in her right hand while guiding the simple snaffle bit into Gounda's mouth with the left, slipping the brow band over his forehead and the crown piece over his ears in one fell swoop.

She pressed her brow to Gounda's forehead, big as a dinner plate. "Just you and me, big guy," she said, remembering too well the last time she had said those words—sitting on the floor of his stall, trying on the word *widow* for size, and how it seemed to fit like a too-small dress, itchy and stifling.

Gounda shook his head free of hers and nudged her shoulder, as if to say, "Come on; let's go already."

Macy held the reins at arm's length, taking one last look at her horse. Gounda's seal brown coat seemed to shine with added intensity, independent of the fading sunlight. He towered above her with chiseled muscles stretched over a refined frame. And his head—his head was perched elegant and regal atop a thick, powerful neck lined with tiny veins. He was stunning. Gorgeous. Wholly and completely beautiful. Macy wondered if this was how parents felt about their children; every time Macy looked at Gounda, she was awestruck by what she saw. His elegance, his softness, him.

She patted his neck twice, and Gounda moved forward with her, taking their first steps toward the show ring together.

Martine was waiting for her in the chute. Macy let him give her a leg up and, once aboard Gounda's broad back, she took in the course as a whole one last time.

"Okay?" Martine asked her.

She was not okay. She still didn't want to be here, to be doing this. Her stomach seized. She felt dizzy, fought the urge to vomit. Macy nodded in spite of herself.

The gate steward's voice boomed: "Painter on course. Armstrong Allen on deck. McGill, Farell, and Jensen to follow."

Oh, sweet Jesus, Macy thought.

"This course is straightforward, Madame Armstrong. Nothing to trick you up." He fixed Macy with a hard, serious stare. "Now," he said, "you ride." With a pat on her boot for encouragement, Martine excused himself to find a seat.

If only it were that easy, she thought.

Macy reached down to check the girth, pulled the billets up one more hole, and fastened the chin strap on her helmet. Then she reached into her coat pocket for her gloves and pulled those on.

She closed her eyes and breathed deep. Every time she visualized the course, rogue scenarios sneaked their way in: Gounda refusing a fence and her flying into it; her pulling Gounda up, too hard, before a plank vertical and him crashing through, sending the whole thing toppling down around them; Macy losing her balance and getting behind the motion, only to be bounced off of Gounda's back like a rag doll upon landing and watching from the ground as her horse tore riderless through the ring.

She heard clapping, which meant that Ian Painter had just finished his round. Clean, of course.

"Macy Armstrong Allen? You're up," the steward said, standing with a clipboard by the gate.

She clucked to Gounda and adjusted her reins as they walked up the chute. An argument raged in her head: *Just breathe. Oh, my God I can't do this. Just breathe. I don't want to breathe and I don't want to do this. Breathe. Oh, God, look at all of those people and fence seven looks gigantic and the bicycle fence looks airier than it usually does and what if he runs out on it? Breathe. Just breathe. Oh, God.*

Ian Painter walked Rosetta out of the arena on a loose rein and toward them. "Nice go," Macy said, so quietly that she didn't know whether he had heard her. As soon as the words escaped her lips, she wished he hadn't. Then she could have just sneaked on by him.

"Be careful out there," he said with a wink. "That last combo's a real doozy. If you get long . . ." Ian Painter shook his head and drew two fingers across his throat and whistled ominously.

Macy glared at him. *You jackass*, she wanted to say, but she held her tongue. She probably had that much coming, if not more.

Riding into the ring, she heard the announcer boom, "Macy Armstrong Allen from British Columbia and her Hanoverian, Gounda." She squeezed her legs to Gounda's sides and they were off.

She pointed Gounda at the first jump, a straightforward ascending oxer with green-and-white-striped rails and a small forest of miniature evergreens on either side. Macy pitched the reins at Gounda and closed her eyes, but he took the jump easily, seamlessly. She exhaled. *Time to ride*, she thought. Then it was on to a simple vertical painted red and white like a candy cane, with a long distance leading up to it and no set number of strides to make the distance in. *Ride with impulsion*. Martine's words—a small stock of them that he used often—rang in her ears. But Gounda's head was up, his ears pricked forward. He lived for this. For jumping. Macy didn't need to help him in the least with his impulsion. So she held still, waiting.

Land. One-two-three, Macy counted in her head, each word matching one of Gounda's strides. Almost always, riders had to cover a specific, preferred distance between the jumps. One of Macy's first riding instructors had taught her to count the landing, which wasn't a full stride, and then continue the count to help her gauge the distance. She didn't need to anymore, but the counting was habit, security.

From there it was on to a bending line from jump three to jump four, a box oxer and a Liverpool. *Keep his eye up. Keep his focus on the top rail. Use some leg in the air.* Martine's voice inside Macy's head was calm and assured. She felt herself starting to settle in. The rhythm, the constant evaluation of distance, and Martine's meditative voice all demanded a level of concentration that didn't allow for stray thoughts.

The rest of the course flew by, with Gounda seeming to float over the jumps. A tight rollback, a triple combination that could trip up inexperienced horses or those with a tendency to jump flat, another couple of verticals and an oxer across the diagonal with a gigantic spread. Through it all, Macy focused on the basics: keeping Gounda's inside shoulder up through the turns, not letting him rush, letting the distance come to her instead of trying to force it—and letting Gounda do his job. *Breathe*, she had to remind herself, and she gulped in a lungful of air. Galloping up to and over obstacles that loomed well above her line of sight, even atop Gounda, never got old. That thrill, that rush. That was what she rode for. But it required a level of concentration so high that at times she finished riding a course as out of breath as if she had sprinted a mile.

And it dawned on Macy, coming out of the final turn with only a triple combination striped loud like a bumblebee left to go, that they were on the brink of a completely clean round. Not one takedown, not even a rub.

Macy gave herself over to the rhythm. She let her concentration drift. And then Ian Painter's words landed in her mind like cannonballs of snark and doubt: *That last combo's a real doozy.*

And right then, with the whole of Canadian show jumping as witnesses, Macy forgot how to ride.

She gulped for air. Panicked, she legged Gounda forward. Then, at the last minute, pulled him back hard. *Combo's a real doozy.* Gounda took off long, farther from the first fence in the combination than he should have. That put them landing too close on the other side of it, with three strides to get in before the second. Macy could see there was far too much distance stretched before them to make it happen. *Combo's a real doozy.* Gounda did the only thing he could: jumped long into the second fence. It was a short, friendly jump—one that on a normal day in normal circumstances they would've sailed over with all four of their eyes closed.

But he had jumped long, which meant that Gounda again landed too close to the base of the second fence. It was one stride to the last and final fence, but they needed one and a half, which wasn't a readily available option.

Macy closed her eyes then. Against what she couldn't make happen. Against what she knew was coming. Against the whole world at that one, brief moment.

She didn't know what to do. She didn't know what to tell this horse beneath her who, day in and day out, placed every ounce of his faith and trust in her without a fight and without question. She didn't know because Ian Painter's sneer had filled her whole head.

And just then, another voice stepped in. Quiet at first, then louder. Until it drowned out every last murmur of Ian Painter. *You can do this, munchkin. Giddy up now!*

Nash.

Macy gathered the reins and closed her legs hard around her horse. Gounda surged forward, then lifted up with his shoulders. Up . . . up . . . up.

And over.

That's my girl, the voice said.

Macy heard the sound of a repeated shrill whistle. Martine. He was jumping up and down with pinkie fingers sticking out from either side of his mouth. And if she hadn't known better, Macy could have sworn that right beside him sat Nash, elbows on knees, smiling in approval. Just as he had all those years ago.

But something was wrong. Gounda wasn't galloping away from the base of the fence. He stumbled and his neck disappeared under Macy. She saw ground in front of her where brightly colored jumps and a cheering crowd and sky should be, right before she felt herself leave the saddle and her world went black.

Chapter Ten

JACK WOKE TO BRIGHT LIGHT STREAMING THROUGH HIS BED-room window and a loud knocking on the door.

"Yeah?" he called out.

"Jack? You up? We've gotta get going."

He rubbed his eyes, put on his glasses and pulled on a pair of jeans, and opened the door of his room to find Macy standing there, looking impatient. For what, he wasn't sure. He had gotten used to Macy being gone to horse shows. But after she had returned from Spruce Meadows the week before with a broken collarbone, not only was Macy around more, but she was around with nothing much to do. Boredom didn't suit her.

"What time is it?" he asked.

"Almost three. I've been checking on you all afternoon to make sure you weren't dead. Are you sick?"

"No." Jack yawned and shook his head. "Not sick. Just didn't get to bed until after seven."

"Again? That crazy old bat is going to get herself killed one of these times, out fishing in the middle of the night, and now she's taking you right along with her."

Jack eyed Macy, her arm still in a sling and the leftovers of a black eye, now yellow, still obvious from her and Gounda's crash. "You fly a horse over five-foot obstacles and we're crazy for fishing at night?" He chuckled, but Macy didn't. "Listen, everyone's A-okay and we've got a great slab of salmon for dinner tonight. No harm, no foul."

"You're welcome to have salmon tonight, but you'll be eating alone," Macy said. "Mama Sophie and I are going to the extravaganza."

The "extravaganza," as Macy had explained to him the week prior, was actually the Campbell River Salmon Festival—a fitting celebration, given that their small town had rightfully earned its place as the salmon capital of the world. Long before the HMS *Plumper*—carrying Captain Vancouver and surgeon Dr. Samuel Campbell, who would later map the Vancouver Island coast—ran ashore, the First Nations people who had settled there had been fond of saying that you could cross from present-day Campbell River to Quadra Island across Discovery Passage on the backs of the salmon. Since then, salmon fishing—and other related tourism oddities, like swimming in the Campbell River with hordes of salmon that returned every August to spawn—had secured the town's place as a salmon mecca.

Jack had always thought of Campbell River as his own well-kept secret. He loved telling people his son lived there and watching them try to figure out exactly where this place could be. He loved knowing he had a reason to keep going back to it. But while waiting for Sophie to check her guiding schedule at Painter's Lodge the week before, Jack had come upon picture after picture of celebrities, from Bob Hope and John Wayne to Goldie Hawn and the Prince of Luxembourg, adorning the

lodge's walls. Apparently, people had been coming there for decades to try their luck at bagging a sockeye, coho, chum, pink, or
chinook. It shot Jack's "well-kept secret" theory to hell, but he
gave selfish thanks that the town had managed to maintain a
good deal of obscurity.

In any case, the extravaganza—as only Macy and Sophie
called it—apparently didn't really have a whole lot to do with
celebrating salmon. There were fishing derbies, but that was
about the only direct tie. The festival also featured a parade, a
logger sports competition, and a driftwood carving competition
called Transformations on the Shore, in which carvers scraped
away at discarded logs with chain saws, mauls, knives, and chis-
els until gnomes, seagulls, Puss in Boots, Hamlet and various
other creations emerged from the wood.

But the real highlight of the festival, according to pretty
much anyone you might talk to, was the same raucous party that
took place in most small towns throughout the world throughout the year. Here, the Old Island Highway that ran through
downtown closed, the beer vendors (who, Jack had heard, out-
numbered the food vendors by roughly four to one) set up shop
on the street, and local live bands took turns trying to entertain
the crowd on a makeshift stage erected behind Discovery Pier.
Macy said there was always at least one good brawl, and for
weeks afterward, the events of the extravaganza fueled a tornado
of gossip that left few unscathed. It was debauchery, plain and
simple. And neither Macy nor Sophie would ever think of missing it. From Macy's determined stare, it didn't seem as though
Jack had the option either.

"What time is the train leaving?" Jack asked.

"I just have to dump the horses their grain and shower.
Which, with this thing, is going to take me a while." She raised

her sling like a chicken wing. "So I'd say five or so? Mama Sophie's coming around half past four."

"I'll be ready," Jack assured her.

"Great. I got you a shirt. It's hanging on the towel rack in the bathroom."

Somewhere along the line—perhaps back when the Christmas in July celebration and the extravaganza had shared the same weekend—someone had made it tradition to attend the event in borderline-gaudy holidayish wear. Macy and Sophie had continued that tradition. It was closer to quarter of six by the time Sophie actually made it to Macy's, wearing a risqué, low-cut silver sequined tank top. *God bless the extravaganza*, Jack thought.

Perhaps Sophie had caught Jack gawking, because she said, "Since when has the extravaganza involved any semblance of tact or propriety?"

"Uh, never?" Macy said. She had chosen a red satin top with a sash that draped loosely over each breast and tied halter-style behind her neck. Most of her back was bare, the material swagging only across the lower part of it. To counter the amount of skin revealed on top, Macy had donned a long, flowing black skirt that just grazed her ankles.

"You like?" asked Macy.

"I don't know," Sophie said, shaking her head. "You have anything else you could wear?"

Macy's face fell. "Why? Too much?"

"Hell, no. I was just thinking that if you were at all serious about saying you never wanted to date again, then it's really not fair to the eligible bachelors of Campbell River, you going out in that getup. You'll make them all ache for something they don't have a prayer of getting." Sophie laughed mischievously. "Ah, what the hell. Those boys deserve a little taste of their own, don't they?"

"They sure do," said Macy in mock seriousness. "Especially Jake Zigman."

Sophie and Jack both looked at her, heads cocked.

"He broke up with me for Laura Camber in third grade because I didn't give him candy with my Valentine and she did."

"Ohhh," Sophie said.

"*Especially* him," Jack chimed in.

"Whatever happened to ol' Jake?" asked Sophie.

"He married Laura Camber a few years back." Macy sighed.

"Hmmm," Sophie said. "Another one bites the dust."

"I'm meeting up with them all tonight. Going to bury that hatchet from third grade once and for all," Macy said. She laughed, but Jack had been around her enough lately to see through it, to see it was an act. He wondered, if he and Sophie hadn't been here, whether Macy would have even gone at all.

Macy rummaged through a drawer full of batteries, rubber bands, superglue, pens that didn't work—Jack knew because he had rummaged through the very same drawer the previous day looking for a functioning pen—and pulled out her truck keys, holding them up in a sign of victory.

"You do have some double-sided tape under there, though, don't you?" Sophie whispered, pointing at Macy's chest.

Macy shook her head in mock exasperation and threw Sophie her keys. "Let's go."

Jack wasn't sure how he had ended up down on the beach with Sophie. She had asked him to dance, certainly; and she had been overserved—a rarity for her, from what he could tell, in spite of her proclivity for straight bourbon. But it amazed him how situations like this happened—how someone, a married man like himself, ended up on a beach with a woman like Sophie McLean.

It wasn't like jumping from a bridge or being hit by a car, where one nanosecond changes things suddenly and completely. This was a quieter sort of progression. More like trying to figure out, on a clock with no second hand, where each minute begins and ends. Sure, there were big moments—the five- or ten-minute marks, like when Jack asked her to dance, and she absently tousled his hair while they swayed. But what had happened in between to bring them here, to this moment?

Jack offered her his canteen. It was small and silver with the letters "JDA" on it. A Charlie Daniels cover band, on the stage behind and to the left of them, was belting out "The Devil Went Down to Georgia." Jack hummed along. He'd always loved this song, the build of it, and its intensity.

Sophie accepted the canteen and took a long swig. He saw her mouth pucker.

"Sorry. We were fresh out of bourbon," he said. "Had to resort to whiskey."

"What's the 'D' for?" she asked, waving the canteen toward Jack so he could see the monogram.

"Donahue."

"Ah. Like that good-looking American talk show host you all used to have on," said Sophie, nodding her head for no apparent reason. "I lived in Seattle for a brief stint and watched him every day. Called him the Silver Fox."

"Like the old family name," Jack said.

Sophie shrugged and kicked off her sandals, burying her silver-painted toenails in the sand. "Old family names are nice."

"If you're into that sort of thing," Jack bantered.

"What sort of thing are you into?" Sophie blurted.

Jack looked over at her. "Ah . . . ah—" he stammered.

"I mean, what's your story?" Sophie said.

"My story?"

"Well, I know why you're here, and I know a bit about you from Macy, but what are you still doing here? It's going on a month now and it doesn't seem like you've given much thought to going back."

"I'm going back," Jack said. "Believe me, not a conversation goes by when Magda doesn't try to pin me down on a date. But I'm not quite ready. Not yet."

Actually, the thought of going back home right now made him shudder. And he couldn't be certain whether leaving this wild, crazy-beautiful place—the place where his son last lived—without getting some feeling of closure, or the thought of going back to his wife, were the only culprits.

"If you want my professional opinion, I don't think you really want to go back."

"And who asked for your professional opinion?"

"No one. But that's never stopped me before, Jackie-boy."

Jack could hear her words starting to slur, just a touch.

"If you wanted to be back home, you would've gone already," Sophie said. "You have a successful business that you enjoy running, and a wife, and friends, I assume. You're a likable enough guy." Sophie tried to chuck him on the shoulder, but whiffed, her fist making contact with air. "Whoops!" she said, dissolving into a brief fit of laughter before continuing on. "Anyway, instead of being home where you belong, you're sitting on this little island with two women you barely know, and you're all content. Now, what does that say to you?"

"Not sure. You seem to be the expert. What do you think it says?" Jack sat with elbows on knees, dangling the canteen between his legs with both hands. Somehow, somewhere, Macy had found a Hawaiian-style shirt for him that had flowers sporadically highlighted with sequins. Its tails had come untucked from his shorts. He thought about tucking them back in, then decided that this was a perfectly appropriate look for this time of night. Plus, it wasn't like a tucked-in sequined Hawaiian shirt was so much less conspicuous than an untucked one.

"That you're full of shit," said Sophie.

"Hmmm. Maybe you're right."

"See. Just listen to the expert." She took another swig. "You unhappy with your wife?"

Jack wasn't sure whether this was supposed to be a statement or a question.

"My wife is a good woman."

Sophie pointed a finger in the air, pondering. "So why are you sitting on some beach in another country celebrating a big fish with a strange woman?"

Jack snorted. "It's not that simple." And as an afterthought he added, "And you're not *that* strange."

She ignored his dig. "It *is*," Sophie said. "Why wouldn't it be?"

"What happened to us, what we've been through—it changes things."

Sophie had reclined back onto her elbows. Her knees were bent, her left ankle slung over her right knee. Her left foot was keeping a beat to a song Jack didn't recognize. It sounded James Taylor–ish—folksy and subdued.

After a long while, Sophie spoke again. Her voice sounded

quieter and more distant than it had only a minute before. "Everyone's is so different."

She let her head fall onto Jack's shoulder.

"What's that, Ms. McLean?"

Sophie didn't say anything. She simply breathed. Two deep breaths, the last punctuated by a long, forceful exhale. Finally, she whispered, "Our lives."

"Mars," Jack said.

"No. *Lives*, I said."

Jack nudged Sophie so she opened her eyes, and pointed at the night sky. "I heard you. But that's Mars there I'm trying to point out. Just a bit over from the moon—right there. It looks like a star, really bright. A little pinkish. You see?"

She followed his finger and found Mars with her eyes. "Hmmm," she said. "Yeah. Saw that about a week ago. Wondered what it was."

Jack raised his eyes to the little red blur in reverence, straining to see it better. "You know this is as close as it's ever been to Earth? We won't see it again for almost three hundred years. *Three hundred years*. Last time it was this close was something like sixty thousand years ago. Neanderthals were hunting mammoths back then—that's how long ago that was."

"We won't see it ever again," said Sophie.

"No," Jack said, "I suppose we won't."

She nodded. "Wow."

"The next time that planet shows up there, in this same sky, we'll have been gone almost three lifetimes over." Three lifetimes. And where would he be then? Part of that cosmos? Part of the earth's crust? With his son at long last? "It's hard to get your head around."

"I don't know about that," said Sophie. "It's easy enough to understand. But it sure makes you feel small."

"Lives like paper," he said.

" 'Lives like paper'?" She raised an eyebrow at him. "Jackie, you're either a closet poet or hitting the canteen a little harder than I thought." Sophie stopped to think a moment, then added, "Like the sands of an hourglass," in a deep mock announcer's voice.

Jack just looked at her. How was it that he could never follow a blasted conversation with this woman? She was all over the map, and the whiskey surely didn't help.

"Another one of your American shows I used to watch," Sophie said. She took a deep breath and exhaled. "How 'bout we just give it up?" She gave him what he thought might have been a seductive smile.

Jack looked at her, again confused.

"The art of Mars," Sophie said.

Jack cocked his head to one side.

"You know, Mars—the god of war?" Sophie asked.

"Oh," Jack said, "right—got it."

"Never mind. Bad pun—like 'give up the fight,' you know—give in." She brushed her feet against his, probably deciding he was not, in fact, a closet poet. Just half in the bag. "Was thinking maybe you could start by going home with me."

Jack sent a crooked smile her way. "I'm flattered by the offer, Ms. McLean," he said, taking her hand.

"But no?" asked Sophie.

"But no," repeated Jack.

Silence hung in the air between them.

"A girl's gotta ask," she finally said.

Jack pushed himself to his feet. "She absolutely does." He

stuffed the canteen in the pocket of his shorts, and offered both hands to her. "C'mon," he said. "Let's get us home."

"You have to steer, though," Sophie said, looping her arm through his.

"I'll steer." He picked up Sophie's sandals for her. "If you'll let me, I'll steer."

The girl was maybe seven, eight at the most, Jack guessed, and curled like a puppy on Macy's porch, on the mat in front of the door. He hadn't seen her at first, not until he started climbing the few short steps, and she hadn't moved until he and Sophie were standing over her, debating whether they should wake her.

The girl had dirty blond hair—not dirty blond as a color, but blond streaked with grime. She had on a white T-shirt with a large pink flower on the front and jeans with little pink flowers that circled the bottom of each leg. The jeans were worn at the knees, and filthy, as if she had been kneeling in mud. Under her head she had wadded a spring satin jacket for a pillow. It looked light gray now, but Jack could tell that it had been pink—with white piping—at one time. Under the jacket lay a flat plastic box.

She didn't sit up when she woke, just opened her eyes, blinked a couple times, and waved up at Jack and Sophie—a baby wave, where she opened and closed her fingers, as if feebly grasping at something.

Jack took Sophie's arm from his and planted it on the porch railing to steady her swaying. He knelt down by the girl.

"Hi, there, sweetheart. How ya doing?"

The little girl smiled up at him, then yawned.

"Have you been here long?" Jack asked. "You been waiting a long time?"

"Little while," the girl said.

"Who're you waiting for, sweetheart?" Jack asked, helping her to sit up.

"My daddy."

"I think you have the wrong house, baby girl."

The girl shook her head. "What's your name?" she asked Jack.

"I'm Jack, and this pretty lady back here is Sophie." He gestured behind him as if the girl weren't just young, but stupid. Obviously she could see that the only other person on the porch would have to be the Sophie he was talking about. This thought came too late, though, for Jack to stop it.

"Hi." The girl waved to Sophie. Sophie waved back. Then the girl looked at Jack. "Do you live here?" she asked.

"No," Jack said, "I'm just staying for a while. Just visiting."

"Oh," the girl said. The hamsters were running—that was what Nash would say. Anytime Jack was thinking about something, usually work related, Nash would ask him why his hamsters were working so hard.

"Do you live here?" she asked Sophie.

"No. I live down the road a ways," Sophie said. "I'm just stopping by on my way home."

"Oh," the girl said again. Jack could see that she was still thinking—hard. He also noticed she was shivering—mini-convulsions rippled her skin every now and then, with a few seconds' reprieve between. "I'm a little confused," she said to Jack, leaning toward him and lowering her voice to a whisper.

"That's okay, sweetheart," Jack said, whispering back at her. "Why don't we all go inside and figure out where you're supposed to be, okay? It's too chilly to stand out here on this porch." As warm as the island could be during the day, the air at night could get damn cold.

The little girl stood up, gathered her jacket and box, and watched as Jack fished the spare house key out of the light fixture next to the door. He leaned over to her and whispered, "Now, you can't tell anyone about that—it's the secret hiding place."

She smiled up at him, then pursed her lips and drew her finger across them as if closing a zipper.

"Atta girl," Jack said, opening the door.

The girl marched purposefully through the door and into the house, as if she had been living there all along. Bold kid, thought Jack. When Nash was young, Jack had always tried to instill a healthy amount of fear in him—don't talk to strangers, look before crossing the street, all of the typical stuff. But he also taught Nash to play a little game they called "casing the joint," where Nash was supposed to be aware of his surroundings all the time: Look for suspicious-looking or suspicious-acting people, pay attention to exit placements or locations of security guards, avoid dark areas of parking lots, and steer clear of vans or cars with tinted windows.

When he and Magda would argue about it—she thought "casing the joint" was the type of thing that would only make their son neurotic; and besides, they lived in rural Wisconsin, and just what did he think could happen to their son in *Wisconsin?*—he'd tell her that only God could prevent accidents, and only parents could prevent everything else. To prove his point he'd clip missing children stories from the *News Chronicle* or the *Press Gazette* and turn the missing-children side of the milk carton toward her at breakfast. If he was feeling particularly zealous, he'd highlight the portions of the newspaper articles that proved his point: "Suspect believed to have driven a white utility van," and such.

This fervor over his son's safety had taken him by surprise by showing up fully formed at the same time Nash was born. He was anything but uptight in any other area of his life—not his business, not his friendships, and certainly not his marriage. Lord knew his and Magda's relationship would never, ever work if they were both as high-strung as she tended to be. Lord knew it barely worked as it was. But his son, now, that was a whole different ball game. He had never wanted to protect anything like he had wanted to protect Nash.

This dirty little girl in front of him, though, hadn't seemed to have learned even the basics of child survival. Going into a strange house with two strangers, and absolutely no apprehension about doing so. Her parents must be frantic. Jack knew he would've been; that was for sure. But the girl was calmly sipping on a glass of orange juice Sophie had poured—albeit sloppily—for her.

"Wonder where Ms. Macy is," Sophie said, wiping up the mess she had made on the counter.

"I wonder," said Jack, although he really hadn't until that moment. Macy had found them making their way home. She was going to get a ride back with her high school friend and was plenty old enough to take care of herself. Jack hadn't given her whereabouts a second thought. Though, in a flash, he pictured Macy with another man—a man who wasn't Nash—and the image made him both uncomfortable and angry.

"Who's Macy?" the girl asked. "Does she live here?"

Jack nodded. "It's her house."

"Oh," the girl said. Then she squinted at Jack. "Does anyone else live here?"

Jack shook his head. The girl rooted around in the pocket of her jacket and pulled out an equally grimy envelope that had been folded in fourths into a fist-size package. She smoothed it on the table, studied it, and sighed audibly. "Is this 8254 Galley Road?" she asked.

"It is," said Jack. "But we're the only ones who live here. Why don't you let me take a look at that address. Maybe you're just reading the numbers wrong."

"I'm not," she said. She jutted her chin at Jack but handed the envelope to him anyway.

Even before he had unfolded the envelope completely, Jack gasped. There, in the upper left corner, was Nash's handwriting. Jack knew it in a second—the short, deliberate, choppy strokes. The letters in all caps. Nash didn't write in cursive, ever. Not even his signature. The all-caps style of Nash's handwriting always seemed to Jack like it was yelling, like it was so much louder and angrier than Nash ever was.

Jack could feel his heart beating all the way up in his ears. He held the envelope up in front of him to take a closer look, but the letters kept jumping around. He smoothed the paper out on the table, just as the girl had, to keep it steady.

He looked at the girl, who was looking back at him, wide-eyed.

"Honey, where did you get this?" he asked. His tongue felt heavy and dry and huge. "Where did you find this? Tell me *where*." Too late, he thought he maybe sounded too harsh, too intense for this sweet little girl.

"My mom," the girl said matter-of-factly, almost annoyed. She had clearly been expecting more substantial information from him.

Sophie had ceased trying to make coffee and had sat down at the table opposite the girl. "Jack?" Sophie asked.

He ignored her, focused on the girl. Everything in the room except the letter and the girl had gone fuzzy.

"What's your name, sweetheart?" Jack asked the girl.

"Glory Jane Gibson," she said, proudly, as if Jack had finally asked her a worthwhile question. "And I just turned eight on June twenty-third."

He looked down at the letter. Addressed to Glory Gibson. Well, at least that added up. Because the rest of it sure as hell didn't.

He should say something nice to her, Jack thought. He should tell her she had a pretty name. That was what he always said to kids—"Wow, what a great name!"—whether it was or not, because it was so much work for most kids to own up to their names, to say them out loud. You had to toss them a little encouragement here and there at those young ages—for being "this many" or for having a name, even. The praise was the thing; it didn't matter much what the hell it was for.

But he couldn't say it now. It just wouldn't come out.

Instead he stared at the kid like she was a talking kangaroo.

"Jack?" Sophie asked again, concern creeping into her voice. "Ja-ack."

Jack turned his head to look at her. Right about then, he wished he had given Sophie a few more swigs off his canteen. He wished she would just pass out already. He turned slowly back to Glory. "Glory, honey, who's your daddy?"

Instantly, Jack started thinking of ways he could have better phrased that question, so as to make it sound a little less like he and Glory were playing a game of pickup basketball in which he had just scored on her. *Who is your father?* maybe.

"Nash Allen."

Jack looked at her. Had she said what he thought he heard? "What?" Jack asked.

"Nash Allen. Or maybe Alden, or something like that," Glory

said. "It's at the bottom of the letter. But reading is my worst subject, so that might be a little wrong."

A little wrong? More than a little *wrong, darling.* Not Nash. Nash, this girl's father? No way.

He stared at Glory. Then he looked back at the letter on the table. Then back at Glory. She did a quick nod of her chin toward Jack, as if to say, "Go ahead; open it."

Jack pulled several sheets of yellow legal paper out of the envelope, unfolded each one, and tried to organize the pages into the correct order. The pages were smudged and the paper around the creases had grown thin from being folded and refolded. Jack found the first page and began to read.

Dear Glory,

I've been sitting here staring at a blank piece of paper, thinking of ways to start this letter, thinking of ways to introduce myself to you. But there is no easier way than to just come right out and say it: I am your father. (Later on, after you've seen all of the Star Wars movies, which you absolutely should, go back and read that in the Darth Vader voice, and laugh, because I just did after writing it.) I have never seen you, and I don't know if I ever will. I don't know what you look like. I don't know if you have my eyes, my red hair, my funny-looking ears that I got teased mercilessly for as a kid (I hope you either don't have my ears, don't get teased for them, or at least grew your hair long enough to cover them up), or my freckles. But whatever you look like, I know that you are the most beautiful little girl in the whole world. You are my daughter, and without ever having met you, I love you more than I've ever loved anything or anyone. That is the truth.

I suppose that I should tell you a little about myself. Here are the basics: I am thirty-three years old, but I don't feel that old. I still feel like I'm nineteen. I'm a photographer. I quit my job in a bank, helping people secure loans and mortgages, because it made me feel sort of like a robot, and more than a little bit empty. Now I capture people's weddings on film, and once in a while, I shoot photographs for ads. That is how I met your mother. But growing up, I always wanted to be a fighter pilot in the Air Force. I used to read all the books I could on pilots and planes. I had memorized each kind of plane and what its job was, what it could do, although I couldn't tell you about one of them now. My dad used to take me to this huge air show in Oshkosh, Wisconsin, not far from where I grew up, every summer. We'd get there right when it started in the morning and walk around looking at the planes until the show ended in the afternoon. They amazed me. I even applied to the Air Force Academy after high school. I got in, but my eyesight was so poor that they told me I'd never be able to actually fly a plane, so I went to the University of Wisconsin—Madison instead and went into finance, working with money in a bank. I don't even know why. One year I had planes on the brain and the next I was studying business law and economics. But that's a life lesson for you: Sometimes you don't plan things; they just happen.

As it turns out, I was on a business trip a few years back, and on that trip I met a really great girl. When she came to visit my family in Wisconsin just more than a year later, I took her to see that same Oshkosh air show that my dad had always taken me to, and just as the Blue Angels did their final maneuver, with the vapor of their planes leaving wispy lines across the sky, I propped myself up on one knee and asked her

to marry me. She said yes, and now we live on an island off
the west coast of Canada together.

But those are just the basics. The rough outline of my life.
Here are the more important things, though: I'm deathly
afraid of birds. I make a mean loaf of banana bread. I don't
like to golf—I'm too impatient for it. I'm the only one of my
friends who doesn't like golf and they tease me about it. My
favorite movie of all time is The Godfather—the original, not
either of the two sequels. The only movie I have ever cried
during was Steel Magnolias. My mother was watching it, and
I started watching it with her, and during that scene in the
graveyard—just watch it; I'm not going to tell you any more
about it—I had streams of tears running down my cheeks
and I ran up to my room and sobbed into my Star Wars
pillow. I have never told anyone this; I wouldn't know how to
explain it. But don't ever let anyone tell you that men don't
cry; the good ones do sometimes.

My favorite book is Where the Red Fern Grows. It is
impossible not to love this book. Read it as soon as you're able
to, and often. I play hockey in a men's league during the
winter. I played goalie in high school and college, and I still
do. My favorite holiday is Halloween, probably because I love
fall. I don't have a favorite color; I think it's wrong to show
favoritism toward colors, because where would the world be
with even one less color available to us? When I'm not at
work, I like to wear jeans and sweatshirts and my red Pumas.
My wife hates these shoes. I couldn't care less. I drink too
much Coke. My wife also hates this. I also couldn't care less
about that. If I had my choice, I'd eat pizza with olives and
anchovies every day, followed by Cherry Garcia ice cream.

I suppose, Glory, that I could do this all day long—list off *things about myself that I think you should know or that I think you might want to know someday. I could suggest certain things that you should and shouldn't do in life. But I won't.*

That isn't really the reason that I'm writing this letter to you. Like I just said, there's a good chance we might never get to meet. Your mother and I barely know each other now, and life has taken us on very different paths. She has made certain choices and so have I. And I hope that someday you'll forgive us both for not making better ones.

It's not so important that you know me, but that you know if anything ever happens, or if you ever need me, I will be there for you.

I am your father, but I am far from being a dad to you. And for that, I am sorry. I suspect that you are not only going to be beautiful, but smart, too. You come from good genes. I know that you will find your way through this life. You'll make some mistakes, and you'll learn so much from making them, so don't be afraid of that. One of the biggest mistakes a person can make, I think, is being scared of making one. And you'll have some huge successes, too; I know you will. I'm expecting great things from you. All of these things—the mistakes and the successes—will shape who you are.

I have no reason to believe you'll ever get this. But if you do, remember this: There is nothing better for a person than to have to chop her own path through life, but if that path gets too rough, or if you're getting lost on it and don't know what to do, I will be here. You just let me know, and I'll come walk that path with you.

Love,

Your father, Nash

Jack's chest felt rubber-band tight. He looked up toward the ceiling, inhaled, and exhaled forcefully, as if to prove to himself that he still had the ability to breathe.

Glory and Sophie were both looking at him expectantly. At the same time, Glory asked, "So where is he? Where's my dad?" and Sophie asked, "Jack, what is going on? Who is that letter from?"

He pushed the letter across the table toward Sophie, half doubting that she could focus enough to read it anyway.

Again, Glory asked him, "Where is he? Why doesn't he live here anymore? Did they get a divorce—him and the Blue Angels girl? My mom and her boyfriend got a divorce a while ago. I didn't like him all that much, but my mom did. She said lots of people split up. That it's 'not uncommon.'"

Jack inhaled deeply again, trying to figure out what to say, or how to say it. "Nash," he started, then stopped. "Nash, the person who wrote that letter, is my son, Glory." He had to force each word out, his voice choked. "Do you know what that means?"

She shook her head no, looking at Jack with rapt attention.

"That means that I'm your—your grandpa."

Jack brought his hands together, as if in prayer, held them in front of his nose, and closed his eyes for a second. "And," he started, opening his eyes again and gesturing out in front of him with his palms still together, "Nash doesn't live here anymore because there was a terrible accident and he passed away. Do you know what that means, Glory?"

She looked at him and rolled her eyes. Of course she knew what it meant. How stupid of him. But the last time he had raised a child was decades ago. Amazing how fast a person could forget what developmental stages children went through and when. There was a time when he thought the range of normal for rolling over, speech development, and potty training would be forever stamped on his brain.

"Dirt nap," said Glory.

Jack raised an eyebrow.

"Duh. It means he's dead. My friend from home, Jilly—it's short for Jillian—" she explained, "calls it a 'dirt nap' when someone dies."

Jack wasn't at all sure how he felt about that expression. "Where are you from?" he asked her.

"California," answered Glory.

"And how did you end up here? I mean, how did you get way up here?" Jack asked.

"Took a bus," Glory said, as if taking a bus straight up the western coast of North America at eight years old was a perfectly normal thing to do. She held her glass with both hands and finished up the last of her orange juice with a loud slurp.

Sophie, perhaps more lucid than Jack had been able to give her credit for, chimed in. "I think we need to call Glory's mother, Jack."

"You're right. You're right. We do."

Sophie nodded, her lips pursed. "Glory, do you know your phone number?" she asked the girl.

"I'm *eight*," Glory snipped.

"Okay, well, do you want to call your mum, then?" Sophie asked. "The phone is right there on the wall." She pointed behind her to the far side of the kitchen.

"Nope," Glory said.

"Do you want Jack or me to call her?" Sophie asked.

"Nope," Glory said.

"Well, someone's going to have to," said Jack sternly. "Either you or me or Sophie. But you can't just run away from home. Your poor mom is probably worried sick about you."

"Don't think so," Glory said in a singsong voice.

Jack looked at her, raising his eyebrow. He could see already that this little girl was turning out to be quite the handful.

"Worried? I'm *sure* she *isn't*," Glory said, glowering at him.

"And what makes you so sure?" Jack asked tenderly.

"Why do you think I'm here?" Glory volleyed.

"Why don't you tell us?"

"Well, brainiac, what did the letter say?" Glory asked him.

Jack's initial impression of the girl seemed to be right on. She was precocious as all get-out.

"It said to contact your father if you needed help, so I'm assuming you need help. But first you need to tell us what happened. Did you get in a fight with your mom?"

Glory rolled her eyes at him and then stared down at the table. She shook her head slowly back and forth. "Oh, boy." She sighed.

"Well, why don't we talk about it?"

"Don't think so," said Glory in that same singsong voice.

"I'm sure whatever it is, we can sort this out," said Jack. "But your mom is probably worried about you. So first let's hear what happened, okay? Then we'll call her and let her know you're all right."

"Okay. But you asked for it." Glory leaned back in the chair and drew her knees up so that her feet were resting on the seat; then she crossed her arms over them, and the words came tumbling out like water through a burst dam. "So, my mom has some issues. She used to be fine. She was a model, you know. Her picture was on a couple of the buses, and on a billboard for a car seller, too. But that was a while ago. She got into some bad stuff. *Drugs*," Glory said, as if the word were a secret, a juicy bit of gossip, not to be shared.

"Anyway, she leaves a lot lately. Probably to score. At least, that's what Jilly thinks, and Jilly's right about a lot of things. Most everything, actually. My mom always comes back, though. Before, when she'd leave, I'd just go down the street to Jilly's house and stay there. But then the last time I heard Jilly's mom tell her that if my mom left me again, even for an hour, Jilly's mom would turn her in. This time, when she left, she told me that her friend Sasha would be coming to watch me. But I waited three sleeps and Sasha never came. And I didn't want to tell Jilly because of her mom. So here I am! Voilà!" The word came out *wah-lah*. Glory made a wide, sweeping gesture with her arm and fixed them with a proud smile, but Jack was having a hard time taking it all in. Her *mother* was on *drugs*? Nash, his clean-cut son, had had an affair with a *drug addict*? This beautiful little girl had a mom like *that*?

Jack couldn't help himself. "Honey, are you *sure* about all of this? That it's the honest-to-God truth?"

Glory rolled her eyes at him again. "Big people are so *clueless*," she said, exasperated. "My mom never thought I knew about half the stuff she did, but I do. I'm plenty old enough. My third-grade teacher, Mrs. Klaus, said that I was one of the most observant kids she ever knew. And I think that's pretty much right. I notice lots of things. Lots. And I don't lie."

"Okay," Jack said.

"But how did you get across the border?" Sophie jumped in. She had either sobered up quickly or was a more detail-oriented person than Jack originally suspected. Maybe both. He hadn't even thought about Glory having to cross from the United States into Canada alone.

Glory shrugged. "Easy-peasy. I was in the way back of the bus and I just curled up on the seat. If anyone came all the way to the back to check, which they didn't, I was going to tell them that I was sick and my mom had my papers to check me in."

"Check you in?" Jack asked.

"Yeah. Check me in to the country," Glory said, impatient with Jack for not seeming to keep up with the conversation. She might as well have added, "Dummy," afterward.

Jack chuckled at Glory's attempt at adult terminology. But somehow this little eight-year-old who talked like she was sixteen and acted like she was forty had gotten herself on a bus in California and ended up in Campbell River. And now what were they supposed to do with her? How was he going to explain this to Magda, or Macy for that matter?

Fuck, Jack thought. *Fucking FUBAR. Fucked-up beyond all recognition.* It was the only time since he'd been in Vietnam when that expression seemed to fit perfectly. He couldn't think of a better way to describe the nightmare unfolding in front of him.

"She's a little young for you, Jack, don'tcha think?"

Jack jumped at the sound of Macy's voice. He hadn't even heard her come in the door. He had forgotten that Macy was supposed to be there. Forgotten that she even lived there.

Before he could say anything, Glory jumped out of her seat and extended her right hand to Macy.

"Hi! I'm Glory Jane Gibson. Are you the Blue Angels lady?"

Macy smiled blankly. She turned to Jack without taking Glory's hand. "Who is this kid? And what the hell is she talking about?"

Sophie, sensing what was to come, scooped Glory up. "Let's go wash your hair and your face, little one," she said. "We'll get you all cleaned up, okay?"

"Jack," Macy said sternly, "what is going on here? Why is there a kid in my kitchen?"

Every inch of Jack's skin quivered. He couldn't look at her. He had been hoping Macy wouldn't notice Glory for a little while, at least, give him time to come up with something. Anything. As it was, he had no idea what to tell her. So he just handed her the letter.

Macy read the first paragraph, then skimmed most of the rest. After she was finished, Macy folded the pages and slipped them back into the envelope.

"Where did she come from?" Macy asked.

"California." Jack couldn't look at her. Instead he studied his folded hands. He suddenly had a strange desire to do the Here's the Church game. He would do it with Nash when he was a baby, probably hadn't done it since. *Here's the church, here's the steeple, now look inside and see all the people.* He'd turn his hands upside down and Nash would laugh and clap. "Again, Dada," he'd say. "Again!" And Jack would do it over and over, neither of them tiring of it.

"How?" Macy asked. The word fell out measured and icy. She didn't look at him.

"She caught a bus," Jack said.

"Why?"

Jack told her, then, about what Glory had told them: about the supposed drug deal gone awry, about how the little girl waited for her mom to come back for three nights, about how she got herself across the border, and about how they had found her on the front stoop.

Macy shook her head, her lips pursed to the point of puckering. "And how old did you say she was?"

"I didn't," he said. It was the one question Jack had been

afraid she'd ask, and the only one he didn't want to answer. "She's, ah—she's eight, Macy. On June twenty-third, she turned eight."

Macy chewed on her bottom lip. Jack thought maybe she was doing the math, trying to figure it out, but really, he knew she didn't have to. Hell, it hadn't taken him very long, and Macy would be the last person to forget how, the first week he had arrived on the island, they had all danced awkwardly around the fact that it had been her and Nash's tenth wedding anniversary.

Chapter Eleven

"YOU GET THAT KID OUT OF MY HOUSE, OR I WILL. UNDER-stand?" And then Macy walked away from Jack, who stood there opening and closing his mouth like a guppy but not saying a goddamn thing.

As if she were watching someone else's hands, Macy saw her own reach out and grab the silver-framed wedding portrait in which two people who used to be her and Nash sat facing each other on a carpet of green with the Fox River shimmering in the background, both of them with heads thrown back in open-mouthed laughter. She remembered that moment. She remembered what had been so funny: Nash had whispered to her that she was one hot burrito. He was forever doing things like that—mixing metaphors, or massacring them completely. She told him it was *hot tamale*, not burrito, and they erupted into laughter, unable to take even minor direction from the photographer, whose exasperation just made them laugh harder.

For good measure, she also swept up the mosaic-framed picture of her and Nash on Long Beach, on the west coast of the island, the two of them draped in ponchos post–whale watching and grinning at the camera in black and white with troubled swells crashing far behind on a giant expanse of beach.

Macy could feel Jack's eyes on her, boring into her back as she walked through the living room, snatching the photographs and continuing down the hall and into the bedroom, where she shut the door behind her, dropped the pile on the bed, and let out a wail that originated so deep down it felt as if it were coming from beneath her. She took aim at the opposite wall, holding their wedding photo by the stand, and heaved it like a discus.

She followed that up with the Long Beach picture, holding it with her palm flat against its back and flinging it like one might a pie at the same wall. It shattered, glass and shards of green and silver and blue tile raining down. And it only made her feel worse.

Because what she really wanted was to throw things at him. To pummel Nash with her fists. To yell at him and scream at him and ask him why, and when he answered, to pummel on him and scream some more. There was no answer he could give that could make this right. But at least he would have been there. At least she wouldn't be hurling photos at a ghost.

She smashed another picture, and then another, and another. And when the floor glistened like sharp water and there was nothing more to break, she tore the covers from their bed and then the sheets. It didn't matter that these weren't the last sheets that Nash had slept on; he had slept on them once upon a time, and they needed to go.

But then there was the matter of the mattress. How to erase him from that? How to erase him at all?

Macy left the sheets straggling off the bed, as if they had been victim of fierce lovemaking instead of quite the opposite. She gathered Nash's baseball hat, taking time to wind up like a pitcher on the mound and whipping the watch inside it at the wall of their room that seemed to be the best stand-in she could find at the moment for her cheating, son-of-a-bitch husband.

"You're damn lucky you're dead, Nash," she muttered. Then she burst into tears.

Macy opened drawers, pulling out Nash's old T-shirts from concerts and hockey tournaments that had survived this long on sheer nostalgia. She piled his favorite jeans on top of them, stopping to think that his legs would never fill them again. Right then, she couldn't put a finger on how she felt about that, so she moved on to the closet, tossing shirts and ties onto the growing mountain of clothes in the middle of the bedroom floor.

And somewhere in the midst of the mad pulling and yanking and piling of clothes, Macy's fingers closed around something as familiar to her as her own skin: Nash's UW sweatshirt.

It was gray with red lettering. A hoodie with WISCONSIN arching over the figure of a sweater-clad badger. The kind of sweatshirt that was once heavy but was now threadbare, the front pocket ripped almost clear off, the neck cut into a vee to make room for Nash's 17.5-inch neck and now comfortably frayed.

It was the one item of clothing that the Nash in her mind always wore. His parents had given it to him the day they visited the Madison campus for the first time. He had probably worn it weekly, if not more often, until the end.

Macy brought it to her nose and inhaled. It smelled faintly of him: musky and spicy and with a hint of something rich like leather. She smiled, thinking about how she used to bury her head into the crook of his neck to fill her nostrils with exactly this scent. And then she thought of that little kid sitting at her kitchen table and just how she came to be, and Macy found herself growling hard and low like a junkyard dog.

She had the urge to get back at him. To hurt him like he had hurt her. The impulse settled in her stomach like hunger. It parched her throat like thirst.

Thirst.

It came to her then. His wine. Nash's precious collection of wine that she knew, in an unspoken directive, she wasn't to open. He had started collecting it in college, back before he even appreciated it, because he admired his roommate's dad and, by proxy, the man's collection of and knowledge about wine. By the time he moved to the island to be with Macy, his collection took up almost a larger portion of the U-Haul than his couch. It was for special occasions, he said. He knew which bottles should be opened when, and how much they would be worth. In Nash's own kind way, he had made it clear that the wines downstairs in the basement were for appreciating, savoring at special mo- ments, and that they were largely lost on Macy's unrefined pal- ate. But those special moments rarely, if ever, materialized. The wine collection was just that—a collection. A museum piece.

Now, though, Nash wasn't there to lecture her if he found she had cracked open a bottle. He wasn't there to say that they really should save this one or that for whatever reason. Now she had the whole damn cellar to herself. And she could sip or swig her way through it without anyone muttering one single word of disapproval. In fact, that was exactly what she was going to do.

Screw you, she thought. *You want to mess around. Well, watch this.*

Macy pictured herself selecting the most expensive bottle of wine, and if she didn't like it, she'd simply pour it down the sink and open another. No matter that she hadn't a clue as to how to pick out the most expensive bottle; she hoped the fanciness of the labels might help guide her.

Macy eased open the door of her bedroom, peering down

the hall to make sure everyone had gone to bed. The house lay dark and quiet. Only the light above the kitchen sink spilled out into the foyer area and living room as she made her way toward the basement. Macy didn't know what she had expected to find, but it wasn't this. The silence put her on edge. She would rather the scene from her bedroom, or the chaos of the kitchen before that. Both better matched her mood.

She opened the door to the basement, expecting to have to feel her way to the light switch, and was surprised to find she could see straight down the stairs. And then she heard voices. Muffled voices.

Macy decided to leave the light off and pulled her hand back from the switch. She picked her way down the stairs one at a time, trying to make her footfall as light as possible.

From her perch, hidden behind a half wall, she could see that while she had been smashing everything that hadn't been nailed down, someone had pulled out the couch in the basement for Glory and tucked her in with a raggedy stuffed monkey. Macy had no idea where the monkey had come from, but the girl was holding it tight to her chest and staring up at Jack. Someone— Macy figured it had been Sophie—had also found a night-light and an old T-shirt for the girl to sleep in.

"She said she'll come by tomorrow—early," Glory said. "She said she was just going to leave out the basement door."

So Sophie had left her here. And then sneaked out. *Coward*, Macy thought.

Macy saw Jack nod absently. "You need anything, baby girl?" he asked her.

Glory shook her head. Jack patted her tiny feet poking out from under the blanket. "Okay, then. I'll see you in the morning."

Jack got up and moved toward the stairs. Macy held her breath, wondering what she'd say to the two of them if they found her sitting there.

"She doesn't like me."

Glory had pushed herself up in bed, still clutching the monkey.

"What's that?" Jack asked her.

"She doesn't want me here," Glory said. "The Blue Angels lady—she's mad at me."

I'm not mad at you, Macy thought, though she wasn't wholly sure she believed that.

"It's just a surprise, your being here, that's all," said Jack. "And some people don't take too well to surprises. Macy's very nice. You'll see. Just give her a little time."

"Okay. B-but—I just don't want to go home," Glory said. "I can still live here, right? Even if my dad doesn't live here any-more? I mean, he told me I could—in the letter."

Oh, my God, Macy thought. *Don't you dare, Jack. Don't you fucking dare.*

Jack walked over, slid Glory back under the covers, and fluffed the pillow behind her. *"Shhhh,"* he crooned to her, strok-ing her forehead. "Just go to sleep now. No one's going anywhere tonight, or tomorrow. It's going to be okay. This is complicated, and you're just going to have to be patient with us while we grown-ups figure things out. Okay?" He smoothed her damp blond ringlets.

Macy exhaled the breath she had been holding.

It occurred to Macy at that very moment that the daughter she and Nash would have had might look strikingly like Glory. This thought came to her with no real confirmation that the child she had been carrying was a girl, and with no knowledge of Glory's mom's coloring or race. But the simple possibility of it—of their child looking like the beautiful one now tucked into the ratty old couch in her basement—would have brought Macy straight to her knees had she not already been on them.

"Grandpa?" Glory asked.

"Yeah, ladybug?"

"Can I give you something?"

"Right now?" Jack asked.

Glory nodded.

"Sure," he said. "Let's see it."

The girl reached down under the bed and pulled out a plastic box. She rooted around in it, among what looked like spools of needlepoint thread, and pulled out a red-and-white bracelet.

She handed it to Jack. "This is for you."

"Did you make this?"

She nodded. "It took me from California all the way to Washington to finish it," she said. "It was for my dad. But he's dead, and you're my grandpa. And I never had a grandpa before. So now it's for you."

She reached out for Jack's hand, set it in her lap, and tied the bracelet onto his wrist.

"Does it say . . . Hmmm—let's see here," Jack said, seemingly trying to make out words on the bracelet.

"It says, 'I love you,'" Glory said, saving him the struggle of deciphering it.

"Oh, Glory. This is so special. Thank you," Jack said. Macy thought she heard his voice break. But he reached down and took the girl's face in his hands and said as sure as anything, "I love you, too. And I'm glad you're here."

Jack kissed her forehead, turned out the light next to the girl's foldout bed, and then turned back toward the stairs. Macy eased herself up and silently took two stairs at a time, carefully closing the basement door behind her. She hurried toward her room.

Even from the hallway, Macy's bedroom looked like it had been the scene of either a rowdy party or a crime. Fragments of glass and ripped pieces of photographs littered the floor like confetti. Some drawers hung open. Others had been ripped clean out of the dresser and thrown about the room. And in the middle of it all was a mound of clothes that her once-husband had worn. As Macy stood there, hand still on the doorknob, surveying the scene, she wondered if he had worn anything in this pile when he fucked some other woman who was now Glory's mom. She'd never know that one random fact, and she couldn't decide whether that made her feel better or much, much worse.

Macy felt her hand close around something hanging on the doorknob. She slipped it off, and by the soft glow of the hallway night-light could see it was a bracelet just like the one the girl had given Jack, blue and yellow, with the words *Blue Angel* woven unevenly into it.

Chapter Twelve

MAGDA SAT AT THE KITCHEN TABLE HOLDING A STEAMING MUG
of water. A lemon wedge bobbed near the top. She had read several interviews with celebrities who claimed that hot water and
lemon were the key to weight maintenance. Supposedly it took
away cravings. Magda figured it couldn't hurt to try. So far, she
had yet to see the effects.

The morning sunlight—more of a gray haze than real light—
filtered through a frosty coating on the sliding glass doors. It
seemed as if fall were starting already. Only in Wisconsin could
you go from can't-breathe-hot-and-muggy to frost in a matter of
days. The rest of the country was still in the throes of summer,
but the early August mornings in De Pere were sneaking toward
winter. Magda usually dreaded the snow and cold, but she didn't
mind the recent turn in the weather. It had been a hot, hard
summer. She was ready for a change.

The house lay quiet, the frost on the doors cocooning her.
She thought of the *Storm Stories* episode on the Weather Channel she had been watching last night when Ginny called to prat-
tle on about her problems with Frank.

Magda had thought about disconnecting the phone before the show started—it was a good episode: avalanches and tornadoes, her two favorite natural disasters—but she didn't want to miss Jack if he decided to call. She didn't much care for floods or earthquakes, except for the History Channel special she'd seen a while ago, *Modern Marvels: Engineering Disasters 5*, in which an oil rig on a lake in Louisiana dug into a salt mine beneath it and created a whirlpool so powerful that it sucked down into the salt mine the entire lake, the handful of tankers on it, and more than sixty surrounding acres of land—all because of a fourteen-inch drill bit. Even the flow of the river that fed the lake reversed directions. It actually started flowing *north* from the Gulf of Mexico into the lake and created a massive waterfall. Magda had never seen anything like it. She was so fascinated by the whole debacle that she ordered a copy of the episode and kept it in her bedside table for safekeeping. After all, who knew when they'd air it again, if ever?

Last night, the Weather Channel's *Storm Stories* was just getting interesting—two skiers had been covered by the avalanche and a reenactment had been set up to demonstrate what it was like to be buried under tons of snow and what smart tactics the buried skiers had used to survive—when the phone rang.

Not again, Magda thought when she heard Ginny sniffling on the other end.

As it turned out, Ginny had checked Frank's cell phone, found a strange number listed under *Fishing*, and in a very un-Ginny-like moment, mustered the gumption to call the number and berate the floozy who answered. But honestly, what did she expect from Magda? And at that hour, besides?

So when poor Ginny started wailing, yet again, about how she didn't know what to do about her disintegrating marriage,

Magda snapped at her, "For the love of all that is holy, Ginny, just do *something*, will you?"

Then Ginny, obviously hurt, and classically passive-aggressive, made up an excuse about forgetting a load of laundry in the washer and having to run and get it out right that second. Magda had chugged the remainder of the glass of white zinfandel she'd been sipping and two more after that, all the while cursing Ginny's meekness, Jack's selfishness, and her own brashness. "You can attract more flies with honey, darling," Magda's mother used to tell her. But the saying had been lost on her. She couldn't for the life of her imagine why you'd want to attract flies in the first place. Not until she had a child of her own did Magda learn that her mother had gotten the saying all wrong, and that she was supposed to be attracting bees. Regardless, she had tried hard and failed to apply the general theory to her life many times, the previous night among them.

Now Magda lay prone on the living room couch. Early-morning light filtered in and the grandfather clock ticked rhythmically, muted by the distance between the foyer where the clock stood and the living room. Magda thought what it must feel like to be surrounded by snow, to be buried alive in it—to be laid out flat, the snow molded to each curve of her body, embracing her legs, her bottom, her back, her neck. To have only her own heartbeat and breathing to break the silence, and nothing else. To be enshrined in pure, unadulterated quiet.

From her imaginary snow cave on the living room couch, Magda let her eyes wander around the room and into the formal dining room and beyond it, to the kitchen. Everything was right where she had left it. Everything was still spick-and-span more than a week after she'd cleaned. Not a single crumb out of place. Oh, to remember the days she had wished for exactly that! The days she hadn't wanted to be a wife, mother, cook, maid, chauffeur, family strategist, and event planner. The days when she wanted nothing more than to go back, way back, before Jack or Nash, to a time when the only person she was obligated to was herself. To a time when she didn't feel used up, wasted—when her future was bursting with possibility. Way back when she felt whole.

She had gotten it all—all that she had ever wanted: a marriage to a handsome man who made sure she never had to work. A beautiful child—a son to boot. A modestly elegant home in a town that was neither too big nor too small.

And look where all that had left her: by herself, with a twinge of a hangover from boxed white zin, and not a thing that she was required to do or a place that she had to be. She could go shopping for a new outfit for next month's golf outing. She could read a book. She could go to the grocery store and whip herself up a nice meal. She could call Jack. She could watch the sun continue to come up through the frosty patio door. Or she could just lie right there on the couch and scream her pretty little head off.

When she was younger all she wanted was to be married. Once she was married, she wanted kids. When her house was full of kids and bills and toys and laundry, she longed for her single days, or to be transported to a desert island. To be completely alone, quiet.

And now she had that very thing. But the weight of nostalgia for those days—when she had to get up before dawn to make Nash's and Jack's lunch and start laundry, when she had to rush through picking up the house and errands and appointments to make it to Nash's school by three-thirty to drive him to hockey or baseball practice, and then some nights to piano lessons, and after that picking up or making dinner, and then staying up late

into the night to get ready to do it all again the next morning—
the sheer weight of wanting it all back had pinned her flat on her
back.

Magda looked at her milky-smooth hands, examined each
knuckle and the myriad minuscule grooves and wrinkles that
spidered over each one. She took exquisite care of her skin.
Lately, though, she could see her age creeping onto it. The skin
of her hands seemed to be growing thinner by the day. Instead
of a soft, luxurious satin stretched over the bones, it looked more
like delicate chiffon. Soon it would be transparent. Soon she'd
have the hands of an old, old woman, with soft blue highways of
veins running just beneath the papery surface.

She ran those hands over her toes, over each ankle, and up
her calves, which were badly in need of a shave and littered with
puffy varicose veins. Her calves were fleshy, Rubenesque. Her
fingers explored, for the first time ever, how exposed the backs
of her knees felt in comparison to the fronts, like the underside
of a turtle.

She let her hands run up to her thighs and linger in the hot
flesh between her legs before continuing over the dimply mound
that, after a C-section and a lifetime aversion to exercise, now
formed her stomach and stretched from hip to hip just below
her belly button. Those same fingers and hands dug deep into
the thickness of her torso, pressing hard to find each rib and
working their way up as if on the rungs of a ladder, and toward
the top, pushing aside her breasts, which naturally slung themselves toward her armpits these days. She took each breast in her
hands, for the first time ever taking note of their consistency,
despite years of urging by her lady doctor to do just that. She
drew her palm across her clavicle and ran her thumbs up her
neck, feeling what seemed like a cluster of wires and tubes sit-

ting underneath the skin. She felt her chin, her jaw, her cheeks, her ears, the orbs of her eyes, and finally her scalp, as a blind person would.

Magda didn't recognize any of it. Her hands were a stranger's. She felt almost violated by their touch.

They had always been at odds, she and her body. She had treated it with a kind indifference; her flesh and bones were responsible for getting her to and fro, and for that she was grateful. But she hadn't ever felt at home in them. For her, being in her body was akin to living in a hotel room her whole life. She knew far less about her body—its contours, how it felt under the skin—than Jack did. And even he hadn't paid it much attention in a while. It had been many months since she and Jack had been intimate, and he hadn't ever given her that—well—that *feeling* that was supposed to overwhelm you during one of those encounters. She had tried talking to him about it once, long ago. But Magda quickly found that it was a conversation with no winning sides. When they were intimate, she made sure he enjoyed himself, and she made sure to enjoy being close to him, the feel of his skin against hers. Afterward, she told herself that this was just life, and there was a lot more to it than s-e-x. *Look at your life*, she would say. *Just look around at how lucky you are. Don't dwell on silly things you can't control.*

And for so long, she had. Magda had been down the road of real, devouring love once before, which had dead-ended in a big, painful, fiery crash on Valentine's Day in 1959, when she found her fiancé, Jimmy Wallis, snuggled in a booth at the back of Kroll's restaurant with a girl who was not her, while he was supposed to be held up at school in Michigan. Then Magda found Jack. She found that he loved her in that dependable, solid way he had. And she found that she loved him, too, only not in the obsessive, jittery, unhealthy way she had Jimmy. With Jack, Magda felt as though she had been wrapped in an old quilt and set by a fire on a cold winter's night. She felt safe and valued and, in the truest sense of the word, like Jack's partner. Like they were forging their lives together, shoulder-to-shoulder.

Back then, she couldn't help but believe that having chemistry with someone was a minor nonfactor in happiness. One had to be practical in matters of the heart, after all. One had to have priorities. One had to think about self-preservation.

But that had been long ago. Magda had self-preserved her way right into boredom and monotony. She wanted to miss Jack when he was gone. She wanted to want to call him each night before she went to bed and look forward to hearing his voice. She wanted to be more reliant on him, on what they had together. She wanted her body to be overwhelmed right along with his in those intimate moments. She wanted to be admitted to that secret club she had been denied from entering, despite trying like h-e–double hockey sticks her whole married life to get in.

She didn't need to feel all of that, even; she'd settle for just a bit. She'd settle for feeling any one of those things just once in a while. Just one time.

But her life was almost three-quarters over. And there was a very real possibility that she'd never felt as utterly sad as she did at that moment, lying on that couch with a dead son and a husband gone in more ways than one. She wasn't Nash's mom any longer. Now she was just Jack's wife. And what was that, really?

It was, Magda decided, the only thing holding her here. To this place. To this version of herself.

The fingers of her right hand found their way into the still-steaming mug of lemon water. She mindlessly let them drop back down between her thighs. The skin down there revolted against the water, or perhaps against her own hand. But she held it fast, the standoff ending when her lower half brushed slowly up against her touch, hesitantly at first, then again. And again. Each time with increasing assertiveness. Until, finally, she felt herself come into her own skin. Until she felt herself come home to her body. At long last.

Magda had chosen the Wisconsin Union hotel for two distinct reasons: its classic charm and the fact that no one really went there anymore. There was always a scattering of patrons, usually in their seventies or eighties, who had been regulars during the hotel's heyday, when it was the hallmark of Green Bay high society. She sat down at the bar and ordered a gin gimlet, three olives, because she liked olives and because it was the kind of place where one should drink gimlets.

The bar and most of the restaurant were both deserted, just as she had hoped for at eight o'clock on a Wednesday night. The Union's big rush was around five o'clock or so, given the average age of its clientele. Most of them were home in bed by this time.

"Thought I'd be closing early tonight," the bartender said, setting Magda's drink in front of her. He looked older than God, and moved so slowly and painfully that Magda felt awful about him waiting on her.

"Oh," said Magda. "Sorry. Do you usually close early?" She sipped her gimlet. It had been decades and decades—the last time she had been in the Union, actually—since she'd had one. The tang of it made her pucker.

"Usually," he said, wiping the bar down with a perfectly folded, perfectly white rag. "We're just not that busy anymore. Not like the old days." He frowned and shook his head. "But I have some office work to do tonight, so you, young lady"—he smiled at Magda and patted her hand—"you just relax and stay as long as you'd like."

"Thank you," Magda said, more pleased at being called a "young lady" than anything. The mood of the place, the gimlet, his age, almost made her add a *sir* at the end. Instead, she waved him off. "Don't mind me. You go ahead and do what you need to do—this drink will last me a while. I'm just going to go relax over there." She pointed to a cluster of chairs and cocktail tables behind her as she shimmied off her stool.

She settled herself at a table by the window. The old days. The bartender was right—this place really had been something back then. She looked around, remembering how it had looked the last time she'd been here. New Year's Eve, 1958. The night that Jimmy Wallis had proposed to her.

They were on Christmas break from college and hadn't seen each other since September. There were wall-to-wall people, and the place smelled of Scotch and Estée Lauder's Youth Dew. Magda and Jimmy were having after-dinner drinks in exactly the same area in which Magda was now sitting. Jimmy had asked her if he made her happy. But it was so loud that she couldn't hear him over the band and the boisterousness of the crowd. He had to repeat the question, yelling into her ear: "*Do I make you happy?*"

Magda told him that of course he made her happy and what kind of question was that? He had leaned into her ear again, then, and said, "I think I can make you happier."

"Oh, Jimmy," she had said, brushing him off. The band announced they were taking a brief break and would resume in 1959, and Jimmy abruptly excused himself to use the restroom. Magda remembered looking at the clock, annoyed. It was eleven fifty-five. Couldn't he wait just five more minutes? If he didn't come back in time, she'd be the only person in the entire room left without someone to kiss at midnight.

It was then that she had heard Jimmy's voice on the microphone. He introduced himself and introduced Magda. He said that he and Magda had been having a little disagreement, and he wanted to settle things once and for all. He told the crowd how he thought he could make Magda happier, but that she didn't think so. Magda's breath had started coming in short bursts, her heart fluttering like a wild bird within her chest. Oh, if this was what she thought it was! Jimmy pulled a box out of his jacket pocket and said, "Magda, I *can* make you happier. Instead of being the best boyfriend possible to you, I want to be the best *husband* possible. Will you do me the honor of marrying me?"

Little more than a month later, after she had already found her dress and booked the church, she had found Jimmy in Kroll's.

She couldn't bear to drive by the Wisconsin Union hotel after that. She'd go miles and miles out of her way just to avoid the sight of it, even after she married Jack. But when she and Jack bought a house just down from the Union, Jack called Magda on her tendency to go the wrong way out of the driveway to keep from driving by it. Embarrassed, she relented as far as driving routes were concerned, but Magda vowed she would never step foot in the Wisconsin Union again.

Yet here she was. Only a few decades, give or take some years, later. And it was okay. She was okay—mostly. Magda felt a stirring of something sad and wistful down inside of her. She peered into her gimlet, studying the liquid, weakly tinted green, as if she might divine the answer there. Jimmy Wallis, New Year's Eve, a chip of diamond shimmering up at her in the soft light, a head fuzzy with bubbly and a whole life to be lived, stretched out as far as Magda could see. The memories were the same, but with a different sting. It was, Magda realized, because she couldn't remember feeling as happy as she had that night. Even the birth of her only child—fueled more by relief and apprehension and then afterward by an intensely pure emotion grounded in fierce devotion and protection—didn't quite qualify. What she was after, what Magda was trying to remember feeling ever since Jimmy, was that sheer giddiness that made a person want to skip and sing her way down the street.

"Well, well, well. Magda Allen. It sure has been some time."

She had expected Peter King's voice to sound different, changed with age. But Magda knew its low, gravely timbre before she ever raised her eyes. They had been classmates from kindergarten all the way through high school, and there was never a time, in all those thirteen years, that Magda couldn't remember him sounding just that way. When all the other boys' voices were cracking and squeaking toward adulthood, Peter's resonated with the deep and steady lilts of a Wisconsin farm boy. Even the kindergarten version of Peter, in her mind, had the mature voice of the almost sixty-year-old man standing in front of her. That his voice hadn't aged with the rest of him— peppery black hair and an obvious paunch—immediately brought Magda back to the days when she knew Peter King oh so well.

"Please," Magda said, gesturing to the chair opposite her. "Please sit down."

"I think I'll grab a drink first," Peter said.

Instead of walking over to the bar, he came around to Magda's side of the table and pulled out a chair next to her. He trailed a finger, letting it brush her forearm as he walked by.

Magda stiffened, then thought to herself, *Oh, Magda, he's an old friend. Loosen up a little for once.*

Peter returned, holding a glass of red wine by the stem with two fingers. "It's good to see you again, Magda," he said.

It was good to see him, too, she had to admit. She had always liked Peter. They had played Kick the Can growing up and had been each other's dates for prom and homecoming because neither had wanted the fuss and complication that came with asking someone else. But Peter had gone off to law school at Notre Dame and had kept right on going. Magda had run into him one year in the pop and juice aisle of Cub Foods—she had a screaming toddler on her hip and he was home visiting relatives for the holidays. They promised to get together for lunch or drinks sometime, knowing full well that it was just something to say.

Until now. Magda looked at the man reclining in the burgundy leather chair across from her. He was a rough sort of handsome. Tall. A few pounds over sturdy. Dark hair, balding around the crown of his head but longer toward the back. Dark suit, purple tie. Crisp white shirt with the long type of collar that gangsters in the movies always seemed to wear. He looked expensive. Not at all like the gangly-limbed, braces-wearing boy of her youth.

He took a long sip of his drink, put it down, and smacked his lips a bit loudly for Magda's taste. He leaned forward and clasped his hands on the table. "So you're sure about this, Magda?" he asked.

It was asked without judgment. Merely a formality, as if he asked each of his clients that very thing.

Was she sure? It was a good question. How could one really be sure about such things, after all? All Magda knew was that she had made a decision and she was going forward with it. That was that. The only thing she could be sure about was that this was the most spontaneous thing she had ever done, and she was increasingly proud of herself for doing it.

"Final answer," she said. She gave him a wide smile.

Peter pushed three piles of papers toward her. "Okay, then. Go ahead and fill these out—all the areas I've highlighted. And sign by each 'X' I've circled."

Magda nodded and started to work her way through each stack. Most of it was basic information: name, address, Social Security number, date of birth, date and place of marriage, so on and so forth. She looked up at Peter. He had draped his arms across the back of the chair, right ankle resting on the opposite knee, right foot tapping out a rhythm in his head.

He caught Magda's stare. "Everything all right?"

"Oh, yes. Yes. Of course. Just taking a breather," Magda said. Truth was, the more boxes and lines she filled out, the more final everything seemed to get. She felt jumping beans inside her where nerves used to be. She was going to start her life, once and for all. After years of hemming and hawing and making do, this was it. This was her beginning.

When she finished, she piled the papers into one neat stack and pushed them back to Peter. He paged through the documents. "Have to make sure all the 'i's are dotted and 't's are crossed," he said.

Magda watched him intently, holding her breath.

"Everything looks good. All in order," Peter said, sweeping the documents into his briefcase. He looked at Magda while he buckled it. "I have to say that I was pretty surprised to get a call from you."

"Me too," Magda said. She felt heat sear her cheeks. What a ridiculous response. Why couldn't she ever think of charming—or, at the very least, appropriate—things to say? She would think of just the right thing tonight, just before drifting off to sleep. That was the way it always was. She was sophisticated and witty and tough as nails in her almost-dreams, but never in real life.

But if she thought about it too much, gave the thought of leaving Jack too much air, it might just up and start breathing on its own. At least by keeping it quiet, by not talking about it, she could manage it. This act, the freedom it brought along, was hers and only hers, and she wanted to keep it that way. So she smiled up at Peter, and in the nicest possible way, asked him if they could possibly talk about something else. Magda was sure they could fill the space of a dinner with enough conversation after not seeing each another for oh so long.

And they did. They covered what their old classmates were up to, who was still in touch with whom, Green Bay's real estate market, the upcoming mayoral race, and, of course, the Packers. Before Magda knew it, dinner was over, she had sipped her way through most of another gimlet, and she and Peter were still reminiscing. Magda felt tingly all over. Not only from the gimlet. But from remembering the old her, too: the girl who lobbied to join the all-boy debate team; the one who belted out Sinatra's "My Way" at the school talent show without a hint of stage fright; the her who took a road trip to California, by herself, the day after their high school graduation, because she wanted to see the ocean before she got roped into a job as someone's secretary. The tingling made her shudder. That girl was back.

"You okay?" Peter asked.

Magda nodded. She had spent her summer wallowing, trying to act like nothing was wrong. Like someone Jack would want to come home to.

She had waited so many nights for the phone to ring, for it to be Jack. Only to hear that he wasn't ready. Well, *she* was ready. How about that? She was tired of waiting and she was going to do something about it.

Peter got up from the table and made a sweeping gesture across the dining room. "Looks like we've got the place to ourselves," he said. "How about a dance before dessert?"

She could hear elevator music drifting faintly through the dining room. It didn't seem the danceable kind.

"Oh, I don't think I could," she said.

"Oh?" Peter raised an eyebrow. "Have your legs quit working?" he asked.

"No." Magda chuckled. "No, of course not. There's just not any music, and I don't think I remember the last time I danced." While her mouth protested, Magda's stomach flipped. It had been so long. So long since someone had flirted with her. She wondered how many women Peter had slept with, then decided she didn't want to know. She had heard through the Green Bay grapevine that he had been married five times. That was three more than the number of men she had ever been with. But if one of the middle wives, with whom she had seen him pictured within the *Press Gazette* after they donated a chunk of change to one of St. Norbert College's capital campaigns, was any indication, his tastes ran toward twiggy, beautiful blondes. That he would flirt with her in the first place struck Magda as both preposterous and exhilarating.

"It's like riding a bike," Peter said, pulling on her hand. "C'mon, I'll show you."

Magda let Peter tug her to her feet, let him pull her close to him, his arm tight around the small of her back.

"Just like homecoming," Peter said.

Magda threw her head back and laughed. "Oh, Peter. You are something else."

He was weaving them through the gathering of tables, his feet knocking hard against Magda's. He might look the part, Magda thought, but he sure hadn't gained an ounce of coordination over the past three decades.

"*We* were something else," Peter said. His whisper skipped past Magda's ear, leaving a vapor trail of alcohol in its wake.

Magda pretended she hadn't heard him.

"We were, Magda. We had chemistry. Doing *The Glass Menagerie*—do you remember that?"

She couldn't tell if he was kidding.

"You played my *brother*," she said.

"I *know*," said Peter. "Almost incestuous," he hissed, then chuckled.

Magda's normal reaction would be to push Peter away. It would be the proper thing to do, after all. But where had that gotten her, exactly? Since she had walked into the Kroll's that day and saw Jimmy Wallis gently stroking a hand that wasn't hers, she had reformed herself. Not that she thought she was to blame, per se, for Jimmy's philandering, but a specific doubt had always nagged at her: If she were just a little thinner, a little more together, a little more proper, then maybe boys would see her the way Jimmy Wallis had looked at the prim blonde sitting across from him that day. But it hadn't ever really worked.

"You are, for all practical purposes, a free woman, you know." Then Peter started to sing, his voice falling off-key and stepping back on, like a drunk walking a curb.

She could still see glimpses of the Peter she knew as a girl. Cute in a gangly way. A mischievous grin that made whomever he aimed it at an instant accomplice in whatever he happened to be planning. Kind, witty, a whiz at geography. So cocksure that she often forgot he wore thick glasses and, for a spell, braces. She supposed that those same glimpses were there in her, too. Probably in everyone.

"Let's go *swimming*," she whispered in his ear.

"Swimming?" The word tumbled from his mouth like a boulder.

Hot summer nights like this one, when they were young, were spent at Lost Dauphin State Park, on the other side of the Fox River. They roasted marshmallows, drank beer, and leaned up against each other next to campfires, drying themselves from occasional dips into the river. Most of the other girls would only dip a toe into the water, afraid of messing up their hair or of what the opaque water might hold, but Magda—Magda loved it. She loved the way the surface shimmered black and silver, the way it felt against her skin, the freedom of lying on her back in the middle of a river in the middle of the night. No adult she knew did things like that anymore, and suddenly, she couldn't comprehend why.

"Swimming," she said. "Down by the old state park. Just like the good old days."

Peter held her at arm's length, trying to gauge her sincerity. "Skinny-dipping?" he asked.

"No, silly. There are houses there now," she said. "It'll still be fun, though. Promise."

She was genuinely excited about the prospect of going night swimming, though it seemed as though she was the only one. Magda saw a cloud settle over Peter and guessed this wasn't where he had seen his evening headed.

Peter made a grand show of looking at his watch. "Aw, Magda. I didn't realize how late it was. I need to be up for a deposition in Shawano early tomorrow." He pulled her into an awkward hug. "I'll get these papers filed for you first thing on Friday. Let's do this again soon."

Magda knew that she wouldn't see Peter King again unless she was paying him. And that was just fine.

Magda pulled her car into the gravel parking lot, which was little more than a widening of the road's shoulder. The air hung heavy and still, without even a rumor of a breeze, and she had driven down Lost Dauphin Road with all four windows down. The wind in her hair, the fact that it was after ten o'clock at night and she had nowhere to be and no one waiting on her to be there—it all felt scintillatingly good.

She looked in both directions before crossing the road to the shore of the Fox River, even though she would have known without looking that a car was on its way by the swath any head-lights might have cut through the dark.

A thin line of young-looking trees stood guard on the river's bank. Not much privacy, but no matter. Magda unbuttoned her blouse, slipped her capri pants over her hips, and kicked off her sandals. The moon fell on her like soft stage lighting, and made the river's still surface look like a giant serving tray. She picked her way over gravel and through long licks of grass and weeds. At the river's edge, she dipped one foot into the water and found the temperature to be nearly warm to the touch. Magda took a few steps in and then dived under. She surfaced, flipped to her back, and looked up at a star-studded sky.

The water was the same temperature as the night air, giving Magda the distinct feeling of floating, almost apart from her body. Freedom, she thought. This was freedom at its most basic level. Primitive, natural, solitary. Suddenly she didn't feel so far from her teenage self, the "her" defined not by her relationships to other people—friend, wife, mother—but by what she wanted out of life. And what she wanted, at that exact moment, was to pucker up and suck the very marrow right out of it.

There was so much she could do, so much she could explore. So much she could learn. *Do. Learn. Explore. Discover. Do.* The words lapped at her like gentle waves. She could finally visit Greece. And not just visit, but stay: six days, six months, six years. It no longer mattered. She could pick up tomorrow and see the Eiffel Tower. She could eat pasta carbonara in Rome, paella in Valencia, pad thai in Bangkok. She had always, inwardly, fancied herself a child of the world. But outwardly, she had been tethered. She had been the mother to a child she had loved as if he were the whole world. She had partnered with a man who had been most interested in bringing the whole world to her, in creating their own little life together. Each of those roles had had little to do with what she longed, in her heart, to do. It seemed almost silly when Magda ran through it in her head: trade a good man for a few good international trips? But it was more than that. She and Jack were different people at the core. Both good. Both trying to do the right thing. But different. Magda longed to feel the wind at her back. Jack longed to build a shelter to block it all out. And Nash had been their compromise. But now Nash was gone. And Magda had, as best as she could tell, a little more than a quarter of her life left to live. If not now, then when?

Magda felt the water on her skin, but only barely. Only when she fluttered her arms for balance, for buoyancy. She gave thanks that Peter had declined her invitation. Out here, floating aimlessly in the wide expanse of the Fox River, she regretted the flutter of excitement she had felt at his touch back at the Wisconsin Union. Or maybe, she didn't regret *it*, but the fact that she had originally assigned it to Peter King instead of to where it really belonged: to her rediscovered self's sovereignty now budding within her.

She thought then about Jack. About how he would react, seeing those papers. Would he think her motives malicious? Or would he see her actions for what they were: a cease-fire? A truce. An acknowledgment that she wanted to be happy; she wanted him to be happy; and they had never quite figured out how to be happy together.

It wasn't as if things had been bad. In fact, quite the opposite. They had had a good life. A darn good life. But Magda yinged where Jack yanged. She golfed not because she loved chasing that little white ball all over a lawn that was better manicured than one she could ever hope to have, but because it relaxed him. Yet he knew—he had to know—way deep down, that she didn't really enjoy it. And he traveled, but only short trips that barely spanned a weekend, and only within North America's borders. Where Magda saw opportunity and adventure and the chance to expand her cultural horizons, Jack feared being unable to order a whiskey and Coke in the native tongue and looking like the quintessential ugly American. "We have everything we could ever need right here," he would say whenever she presented him with a pamphlet for a European cruise or a new eco lodge in Costa Rica. "Why do we need to go chasing halfway around the world to try to find something more?"

Floating there, half-naked in the middle of the night in water that made her feel disembodied, Magda hoped that Jack would see those papers and think that finally he, too, could just go ahead and be himself.

.   .   .

Magda's car accelerated, cutting through the night. Her body felt wholly relaxed, as if she had just finished a daylong massage, and her mind had followed suit. For the first time in longer than she could remember, she was looking forward to tomorrow. First, though, she was looking forward to crawling between her freshly laundered sheets—one of the most underappreciated and underrated little pleasures in life—and falling fast asleep.

Without a towel to absorb the extra water, stray drops dripped intermittently from her hair, pinging off her shoulders. She ran a hand through her hair to ruffle some of it loose. She rounded a curve in the road and felt the car jerk as if it had tripped. She had been lost in thought, still reveling at her bravery in going swimming late at night, all by herself, and for a split second thinking that she couldn't wait to call Jack to tell him about it. That was followed by another split second when she realized that this wasn't something she could do much longer, if at all, and her mind went to a sad, reflective place.

That was when she heard the thud. The steering wheel lurched under her loose grip. Magda looked up, and for the briefest instant two beady black eyes met her gaze, right before she jammed on the brakes and the deer careened off the hood of her car.

Magda had never hit a deer before. In northern Wisconsin, where the deer seemed to outnumber people and were prone to kamikaze missions, this was like saying that she had never come upon a red light. Magda had always imagined how positively awful it would be to hit one, with their spindly legs, graceful bodies, and oh, so gentle faces. After reading *The Yearling* as a little girl, Magda had wanted a pet deer like other kids wanted dogs or goldfish, and she tried luring them to her parents' yard by hanging carrots from the fence posts and stockpiling discarded cabbage from her father's garden just outside the alley gate. All she ever got was a stern lecture from her father regarding the rabbit problem she had created.

Growing up, she'd notice the dead and bloated deer carcasses that dotted the roads' shoulders, and she would say a prayer for each one. But as she got older, she prayed less for the deer and more to thank God that she hadn't been the one to take one of their precious lives.

She'd be skipping that prayer tonight.

Magda's hands shook as she pulled her car to the shoulder. Her breath came in raspy gasps. She didn't have the first clue as to what to do. This kind of thing didn't happen to her. Or it never used to.

Magda tried breathing deeply: in through the nose, out through the mouth. *Think rationally, think rationally.* What would she do if it had been a person? What would she do first?

Magda's trembling hand found the door handle and she kicked the door open with her foot. She balanced herself between the car and the open door, willing her legs to stand firm, then took one more deep breath and marched toward the front of the car.

There, just on the edge of the headlights' harsh glow, lay the deer. It had been slung like a large beanbag. One front leg was clearly broken, lying at an unnatural angle, its hoof pointed toward its hip. The other was twitching at odd intervals.

Oh, dear God. It was still alive.

A whining, squealing sound escaped from the poor thing—a cross between an asthma attack and an injured cat. It was eerily primal, and it unnerved Magda—out in the pitch dark by the side of the road all alone with a nearly dead deer—to her very core.

She knelt down, picked its head up, and laid it in her lap. She stroked the wet, matted fur. Blood ran freely from a gash in the deer's neck. Magda placed one hand over it, trying to stop the flow, but it kept coming, dripping warm through her fingers.

Oh, God. She sobbed, pressing her forehead between the deer's floppy ears. *Oh, God, what have I done? What have I done?*

Magda listened for, hoped for, the approach of another car, a person. Anything. But the night just sat there, silent. She could see that one house had a light on over the sink. She could almost make out the suncatchers that dotted the window. But the light was just for show. No one stirred behind that pane, and those of the surrounding houses looked inky black, like gaping holes. A wind moved through the tree branches above her, but nothing else did.

She didn't know how long she stayed there, talking to the deer. Petting it. Apologizing.

Eventually, though, she knew there was nothing left to do. Its breaths grew increasingly labored. Its eyes more and more wild, even though its body seemed immobile.

The thing was beyond saving.

Magda laid its head back down on the ground and tried to close its eyes. She didn't want it to see her, what she had to do. But as soon as she took her hand away, the eyes crept open again. They fixated on her.

She stumbled to her car, wiping away blood and tears and dirt from her face. The sweet smell of blood and the acrid scent of wild animal pelt followed like a shadow.

Maybe she hadn't really been brave, way back when. Maybe that was just the way she liked to remember herself. What was so

brave about driving cross-country or swimming in the dark, after all?

She closed her eyes then, and shifted into drive. She pressed
her foot on the gas pedal, and felt the horrid crunch beneath the
tires right into her own bones.

Magda Allen didn't look back.

Chapter Thirteen

"You smell like the beach."

Sophie's voice floated to Jack as if it had traveled a great distance, and just barely nudged his thoughts aside enough for him to hear. But he turned his head and nearly ran it straight into Sophie's. She had come up the back side of the porch and was leaning over him, her face moving to bury itself in the crook of his neck.

It had been a little more than a week since Glory had appeared on Macy's doorstep, but it felt so much longer. Jack and Sophie had spent most of their waking moments together, attempting, and mostly failing, to manage the whole mess. It had created an intimacy between them that Jack wasn't wholly comfortable with, and did absolutely nothing to discourage.

"SPF thirty," he said, not looking up.

"I don't think you're going to need that."

"Hmmm," he said.

"Something wrong, kiddo? You look like you just lost your dog."

"Nope," he said. "Just my wife." He knew it was inappropriate but he laughed anyway. For effect, he fanned the thick folds of yellow and white papers, which had arrived just before Sophie, in front of him.

"What in tarnation?" Sophie said. She squinted her eyes, turning her whole face into a question mark.

"Here," Jack said, and jabbed her with the papers.

It wasn't hard to miss the "Complaint for Divorce" looming bold and angry at the top of the page and Magda's pointy signature toward the bottom.

"Oh, Jack," Sophie said, reading and then rereading. She coerced the papers back into a reasonable pile and handed them to him. "I'm so sorry. I don't know what to say."

Sophie wore her customary uniform: a ratty, long-sleeved T-shirt, fraying jeans shorts, and, from the looks of it, even older sneakers. The kelly green bow around the bun in her hair matched the shirt, across the front of which previously glittery gold letters proclaimed, TWELFTH ANNUAL RIZZO ROYSTON MEMORIAL MARINA CUP. She was the only woman over fifty Jack had ever met who wasn't afraid to bare her legs. They stuck out the bottom of her shorts like knobby brown twigs.

"Nothing much to say," Jack said, wagging his head back and forth. "Sure didn't see this coming, though."

Sophie only nodded. She held one hand against her lips, fingers folded inward as if she were kissing her fingernails. She let out a loud breath.

"So I assume she doesn't know about her?" Sophie asked. She was referring to Jack's wife and his granddaughter.

Jack shook his head. "Magda doesn't take well to surprises, and she's been through so much already. I was waiting to get to the bottom of things first, to make absolutely sure." Sure of what, he didn't know. That Glory was their flesh and blood? That she wasn't? He could see her in the backseat of Sophie's parked station wagon loaded down with camping equipment, rummaging through a box in the hatchback. She had moved in with Sophie after that first night, sleeping on a hideaway bed on her sunporch.

"You sure get yourself into some pickles." Sophie stood. "Still want to go?"

Jack nodded. He would have challenged Sophie on her pickles accusation, but it was all he could do to gesture.

They had decided on this trip soon after Glory arrived, though it had taken Sophie more than a week to clear her guiding commitments. Jack had been wanting to get over to the west coast of the island, and Sophie suggested they take a camping trip to Long Beach, a supposedly picturesque stretch that she liked to call a "real beach" (meaning that it had true white sand, as opposed to the gray gravel that coated most of Campbell River's beaches) on the very southwest tip of Vancouver Island. It was supposed to be one of the great surfing destinations outside of Hawaii and Australia, and ever since Darrin Ott had sauntered into Green Bay West High School with his shoulder-length locks and seashell necklace and sun-kissed skin straight from California that made girls swoon at the sight of him, Jack had been mesmerized by the idea of surfing. Never mind that he couldn't swim too well and had no desire to actually learn to surf. Regardless, Long Beach, with its surfer crowd, intrigued him enough to want to make the trip.

But the other—and, if they were all being honest, more urgent—reason for heading west for a few days was that Macy hadn't handled Glory's arrival all that well. They had yet to get hold of Glory's mom. And to top it all off, before Jack could decide whether he should call Magda and tell her about the long-lost granddaughter who had materialized on Macy's front porch, he had received divorce papers from his wife with equally scant forewarning. The timing for a getaway really couldn't have been more perfect.

"Yeah," Jack said. "Yeah, of course. This can wait. Just let me grab my things, okay?"

Sophie nodded. "Sure. But just bring what you need. I've got everything else."

"Sure looks that way," he chided.

Sophie rolled her eyes, but didn't bite. "Where's Macy?"

"Not sure," Jack said. "Barn, maybe? Or town? I honestly can't say I've seen her."

"Well, I'll just wait in the car with Glory. Get going now," she said, shooing him toward the door. "We've got a few hours' drive ahead of us and I don't want to do it in the dark. Not on those roads."

The last stretch of road unfolded behind them and Sophie steered the teetering station wagon into the Pacific Rim National Park Reserve. The dusk of early evening started to ebb into a cool summer night, and Jack could see why Sophie hadn't wanted to drive much after dark. The road curved back and forth onto itself again and again over an almost three-hour stretch, its width scarcely enough to hold two midsize cars. The other side of the road butted up against a vertical rock face, while the side they had traveled dropped off after only inches of shoulder into a valley so lush and cavernous that it seemed as though the station wagon were flying above it all.

Jack and Sophie set up camp by light of the waxed-paper moon that shone through the trees. Glory had fallen asleep just as they reached the campground, and Sophie left her in the backseat—

covering her with a sleeping bag to keep her warm while she and Jack shuttled supplies from the car to the campsite.

The site was in the shape of a keyhole that had been cut into the thick brush. Jack couldn't see the other campsites except for the brief shadow of a fire flickering here and there, and he couldn't hear the other campers. When Sophie had suggested this place, he was skeptical. Most campgrounds in Wisconsin were fields packed tight with travel campers, littered with clotheslines, and teeming with the sounds of drunken parents and screaming kids. They were like shantytowns or tenement villages. He hadn't ever understood the desire to camp like that, what the point of it was.

Here, they had to keep all food locked in the car or away from the tents, and keep a "clean" campground so as not to attract bears or cougars. Cutting wood from the surrounding rain forest was prohibited, and campfires were limited to the tiny, steel-lined fire pit toward the rear of the keyhole. Jack could hear scurrying in the woods behind him and the continual crashing of surf on the beach below.

They set up two tents: a tattered blue one-person, triangle-shaped tent and, on the other side of the keyhole, a newer yellow three-person dome tent with a "foyer," as Sophie called it. Sophie had decided that having a "girls'" and "boy's" tent would be best—the most proper option. Jack was in no mood to argue.

It was obvious that Sophie wasn't new to this. She had the essential gear, and just enough of it. Despite the looks of the station wagon, he realized there had been little overpacking, no excess. She had thought to bring kindling, a hatchet, tarps, rope, a small tin coffeepot, and a frying pan. Wide, shallow mugs would serve double duty as bowls or plates, and smaller-than-average forks hung from the handles, fastened by leather strings that had grown smooth, almost slick, with time and use. Those things, according to Sophie, were all they needed. Pretty much anything else could be skewered on a stick for cooking.

In the time that it took Jack to hang two tarps, one on either side, Sophie had started a fire, erected a tent under each tarp, and bedded them both. She had turned the station wagon around and backed down the short, narrow "driveway" to their campsite, then organized the coolers and food to be within easy reach of the rear window. Some people brought footlockers for their food, but Sophie claimed this was too dangerous. Besides, she said, there was not much an old bear could do to that car that hadn't been done to it already.

Jack pulled a folding chair close to the fire. The temperature at night dipped more sharply here than in Campbell River. Sophie was right that he wouldn't need much sunscreen. It seemed as though the wind gained ferocity with every mile it covered across the vast, empty expanse of the Pacific Ocean, hitting the west coast of Vancouver Island in a constant scream. Even if the sun decided to make an appearance during the day, Jack didn't think he'd be stripping down to much less than a sweatshirt. He was chilled to the bone, and even though the fire's heat seared his skin, it felt good.

He watched all but Sophie's legs disappear into the backseat of the car and reemerge with a bundled, fast-asleep Glory. He saw Sophie stare down at the girl and bury her lips in Glory's tousled curls. Only as Sophie struggled to get Glory into the yellow tent without waking her did Jack realize that maybe he should've offered to help.

"Wanna beer?" Sophie whispered, zipping the tent behind her.

Jack smiled, nodded.

Sophie grabbed two Kokanees, cracked one, and handed it to Jack. She pulled another folding chair to his side of the fire, opened her own beer, and took a long swig.

"Didn't think you were a beer drinker," Jack said.

Sophie shook her head. "Only when I camp."

"Why's that?" Jack asked. He'd never met a woman with so many quirks.

"Don't know," said Sophie. "Just always been that way."

They fell to silence then, listening instead to the fire's monologue of sputter and sizzle. A million and one worries should have been clamoring through Jack's head, but for the moment they were quiet. He closed his eyes.

"You lonely, Jack?" It was a sudden, forceful question.

"Yep," Jack answered. He didn't hesitate. He didn't have to. Not with Sophie. He was starting to see what Nash saw in these blunt and slightly wild island women.

He'd had to think a lot about loneliness lately, about being alone. He had long ago decided he didn't mind it much. It didn't make him happy, being lonely—that was certain—but he didn't mind it. Not like other people seemed to.

"You okay, though?" Sophie asked.

Jack paused before finally answering, "What's okay, really? I'm not sure what that is."

Sophie looked as though she might be mulling over an answer to his rhetorical question. Then she shrugged.

"What?" he asked.

"Nothing," said Sophie

"I guess," said Jack, stretching his legs in front of him and crossing them at the ankles, "what I meant is that I don't know what I am. I might be lonely. I might be fine. It's hard to tell sometimes." He looked at Sophie, who nodded in agreement.

"That sweet little thing in the tent sure doesn't hurt either, though, huh?"

"That she doesn't," he said.

"Jack?"

"Sophie."

"It would be great if she could just stay, don't you think?"

He had never agreed more with anyone in his life. And it would be dishonest of him to deny entertaining the occasional daydream of all of them continuing right on as they had been over the past week or two—afternoons bobbing along in a rowboat with lines cast; hiking the Beaver Forest trail, Glory's incessant questions a sound track to every outing; cooking dinner and then sitting down to eat together, almost like a real family; nights on the back porch after the dishes were washed and the leftovers put away, sipping on bourbon, careful not to disturb a sleeping Glory against his chest. But Jack didn't want to get his hopes up.

It felt more than a little off—Glory there with them like this, all of them pretending like this was simply their new reality and everything would turn out A-okay; all of them except Macy, who wouldn't even look in his granddaughter's direction. It was such a perfectly imperfect situation, like a beautiful cupola placed atop a house of cards.

"I hope she can," he said. "But how selfish is that of me? My son is gone, so I'm going to hope to take someone else's kid? That's all sorts of screwed up."

Sophie shook her head. "She is your *granddaughter*, Jack. And she adores you. Of course you want her to stay. I want her to stay. But she can't sleep on my porch forever. It's going to get cold, and this guiding business of mine can get pretty unpredictable."

"We'll figure something out. I'm sure it won't be for long. Her mom is going to turn up here at some point. She has to. No mother just disappears and leaves their kid, do they?"

"You'd be surprised."

The fire and Jack groaned at the same time. "I've had enough," Jack said.

"Oh?"

"Surprises. I don't want to be surprised anymore."

"I hear you," she said. Sophie took a long, hard swig of her beer, finishing it off. She closed her hand to crush the can and a loud rumbling escaped her throat. Her hand flew to her mouth, while Jack gaped, laughter bubbling out.

"That's why I don't ever drink this crap," Sophie said, eyeing the can with disgust. "Makes me look unladylike."

Jack raised his beer can as if he were preparing to give a toast. "You think *this* is what makes you unladylike?" he asked.

"That's quite enough," Sophie said with mock seriousness. "I'm turning in." She patted his knee as she got up, walked to the car, and tossed her can into a garbage bag in the back. Then she walked back over to the fire, bent down, and brushed Jack's cheek with her lips. They were soft and moist, like a cow's nose, and lingered against his stubbly skin a second longer than they should have. "Good night, Jack Allen."

Jack didn't take his eyes off the shuddering flames of the fire. "Good night, ma'am," he muttered. But he was too late. Sophie's ankle and ratty shoe were all that remained, and just a split second later those, too, had disappeared into the tent.

It was the birds that woke him. Those birds with their doleful, unrelenting caws. It wasn't even light out yet—though not completely dark either—the night sky infected with just a rumor of dawn. Enough to give the inside of the tent an eerie blue glow. When Jack raised his hand in front of him, it looked as though his heart had failed to circulate any blood during the night.

He dressed quickly, pulling on jeans and a heavy sweatshirt over his head, and slipping his feet into a pair of hiking boots he had found just in time for this trip at Island Outfitters' summer clearance sale a few days before. Then he slipped out of his tent, quietly zipping the flap.

The trail to the beach was a steep, rocky descent, and shrouded in darkness on account of the thick foliage it had to sneak through. Jack picked his way over the rocks and roots, placing one foot nearly in front of the other on the narrow path. As he walked, the muffled grumble of the ocean grew louder, and just when it seemed to almost totally surround him, just when he felt as though the trail would never end, it spit him into the open, onto the longest expanse of beach he had ever seen.

He stood there for a while, he didn't know how long, trying to register it all. A hundred, maybe two hundred feet in front of him, waves met sand, then retreated, clawing at the beach with foamy hands like a rake. This happened all up and down the shoreline, as far as he could see. The steady crumpling and clawing created a quiet roar that filled Jack, lifted him in that fullness.

And past the shore, past the rocking waves working their way inland, there was nothing. Nothing and nothing and nothing. Until the Kuril Islands or the north end of Japan, depending on how far north or south one might drift. It made the world seem so small, so intimate, to think that the only thing that separated him, Jack Allen, from the coast of Japan was a couple hundred feet of sand and a few thousand miles of water. But there was the volume of water to consider, too. The thousands of feet it descended below the surface; the fish and sharks and whales and octopi and masses of unknown creatures it contained; the totally foreign, wholly complete world that functioned just below the waves. It was too much, then. Too much to even try to fathom. And just like that, just like the night at the extravaganza sitting next to Sophie and looking at Mars burn red in the night sky, he was back to feeling like a tiny crumb on that beach.

Large outcroppings of rocks dotted the beach to Jack's left. In the waning shadow of night, they looked like haystacks looming, like miniatures of the rocks from *Goonies*. Jack should know. He had watched that movie, endured that movie, endlessly on account of Nash. The wind whipped at Jack as he clambered up onto one of the smaller, flatter rocks. It stood about the size of a two-car garage and had deep grooves that formed a natural ladder up the back. A plaque hung from the side, though he couldn't make it out in the thin predawn light.

So he sat there atop the rock, letting the wind whistle at him, into him, and wondered what the hell he was supposed to do. It would help if he knew what he wanted, or if he felt like he really wanted to do one thing as opposed to another. But that wasn't the case. He just didn't really care anymore. He knew he'd have to call Magda eventually. He knew he'd have to go back to Green Bay at some point or another. Those were absolutes. But the rest was clear as mud. He suddenly, for the first time that he could remember, didn't belong anywhere. He didn't have a home to go back to—not his home, anyway. Not the way it used to be. And he knew he was overstaying his welcome with Macy. Especially now, with all the added stress of late.

Jack's second-in-command at the concrete shop had e-mailed him a few days back, wondering whether he'd consider selling the business. At first the idea had seemed crazy. What would he do with no job, nowhere to be each morning? He had built that business from scratch with his own two hands. He had sacrificed time with his family and a decent golf swing to see it succeed. But just then, sitting atop a rock in the fog of early morning, Jack saw the business, his life's work, for what it was: work. Goddamn concrete. It wasn't like he was curing cancer or feeding the hungry. And if he wanted to, really wanted to, he could do anything, go anywhere.

The sky matched the water below it, and both of them melded into a solid wall of slate. But there was motion beneath the gray haze. Jack could hear it. Feel it. His bones buzzed with it.

Because it's their time. Their time! Up there! Down here, it's our time. That one line echoed through him. Nash might be gone, his wife might be divorcing him, he might have a granddaughter who could melt him with one look and whom he'd probably have to send back to a drugged-out version of a woman his son had had an affair with way back when, but here, this was Jack's time. He was sure of nothing if not that.

The vista looked positively empty to him. Empty and still and indifferent, and in a flash, Jack knew that he wouldn't ever leave here. Not for good, anyway. If he left, he'd come straight back. Back to where angry wind fought unruly water to make music composed just for him. Music he finally understood.

The fog had started to lift as Jack ambled toward the campsite. Even before he reached it, he could hear a woman's voice floating in the air in front of it. Jack stopped. It took him a moment to place the song. Sophie's voice. Who would've guessed she'd have a voice like that? Throaty and heavy and soulful, just like Janis

Joplin but without the edge. He got chicken skin—that was what Nash called it his whole life—the hair on his neck prickled. Glory's voice joined in at the chorus. "Freedom's just another word for nothing left to lose." It floated up, light and tiny and hopeful, sliding in just under each of Sophie's words like a napkin beneath a glass. As Jack stood there, transfixed, he felt his eyes smart, his cheeks dampen. And his chest . . . his chest felt as though it were suddenly a size too small.

Sophie was sitting in one of the folding chairs near the fire, her back mostly to the campsite's entrance, Glory on the ground beneath her between her knees. Sophie's fingers had buried themselves in Glory's blond ringlets, weaving the fine, wispy hair into a petite plait down the center of Glory's head. Sophie didn't even look down. She stared straight out into the forest. At what, Jack couldn't be sure.

"Hey," Jack said, maybe a little too forcefully, because Sophie jumped and put her hand over her heart. "Sorry," he said, more quietly this time.

"I thought you were still sleeping," she said.

Jack shook his head. "Naw. I was up early. Went for a walk."

"Oh," Sophie said. She turned her attention to Glory's hair, smoothing a bump with her fingers like a comb.

"Hi, Grandpa," Glory said. She couldn't turn her head, so she just raised her hand and waved backward at him.

Grandpa. The word fell on him like ash. Would this island still feel like home if she weren't there with him?

"Hi, sweetheart," he said, sitting himself down in a chair by the crackling fire.

Sophie wound an elastic band around the hair at the very nape of Glory's neck. She ran her fingers through the remaining tail of hair, fluffing and separating the ringlets.

"Can I see?" asked Glory.

"There's a mirror behind the passenger-side visor," Sophie said, and nudged her toward the car. Glory skipped to it, feeling her braid the whole way.

"What should we do today?" Sophie asked.

Jack shrugged his shoulders. He didn't want to *do* anything. "Nothing touristy," he said.

Sophie reclined in her chair and ran a finger along her teeth like a toothbrush. "Yuck. Feels skuzzy," she said. She cocked her head, thinking, and then added, "There're whale-watching tours, or bear-watching tours. Or we could knock around town a bit. Surfing, too. There's surfing."

The thought of the three of them, the most unlikely trio of surfers in the world, attempting to ride the waves made him laugh.

"What's so funny?" asked Sophie.

"Nothing. Just the thought of . . . Ah, never mind. Tofino or Uselet?"

Sophie laughed. "It's Ucluelet—U-clue-let—not Useless, Jack."

He hadn't said "Useless." "Whatever," he said.

"Well, there's a little more to Tofino—more shops, more to do."

"Where are the whale-watching tours? I know Glory wanted to do that."

"Mostly in Tofino," Sophie said.

"Then we'll go there."

At one o'clock, Sophie and Glory boarded the Zodiac boat for their whale-watching tour, and Jack had the next few hours to himself. Glory had begged him to go, but he'd seen enough whales with Macy the few times they had visited her and Nash. But he couldn't tell her that—that it wasn't all that spectacular anyway, that he was all whaled out from the last couple of times—so he just said that he got seasick easily and would meet them afterward for dinner. Neither of them was any the wiser.

He crossed the busy two-lane road running straight through Tofino, walked up a few blocks, and bought himself an Americano at the town's only coffee shop. It struck him as odd, ordering an Americano coffee in Canada. He thought the Canadians were more resourceful than that. Figured they'd at least change the name to Canadiano to make it their own. He'd noticed how fiercely proud of their country Canadians were, and how they seemed to get their collective dander up at the idea of being considered United States north.

He perused the streets of Tofino, but even though Sophie had said it had more going on than Ucluelet, Jack covered most of it in twenty short minutes. Finally, after the third pass just to make sure he hadn't missed anything, and for lack of other ideas on what to do with his time, he got directions to the marina a few blocks down and hoofed it over there.

Tofino curled itself at the feet of the ocean like a dog to its master. Fishing and crabbing boats sauntered in and out of the marina. Whale- and bear-watching tour boats buzzed out toward the horizon and back on regular schedules, and sailboats and the occasional yacht bobbed contentedly in the harbor. Jack walked up and down the docks shaped like combs, among boats lodged like bugs between the teeth, watching the activity. Or at times, the inactivity—three gruff old fishermen in matching yellow rain-slicker overalls, sitting like statues on crab traps and mostly just staring at one another. A young woman bundled in a sweatshirt and blanket was reading on the deck of a sailboat. A couple who seemed about Jack's age—who looked sort of like him and Magda—played checkers on their yacht. Him and Magda. There wasn't any such thing as him and Magda now . . . no. No. He wasn't going to do that. He wasn't going to wallow. Magda had been a hard woman to love, and he had tried. Lord, how he had tried. Now he didn't have to.

He'd often imagined this day. In the sagging middle of their marriage—didn't every couple have one of those?—he'd try to stimulate interest in his relationship with Magda, by imagining what would happen, in detail, if they split up. He thought through how he'd have to make dinner for himself night after night, and how often he'd rotate through the painfully short list of things he could cook. He considered who might get what furniture, how aggravating it would be to move from their beautiful house into an apartment, what it would be like to sit across from his wife in a courtroom, the fees they'd have to pay, how he'd have to work twice as hard to live half as well when you added it all up. And this long list of inconveniences was enough to make him realize that Magda was difficult, but rewarding at times. Turning life as he knew it on its ear would not be.

But with some words printed on a paper and a signature at the bottom, he had been set free in a way that many people longed for, knowing it wouldn't ever happen. It should have made him feel light. Perhaps, though, it wasn't so easy, or so quick. Jack had spent a whole lifetime loading himself down with obligations and duties; it only made sense that emancipation would take some getting used to.

"I've lowered the price on her a bit."

The voice startled Jack. He looked to his left to see one of the old men from the crab traps standing beside him. The man thrust his hand toward Jack. "Name's Will Carey, but most 'round here call me One-ear."

Jack offered his hand tentatively. He noticed that beneath the random, thick growth of beard that merged with an even wilder mane of steel gray hair, almost all of Will Carey's right ear was missing. Jack looked away.

"I saw you 'miring her and thought I'd let you know she's on clearance now."

Just then Jack noticed the homemade For Sale sign in the window of the sailboat. He had simply been lost in thought, not admiring Mr. One-ear's boat. But he was curious as to why a weathered old fisherman like Will Carey owned a sailboat.

"Why's that?" he asked.

Will nodded as if Jack had asked a yes-or-no question. "She was my daughter's. Loved this boat, that girl. She used to come back here from college in Vancouver, live on this here boat all summer long—breaks, too. See, her mum's been gone for some time now. She left town when Lila was sixteen, and to make ends meet I sold the house and we lived on the fishing boat for a bit. But a fish boat filled with cranky old men ain't no place for a pretty young girl, so Lila and I found this here sailboat and fixed 'er up nice as can be and parked her right across from where the guys and I docked our boat, and that was that. But then Lila found a husband and a job up there in Van. They still come back to visit now and again. But they stay at the motel down the road when they come here now, or they camp, because the husband gets seasick," Will said, rolling his eyes. "Isn't she a beaut, though?"

Jack nodded. It was a nice boat. Nice size. Thirty-footer, maybe. He couldn't be sure. It could've used a paint job—the red part of the boat, the hull, was flaking off, but it had a beautiful, shiny wood-finished deck that was the most appropriate visual of elbow grease that Jack had ever seen. "I like the deck," he said.

Will Carey tossed his head back and laughed a booming "ho-ho-ho," and Jack wondered whether he'd really said something all that funny—either funny ha-ha or funny strange, as far as boating went. "That was Lila's favorite part, too. She insisted on refinishing the deck. Wouldn't stand for anything else. Took us months to refurb it."

"So you can just live on these things, these boats, all the time?" asked Jack.

"Sure. Lots of people do. As long as you don't mind small spaces. Or get motion-sick. Although that goes away after a while. Honest. You get used to it so much that when you're on land, you miss the rocking and rolling. I can't even sleep on land anymore. Want to take a look at 'er?"

"Oh, I don't—I mean, I'm not really—"

"Aw, c'mon," said Will, already on the deck. "Let me show you around. I know she don't look like much from out here, but wait till you see what's belowdeck." He didn't pause for an answer, and Jack, with nothing much else to do, followed him.

One-ear Will Carey was right. The living area, or "belowdeck," was spectacular. Everything—from the booth-style table at the bow, to the cabinets, to the three-foot-high base for the full bed at the aft, and anything else made of wood between—was fashioned out of a rich, almost black-looking mahogany. Miniature red Roman shades adorned each of the windows (Jack had endured enough of Magda's redecorating whims to distinguish between styles of "window treatments," as she called them, and even to know that ecru was not "more or less the same" as white), and a red couch almost large enough for Jack to stretch out on, and softened with overstuffed red-and-white-striped pillows, along the opposite wall of the kitchen. The kitchen was tiny but functional, as was the bathroom. Everything on the boat had its place—cup holders carved into the table and countertops, a magazine rack fastened to the left side of the couch, a drawstring velvet pouch tacked neatly to the anorexic bedside table, for loose change or jewelry or one of those mo-bile phones, as Will called them. Lila used it for jewelry, though, he said.

"This is great workmanship. I'm impressed."

"Thought you'd be," said Will. "Did it all ourselves, Lila and me."

Jack raised an eyebrow at him.

"Used to be a cabinetmaker long time ago," Will said, situating himself on the couch. "Yep, I was. But the cabinetmaking fell off a bit and the fishing got good, and when we moved here to Tofino the cabinetmaking went by the wayside altogether. Lila did all the decorating, all the sewing. Only thing she and I didn't do was this couch. One of my buddies does some furniture making on the side—hobby of sorts. He did this for us. Not many boats this size have a couch this size in it, but he worked some magic, boy. Whaddaya think?"

"Seems like a real good boat," Jack said, as emphatically as he could.

"Seems?" Will scoffed. "*Is*. She *is* a good boat."

"I'm just not all that familiar with boats," said Jack. "What makes a boat a good boat and all that. But I sure like it."

"Sure like *her*," Will said.

"Her," Jack repeated. "I sure like her."

"Enough to buy 'er?" asked Will.

"Yes," said Jack.

The word sneaked out of him like a teenager at midnight. It

was as if he had no control over his mouth. What the hell was he thinking? Buy a boat? *Live* on a boat? He didn't know the first thing about boats. Hell, he couldn't even keep the difference between port and starboard straight. Had he finally, completely, lost his mind?

But his mouth was paying him no mind. It had asked Will Carey, already, how much he wanted for the boat, and when Will Carey said eight grand American, Jack heard his mouth say, "That's not bad. Not bad at all."

And then there were Jack's hands reaching into his wallet and pulling out one of the handfuls of checks he had stashed there just in case, and making check number 1098 out to William Carey for eight thousand dollars while Will signed a handwritten contract transferring ownership.

And just like that, Jack had his very own boat.

"Somehow I have to get it to Campbell River," Jack said as they climbed up onto the deck from below. "I suppose there's nowhere around here to rent a truck and trailer?"

"Her," Will said. "If you're gonna be a boatman, you gotta learn to talk like a boatman, eh?" He waited for Jack to nod, then continued. "And *think* like a boatman. This here's a boat, which means it travels by water. Which means you don't go lugging it all over the road."

"But I don't know how to sail," Jack said. "Hell, I can't even get the terminology right."

Will waved him off. "Forgot to tell you: included in the clearance sale price is delivery. I've gotta guy who needs to go to your part of the island first thing Monday to pick up a fishing boat we just bought. He'll sail this on over to you and then motor back on our new purchase. Everyone wins."

"Sure?" Jack asked.

"Sure," Will said.

The two men shook hands. Jack thanked Will. "I'll take good care of her," he said.

Will grinned and nodded.

Jack was almost to the edge of the dock when Will One-ear Carey called out to him. "Hey, don't you want to know her name?"

"Whose name?" Jack called back.

"Your boat's!" Will yelled, his hands like a megaphone around his mouth.

Jack raised both hands in a slight shrug. "Sure," he said.

"*Nowhere Bound*," yelled Will. "That's her name: *Nowhere Bound.*"

"Perfect," Jack yelled back to him with a wave. "Couldn't be more perfect," he whispered to himself as he walked up the steps to the street.

While Sophie put together tinfoil packets of potatoes and onions, pouring part of a beer in each one before closing the top like a tent, Jack taught Glory to play Go Fish and Hearts. How the girl had spent eight years on this earth without learning a single card game was beyond Jack. Yet she had just schooled him at both.

"How 'bout Uno?" he asked. After buying *Nowhere Bound* that afternoon, Jack had stopped in one of the downtown shops to pick up a deck of cards and saw a used game of Uno that he paid two loonies for, thinking that would be just the thing to do with Glory.

"Huh?"

"Uno—you know, colored cards and numbers. Haven't you ever played Uno?"

"Nope. Is it hard?"

"Where'd you grow up, under a rock?" Jack teased her.

Glory's face went hard. She set her jaw. "I lived in a house. It was nice," she said.

"I was just kidding with you," Jack said.

Like all women, Glory was a mystery to him, a child who at times seemed like she was either eight going on twenty or eight going on five. There was so much Jack wanted to know about her.

"I think I want to go home soon. My mom probably misses me," she said.

Jack didn't want to tell Glory that her mother had all but vanished. That every one of their calls to her had gone unanswered. That she hadn't returned even one of the by now hundreds of messages they had left for her. That they had given up trying to reach her themselves, and had turned things over to the authorities in LA. "I'm sure she does," he said.

"Did my dad like this game?"

Jack had to remember back. "I think so." He shuffled the cards and started to deal, his thoughts lagging behind on Glory's mom, wondering how she could leave her child. This child.

"But how could you not know? Was he adopted?" Glory asked.

"Who's that? Nash?" Jack asked.

Glory nodded.

"No, not at all. Why?"

She shrugged. "Dunno. Just thought you'd know, being his dad."

It wasn't an accusation—she was eight, after all—but Jack reeled as if she had punched him.

"I worked a lot, and I guess I missed things that way. Moms

and dads don't always know their kids as well they'd like, or as well as they think they do. I'm sure there are things about you that your mom doesn't know."

"Bet your ass. My mom's a piece of work."

Jack tried not to laugh. "Glory," he said sternly. Then, almost as an afterthought, he asked, "Do you miss her?" That she nodded surprised him.

"We'll get this all sorted soon, see what's what. But for now, how about we play some Uno?"

Glory smiled a toothy, gapped smile. "Game on," she said.

He dealt seven cards to each of them. Glory organized them into a lopsided fan. It took two of her hands to hold them all.

"I want to play cridage after this—the one my dad liked," Glory interrupted him.

"Aw, we can't."

"Why?"

"Well, for starters, little one, it's called cribbage, and it's a game that you need a special kind of board for, to keep track of the score. And second, it's kind of a big-people's game. It's all about counting and adding."

"Okay. But can you teach me—when I'm big people?"

"Yes." Jack laughed. "When you're older, I'll teach you."

"Pinkie swear?" Glory stuck her tiny hand out, pinkie extended.

"What's that?"

"Pinkie swear. You know, you lock pinkies and it seals the promise you made? Pinkie swear?"

That was a new one for Jack. Nash's thing had always been "Scout's honor." Perhaps this was the girl version. He hooked his pinkie around hers.

"Even when I go home?" she asked.

"Even if you go home," he said, conscious that he had changed his echo to her question. "Your mom will come get you, I'm sure. And when she does, you'll come back and visit all the time." It hurt him, physically hurt him, to say those words.

"You can come visit us, too!" Glory said. "I'll show you my room, and the park where Jilly and I go to play, and my school, and Jilly's house, too."

Jack hoped he never had to make that trip. He hoped that his granddaughter could stay right there, with him. Jack felt a pang of guilt jolt through him. But was he really so selfish to wish that for himself? For Glory? "Sure, baby girl," he said. "I can't wait."

Glory turned her attention back to the cards, ordering them in her hands. Jack explained the rules and they played a practice hand. He was amazed by how quickly she caught on. Even more amazing, though, were the little glimpses of Nash he caught in her. The way she cocked her head to one side when she was thinking, or how she drummed her fingers against her chin when waiting. Her lopsided smile. The same shoulders, in miniature, rounded in concentration.

And try as he might, he couldn't seem to peel his eyes away.

Chapter Fourteen

FOR THE FIRST TIME IN HER LIFE, MACY HAD NOWHERE TO BE and nothing to do.

She was a person prone to perpetual motion, one who drowned herself in its rhythms and flow. But all around her, the house sat defiantly still. Jack and Sophie had taken the girl camping under the pretense of whale watching, but Macy knew the real reason was to get them all out of her hair. With her collarbone still on the mend, she had to admit that getting anything out of her hair had literally been an effort in futility. She had long ago tired of wrangling her barely combed locks into a ponytail, only to have it look like a bird's nest attached at an odd angle to her head. Now she tamed it under a baseball cap whenever she needed it out of her face.

Macy didn't know what to do with herself, not riding. She could take not showing. Fine. But she at least had to saddle up, feel the reins in her hands, the bundled will of a half ton of horse underneath her, working with her—and she with it. She had once heard "to ride a horse is to borrow freedom." But after she and Gounda had crashed at Spruce Meadows weeks ago, Macy's freedom, borrowed or not, had been stripped from her. Gounda had come up lame with an avulsion fracture in his hock, and even though the veterinarian had started him on shock-wave therapy, little more than rest, time, and patience would be able to heal him. And Macy.

Unfortunately, none of that played to Macy's strengths.

Her stomach growled and she realized she hadn't yet eaten. She thought maybe she should try cooking something for dinner. That would take time, stretch the hours until she was tired enough to slip into sleep. Though everything she thought to make required two hands, a working set.

She had stopped going out to dinner or getting takeaway months ago, after one too many awkward conversations. Campbell River was a small town, and running into someone she knew was the norm, not the exception. People either didn't know what to say to her, and so avoided saying anything at all, or they gushed to her about how sorry they were and what a great guy Nash was, and wondered how she was getting along. They were never people she knew well, and although she was sure they were well intentioned, Macy didn't want to update every single one of them on how she was holding it together. Or not. Besides, those conversations turned even a quick pickup into such a span of time, she might as well have sat down at a restaurant.

She wished right then that she had someone to call to have dinner with, a buffer between her and the rest of the world. She had always wondered whether pregnant women minded having strangers place a hand on their swollen bellies, unbidden. She was now sure she had an answer: They minded. If they were like her, they minded a hell of a lot.

So when Macy climbed into her truck and started toward

town, she pointed it toward Thrifty Foods in the Ironwood Mall. They had a hot Asian deli right at the front of the store—easy in, easy out—and it made a mean sweet-and-sour chicken that used to be Nash's favorite.

Nash.

The girl.

Nash.

Nash and that damned little girl. Nash's daughter. *Daughter*. The word sounded as foreign rattling inside her head as the word *widow*. How had she gotten to this place? To a place where she had to use such words, apply them to her life?

Macy wanted to know everything about the girl's mother (or, more specifically, Nash and the girl's mother). At the same time, she didn't want to know a damn thing. Now and then, sticking her fingers in her ears and closing her eyes and chanting, "La-la-la-la-la," at the top of her lungs seemed as good a plan as any.

It was what she had done before—four years before. When she had picked up the phone in the barn at the same time Nash had picked up the house line, and heard a woman's voice say, "Well, hello, there, handsome," in a breathy, "Happy Birthday, Mr. President" sort of way. It was what she had done since then, because, had she asked, she would have known more. And there would be no way to unknow any of it.

Macy had held fast to not knowing, even as it chewed at her from the inside out over the past weeks. But driving up on the DD—pronounced "the Double D" by locals—a dive bar with passable burgers, she felt the tires of her truck turn almost of their own will. Before she fully realized what was happening, she had pulled into a parking space and grabbed the keys from the ignition.

She shut the truck door behind her and started across the

parking lot, only slightly ahead of her own feet. Her mind barely contained a complete thought. She stared down at her red flip-flops meeting the pavement with each step. First one, then the other. Step. Step. Slap, slap. Things had gotten that basic.

Macy heard men's voices, and glanced up to see a trio walking toward her. It was a trio she recognized—teammates of Nash's. *Former teammates*, she reminded herself, then wondered if that was really correct, since Nash was the "former," not them. Not Walzy, Jonsey, and Pratter. Their last names were actually Walz, Jones, and Pratt, but there was something about hockey players calling one another by only their last names, and always adding a -y or -er to the end to form the guy's anointed nickname. Rarely did they get more creative. Nash's teammates had called him Allen Edmonds, but Macy assumed that stemmed more from desperation about how to alter a name like "Allen" than any sort of true desire to branch out on nicknaming convention.

"Macy? That you?" one of them said.

She looked up at them and tried to smile. She knew she failed, but they walked right up to her anyway. Jonesy leaned in as if to hug her. Macy stepped back. He dropped his arms and shuffled sideways, like he had meant to do that.

"Are you—"

"How are you—"

"I'm so sorry—"

The three of them talked at once, tripping over one another's words. Tripping over what to say to her. This was the part she hated: having to be the one to put them at ease. She had come to appreciate those who ignored the elephant leering over her shoulder. The ones who didn't make her tragedy the centerpiece of every conversation. Most people chose not to say anything about Nash and looked just as uncomfortable as the threesome standing in front of her, but at least they didn't make *her* uncomfortable right along with them.

After Nash died, Macy had tried to tighten the already small circle of people she enjoyed having around her. "You can't run from it," Mama Sophie had told her. She was right, but Macy had learned to minimize it. When she absolutely had to face the rest of the world, she had developed a stump speech that she would recite nearly word for word: "I'm doing okay. Hanging in there. Good days and bad. Kind thoughts and prayers help so much—I really appreciate it. I have my moments, believe me, but I have a lot of help and support, and good friends to get me through."

She would smile a thin smile at the appropriate places and purse her lips into a sad, solemn look at others—most often when the other person began listing Nash's many good qualities and how much he'd be missed, which they almost all did. Often, the "good friends" bit, strangely enough, was what helped end most conversations. Maybe it made people wonder if they were a good friend, and if that was a role they played in her life; yet no one would ever feel comfortable asking that. Or maybe it sounded to them like, "I have friends who are helping me through this and they are not you." Either way, Macy hardly cared as long as her words had the effect they so often did, like just then.

Walzy, Jonsey, and Pratter wished her well, told her to call them if she needed anything at all—also something everyone said—and walked off, muttering, as most people did, about what a "stand-up guy" Nash was and what a shame it was for her.

She breathed a sigh of relief—that run-in had gone much more quickly and smoothly than many—and turned to head inside.

The Double D was a study in dingy. Cracked black leather

booths in the shape of horseshoes skirted the perimeter, and a smattering of tipsy cocktail tables dotted the area in front of the bar. The place smelled of stale beer and bleach and broken dreams, and was owned by Nash's best friend in Campbell River, Tommy Morgan. They had played men's league hockey together and shot pool on a weekly basis. Macy hadn't seen Tommy since the funeral, though it wasn't as if she ever saw him all that much to begin with.

She looked around at the mostly empty bar and didn't see Tommy. *What am I doing here?* she thought. She felt jumpy and sick and disoriented. The problem was, the bar wasn't to blame. Her life was. Those feelings would follow her right out of there. They'd follow her right back home. And then they'd move in with her, put down roots. Unless—

Macy waved the bartender down. She didn't recognize him, fortunately. "Tommy here?" she asked.

The bartender shrugged. "Dunno."

"But his truck is parked outside."

The bartender shrugged again before turning to the cooler behind him and retrieving a can of Lucky. He cracked the beer and set it in front of a guy on the opposite end of the bar with a low-pulled camouflage baseball hat before coming back to talk to Macy. "Sorry," he said. "Tommy doesn't say where he's going. He just goes. And sometimes he comes back."

"I'll wait, then," Macy said.

The bartender shrugged again. Macy wondered if it was some sort of tic with him. "Suit yourself," he said.

She chose a booth that faced both the DD's entrance and the kitchen door, to the left of the bar, so she could see if Tommy materialized.

Cher's voice boomed over the speaker system, too loud for

the quiet conversations and jostling of the early-evening hours. She was singing about someone being the lonely one and wondering if the listener believed in life after love.

The lyrics struck Macy as odd. Life after love—as if it had an expiration date. As if there could distinctly be a before and an after instead of the shadowland that so often stretched between those two words. Because unless something happened in a split second—a car crash, a dropped glass, power going out or coming on—before and after didn't apply. Especially not to love, which, if someone was lucky enough to even recognize it, looped in on itself so often that cause and effect, before and after, blended into an imperceptible haze. A person might as well try to separate fog from air.

Macy felt a tap on her shoulder, and turned to find the bartender holding a shot of tequila. "From them," he said, setting it on the table in front of her and pointing to the bend of the bar, where a handful of men roughly her age whom she didn't know had camped.

One of them saw her look over and called out, "Hey! Nice bum, where ya from?" They were young—much younger than her. Twenty at most. Full of themselves. *Just wait ten years*, she wanted to tell them. *You live another ten years, and then we'll talk.*

Macy smiled a weak smile as she delivered the standard return line, "Campbell River, wanna giver?" and downed the shot. She didn't drink much anymore, and she definitely didn't drink tequila. The taste of it made her whole body recoil.

Before long, the bartender had returned with a bottle of Kokanee. "From Big Jim," he said. "In honor of Nash."

Macy followed the bartender's finger, which pointed at a very large man indeed, who had completely obscured the barstool beneath him. The man raised his can of beer in Macy's direction and nodded solemnly. Macy mimicked the gesture.

She ran her finger through the water on the table that her beer had sweated off, then reached for a napkin to put under her drink. That was one thing that always drove her crazy and never seemed to bother Nash in the least—wet rings on the coffee table, kitchen table, bedside table.

At least Nash's bedside table was always strewn with books, and he'd place his glass of water or the occasional beer he brought with him to bed on top of those. Lately, though, it had been *What to Expect When You're Expecting* on top of *The Expectant Father*, which hung precipitously off the edge of his previous reads, like *Alexander Hamilton*.

When they were first married, Macy used to read along with him at night. She never had enough stamina or follow-through to actually pick out and read a book herself, especially the thick-spined biographies and autobiographies that Nash was drawn to; but each night she would lay her head on his chest and let the words plod along the page to the rhythm of his muffled heartbeat, and the snippets of stories that came her way were just right. Like commercials. Just enough.

She had stopped when the pregnancy and parenting books arrived on his nightstand. "Aren't you excited? Or even a little curious?" Nash had asked.

"My broodmares don't have books. They all seem to get along just fine," she told him.

In reality, she just didn't want to know. Because if she had let herself imagine it all, she might have brought a tiny little being into the world who deserved so much better.

Another shot arrived, and then another, and then a can of

beer. Each from a different patron, but with the same message: "In memory of Nash."

In memory of Nash. She wondered what kinds of memories each one of them had of him. She wondered what they knew. She wondered whether any of them knew any of the things that she didn't.

She also wondered whether she'd be able to walk out on her own volition if she didn't eat soon. "Can I order some food? Chicken sandwich and fries?" she called after the bartender.

He turned around but didn't walk back toward her table. "We don't have chicken sandwiches. Only chicken strips. Or burgers."

That sort of lack of ingenuity always stunned Macy. Couldn't they slap the strips on a bun with some tomato and lettuce and call it a chicken sandwich? But she was in no mood to argue with convention. "Cheeseburger," she said.

Her food showed up at exactly the same time Tommy Morgan did. She spotted him first and trained her gaze on him until he looked over at her. She motioned to him and he waved at her, his brow furrowed.

She saw him ask the bartender for a beer and then he started toward her. When he arrived at her booth he stood in front of it for a moment, his head cocked like a dog might. "What are you doing here?" he said, not unkindly.

Macy couldn't answer his question directly, because she didn't know. *Because I'm lost*, she thought. *Because I'm barely hanging on. Because someone needs to tell me what to do or what to think, and before, that was always Nash, but Nash is gone now. And as it turns out, he was a cheating bastard, too.* She had no reason to think Nash would have been any different.

"I thought you might have a minute to talk," she said.

He bobbed his head, lips pursed, as if to indicate that how long he had depended on what the topic was going to be. Tommy Morgan had always been a person of painfully few words. He said most of what he needed to with his eyes, his shoulders, and the carry of his six-foot-four-inch frame. Those around him tended to get the message. But she had regularly marveled at how animated both he and Nash were in each other's company, belly laughing and knee slapping and conversing like a couple of teenage girls. Once apart, they each reverted back to their stoic, quiet ways. It was as if each of them held the secret key to the other. They had been two parts of one whole, even if to her, Tommy had always been intimidating and Nash had felt like a flannel blanket on a cold, cold night.

"I was hoping you could tell me . . . about Nash," Macy said.

Tommy took a sip of beer, placed the bottle on the table, looked up at her. "You knew him better than anyone, Macy. I don't think there's much I could tell you. Other way around, maybe."

Macy shook her head from side to side. "I don't think so."

"What's this about, Macy?"

She steeled herself. She breathed in deep, held the breath for a second, and exhaled. She met his eyes. "I know there was someone else," she said.

Tommy chuckled, though not as if she had told a bad pun, not in good humor. This chuckle echoed with disbelief, exasperation, annoyance.

"Come on, Macy. Don't do this. There's no need."

She stared at him.

"There was no one else."

She kept staring.

"I'm serious."

Macy kept looking at him.

Tommy shook his head, sighed, and held up both hands in a conciliatory gesture.

"So what if there was?" he asked. "It doesn't matter anymore. Not now."

Macy bit her lip. The hell it didn't. Easy for him to say. He didn't have to hit the reset button on his life four months prior. He hadn't had to keep hitting it over and over again. "It matters," she said softly. She willed the tears threatening the edges of her eyes not to spill over. Not in front of him.

She calmed herself by placing both of her shaking hands on the table. "Did you know he had a daughter?"

Tommy had just taken a sip of beer. He swallowed hard, his eyes as big as a cartoon character's on springs. "Shit," he said, almost in disbelief. It was directed at the table, not her. He repeated it, this time with more oomph: "Shit!"

"So who was she?"

"I don't know."

"Goddamn it, Tommy. He was your best friend. He had an *affair*. He had a goddamned *daughter*. And you didn't know?" Macy slammed her open palm against the table. "Bullshit!" she said. "How could you *not* know?"

"How couldn't *you*?" he shot back at her.

Macy set her jaw. She breathed out through her nose. It felt as though he had just clocked her with a roundhouse. And she thought at that moment of the phone call. The breathy, singsong voice on the other end. And she was right back there—her insides seizing up, letting the phone drop softly, leaving it to dangle by its cord. Padding out the back door of the barn, cutting across the rear pastures, and ducking into the woods that separated them from the Oyster River before the woods spit her out onto a tiny triangle of beach littered with oversize driftwood weathered white by salt and sun and wind and waves and rocks.

She had settled herself onto the gray sand, her back against one smooth, white log and her feet propped up on another. It had been spring in Campbell River, and cool. A halfhearted rain had drizzled down all morning, and although the sky had cleared, that same rain seemed to rise like steam up from the ground, dampening Macy's legs and seat.

She could still see them, even now: A family of ducks waddled along the forest's edge, not fifteen feet from her. Mother in front, six ducklings behind, father behind them, and bachelor uncle off to the side. Macy had studied them, the plainness of the mother with her brown feathers, the hapless ducklings, the brilliant emerald heads of the father and uncle. Handsome. They all toddled along dutifully until a branch broke somewhere in the woods. The mother, father, and ducklings had looked around frantically and closed ranks, but the uncle spread his wings and skimmed back toward the river. His decision to leave was instantaneous, its rashness alarming.

That night, Macy had drawn Nash on top of her, taking his face between her hands the whole time. "Look at me," she had said to him sternly. "Look at me, handsome."

She had known. Tommy was right about that much. She had let herself pretend, when Nash would tell her he loved her while he traced a finger lazily over her scarred arms in bed at night, that he was telling the truth.

"Did he love her?"

"We didn't talk about that kind of stuff," Tommy said. "Neither of us were really heart-to-heart-type guys. That was his business. I wasn't about to butt in."

"How convenient for you," Macy said. She looked away, more shocked than usual at how Nash could have been friends with Tommy.

"Listen, he loved you, okay? I don't know if he loved her, but he did love you. Isn't that enough?"

Macy glowered at him. She didn't know. What was enough?

Tommy had offered to drive her home. He said he'd have someone drop her truck off in the morning. It was a hard deal to refuse. Even though Macy hadn't so much as sipped some of the last drinks sent her way, it seemed that her body's processing of alcohol had pulled far ahead of any roadblocks the cheeseburger and fries were able to erect. She had to squeeze an eye shut to see only one of Tommy.

While their conversation at the bar had worn Macy down, it had had the opposite effect on Tommy, like a door crowbarred open. As he steered his truck along the winding Old Island Highway, he reminisced about Nash—how he loved playing practical jokes on the rookies, like putting ink on the brow bands of their helmets or bringing them doughnuts dusted with baby powder; how he'd laugh the loudest and hardest at his own jokes, but if someone got him back, he'd "give 'em a high five and congratulate 'em on a job well-done."

Tommy laughed, to himself, at the memory. Macy stared past him out the window at the moon lighting up the Strait of Georgia like a stage. The Tragically Hip belted "Bobcaygeon" from the speakers. Nash had adopted the Hip as a favorite band. He was more enthusiastic about them than any Canadian Macy had ever met, tracking their concert schedule the way she imagined some Americans followed the Grateful Dead. Macy wondered whether Tommy had played that particular CD to remember Nash, because she had done the very same thing once she could finally bear to listen to music again.

"He was such a pack rat, wasn't he?" Tommy was saying. Macy had lost the thread of the conversation, but couldn't help but agree with him. No one saved useless items quite like Nash.

"This road, right?" Tommy asked.

Macy nodded and yawned. It felt like months ago that she had headed out for sweet-and-sour chicken from Thrifty's deli.

No one could save useless things quite like Nash. The words bounced around inside her foggy head. *No one could save quite like Nash.*

He was right. And what if Nash hadn't just saved useless things?

It was an interesting position to be in—the jilted lover, the scorned spouse. She'd seen it happen with friends over the years, and then again with the girlfriends of several of Nash's hockey teammates. Even if the girlfriends knew, even if they tried to confront the infidelity, no one would say a word to substantiate their intuition. One of the girls had asked Macy once, directly, if her boyfriend, who everyone knew was cheating on her, had been unfaithful. Macy told the girl the truth. The next day, Nash lashed out at her. "Why would you do that?" he said. "It was none of your business!" It didn't make a bit of difference what Macy said in her own defense; Nash's response was the same.

"It's a freaking code," one of the wives had told Macy the following weekend, "and it goes something like this: Let cheating dogs lie. They all live by it."

In the past weeks, Macy had found herself railing at an imaginary Nash, having full-on arguments with him in her head. She ached for an outlet for her questions. But she knew better than to turn to his friends.

She'd thought—hoped—that Tommy might be different. But what she hadn't accounted for was that she wasn't simply the jilted spouse. She was on a whole new plane: that of the jilted widow. And she knew that no one, even Tommy, would ever part with a single damn detail for two very good reasons: One, Tommy wouldn't have done it even if Nash had still been alive; and two, Nash was dead, and neither Tommy nor any of the rest of them would stoop to sullying his memory just to provide Macy with peace of mind.

She wondered now, had Nash been alive, how much even he would have told her. How honestly he would have answered the questions that burned so hot they seared her from the inside out: Was it one single rushed quickie in a dank alley outside a club, or an evening in with Chinese takeout and wine followed by scrambled eggs and coffee in the morning? Had he seen her bedroom, or did they meet at a hotel? Did he turn away from her before he drifted off to sleep, as he did with Macy, or did he let her spoon against him and drape an arm around her? Did he love this woman? Did he ever tell her that? And just once, or how many times? Did he feel guilty? Did he regret it? Or was he planning to leave Macy anyway? Was he running away from Macy? Or was he running toward this woman, whoever she was?

Macy decided that even if she could go right inside the house and ask Nash every one of those questions, even if she could look him straight in the eyes and watch as he answered her, even then, she would never know what she wanted—what she needed—to know. But Tommy had given her an idea.

Tommy pulled into her driveway and shifted into park. He

was reaching for the ignition, about to turn it off, looking like he had something he wanted to say. But Macy didn't give him a chance. She didn't invite him in. In a rush, she thanked him, poured herself from his truck, and almost ran to the house.

Basements unnerved Macy.

They were creepy, for starters. Not that she believed in ghosts—she was more afraid not to. Afraid that if she were up front about not believing, they'd try to prove her wrong. More than that, though, was all that space dedicated to storing "things" not in use, which translated loosely into things that had never been, or were no longer, useful. Things that would have to be sorted through, taken elsewhere, disposed of. A basement was the embodiment of future work waiting to be done, and she always had plenty to do aboveground.

Macy flipped on the lights illuminating the rickety basement stairs. They led down at an angle that, along with a myriad of other things in their house, most likely violated all sorts of building codes.

A bulb had burned out (or maybe had never actually worked) and the dim light only exacerbated the creepiness factor. Macy felt along each step. She held the wall with her right hand, since the only railing lined the left wall and she couldn't grab it with her left arm, which hung limp and useless in the sling.

For years, she'd ignored the fact that their home had a basement, and that she had a husband who insisted on saving things like empty shoe boxes and a spare washing machine motor. Anything that descended below the first floor of their house, in her mind, ceased to exist.

When her grandfather died, then her father, Nash hauled their boxed things to the basement at Macy's request. She told him she didn't have time to deal with it all right then. He knew she meant she couldn't deal with it at all. Probably ever.

"Whenever you get to it, you get to it," Nash had said. "None of it is going anywhere."

And there it all was, lining one whole wall. Boxes labeled "books," "china," "shoes," and "files and papers." A mismatched set of lawn furniture. The body of a lawn mower. A shelving unit full of tools waiting to be made whole—rake heads, buckets, shovels with missing or broken handles. Boxes of cassette tapes, psychic readings Magda had commissioned for Nash each year on his birthday. Magda liked to call them "astrological insights." Macy liked to call them what they were: complete and utter crap.

Macy wanted to be anyplace but there, doing anything but what she was about to do. But this was the only option.

She started with a giant clear plastic Tupperware container capped by a purple lid. The cover gave way with a loud pop that made Macy jump, despite knowing full well that sound was coming.

Inside she found layer after layer of paper: old mail still un-opened, addressed to Nash's apartment in Milwaukee. An essay titled "Adam Smith and Pareto Optimality" written for an Intro to Economics class with a glaringly large "C+" scrawled in green ink at the top right corner. Receipts in no apparent order, for items of no particular worth. One for Best Buy for $201.09, and another for McDonald's for $5.62. Pamphlets that defied classi-fication, ranging from "Weatherproofing Your Home for Better Energy Efficiency" to "Duck Boat Tours in Wisconsin Dells" to the Royal BC Museum's "Eternal Egypt" exhibit in Victoria that they had taken Nash's parents to see three years back.

Good God, she thought. *Who saves such things?*

The second bin—this one an all-over opaque blue—held a

handful of concert and hockey tournament T-shirts that, from the looks of it, Nash had long ago outgrown. She picked one up. It was green with yellow lettering. Packers colors, that much she knew. Hell, anyone who had longer than an hour layover in Green Bay could come up with that bit of trivia. But the front showed a medieval knight in full armor atop a horse, charging at something over her shoulder with his lance leveled at whatever it was. Words above and below the knight announced, GREEN KNIGHT SUMMER HOCKEY CAMP. The seams along the sleeves and neck had come apart with use, leaving dime-size gaps. Macy drew it to her face. Inhaled deep. Nothing.

The T-shirts had been loosely folded over a menagerie of knickknacks that she imagined lining the shelves of Nash's boyhood room. Matchbox cars, Transformers, GI Joe figurines.

More bins, more useless bric-a-brac collections in each. Finally, one bin remained. It had been labeled, "For Sorting," with Nash's scrawl in black marker on duct tape. And if the rest were any indication, nothing here would tell her anything. These were useless remnants of Nash's life. Remnants of Nash.

She hoped, suddenly, that that was exactly what she would find. Then she could simply close the lids, store the boxes, and stop looking. Stop wondering. Stop waiting.

The lid of the last bin gave way just as the others all had: with a loud pop that seemed to announce the opening, though Macy had long ago stopped jumping at the sound.

She looked in to find a sea of photographs.

Not in envelopes or boxes. Not bound by rubber bands. Not separated into orderly, ready-to-file piles. They were like snowflakes, huge pieces of confetti, looking like a mess packed in together, and each one holding the story of that brief snippet of time. Nash used to say that that was what drew him to photography in the first place, the thing he couldn't let go of: that he was responsible for capturing the moments that people would otherwise miss, never to remember them or even know they had forgotten them. He had started out doing weddings before moving on to shooting advertisements and working now and then for a smattering of travel publications. Most would see it as climbing a few career rungs, but when asked about his new assignments, Nash's voice would register a sad note. Unlike many photographers, he never seemed to approach weddings as a means to an end. "I get to be a part of the happiest day of these people's lives," he'd tell her. "And if I do it right, well, isn't that probably one of the best things I could do with my life? Give them something to remember it by?"

Now she wondered whether Nash would say the same thing about their wedding day—whether it was one of the happiest days of his life. She used to hope so. Now she'd settle for top three. Top five, even.

The basement's dampness had worked its way into her, and she shivered. Macy wished she could carry the bin upstairs, spread the contents out in front of the fire, and surround herself with these images. But it was too heavy to maneuver, one-armed, up a steep set of stairs. And so she pulled up a lawn chair, tugged the cord on another bare bulb for extra light, and started sorting.

Nash was the rare young photographer who didn't prefer digital cameras and processing. He used them when it made sense for him to do so, mostly on official shoots that required quick turnaround—those for advertising inserts or Web sites or weddings. When he photographed her, or the landscape of the island, or gatherings with their families or friends, he'd do things the old-fashioned way: in his darkroom.

Macy realized, looking into the strata of images below her fingers, how little she had actually seen of his work. She understood, maybe for the first time just then, how intensely solitary their worlds were. Hers in the barn, Nash's behind the lens. They'd reconvene at the end of the day and meld their lives back together again, but she didn't have the faintest idea of how he went about doing what he did. She knew Nash knew the difference between a halter and a bridle, or a vertical and an oxer, but not much more. At one show, she was riding two sorrel horses back-to-back—youngsters she was slowly bringing along. One had a solid blaze down its face, while the other had brown spots that broke up the white. Nash turned away to take a phone call while Macy switched horses. When he hung up the phone and looked at her, he couldn't have been more confused. "What did you do with its spots?" he asked. She and Martine had laughed then. She smiled now, thinking back on it.

Through her fingers ran pictures of her getting Gounda prepped to go into the ring—a series of her fastening the billets, tightening the girth, oiling his feet and face, brushing his bushy black tail, and finally, Macy giving him a private, quick kiss on the soft skin just above his muzzle. There was another that she lingered on—Macy atop Gounda just before their number was called, waiting in the chute, backlit by the bright lights of the arena and the vibrant jumps beyond, all the colors of a rainbow. Macy was a study in concentration. Slumped shoulders, one hand resting on the giant horse's seal brown withers, eyes closed, and chest inflated with a long inhale. Gounda's ears focused forward, his eyes open wide.

There were others, no rhyme or reason to the order in which they found her hands. One, seemingly retouched, of Nash as a boy. Freckles loud as ink stains across his nose and cheeks. He wore blue corduroy bib overalls and a giant pile of leaves, and a laughing smile so big that his eyes had narrowed to make room for it.

Another of Magda and Jack in black and white, bent toward each other over a cribbage board, painted Italian tiles in the background tethering the image to the Allen family kitchen in Green Bay.

And on. And on. One after another. These lost moments, captured by Nash's eye. By his fingers.

And then Macy's stomach turned in on itself.

Staring up at her, in her right hand, was a woman she had never seen before.

The photo wasn't the person-on-the-street variety of which Nash was so fond—where he would stake out a spot at an outdoor table or bench and catch people as they went about their days, fixing an out-of-place lock of hair in a storefront window, tucking in the tail of a shirt, staring off at someone else they either knew or didn't. No, this woman knew she was being photographed. And unlike Macy, who was always embarrassed at being in the crosshairs of the camera lens and either challenging it head-on or slinking away from it, this woman clearly knew how to pander to the camera. She had tilted her eyes up at it and her chin down. It was a coy, knowing pose.

Her black hair had been shorn into a tight bob that hugged her ears. Milk chocolate freckles dotted her nose, thin and white as bone. Her lips, parted ever so slightly on the right side, glistened. Raggedy Ann meets Glamour Shots.

And there were others.

This woman, with bony elbows on a Formica table, fingers folded in against her cheeks, looking off to the left, a runny egg, slice of bacon, and half-eaten piece of dry toast in front of her.

This woman on a striped couch somewhere, skinny knees busting up through ripped jeans, holding a glass of white wine and laughing unabashedly, all teeth and joy.

This same woman, reclined back with legs crossed and one hand reaching up toward the camera, sprawled on a quilted blanket spread out over white sand. She wore the same jeans as in the other photograph, ripped in both knees. She also wore Nash's favorite UW—Madison sweatshirt, which was, at that moment, balled under Macy's pillow.

Buried between these photos was a paper napkin from a restaurant called Genghis Cohen in West Hollywood. On it, words unfurled in a scrawl distinctly feminine, and distinctly un-Nash: "I'm struck by the lightning of seeing you after you're gone," it read. It was signed by three tiny letters: K-a-t: "Kat."

I'm struck by the lightning of seeing you after you've gone.

K-a-t.

Macy's head pounded.

To know something theoretically was one thing. To see lines and letters sloping distinctly on a napkin, or blue eyes staring back at you, wearing the same sweatshirt you had been sleeping with every night since your husband had died? That was something altogether different.

A woman not in Macy's particular situation—a woman with a living, breathing significant other—could approach this in another way: yell, scream, cry tears that she hoped would inflict guilt and pity in the betrayer. Ask "why" and "how" and "how was she?" over and over again, ad nauseam. Monitor future phone records and receipts to ensure that what had happened once would never happen again. Use the transgression to leverage assurances of love.

Macy didn't have those little luxuries.

She could scream and cry and kick and scream, and at the end of the day, she would still be alone. A tree falling in the forest.

And that saying? About a picture being worth a thousand words? Complete and utter bullshit. Because there, in that bin, were hundreds of pictures. And none of them told her a single thing other than what she already knew.

Nash and this woman. The woman and Nash. The girl.

Macy grabbed a wastepaper basket, discarded in the basement's far corner. Without thinking about what she was doing, she grabbed handfuls of photographs and stuffed them into the garbage can. When what she forced in had run out of room and sprang right back out, Macy hauled the can upstairs.

There she walked to the kitchen, rinsed dregs of coffee from the "Shoreline Dental: A Smile a Day . . ." mug she had used that morning, dropped a handful of ice cubes into it, and fished a bottle of vodka from the cabinet. But the smile on the mug, which should have turned from gray to sparkling white when anything hot or cold was poured into it, stayed a dreary, noncommittal gray.

She walked back to the living room and sat down cross-legged in front of the fireplace. Then she put the photos one by one into it until the trash can stood empty. She lit a match, and she tossed it onto the pile.

There were photos of her. Her and Nash. Nash's parents. Unfocused, drunken party pictures Nash had taken in college. Flowers in various stages of bloom from Victoria Gardens. Sunsets over Stories Beach and Miracle Beach. Landscapes with sharply focused foregrounds and backgrounds as soft as spun cotton. Macy watched the fire eat each one with hot black teeth—edges first and eventually the whole of them. Then she went back for more.

By the second load, Macy had slurped the remaining drops of vodka from the cup and had done away with more than half of the photos.

She started chewing the ice cubes into bits in hopes they had absorbed something, anything, that might work its way into her bloodstream, into her head, to help her make sense of all this. She knew there wasn't any vodka left, or anything else might do the trick. Macy drew her finger deep around the inside of the cup and brought it to her lips, savoring the bitter sting.

The fire had been slow to catch on, and it would smolder and flare up in spurts. Macy lay curled next to it like a dog, feeling the heat and flipping through the pictures that had never been taken, that existed now only in her head.

There was Nash crying when it came time for the injections, saying that it hurt him to hurt her, and her response, each time, measured and even: "I want to do this—for you." "For us," he would correct her, and she would think of the voice on the phone and repeat, "For us."

There was the one of his lips, soft on the jagged scars of her arms, whispering their quiet promise: that he loved her, no matter what, followed by her silent refrain of, *You don't know what you're saying.*

And then the pictures in her head of her own lips on the unadulterated skin of her baby's stomach, like a sip of warm milk passing them by. Her baby's giggle. Its tiny fingers reaching for hers, knowing hers, wanting hers out of any others. Then finding that same baby, years and years later, the same way she had found her mom—its skin still warm as milk, but leaking the color of crushed cherries.

And then, that baby—her baby—replaced by eight-year-old Glory. Spunky, gregarious Glory. Glory, the perfect mix of Nash and not-her.

She had forgotten to open the flue. Macy's eyes smarted—partially from the smoke, and partially because her life could be summed up in movie taglines: She had been duped. It was all a sham. She had been reduced to that. To this.

There was one more load. If she had had two good, working arms, Macy would have simply picked up the Tupperware container and lugged the entire thing upstairs. As it was, she had to use the trash can, clutching it to her chest with one arm wrapped around it.

Macy thought about being done with it. She thought about letting the fire burn out, putting the lid back on the Tupperware container, going to bed, and waking up tomorrow. But then all of it—all of the potential reminders—would still be down there, lurking. No, there was moving on to be done. This would end tonight.

By the time the wastebasket was half-full, Macy wished she hadn't gone back downstairs. The fervor had left her. Her heart wasn't in it. They were just pictures, after all. She wouldn't miss them—she hadn't even known about any of them until that night—but by the same token, what good was all this doing? It didn't make her feel one bit better, because it didn't change anything. There wasn't any changing to be done. This was her new life. She had no choice but to live it.

The wastebasket was almost full now, the Tupperware bin nearly empty. Macy reached in for another handful of photographs, but instead of grazing glossy surfaces like the last hundred or so times she had reached into the bin, her fingertips felt something rougher. Paper.

She brushed aside the remaining photographs and found the bottom of the bin scattered with thick envelopes, each one addressed to Glory Gibson. Each one postmarked December 31. Each one stamped, "Return to Sender."

She opened a letter dated three years before. It was almost word for word like the one Glory had brought with her. She opened one postmarked the previous year. It, too, read nearly verbatim. Macy thought of Nash ending each year by sitting down in front of a blank yellow legal pad and pouring his heart out to a little girl he had never met. She thought of him folding up the sheets filled with his scrawl, folding it into thirds, and stuffing it into a long, plain white envelope. She thought of him starting each new year with the letter boomeranging back to him, and when it did, how it must have weighed heavy with disappointment in his hand.

She thought of Glory then, too. What would have happened to her if Nash and Macy had moved—to another house, another farm, another city? Had Glory even thought about the risk that she had taken—not just jumping on a bus at eight years old, but putting every last shred of faith in one single letter? Probably not, Macy decided. Impossible-seeming things, for whatever reason, were always easier to take a chance on. It was the normal, day-to-day risks that rendered a person immobile, wholly unable to do a damn thing.

Macy went about gathering the letters, sorting them by date. Seven in all. Until, at the very bottom of the bin, one envelope remained.

At first it looked like the others—long, white, marked, "Return to sender," and addressed in Nash's scrawl. But this one was postmarked July 15, just over three years ago, to the day. And it was addressed to Katherine Gibson.

Macy lifted the edge of the envelope and slipped her finger under it like a letter opener. Halfway through the letter's top, Macy realized an actual opener might have been a good idea. She felt the sting before she saw the thin line of blood materialize on her finger. She brought it to her mouth and sucked on it to stem the blood from bubbling up. It stopped bleeding, but kept right on stinging.

Macy wrestled the letter out of the half-open envelope and unfolded it. Like the others, it was on lined yellow legal paper. Unlike the others, it was one single page.

She started to read.

Kat—

   I'm sorry our talk ended the way it did the other day. I didn't mean to say what I said. At the very least, I shouldn't have said things in the way that I did.

Macy's breath caught in her throat. She couldn't seem to make it go in either direction—up and out, or in and down. Her heart pounded. She felt as if a fist had closed around her stomach. She realized, with a start, that the letter in her hands could answer all of her questions, and at the same time, it could unravel even more of her and Nash's relationship. She didn't know if she could read it.

Reading those words—all of them on that page—could fundamentally change everything about how her world with Nash had looked. She knew only so much just then, and maybe that was best. It was as though she were standing on the bank of a river, and if she crossed, she couldn't ever come back. Her view would forever be altered. Because there was a chance that if she knew more, if she knew everything that she had thought she wanted to, she might have to acknowledge that the last ten years of her life were only one version of reality—only *her* take on it. And it would be like losing Nash all over again. Only this time, she wouldn't have fond memories to buoy her. This time, it would be like lashing concrete blocks to her ankles.

Macy folded the letter and the envelope and tucked both into the back pocket of her jeans. Then she took the letters to Glory and placed them in the plastic bin. All alone, splayed against the bottom, those letters looked expectant, like they were waiting for something. She thought of how Glory clung to that one letter from Nash, how the girl took it everywhere with her, transferring it from pocket to pocket each day, fingering it to make sure it was still there. Macy had seen her do it many times over in the two weeks since Glory had arrived. And if one letter could offer such hope, such promise, what might a complete set—one for every year of Glory and Nash's overlapping lives—do for the girl?

Macy snapped the lid back on the container, sealing the letters inside. "Maybe someday," she said out loud, to no one in particular.

If Gounda hadn't been dead lame, Macy would have tied a lead rope to either side of his halter—since she couldn't saddle or bridle him with only one working arm—and ridden him out through the back pastures, even if it was nearly three a.m. She would have felt his sure stride beneath her, his muscles working, carrying her, calming her. And out there, where she could hear the water just beyond the tree line, as far from her house and that basement as she could have gotten, she would have pulled the letter from her back pocket and read it by the light of the moon.

But Gounda was lame. In fact, he was nearly three-legged at the moment. And so Macy did the next-best thing she could think of: She went to the barn.

The horses would be sleeping, some lying down and some standing up, and Macy didn't want to jolt them awake by flipping on the overhead lights and flooding their worlds with brightness out of nowhere. Instead, she felt her way to the tack room and turned on the inside light, keeping the door open so illumination filtered out into the aisleway. Then she turned on the lights in the wash stall and the bathroom, all in a line along the left-hand side of the barn. The result was a dim glow that fell across most of the walkway, but didn't reach to the stalls on the opposite side.

She looked in the stalls along the right-hand side. In the first was a six-year-old mare, a dappled gray Holsteiner named Zanzara that Macy was bringing along through the lower-level jumper ranks. She was thoughtful and brave, but had a stubborn streak running through her a mile long that Macy didn't altogether mind. Next was Kingston, a sorrel with a spotted blaze. He was a half brother to Gounda, and Macy hoped that in a handful of years, he'd be able to step into Gounda's shoes as her next top mount. In the stall next to Kingston was Brouhaha, or "Brew," as Macy called him, a Dutch Warmblood stallion that Martine had found and imported for her. And across the aisle from Brew stood Gounda. He didn't nicker, but his eyes followed Macy. In the stalls beyond were a couple of horses that Macy had taken on to sell for their owners. They'd be going home now that her show season was over.

Macy breathed deep, letting the sweet smells of hay and manure fill her nose. There was something magical about this place. One step inside and the rest of the world fell away. A million miles away. It was her center, another spine. And as she stood there, the thick fog she had found herself trying to wade through in the basement dissipated. Thoughts clarified, as if she were adjusting one of Nash's camera lenses. There really hadn't ever been a choice. Not for her.

She reached into her back pocket and fished out the letter. Then Macy laid herself down in the middle of the aisleway, knees bent into an upside-down "V," in a weak patch of light. And she began to read.

Kat—

I'm sorry our talk ended the way it did the other day. I didn't mean to say what I said. At the very least, I shouldn't have said things in the way that I did. I was frustrated and mad.

Here's the deal—and this is what I was trying to explain on the phone: You need to separate out the "you and me" from "me and Glory." Things between us shouldn't affect my relationship with her. She's my daughter, Kat. And yet, it feels completely foreign to even write those words, because I've never met her. I've never talked to her. I don't even know when her birthday is. I don't know if I'm on her birth certificate. I have no evidence that she exists other than your telling me that she does. I'm not saying I want a paternity test or anything. I don't. If you say she's mine, then she's mine. But you have to let her be a little bit mine. Using her to suck money out of me, to get me to leave my wife, using her like a pawn—don't you see how wrong that is? She deserves to

*know who I am and that I love her, and then, eventually, she
can make a decision about me on her own. But you don't get
to decide that for her.*

*I don't want to go to court over this. It would only hurt
Macy and I don't want to drag her through that. And I'm sure
it would hurt you, too, and that's not something I want either.
What I do want is for you to do the right thing here.*

*I tried to call you back the other day, but the number I
have for you is no longer in service. I have no way of reaching
you, but I want to. I hope you get this and try to think about
things rationally. And when you do, give me a call. Or send
me your new number.*

*Talking to you the other day, you didn't sound like the
same girl I met years ago on that flyer shoot, all sparkle and
energy—my California girl. Something's happened, Kat, and
I don't pretend to know what, but I miss that girl.*

*I'm not the enemy here. I'm on your side. And I'm willing
to help. You just have to be willing to meet me halfway.*

Enclosed is a check to help in the meantime.

—Nash

Macy lifted up her right butt cheek and pulled out the envelope. She slipped a finger inside as if testing bathwater, and her
finger hit on something she hadn't noticed before. It was a check
from Nash Allen Photography made out to Katherine Gibson
for two thousand dollars.

Macy balled the check in her hand until it was the size of a
small rock and almost as hard. She heard that same voice she
had heard on the phone saying, "Hello, handsome," its breathi-
ness coating Macy's thoughts like a film all these years, haunting
her. She thought of all that she had assumed. All that she had

been too afraid to ask, to know. All that she had been too afraid to tell Nash. What might have happened if she had?

She hadn't needed to tell him all of it, or not at once. She could have started with her grandmother steering her car off the St. George's Bridge into the Bow River, with the beloved family dog in the backseat and her month-old daughter in a crib at home.

Or she could have skipped straight to her mom: how one day in second grade Macy had opened up her My Little Pony lunch pail to find a tiara and a wand made out of a chopstick and a piece of purple streamer where a ham sandwich, applesauce, and a Ho Ho should have been. She could have told him how, even then, it had struck her that normal people didn't do such things.

She could have told him about that Christmas Eve afternoon when Macy's mother decided to draw a bath, climb into it, and open each wrist with the rotary cutter she used for sewing projects, while Macy, her father, and her sister drove around exchanging gifts with family friends. She could have told him that all she could see of that day now was her red-mittened hand waving back at her dad as he parked the car before she ran up the front walk. How she could still taste the metallic warmth on her lips as they pressed tight against the gash in her mother's wrist, sealing it from spilling into the pomegranate red water, still as sleep.

Or she could have simply said that crazy was a sort of family heirloom with them. That she wanted, more than anything, to see the combination of them, her and Nash, in one tiny little being, and to wonder whether it would have her dark hair, his freckles, her pinkie fingers that seemed to be shifted down a joint on each hand, or his laugh that sounded more like a windup to a sneeze. But that passing along the crazy that had attached itself to her family tree, that flowed swiftly through her own veins and that would surely find a home in any baby of hers, terrified her more than anything else in the entire world.

Maybe if she had told Nash everything, he might have understood. He might have loved her anyway.

She should have. But she hadn't. And now, it seemed, she and Nash were more or less even on secret keeping.

Chapter Fifteen

MAGDA HAD A PLAN.

The first step involved taking herself out for lunch, alone, with the exception of a book. Then it was off to the travel agent to book her first world adventure: a cruise through the Greek islands. After that, it was to the store to get a cordless phone so she could draw a bath and relax in it while talking to Jack. He had asked if he could call that evening, and she was almost looking forward to it—both to get it out of the way so they could start moving forward and because she had genuinely missed talking to him in the past weeks. Even if they were different people who wanted different things, Magda was still fond of Jack. He might not spark flutters within her, but in a very basic way, human being to human being, she did love him.

What did cause flutters within her was pulling into Van Dyn Hoven Travel and the thought of what she was about to do, the leap she was about to take. She had always dreamed of Greece. She never thought she'd actually get there. "The good Lord works in mysterious ways," Magda's mother used to say. *He sure does*, Magda thought. *He sure does.*

The receptionist greeted Magda and asked whether she had an appointment. She didn't. So the receptionist wondered whether she wouldn't like to please have a seat and someone would be right with her. She would, and did.

Magda lowered herself to the very small, uncomfortable-looking couch. She surveyed the magazines spread before her on the coffee table, and it was a virtual cornucopia: *Travel + Leisure, Condé Nast Traveler, Afar, National Geographic Traveler*—all of the magazines to which Magda had always longed to subscribe but wouldn't allow herself. Because it hadn't ever been enough for her to simply look. To window shop. And if she was resigned to looking, she would just as well rather not know all these fabulous places were even out there. She would just as well put her blinders on and focus on her little life in Wisconsin.

Magda took in the pictures and framed posters on the wall: Egypt, Thailand, Venice, Iceland, Russia, Australia. Each of them distinctly beautiful. Each of them now open to her. She was surrounded by possibility, and it was exhilarating.

"Magda Allen?" An older woman who looked as though she should perhaps be holding down a bridge table at the senior center, or at her quilting guild meeting, held out a hand to Magda. "I'm Pauline. Follow me. Let's go see if we can get you going on a trip here."

Magda followed Pauline back to her office.

"So, what were you thinking of today?" Pauline asked Magda, motioning for her to sit.

"Booking a cruise to Greece," Magda said. She arranged her purse on her knees, and clasped her hands on top of the purse.

"Oh!" Pauline exclaimed, placing a hand over her heart. "Oh, you are going to absolutely, positively *love* this trip, Magda. It doesn't get any better than Greece. And cruising through the islands is simply the only way to go."

They discussed durations of trips and ports of departure and ports of call. The whole while, Pauline plucked away at her keyboard. Every now and then she'd emit a "hmmm" or an "ooooh" and Magda would lean forward in her chair as if that would help her better interpret Pauline's sounds in response to whatever had popped up on her screen.

Finally, Pauline leaned back and clapped her hands together. "Okay, I have it! Seventeen days, which will cover the islands of Aegina, Poros, and Hydra, and a few others. You'll fly in and out of Barcelona, and all transfers are included. How does that sound?"

Magda nodded excitedly. "Perfect!" she said. She could hardly believe this was happening. She could see in her mind's eye the whitewashed buildings against the bluest of blue skies. She could nearly taste the olives, the dolmathes.

"You have your choice of an interior, ocean view, or veranda suite," Pauline said.

"Whichever one has a balcony," Magda said.

"Veranda it is, then." Pauline smiled and nodded approvingly. "So many people don't think a balcony is worth it, but it truly is."

Magda could smell the salt water. She could feel the ocean spray on her face, blowing through her hair.

"Okay, we're looking at $6,647, including transfers but not airfare. How does that sound?"

Magda winced. That was more than she had bargained for. And she hadn't yet checked into what flying there and back would cost. Maybe she should check with Jack. Though Jack hadn't exactly checked with her on his trip to Vancouver Island.

There was a bit of a difference in price, but the principle of the thing was the same, wasn't it?

Pauline was looking at Magda expectantly.

"Is there anything a little cheaper?" Magda asked.

"Well, remember," Pauline said, "this is all based on double occupancy. So, that's a little under three thousand dollars a person. It's a pretty good rate. All food included."

"But I don't have another person," Magda said. Storm clouds started moving in on her sun-washed, salt-sprayed visions of the Greek isles. "It's just me."

"Oh," Pauline said. "Oh. Well, I should have asked that up front. I'm sorry; I just assumed. We can look at some singles cruises if you'd like." Her tone was unreasonably cheery.

Magda's visions of touring the Acropolis and the Parthenon blurred and faded. In their place were imaginings of a boat full of single people all running from their singleness as fast and hard as they could, probably with a stiff drink or two in hand. It would be the adult version of Baba Louies, the local college meat market where the St. Norbert College kids went to solidify their drunkenness and then sloppily pair off for the evening. The thought made her shudder. She wasn't running from her single status. She wanted to embrace it. Relish it.

"No," Magda said. "I'd rather do a regular cruise, just with a single room. Or rate. Or however you have to do it."

Pauline nodded. "Absolutely. We can do that. It's just that all rates are based on double occupancy. You'll have to pay a bit of an up charge if you're traveling alone. Or maybe you can find a travel companion to go with you?"

Magda couldn't believe what she was hearing. She was being penalized for traveling solo! It was completely ridiculous. Surely Pauline was mistaken.

Pauline assured Magda that she wasn't. Magda also discovered how mistaken Pauline wasn't after she stopped at Fox World Travel and Journeys Unlimited later that afternoon, thinking that the last company should probably change its name to Journeys Limited, or Journeys Unlimited as Long as You Can Afford to Travel Alone.

Magda thought that Ginny might like to go. She didn't anticipate having to dance around the fact that she was divorcing Jack when she called Ginny, whom Magda hadn't yet told about her developing . . . situation. Or that Ginny would say no.

"I'll have to talk to Frank about it," Ginny said. "But I can't imagine he won't be on board. We've been talking about doing a big vacation this year, and he just loves going with Jack. I swear, those two, starting their beer drinking and cribbage playing at noon! But I suppose who knows if we'd even be able to keep track of what time zone—"

"No, Ginny," Magda said. "It would be just me and you. Just the girls! Doesn't that sound fun?"

"Oh," Ginny said. Her voice had fallen. "I don't know, Magda. I can't go without Frank."

"Sure you can!"

"I don't think so," Ginny said. "I mean, I *can*, but I don't know if I want to. Or, rather, I want to. You know I do, Magda. But if I go with you, then Frank and I can't take a big vacation together like we were planning. I won't have enough vacation days left, and that's not really fair to him."

After Ginny, Magda called Susan Forster, Millie Gunn, Martha Vanderwagen, and Sandy Walters. Each of them repeated to her what Ginny had said, slight riffs on the exact same words.

At the end of that litany of phone calls, Magda checked her watch. It was nearly four o'clock: almost time for Jack to call.

They hadn't talked often since Jack had ventured to Vancouver Island nearly nine weeks ago. Neither of them was big on phone calls, and the two of them together weren't prone to long, rambling conversations either. Even in the dawn of their relationship, time spent on the phone was purely utilitarian and rarely exceeded a handful of minutes. And with Jack gone, they had settled easily and comfortably into not calling each other for days at a time. More recently, those days had ebbed into a week's span or more. So when Magda had sent Jack the divorce papers, she had hoped he would have called sooner, but the fact that he hadn't didn't alarm her. Jack needed time to process new developments. Always had. But Magda didn't know what to expect on the other end, and the not-knowing made her nervous. Would he keep his composure? Magda figured he would, because Jack always did, and because he had had time to think it all through. Would he argue with her? Maybe. Beg her? Magda hoped not. She hoped she could make him see her side.

To do that, Magda knew she'd have to be calm, rational, and in control. She couldn't let herself get caught up in Jack's protests, in the emotion of the situation. And so she had thought well in advance of how to put herself in the most relaxed mood possible and had decided that soaking in a hot bath during their conversation would be just the thing.

Earlier that week, when she had decided to finally pony up thirty-five dollars for a cordless phone to enable the bath part of the plan, it had all nearly unraveled. She announced to the boy in the electronics department that she needed a mobile phone, and he responded by showing her a cabinet of cell phones. "No," Magda had told him. "I want a phone I can walk around my house with," to which he responded that these could go all around the house and that they needed only to be plugged in for charging. "I'm not an idiot," Magda had said. "I know how they work. But I don't want one of these. I want a mobile one." Eventually, a passerby overheard their exchange and informed the salesboy that Magda wanted a *cordless* phone, successfully solving the impasse they had come to. "Yes!" Magda said. "That's what I meant!" She had been so thrilled that she had even ignored the boy when he muttered under his breath, "Then that's what you should have said, lady."

Magda grabbed the new *cordless* phone, poured herself three fingers of white zinfandel, and headed upstairs, where she drew a hot bath and lit a candle. She had even dug bath salts out of the bottom reaches of a drawer for the occasion, which she now sprinkled generously over the water.

She shut the faucet and tested the temperature with a finger. It was hot enough to still be comfortable when it cooled, yet not scalding. In a word, perfect.

Magda undressed and climbed in, easing into the water. She checked the clock. She still had eight minutes, and thought that maybe Ginny would want to meet her out for a nice dinner afterward, to celebrate. She also thought that might be a good opportunity to tell Ginny what it was she was celebrating. Maybe she could even talk Ginny into going to Greece with her after all.

She dialed Ginny's number and barely waited for Ginny to greet her after answering before Magda launched into her proposal.

"I was thinking we haven't had dinner in a while, and I was also thinking I'd really like to try Hinterland," Magda said. "Are you up for it?"

"I might be," Ginny said. "Do you mind if I drag Frank along?"

She did mind. "I was hoping we could just make it the two of us."

"Okay," Ginny said, her voice trailing. Magda could tell she was thinking. "Well, I suppose I could order Frank a pizza, but do you mind if we go somewhere else? Titletown, maybe? Hinterland's awfully expensive, and Frank's been wanting to try it, too. I really should go the first time with him."

Magda felt her blood begin to boil. She had wanted to go to Hinterland. She had wanted to dine out for a ridiculous price. She had wanted to celebrate. With Ginny. Why was that so much to ask? Couldn't Ginny cut the cord from philandering Frank for one measly meal? She hadn't counted on having to bargain so hard with Ginny over a stupid dinner out.

Magda checked the time. "I need to call you back, Ginny," she said. She wasn't completely sure she would.

She tilted her head back so that only her nose, mouth, and eyes remained above the surface, and wondered if this wasn't all a giant mistake. Magda was a woman who believed in signs, and she thought that recently God seemed to have rented out billboards just for her—the cruise debacle, for one, and now Ginny's asinine reluctance to eat a simple fancy dinner without Frank. And then there was Peter King: Was he the best she could hope for in eligible men? Even if they didn't have Peter's slimy tendencies wrapped up in look-at-me suits, surely they'd have some other hang-up, some other broken part. Maybe Magda simply needed to take the steps she had to discover the value in a partner who so intimately knew her history. It used to be her and Jack and Nash, and now it was just her and Jack. But maybe that was better than her alone. Instead of answers, silence rang loud in her ears. Then, as if from far away, a phone did, too.

She sat up and dried her hands on a towel, then reached for the phone and answered.

Magda and Jack exchanged pleasantries. Each asked what was new with the other. Responded, "Not a whole lot." This was followed by a span of silence a second too long for Magda's taste, so she started right in on explaining, which she had sworn she wouldn't do.

"I hope you don't think it was awful of me, Jack, to surprise you with the papers the way I did. I would have liked to have done things differently, and maybe I should have. I just didn't trust myself to talk to you about it. I thought you might try to talk me out of it, and I took a long time deciding that this was really, truly the right thing for me to do, but—"

"It's all right, Magda."

"I've been thinking about things since then—"

"Well, I was mad at first, but I've come around."

"I didn't want to ambush you with a phone call, Jack, but—"

"And I think you're a hundred percent right," Jack said.

This wasn't what Magda had expected to hear. She had expected to have to stand firm. She had prepared herself for the possibility of a small amount of begging. She had not anticipated, of all things, such a quick consensus.

"I—I'm *right*?"

"Yeah," Jack said. "You and me, we're two good people. And we're awfully good at getting in each other's way when it comes to what will make each other happy."

"Sometimes," Magda whispered.

"Of course. Of course! Not all the time. I'm not saying that. But on the big things. I love you, Magda. You know that. Somewhere along the line I stopped trying to be who I always wanted to be. And you did the same. We had to, in a way. But we don't have to anymore. Before I got those papers I would have caught a plane back to Green Bay, maybe as soon as last week. I would have settled back into my old routine, our old routine. And it would have been fine. It really would have. But I would have woken up every day for the rest of my life thinking about how good I felt here on the island, how much I wanted to still be here. Does that make any sense?"

Magda had to admit that it did. Still, though, how could he agree with her? How could a part of him not want her back? How could he be so chipper about it all?

"It doesn't have to be like this, Magda. Go live. Take some cooking classes, learn Italian, go travel like you've always talked about wanting to do. Things with us aren't going to change all that much. This doesn't mean we can't still be a part of each other's lives. It's just in a different way. None of it is going to erase the fact that we raised a pretty damn good kid together. We're always going to have Nash."

"Nash is gone."

"Naw," Jack said. "Not by a long shot." He paused. "Are you sitting down?" He waited for an answer.

Magda surveyed her watery roost. "Close enough," she said.

She couldn't imagine what Jack was playing at. How was he so calm? So rational? Rational even for Jack. And then one thought entered her mind and stuck fast there: There was someone else. Already.

"Magda, there's something you should know," Jack said.

Magda's breath caught in her throat. She pictured Jack with some young thing out on that island—a woman with long, sandy blond hair who wore Birkenstocks and no makeup and looked windblown, sun-kissed, and radiantly beautiful. A woman younger than her. A woman skinnier than her. A woman more interesting than her, with the whole balance of her life to spend with Jack. With *her* Jack.

Lord, give me strength, Magda prayed.

"Magda?"

Magda cupped her free hand and scooped a palmful of water to her face, washing away the hot tears threatening to fall from her eyes.

"Magda?"

"I'm here, Jack," she said, her voice quiet, her former resolve nowhere to be found.

"You're not going to believe this, but—"

Magda found herself clutching the edge of the tub so hard that her knuckles screamed in protest.

"—you *are* a grandmother."

Magda drew her mouth into a scowl. Her husband—ex-husband? Soon-to-be ex-husband?—had lost his fool mind. "That's not funny, Jack." Her fingers relaxed. What in tarnation was he playing at?

"Didn't say it was," Jack said. "But she's beautiful. She looks so much like him, Magda."

Magda could barely make sense of the words she was hearing. "I don't understand," she said.

"It's a long story," Jack said, and then proceeded to tell her all of it: about how the girl showed up on Macy's front steps after getting herself on a bus to Canada and convincing a tourist at the Black Creek General Store to drive her to Macy's farm, about the girl's mother and her troubles, and about how intoxicatingly adorable—Jack's exact words—their granddaughter was.

"Can I come meet her?"

"Absolutely!" Jack said. "Whenever you'd like."

Magda wished she could transport herself right then. Were it not a solid two-day drive to Vancouver Island, she very well might have hung up with Jack, thrown clothes in a bag, and taken off for wherever this granddaughter was straightaway.

"What time is it?" she asked.

"A little past five your time. Why?"

Magda stood up and reached for a towel with her free hand. "I have to try to book a flight. I'll call tomorrow and let you know when I'm coming."

She had nearly hung up when she heard Jack say something. "What?" she asked.

"Your granddaughter," Jack said, and that one word that had weighed so heavily on her before now tinkled light and airy, like the music of a harp, in her ears. "Her name is Glory."

"Glory." *Glory, Glory, Glory*, Magda repeated to herself. The refrain formed a song, a silent prayer, in her head.

Chapter Sixteen

JACK HAD NEARLY MADE IT OUT OF THE MARINA CLUBHOUSE when he heard someone calling after him.

This was not an unusual occurrence in the month that had passed since his sailboat had been delivered to Campbell River and he had moved onto it. He had learned early on to assemble all of his things before exiting the showers and walking quickly toward his boat's berth. One dropped shoe, one misstep, and he'd be stuck talking for up to an hour with Old Sammy Hogan— the clubhouse manager who moved at a turtle's pace and talked even more slowly, albeit continuously. It seemed to Jack that Old Sammy's deliberate speech allowed him the time to always think of something else to say, stringing unrelated subjects together like beads and leaving the listener unable to find a break during which to extricate himself.

Today, though, as Jack turned around, it looked like Old Sammy had a little more zip to his step. He was moving, if not fast, then at least at the pace of a normal person, toward Jack, waving a piece of paper in the air.

"Mr. Allen! Mr. Allen! I got a note here for you!"

To expedite the process, Jack started walking toward Old Sammy, meeting him roughly in the middle.

Jack took the piece of paper from him and opened it. Scrawled in thick blue marker was the name Jamie Rodriguez above a barely legible phone number.

"She said for you to call as soon as you could, and that you'd know who she was," Old Sammy said, his eyes open wide, as if expecting—or hoping—Jack would confide in him what was behind this cryptic message.

"Thanks—I've gotta run and take care of this," he said, holding up the note. "Thanks, though, Sammy. I appreciate your getting me this," he called over his shoulder as he strode in the opposite direction toward the pay phones.

He couldn't figure out why Jamie Rodriguez had called here—the marina clubhouse—to try to get hold of him. He had given her Macy's phone number for that purpose.

Jack had to flick the hook switch on the phone a few times to get a dial tone. He fished a prepaid phone card from his back pocket, entered the code, and then unfolded the paper with Jamie Rodriguez's name on it and dialed that number. What was this all about?

"Sergeant Rodriguez, LAPD."

"Hi, Sergeant. This is Jack Allen calling. I just got a message to call you."

"Jack, good to hear from you. I'm glad you got a hold of me. I just need to clear a few things with you."

Jack's feet danced. He couldn't keep still. "Did you find her?"

"Didn't your wife tell you?"

"My wife? No." What in the world did Magda have to do with this? How had Sergeant Rodriguez reached *Magda*?

"Well, we found Kat Gibson last night." Jamie Rodriguez

paused. "Or, rather, she found us. She ran over a cop doing a traffic stop. He's still alive, but just by a thread. She was high out of her mind, and if he dies, she's looking at ten to twelve."

Jack's feet stopped shuffling. "Years?" he asked.

"In prison," the sergeant said. "She had enough heroin on her to charge her federally with intent to distribute, too. So that's another five."

"Oh, my God," Jack said. "So she's going to jail?"

"Prison," Sergeant Rodriguez said. "Even if those drug charges don't stick we've still probably got a dead cop on our hands. Oh, and she tried to flee the scene, too."

"So what happens now? What happens to Glory?"

"Well, that depends. The mother doesn't know where the father is and doesn't have a legal guardian on record."

"But the father is dead," Jack said, then corrected himself: "My son, he's dead."

"Right," Sergeant Rodriguez said. Jack thought he heard a note of sympathy in her voice, but couldn't be certain. "So that leaves a couple of options. The mother can either appoint a legal guardian, or we'll turn the daughter over to the state and put her into Child Protective Services."

Foster care. Jack's stomach lurched. "You mean there's no way for us"—he let himself think, and then say, the very words he'd been trying to bury since the first night he laid eyes on Glory Jane Gibson—"for us to keep her?"

"Well, of course. You could petition to be her legal guardian, or challenge any guardianship the mother decides on, and as her closest known living relative, you'd have a good shot at custody. But I think that's something you and your wife should get on the same page about."

"My wife?"

"Yes. That's why I left the message to call. Your wife indicated that she was happy we located Katherine, but that it would not be possible for you to take Glory in. I know you are attached to this girl, but no social worker in their right mind is going to place a kid who's been through all of this into a home where one person wants them and another doesn't."

My wife? thought Jack. And then, like a switch had gone off, it dawned on him whom Sergeant Rodriguez had talked to. "Thanks, Sergeant. I'll be in touch," he said. He could still hear her as he hung up, but Jack didn't have time to talk just then.

He found Macy in the barn's tack room, sponge in hand, oiling a saddle. From the looks of it—several more saddles tipped on their front ends at her feet and a tangle of bridles on the tack trunk next to her—she had just started her tack cleaning. He suspected she was reaching for horse-related things she could do with only one arm, because she had cleaned tack two weeks before as well, and none of it had been used between then and now. The light was dim, and it took his eyes a moment to adjust when he walked in. She was singing, but stopped when she noticed him standing in the doorway.

"Jack. Hey! What are you doing here?"

"Trying to figure out what the hell you think you're doing," he said.

"Come again?"

"You heard me the first time, Macy."

She looked at him, head tilted like a dog trying to understand a string of baby talk.

"You talked to Sergeant Rodriguez, didn't you?" he asked.

Macy placed the sponge in a bucket at her feet. "I did," she said.

"I can't believe you. You let her believe you're my *wife*? And told her we can't take Glory in? What the hell is wrong with you?"

"I didn't lead her to believe a damn thing, Jack. You gave her my number and she called it looking for Mrs. Allen. Last time I checked that's still the name on my mortgage and all my credit cards. Besides, we *can't* take Glory in."

Jack stared at her. "Why not?" he asked.

"Well, *I* can't take her in because as soon as this bad wing heals"—she flapped her slung arm feebly, like a baby bird testing it out—"I'll be gone most weeks from Wednesday to Sunday. And because she needs someone to love her and I really don't think that's me. That's not the kind of home life a kid like that needs, even if her last one was horrible. Sophie can't because her schedule is more unpredictable than mine. And *you* can't because you live on a boat, Jack. If I'm somehow mistaken on any of this, you go right ahead and let me know."

"How dare you!" he shouted at her. "She needs a place to live. She needs family. She is my granddaughter, and this is our home!"

"No, Jack. This is *my* home. She lives in California. You have a house in Wisconsin. You two feel free to take your little Brady Bunch to either of those locations."

"Well, this was her dad's home. Doesn't that mean anything to you, that she's Nash's daughter? Or are you so selfish that you can't look beyond a simple mistake to see that? To see that she needs us?"

Macy threw her head back and laughed.

Jack could feel the blood pumping through his veins in quick, short bursts. His chest strained against the skin, barely keeping it from exploding. He wanted to take the pitchfork leaning against the tack room wall and smash it against the concrete until it splintered into a million little pieces.

"A simple mistake? Oh, that's rich, Jack. You don't know the half of it, and you sure don't get to judge me for this," Macy said. "You don't get to sit there and tell me to just get over this and move on, or to do the right thing. Because you have no idea what the right thing looks like from over here." Macy pointed toward herself.

"The right thing doesn't have sides, Macy."

She stared back at him, unblinking. He waited for one of her tirades that, like tropical storms, seemed to gather and unleash out of nowhere, disappearing just as quickly. Instead, she dropped the sponge in a bucket at her feet and stood up. "Let's go for a walk," she said to him. Her words were soft, as if she were talking to a frightened animal. She marched ahead. Jack had to double his pace to catch up to her.

She led him out of the barn and toward the southernmost pastures, closest to the tree line and, beyond that, the beach. Macy slid herself between the first and second boards of the fence. Jack, doubting he had the agility or adequate slimness to do the same, scampered up and over. He tried to strike a balance between quickness and bodily safety, but felt a twinge in his knee when he landed all the same. Again he had to quicken his footfalls to catch Macy.

They crossed the field, through ankle-high grass and horse droppings. Something in Macy's determined stride, her shoulders set back, her head nosing out like a tortoise, leading the way, told Jack not to speak until spoken to. Or at least until she decided to stop walking.

They scaled another fence and came to the tree line. Jack was surprised that there was yet another pasture and tree line beyond that one. How quickly he had forgotten every foot of these fences after mending them with Macy back in June. Nearly three months had passed—months that felt now like they might as well have been whole years.

The briny smell of seawater filled Jack's nose, and he could hear a faint rustle of water. They couldn't walk forever. Eventually they'd run into the sea, and if the strengthening smell was any indication, they'd be running into it before long.

Macy slipped through one more fence and led Jack through a copse of trees. The ground beneath his feet turned soft and gave way a little bit with each step. And then they emerged onto a sandbar that a stream ran around and over. Jack caught glimpses of open water a ways beyond, which the stream emptied into.

Macy stopped, looked around, and headed toward a driftwood log. She settled with her back to it, not on it as Jack expected her to. She drew her knees toward her and circled them with one arm as Jack lowered himself next to her.

Still, she didn't speak. That was fine; he would wait.

The stream ran, making metallic sounds like a wind chime carried over the breeze from far away. His ear was so tuned to the stream's quiet music that he almost didn't hear Macy say, "There was a baby, you know."

Jack was about to ask her to repeat herself, or ask what she was talking about, but Macy kept right on talking.

"Nash and I were going to have a baby," she said. She stared straight ahead, not even glancing in Jack's direction. It was as though he were invisible, eavesdropping on a conversation between his daughter-in-law and the stream, the sand, the trees.

Macy inhaled deeply. "I was pregnant," she said. "A handful

of weeks before the accident we had gone to see Dr. Zip—our fertility guru—and found out."

Jack had had no idea they had been trying to have kids, or that they had had problems. He couldn't help but think that this bit of knowledge—that efforts were being made to produce a grandchild—might have helped Magda go a little easier on Macy over the years.

"His name was actually Zipinski, but he liked to call himself 'Dr. Zip.' Kind of cute. Every time we saw him he would whirl into the exam room, kind of like Kramer on *Seinfeld*, and say, 'The Zip has arrived! Let's get rolling on this, shall we?' He wore tie-dyed shirts under his lab coat and listened to Led Zeppelin and the Grateful Dead in his office. He sang along to 'Uncle John's Band' at the top of his lungs one day during my appointment. I'm not the biggest Dead fan, but it put me at ease."

She told Jack, then, about the endless, endless shots. The syringes of Gonal-F and Lupron that Nash had to stick straight into her leg every single night before bed. How she would squeeze her thigh between two heavy coffee-table books of photography to create as much loose skin as possible, and how it usually worked, but once in a while the needle would prick her muscle and she would scream and twist away in pain.

The injections were to prepare her for an operation to harvest her eggs and then reinsert them, fertilized, into her uterus. After that came the estrogen replacement shots, which had to be inserted, with a two-inch needle, intramuscularly, right into her ass. Nash would literally have to sit on her back and lean on her legs to give her the shots. And regardless of whether the shots went well or poorly—meaning relatively pain-free or intensely painful—she could hear Nash sniffling in the bathroom afterward. She said that Nash would try to hide it by running the water, but she knew, and she resented him for it. "I was the pin-cushion," she said.

And when Nash wasn't sticking a needle the length of a ciga-rette into her muscles, she was on strict bed rest so as not to prevent the embryo from implanting. Flat on her back.

"So I should have been over the moon at the news, right? Nash sure was. You should've seen it, Jack. I could barely see it on the ultrasound. Just a pinprick of light on the screen. A little pulsating star. And Nash kept saying, 'That's our baby. That's our baby.' He had both arms around me, rocking me. He was so ex-cited. And I couldn't stop crying. He thought it was because I was happy."

Jack looked at her. He opened and closed his mouth. There were questions he wanted to ask, things he needed to know. Never before had he realized how little you see of someone else's life. Even when that someone was your own child. It was like a glacier, like the ocean. Everything but the surface hidden from view.

"You would have been a great mom," he said. But even as the words came out, he knew they were all wrong. Their aftertaste hung acrid in his mouth.

"No offense, Jack, but you don't know me. Not like that."

He thought of Glory—alone, lost. Not unlike Macy in a lot of ways.

"Maybe I don't. But I know you're strong, and you have a good heart. You're smart and loyal. You didn't ask for this hand to be dealt to you." He saw Macy nod in agreement out of the corner of his eye. "But right now there's a little girl who didn't ask for any of it, either."

Macy parted her lips to speak, but Jack held up a hand. "I don't want to talk about it right now. Even without everything you just told me, I don't blame you for being confused and all sorts of pissed off. Hell, I'm surprised you've held it together as well as you have. But that little girl is the last piece of Nash that any of us have left."

A silence settled over them, not uncomfortable. He could sense Macy relax into the moment. Jack heard the rustle of water, the cry of a gull. Neither of them made a move to go.

Jack broke the quiet first. "I've been pushing you on this," he said, "and I'm sorry. Just think it over; that's all I'm asking."

Macy nodded. Then she said, "Don't be sorry for me. I don't deserve it."

Jack shook his head. He put a hand on her shoulder. "We all deserve it," he said. "Every one of us."

Chapter Seventeen

MACY STARED AT THE CEILING OF HER BEDROOM. THE NUM-
bers on her alarm clock read 5:27.

If she were at Thunderbird Show Park in Langley, where she
should have been right about then, she'd be preparing for the
day—for the chance to make Jump Canada's Talent Squad.
Maybe she'd just be getting to the barn to feed. Maybe she would
have given Gounda his grain and hay already and she'd be sitting
on the tack trunk outside of his stall, zipping on her half chaps
to the melody of his chomping and nose blowing. Or maybe
she'd be waiting for Gounda to finish his breakfast, too nervous
or preoccupied to eat any herself, standing on the hillside overlooking the Grand Prix course, studying the maze of jumps as
the sun inched up.

Whatever she would have been doing, it sure as hell wasn't
this.

But the fracture in her collarbone hadn't yet fully healed, and
Gounda was nowhere near sound enough to ride, much less
compete. And so, she lay there and stared at the wrong ceiling.

Macy knew that sleep had gone for good that morning, so

she maneuvered herself out of bed and began the process of dressing. Pulling on jeans and a T-shirt, and over it a light fleece sweatshirt for good measure, had once been something she did without thinking, almost reflexively. But now, with only one usable arm and one requiring constant vigilance against jostling, getting herself dressed had become something Macy had to diligently strategize: Which jeans had a zipper instead of a button fly? Which shirts were liberally cut or had enough of a stretch to them so as to not require her to lift her bad arm too far from her body, or up in the air? Which fleece was roomy enough to fit over her sling so she wouldn't have to resling her arm after the morning chill burned off and she no longer needed the extra layer?

At the back door, she slipped on the paddock boots that zipped up the front instead of tied, even though they weren't as comfortable. Then she made a quick stop in the barn to ensure all of the horses had water and threw each a flake of hay to tide them over until the morning help got there. Usually she'd muck stalls while the morning help fed, filled water buckets, put fly sheets on, and turned horses out for the day. To her, mucking stalls had the effect that, for most people, coffee produced; she didn't feel centered if the rhythmic repetition of lift, sift, and toss wasn't a part of her day.

Macy left a note that read, "Sorry—useless these days. Hope to have both arms back in working order soon. Please hand-walk Gounda for ten minutes and let him graze a bit. Thanks, Macy." Then she hopped in her truck, felt the engine rumble to life, and started down her driveway.

She could see the lights of Sophie's house glowing through the trees. Not surprising, the old bat was already awake. Macy was sure that no matter what time she woke up, Mama Sophie would have beaten her to it. Hell, half the time Macy couldn't be sure the woman slept at all.

On a whim, Macy turned down Mama Sophie's driveway. She parked in front of the house and jumped out, letting her truck idle. She had stopped knocking on this door long before. Macy turned the knob and walked right in.

Sophie was pouring steaming water from a kettle into a thermos. She already had her yellow rubber bib overalls on. She didn't look up. "What in tarnation are you doing here before six a.m.?" she asked Macy.

"Going to a horse show," Macy said.

Sophie looked at Macy's arm in a sling and then looked out her kitchen window at Macy's truck. "Without a trailer? You tying 'em to the bumper to save money these days, or what?"

Macy chuckled. "No, you crazy coot. I'm going down to Parksville, just to watch for a bit. There's a little show going on there today."

"Can't help but scratch that itch, can you?" Sophie said.

Macy shrugged.

Sophie looked at Macy with narrowed eyes, probably trying to gauge whether Macy was all right. *Good luck*, thought Macy, who could hardly tell herself whether she was coming or going these days. She seemed to float through days at a time on autopilot, or to do things, only to have them register after the fact.

"I'll get there early enough to see the ponies," Macy said.

"Glory would like that." Sophie raised an eyebrow at Macy. She was about to object but Sophie didn't give her a chance. "I'll go ask her what she thinks," Sophie said.

Macy told herself that the girl was probably sleeping, or wouldn't want to head out into the chilly morning so early. But within minutes, Glory appeared in the kitchen, fully dressed and nearly vibrating with energy. She had gone from fast asleep to a hundred miles per hour faster than Macy could usually brush her teeth, though these days even that thoughtless routine was taking her a good long time.

"Where are we going again? Are you showing your horse? Are you sure you want me to come? Are we going to be gone all day? Just me and you?" The girl spewed questions like a busted water main, not allowing any opportunity for Macy to answer.

Finally, she looked up at Macy, who thought right about then that there wasn't enough coffee between them and Parksville—or maybe on the entire island—for her to be ready for that particular morning. The girl's jeans hung from her like off a mannequin, and the sleeves of her shirt nearly covered her tiny hands.

"You have a shirt on under there?" Macy asked her. "It might get hot this afternoon."

"Nope," Glory said, "but I'm always cold. Aren't I, Mama Sophie?"

Macy cast a sideways glance at Sophie, who nodded at her. "That's because there's nothin' to her. Skin and bones. She needs a few pounds on her is all."

Macy waited, thinking that Sophie would grab the girl a short-sleeved shirt. Instead, Sophie tossed Glory her dirty pink jacket. Macy shrugged. "Whatever," she said. "It's your funeral."

She started out the door, only to find Glory stalled behind her. The girl was looking at Macy as though she had suggested roast puppy for dinner.

"What?" Macy said.

"Should you be saying stuff like that?" Glory asked. "You know? Joking about funerals?"

Macy rolled her eyes. "Come on. We're going to be late."

Glory didn't budge. "Aren't you the one who's a big fan of the term 'dirt nap'?" Macy asked.

She must have scored a point, because Glory fell in behind her.

Sophie called for them to have fun, though Macy wasn't quite certain whether "fun" was really the right word for what Sophie had set in motion.

Macy sat on the dusty bleachers of Havenhill Farms watching the short stirrup class. It was a study in miniature—the itty-bitty girls atop their low-to-the-ground ponies, navigating the course of one-and-a-half-foot jumps. A scale model of a normal class.

From her perch, Macy could see the practice ring where girls and a couple of boys of all ages and sizes warmed up their mounts. She had told Nash once that any single guy with two brain cells to rub together should make a practice of scoping out eligible dates at horse shows. For whatever reason, girls tended to outnumber boys by a ratio of roughly ten to one. Nash had agreed that it was, most likely, one of the best-kept secrets from teenage boys everywhere.

A little blur of blond ringlets, toothpick legs, and a pink satin jacket paced outside of the practice area. She had grown bored sitting next to Macy and watching the classes, where only one horse navigated the course at a time, and pointed to the practice ring, saying, "Look! There are six whole horses doing stuff in there. Can't we go and watch them?"

"But they're just practicing, Glory," Macy told her. "This is the real deal, in here." She nodded toward the arena, where a girl who couldn't have been older than six steered a little chestnut pony around like she'd been riding her whole life. Glory told her the "real deal" was boring and she was going for a walk.

Macy had watched her ambling away. She was so tiny. So little. Macy marveled that she had made it from California to this island off the coast of Canada completely on her own. That she had managed to find them all. That the girl existed at all.

You could do this, you know, said a voice in her head. Nash's voice.

At the moment, Glory had moved to the opposite side of the practice ring and was going up to people standing by their horses, presumably asking if she could pet them.

Since she had found the letters, Macy had tested herself, trying to forget that Glory was some other woman's child. She tried thinking of her only as Nash's. And sometimes it wasn't so hard. The nose, the freckles, the smile. Those things did the reminding for her. Besides, Glory wasn't hers. She didn't have her mother's blood or her grandmother's. The girl had been spared all that. And so maybe Nash—Nash's voice in her head—was right. Maybe she *could*.

The little girl on the chestnut pony cleared the final jump and the girl's parents stood to clap. This indicated to the pony, correctly, that it was finished, and it promptly slammed on its brakes. The little girl tumbled onto its neck, then righted herself and nodded at the judge as though nothing had happened. Macy giggled—the girl had such spunk, and at such a young age.

Macy could hear a ruckus behind her, and turned around just in time to see a fully saddled but riderless horse break out of the practice ring at a full gallop and head straight toward Glory.

"Glory, watch out!" Macy yelled, but she didn't know whether Glory could hear her. And once she had jumped down from the bleachers, Macy could see only the top of the girl's head, her tangled ringlets over the ridge separating the practice and show pens. And then she heard a crack as the horse covered the ground where she had last seen Glory.

Oh no oh no oh no oh no. In only seconds, Macy prepared herself for the worst: Glory balled up on the ground, having been run over by four metal-clad hooves attached to a thousand pounds of frantic muscle. Glory bent over from having caught a stray kick to the ribs or, worse yet, the head. Glory with an arm hanging limp at her side, or not attached at all, having been pulled straight out of the socket from trying to reach out and grab the reins of a horse moving at upward of thirty miles an hour.

What she hadn't prepared herself for as she crested the ridge was seeing Glory bounding up the hill that bordered the practice arena after the galloping horse.

"Glo-ry!" Macy called to her.

Macy scrambled up the slope. A few people had made it up from the practice ring and were right behind her in pursuit of the runaway horse, but most were still congregated around the too-still body of the horse's rider, lying prone at the far end of the arena.

"Glory! Glo-ry," Macy called as she ran. She had never been an exerciser and had a brief-but-intense stint as a smoker, and was now paying for both. Her breath came in heaving gasps. "Shit," she muttered. "Shit, shit, shit!" She knew all too well how fickle horses could be, and that the one galloping away from Glory could just as easily spook, change directions, and head back toward her. Loose and scared horses in motion tended not only to stay in motion, but tended also to become increasingly frantic. And Glory didn't have a goddamn clue what she was doing.

In the far-off distance, over the heavy wheeze of her breath, Macy could hear faint sirens making their way down the highway. Good thing, too, given what Macy expected to find at the top of the hill.

What Macy actually found stopped her short.

There stood Glory, with a horse several times her size and the fur of its neck lathered white with sweat, holding the reins and patting its shoulder. Glory, who, as far as Macy knew, grew up, if not smack-dab in LA, then pretty close to it for her whole eight-year life. The closest that little girl had probably ever been to a horse was the kind you dropped a quarter in outside of the grocery store, if those were even still around.

A woman who seemed to know the horse—or at least knew its name: Pim—took the reins from Glory, thanking her, and Macy took the opportunity to grab Glory herself, moving her away from the horse, which was now dancing as a throng of people rushed toward it.

"That was a very brave thing you did," another woman said to Glory, tousling her hair.

"Thank you!" Glory said.

Macy bent down and slung her arm around Glory's shoulders, pulling the girl to her. "You could've been really hurt," Macy said. She held Glory close, and Glory tried to wiggle away from her.

"But I didn't!" Glory beamed, clearly proud of herself.

Macy bent down onto her heels, to Glory's level. "How in the world did you catch him? That horse was going like a bat outta hell, Glory. Weren't you scared?"

A smile crept across her face again. She shook her head. "I gave him grass."

"You did *what*?"

"Like this," she said. She bent down and grabbed two fistfuls of the long grass, pulling it out at the roots, then held it far in front of her. "He stopped and came right over. He seems like a real nice horse."

Macy shook her head. Glory had either never been told she couldn't do something, or she had been and it simply hadn't sunk in. Take a bus across three states and into another country? Sure! Worm her way into a family she didn't know and who didn't know her? No problem! Tame a runaway horse? Might as well give that a whirl, too.

"How did you know to do that?"

Glory shrugged. "Dunno. I think I saw it in a movie once. I guess it works in real life, too. Do you think I was brave?"

Right as Macy was about to answer, she heard a woman behind her say, "Whose kid is that anyway?" The question was not kind or curiously inquisitive. It was angry and hunting for a target.

Macy turned and drew Glory to her. The woman asking was a backyard trainer named Patricia Knettles, and as long as Macy had known her, she hadn't ever not been a pain in the ass. You could count on Patty Knettles to be the first one to stick her nose where it didn't belong, and the last one ever to offer help.

"She's mine," Macy said.

Patty Knettles looked Glory up and down, and then looked at Macy. Her face twisted into a look that could only be interpreted as, "Yeah, right."

"Maybe you'd like to keep an eye on her, then, instead of letting her wander around here and almost get herself killed," Patty said.

Macy felt her face flush hot. She wanted to lob a barb back at Patty, but the only words she could conjure were: *You're right—this was probably a mistake.* So Macy grabbed Glory's arm and marched away. And as she walked, she heard bits and pieces of the exchange between the gaggle of women who had gathered: "Irresponsible," "She was always a little flighty," "Kids can't be expected to babysit themselves."

Some people just shouldn't be parents.

Macy couldn't be sure if it was one of the women who had said that, her mother-in-law's voice in her head, or Macy herself.

Glory jogged to keep up with Macy.

"Do you know anyone here who's going to ride soon?" the girl asked. "There are some really cool horses. I met one named Midnight—because he's black—and Apollo, and Cadbury, and a short one that was my size named Peanut Butter because that's what color he was, too. Oh, and Pim. I guess I met Pim, too, but I didn't know his name when I caught him. He's a nice horse, isn't he? He sure seems like it."

Oh, dear God, Macy thought. There was, without a doubt, some deity sitting on a mountaintop or cloud looking down at her and laughing its ass off right now. Macy shot a middle finger toward the sky.

"What'd ya do that for? Were you flipping *me* off? Because that's not a nice thing to—"

"For crying out loud, Glory. I was not flipping you off. I'm just not having—" Macy was going to say that she wasn't having the best day—or week, or life, for that matter—at the moment. But she realized just in time that that would have elicited another *why* from Glory, and that answer would have elicited a *why* as well, and on and on, until Macy had talked herself right to death at the girl's urging. So instead, she said, "Can we just both be quiet for a bit?"

"Are you mad at me?"

"No," Macy said. "I just don't feel like talking right now."

"That's fine. My mom says that a lot, too. Only she says would I just shut up already or asks if I ever shut up. So then I usually leave and go down the street to find my friend Jilly, and we'll go—"

"Glory?"

"Yeah?"

"Shhhh."

"Oh, okay. Sorry."

Glory was walking with her right arm raised straight up in the air. A few people were staring at her. At them. *Someone just kill me now*, Macy thought.

"Glory, what are you doing?"

"I need to tell you something."

"Well, just tell me then."

"But you said not to talk. So I'm raising my hand. That's what we do in class when—"

"Glory!"

"Fine." She sulked, her shoulders drooping. At least she had put her arm down, but the girl's instant deflation made Macy feel bad for snapping at her. Glory stared at the concession stand, which they had just walked past. "I'm hungry," she said, so softly that Macy almost had to ask her to repeat herself.

"That's fine," Macy said. She stopped and waited, motioning for Glory to go back to the food stand.

Glory hung her head. "But I don't have any money," she said, staring at the ground.

Macy chastised herself for making Glory admit to that. The girl was all of eight years old—of course she didn't have any money. What was Macy thinking, inviting her along and then making her grovel for a handout? Why hadn't she thought of feeding her earlier? Just because Macy could subsist on nothing but coffee until late afternoon didn't mean that was any kind of nutritional schedule for a little kid. Macy fished three loonies from her pocket and deposited them into Glory's hand. "Now you do," she told her. "Pick out whatever you want."

"Anything?" Glory asked, staring at the coins in her hand and then up at Macy.

"Absolutely," Macy said. "If you need more money, just wave me over. I'll wait here." She pointed to a bench.

Glory came back with a hot dog, a bag of Skittles, and a Mountain Dew. Macy thought they'd both probably regret this combination in the near future, but if the girl could get herself all the way from California to Vancouver Island unsupervised, who was Macy to stand in the way of a good sugar binge?

They settled themselves back on the bleachers overlooking the show ring. The children's hunter class was in—riders fourteen to eighteen years old. A short, stout blond girl on a seal brown horse with three white pasterns—two in front, one in back—and a pencil-thin blaze the shape of a lightning bolt on its face glided through the course as if floating. You couldn't see any of the girl's cues to the horse. The horse never hesitated, or at least that was hidden from view, too. It was effortless, their union whole and complete.

It was Macy's favorite class to watch. The girls—and a smattering of boys—were so young, yet so poised and accomplished already. They all had the whole world ahead of them. Macy felt as if she were a banjo being plucked—strings of envy, nostalgia, and wistfulness reverberating inside her.

She remembered being the age of the girls riding in this division. Knowing everything. So self-assured and confident that she could steer not only her horses, but also her life, to the exact destination she chose. Only somewhere along the line things had veered far off course. Even if shown a map of her life now, she'd hardly recognize the place she had ended up. The funny thing was, this—the girl on the seal brown horse, the dusty weekend shows, the sheer promise of what waited on the other side of next week, next year—it didn't feel as far behind Macy as she knew it was. Did it feel like this to be seventy, eighty, or ninety, too? To know you had more of your life behind you than in front of you, yet still feel like twenty was a bit past, like a shadow instead of a far-off memory?

The stout girl on the seal brown horse pulled it to a walk after the last fence and leaned forward to scratch its neck. It was such an intimate gesture. Most people lightly slapped their horses' necks in an attempt to convey that it had done a good job, when in fact the slapping made most horses more anxious. But the scratching—that told Macy that this girl was serious about her horses, and this horse in particular. She had gotten to know her mount, and he her, in a way that went far beyond winning. Macy clapped and whistled for the girl, having no clue who she was.

"He's *so* pretty," Glory whispered. In her voice Macy recognized a familiar note of longing. It was the same one she had felt at Glory's age. When her dad would tell Macy and Regan to pick whatever treat they wanted (within reason) in exchange for helping him out with whatever needed doing around the house, Regan would pick ice cream or a movie or riding go-carts; Macy would ask her dad to take her to feed apples to Bucky, the old Appaloosa that lived down the road. Every single time. "Bucky is the prettiest horse in the world," she would tell her dad, in awe of Bucky's baby pink muzzle, his strong neck, his broad back. Years and years later, cleaning out her dad's desk drawer after he had died, she had found a picture of her petting Bucky through the fence and realized that he wasn't at all attractive as far as horses went. He was swaybacked and overweight, and his wispy suggestions of a mane and tail put him squarely on the equine chemotherapy-patient side of the spectrum. He was, for all practical purposes of comparison, the direct opposite of Black Beauty. Macy had always chosen to picture the Bucky of her childhood memories.

"They're like, like . . . magic," Glory said out loud, but not really to Macy.

"They are," Macy whispered back.

Glory turned to Macy, and something in her movement— the way her chin jutted out toward the person she was about to address, or the slight squint of her eyes, or the way she smiled as if she already knew she had an answer for the question she was about to ask—was as if Nash were sitting there right beside her. It almost made Macy want to reach out and touch her cheek, just to make sure.

Then, like a wave, the girl transformed into looking every bit like Glory's mom, with her smug smile and almond eyes and petite wrists and collarbones.

Glory was as much her mom as she was Nash, if not more. No, worse. She was the exact combination of the two of them: of that woman and a husband Macy no longer had any idea whether she had ever really known. Macy saw that clearly, in a flash, in a way she hadn't all day long.

"Do you think you could teach me? To, you know, ride and stuff?" Glory asked. Her wide eyes fixed on Macy, as if this were the best idea she'd had yet in her short, young life. It was the same exact look Glory's mother had given Nash's camera— Nash—in the photograph on the beach.

Macy thought about the words Nash himself had written: *My California girl.* She thought of him bending down to kiss Kat's upturned face after taking her picture. Him whispering those words. Him running his hands under her sweatshirt—*his* favorite UW sweatshirt. On Kat.

Macy looked at Glory's eyes. She wanted to say yes. She did. But she couldn't. Macy shook her head. And she watched the horse-filled world that Glory had conjured for herself disintegrate in them as Macy uttered one simple syllable: "No."

The hell of it was, she would have loved nothing better than to open up the world of horses to a little girl exactly like she'd once been. She just preferred to do it for one who didn't have Nash's eyes. Or Kat's. One who didn't need a mother right about then.

"I'm sorry," she told Glory. "I can't."

Chapter Eighteen

JACK BEGAN HIS DAY ON THE DECK OF HIS BOAT SITTING IN A rocking chair he had found at a rummage sale the week before, breathing in the summer island air that now had a bit of a bite to it, that now whispered of fall. Back and forth. Forward and backward. One big toe providing all the push necessary to keep the motion fluid, the movement of the water rocking him the other way.

He began his day like that—on the boat, his heart sitting heavy with anticipation in his chest. And then, later, nearly skipping out of the office of Carl Vicker, barrister and solicitor, after being told that his chances of adopting Glory looked "excellent." The Ministry of Children and Family Development would have to do a home visit, and they'd need to get a landing visa for Glory, and immigration might ask for presumption of paternity—all of which conjured in Jack's mind a mountain of paper tied up in a bow of red tape—but Vicker seemed certain that none of those requirements should pose a problem. Jack could hardly believe it was going to work out so smoothly.

He began his day like that, and he ended it, or almost ended

it, after eleven o'clock that same night by practically stealing Sophie's car (she had accepted a last-minute guiding trip, and
Macy and Martine had gone to Victoria to look at a horse) and
driving to the Fanny Bay Inn—or the FBI, as everyone called
it—after receiving a phone call from a trucker named Body who
said he'd picked up Glory somewhere outside Parksville and finally convinced the girl to give him a phone number. He bought
Glory a hamburger with extra pickles and a Mountain Dew, and
waited with her until Jack could meet them at the pub.

On the way home, the road stretched out in front of them
like a black velvet ribbon. Jack cursed the headlights on Sophie's
old station wagon, which were too weak a match for the black
night that had settled around them. Glory sat stoically in the
passenger seat, pressed hard against the door.

"Honey, I wish you wouldn't do that. At least lock the door,"
he said. He wondered if she should even be riding in the front
seat at her age. Weren't there all sorts of laws about that sort of
thing? He quickly reconsidered. Where Glory rode in the car
was the least of the things he should have been worrying about.

Glory didn't budge from the door. She didn't lock it, as he
had asked.

"Lock the door, Glory. Please."

She looked at him and turned away, staring out the window.

"You want to tell me what happened?" Jack asked her, but not
softly.

They were almost home and a mutual haze of something
close to anger had settled inside the car. Jack could almost see it
wafting in the air.

Glory shook her head.

"That's fine. Fine," he said, though the tone of his voice communicated the opposite. "But we've been good to you, and I

think you owe us the respect of telling us what's going on instead of just up and leaving. You can't run away every time something goes wrong."

Jack knew he wasn't talking like he should to an eight-year-old, that he was talking to her like he'd talk to the guys on his staff, but he was out of practice with kids.

"Who's 'we'? You have a mouse in your pocket?" Glory didn't turn to look at him. She stared intently out the passenger-side window instead.

"'We' as in Sophie and Macy and me."

"Hrumph," said Glory.

Jack had slowed down to ease into the long, winding driveway leading to Sophie's house. That was right about when Glory nearly startled Jack off the road by wailing, "Nobody wants me!" before bursting into body-racking sobs. Jack pulled to the road's edge and threw the wagon into park. He took Glory's chin between his thumb and forefinger and said, "You stop that right now. You know there's not a shred of truth to what you just said."

But he didn't sound convincing, because it was true, or at least partially true. Macy? Well, she'd made her feelings well-known. Sophie loved Glory and spoiled her rotten, but she had an unpredictable life, a business that didn't and couldn't revolve around the girl; when a guiding opportunity called, Sophie went. As she should. And Jack? He wanted Glory more than anything, but was it really the right thing to do by her? To bring her into this shim-sham family they had set up here, together barely forming a whole?

"What happened, Glory? Go ahead and tell me. Everything was fine last night."

"No, it *wasn't*," Glory wailed.

"You've got to try to tell me where you're coming from. I can't read your mind." *Throw me a bone here, kid.*

Glory brought her face inside her shirt and swiped at her eyes and nose. "I told you," she said. "No one wants me."

"I want you," Jack said, nice and quiet. "And so does Sophie. She loves you to pieces."

"And what about *her*?" Glory asked. Her eyes were steely as she locked them on Jack. She had stopped sobbing as quickly as she had started. "She won't even teach me to ride."

"Oh, Glory, honey—"

"This wasn't how it was supposed to be. My dad was supposed to be here!" And then it started again. It was like the girl had an internal faucet that she could turn on or off at whim. Glory started hiccuping, her body jumping with each quick breath. She raised her fists, which looked like hammerheads at the end of her spindly arms, and began flailing them against the dashboard. The sound of bone against the unyielding plastic of the dash filled the inside of the wagon and stunned Jack into action.

"I miss my mom!" Glory screamed. "I want to go home! I want my mom!"

Jack reached out and threw his arms around Glory's wild ones, pulling the girl close and holding her so tight that he worried Glory might not be able to breathe. But she was still hiccuping now and then, her doll head pressed tight to Jack's chest.

"*Shhhh,*" Jack soothed. "It's going to be all right. Don't you worry."

But he wasn't sure whom it would be all right for. His heart nearly broke at the thought that the one thing that might torpedo the plan to keep Glory with him would be Glory herself.

· · ·

It might have been the fact that Sophie's house had been shut up tight all day while she was up north guiding and Jack was searching for Glory, or maybe that the weather front that had felt like the end of summer for a week or so was simply a teaser. Maybe he had become acclimated to being rocked to sleep by the soft sway of his boat. In any case, Jack couldn't get comfortable. He tossed and rolled and turned on the couch, but the heavy-wet air that settled all around him wouldn't budge. So he got up, poured himself a finger of the bourbon Sophie kept in the cabinet above her refrigerator, and wandered out to the sunporch—Glory's room, for now—to check on the girl.

Beads of sweat stood like Braille on Glory's forehead. It made Jack uncomfortable, knowing how muggy he himself felt. He cracked the farthest window from Glory's bed, then decided that the long-sleeved shirt the girl had on was probably a worse culprit. He rummaged through the two laundry baskets of secondhand clothes they had scrounged up at the foot of Glory's bed, which was really a roll-away cot, to find something with short sleeves. Jack knew Glory was exhausted—she had fallen asleep in his arms in the station wagon—and knew he didn't need to worry about waking her.

He was right about that. Jack changed Glory's shirt without so much as a night whimper escaping from her. But as he eased her back down onto the bed, he saw something that almost stopped his heart.

The biggest part of Glory's arms was her elbows, which joined the bones above and below them at severe, odd angles. Those bones were covered with the softest, most translucent skin, marred by gashes in various stages of healing—from old scars to flame red ridges that looked like they might break back open at any minute.

Jack gasped. He felt the room start to teeter and spin. She was just a little girl. An itty-bitty little girl. Who could do something like that to her? Torture her like that? What kind of monster? Her mother? Could a mother really do something like that to her own child? Or was her mother's boyfriend to blame? Was that the real reason Glory had braved so much to get to them? Had some guy abused her in other ways, too? Was this simply the physical manifestation of all Glory's mental or emotional scars that she seemed to have hidden so well? Was he prepared to deal with all of this?

Jack wasn't sure. But he sure as hell could use a little help figuring it out.

He lowered himself to the foot of Glory's bed, staring at the girl's mutilated arms. Black specks danced in front of his eyes. His breath skipped like pebbles.

He didn't know what to do, or what to think. Sophie would. She was sensible like that. But she was also far up-island, guiding, out of reach of cell phone service.

Could he ask Macy? Would she come?

She picked up on the fifth ring, her voice groggy. Perhaps the notes of panic in Jack's voice that he didn't try to hide had roused her, because she said she'd be over in five, and hung up.

Jack led Macy to the sunporch, to the edge of Glory's bed, rolled Glory onto her back, and held out the girl's left arm.

"Do you see?" he asked her.

Macy covered her mouth with an open hand. "Oh, God," she said. "Good God."

"Do you see it?" he asked her again.

Instead of answering, Macy knelt beside Glory's bed. "Can I touch her?" she asked.

Jack nodded. "She's out cold." Macy took Glory's arm in one hand, and lightly brushed the other over Glory's ravaged skin.

"I don't know what to make of it, Macy," said Jack. "I mean, what the hell?"

Macy swabbed at her face with the back of her hand. "I used to do this," she said.

"Do what?" Jack didn't have to ask, really. He knew, in his head, that no one else had carved up Glory's arms. But it was just all so god-awful that he couldn't make himself actually believe it. She was *eight*. Only eight years old. Jack pressed his fingertips to his eyelids, feeling the subtle pulse behind each one.

Macy continued brushing her hand back and forth over Glory's arm as if trying to erase the marks.

She stood up and made her way to the steps leading to the house. She motioned for Jack to sit down next to her. Macy told him then, in a whisper, what she had never told anyone—the full story of how it had all started. And she started at the beginning, on that Christmas Eve, just before her dad found them—she and her mother in the bathroom—when Macy's mum had opened her eyes, looked straight at Macy like she wanted so badly to say something, and then closed them. For good.

After that, Macy told him how she took to practicing so she wouldn't be her mother and let Death in on the first knock. She'd make him wait on the stoop until she was good and goddamned ready to open that door. He'd come in on her terms, not by accident.

She had started with her stomach, she recounted calmly. It seemed the easiest—soft and fleshy—and the safest. Nothing vital near the surface that she could accidentally nick.

She described how the little beads of blood that rose to the surface of the cut soothed her. That there was a well of crimson within her, and that she could control its flow fascinated her. That she loved how she could control how and where and how much blood she let see the light of day, or the thin skin of night. She told Jack about how she would place her index finger across the cut, hold for a few seconds, and then raise her finger to her lips. No nightmares, no worrying about being chunky or unpopular or latent-crazy. No thoughts to torment her when she was alone. Just her and a tiny bit of steel. It was almost too simple.

Even better, she said, was the way her wounds bristled against the waistband of her jeans, the buttons of her shirts. The way she endured the stings straight-faced through biology and geometry and English. It made her feel real, alive. She told him that at first it wasn't a frequent thing, but when one cut would start to heal, when it just itched instead of hurt, she'd reopen it, or sometimes make a new one altogether.

He raised his hand to stop her. He had heard enough. But she didn't take the cue. She went on, to the time when, years later, she started sneaking into an abandoned orphanage to entertain boys after school, and right about then she had to switch to her arms and the flesh of her inner thighs; and a year or so after that, when she started to sneak into local bars to pick up unhappily married men, she switched to the undersides of her arms. "Boys and men notice a woman's torso under their hands, but the undersides of their arms they can do without," Macy said.

The men would run their hands down her arms, pinning her wrists to whatever she happened to be lying on—bed, floor, pool table in the back bar—and if they bothered to ask what had happened she'd say, "Barbed wire."

"By that time, it didn't seem like such a lie," Macy said.

Jack's head felt like it had been whipped with electric beaters. Why would anyone do such a thing—on purpose? To themselves?

"Do you . . . still . . . you know?" he asked, his voice shaking.

"Cut?" Macy asked. "No. I stopped. Nash caught me once. The look on his face—I couldn't after that."

"But why?" Jack asked, shaking his head. "I just—I don't get it." Though it dawned on him then that he hadn't seen Glory in short sleeves since she arrived.

Glory stirred in her sleep and Macy moved toward her. She lowered her voice to a weak whisper. "Believe it or not," she said, "it makes the hurt go away."

Jack covered his mouth with the back of his hand. He bit a knuckle. He hauled himself up the half step leading to the living room, turned, and sat down.

"Every time I look at her," Macy said, "all I see is Nash fucking someone else. Like I never even knew him."

Jack shook his head. "You did. You knew him like I did."

"And how was that?" Macy asked. She lowered herself to her knees, leaning against Glory's cot.

"The best we could," he said. "We all did the best we could."

They sat in silence, watching the rise and fall of Glory's rib cage.

"Do you really believe that?" Macy asked after a while.

"I do," Jack said. And he did.

Glory stirred. Her eyes lolled open. "Wha's going on?" she asked, still mostly asleep.

"Your grandpa and I are just talking and waiting for Sophie," Macy whispered to her. "Go back to sleep."

Glory nodded and closed her eyes, but then they popped back open. She seemed to realize, too late, that her arms lay on top of the bedding, exposed. She pulled them back under the sheet, her eyes darting from Jack to Macy and back. Glory bit her lip, as if she were bracing herself for the lecture that would surely follow.

But Macy didn't say a word. Instead, she reached out to stroke the girl's forehead with her left hand, and with the right, she reached under the sheet and freed Glory's scarred arm, setting it back on top. She traced a finger over the mangled flesh, then bent down and kissed the gouges carved raw and bloody into Glory's skin. She let her lips linger there.

"What are you doing?" Glory asked. She didn't pull her arm away, but looked wholly confused.

"Didn't your mom ever do this for you?"

Glory shook her head.

Macy brought her lips once more to the girl's scarred arm. "I'm making it all better," she said.

Chapter Nineteen

MAGDA MADE CERTAIN HER WINDOWS WERE ROLLED DOWN BE-fore putting the car in drive. She had heard about a tragedy years ago when a car ferry in Vancouver—or was it Seattle?—pulled away from the dock as it was unloading and cars trying to make their way to dry land instead found themselves plummeting into the icy North Pacific. The news coverage following the disaster had said that a lot of people would've been saved if they had just been able to roll their windows down. So now, every time she was over water, Magda dutifully made sure to do just that.

But this was Vancouver Island in late August, and the acrid mix of dead fish and seawater and something else equally offensive—barnacles, maybe?—mixed into an aroma that stung her nose. She hated the way this place smelled, and as soon as she felt the tires of her rented Chevy Malibu touch asphalt, the windows went up and she switched the air-conditioning on.

She inched along in the line of cars making its way out of the ferry lot and pushed buttons on the radio, trying to find a station. Magda stopped fiddling with it as she eased her car onto the Old Island Highway, the sight of which made her suck her breath in hard. There was the gourmet kitchen store where Nash had bought her a sushi-making kit, plates, and fancy chopsticks for her birthday during their last visit. Sushi was the thing to eat out here, the thing to do. Everyone seemed to make their own. And Magda didn't mind sushi itself. But she couldn't deal with preparing the raw fish. She had tried once, but the slimy, smelly salmon had made her gag. And gagging was not exactly an appetizing response to the dinner one might be trying to make. So she had tucked the mat and fancy chopsticks and plates into the cluttered cabinet above her refrigerator—the place where once-good-idea kitchen gadgets and gaudy nonregiftable platters went to die in their house. And she lied to Nash each time he asked how she was enjoying her sushi set and whether she had made any for Ginny and Frank yet.

And there was the little bakery where Nash had first introduced her and Jack to Nanaimo bars. Macy had been away at a horse show for the weekend, and it was just her little family together. They had gone shopping for a tent for Nash at Canadian Tire, and then to the Ironwood Mall for eggs, bacon, bread, and feta cheese for that evening's meal. On the way out, Nash had suggested they get some Chinese food from the deli (it was his favorite, although Magda couldn't quite understand why—Chinese food from a grocery store!), and they parked at the marina, staked out a spot on the docks, and had an impromptu picnic. Afterward, on the way back home, Nash had convinced them that they absolutely *had* to try a Nanaimo bar. "Even you, Ma," he had said. "And you're getting your own." Magda tended not to order dinner—less guilt and, ideally, calories. She'd make do with a side salad and satisfy herself with bites from Nash's and Jack's plates. She hadn't realized, until that point, that anyone had noticed her little trick.

"What the heck!" she remembered saying, as she took in the trays of bars striped mocha and white. The simple smell of the bars' vanilla custard, coconut, and chocolate had been sweet enough to pang her teeth. "After all that MSG, why not?"

Nash had thrown an arm around her then, and kissed her on the cheek.

Even though the drive home was a good twenty minutes or so, by the time they had reached Nash and Macy's house, none of them had managed to put away a whole Nanaimo bar. Magda herself had conceded defeat not even halfway through. She was sure she had never tasted anything quite so sweet. Each bite literally hurt her teeth to the point where she thought they might melt from the sugar.

Now she was passing the condo that Nash and Macy had bought as an investment property. Nash had taken out the worn gray carpeting, put in new bamboo floors, painted the bedroom a blue reminiscent of the ocean it overlooked on sunny days. He'd tiled the modest bathroom and put a colorful mosaic backsplash in the kitchen. He sanded and repainted the porch railings a brilliant white, and replaced the vertical railing supports with Plexiglas, common in homes and condos with ocean views in Campbell River. Every week, he would send Magda and Jack pictures of his progress, always so proud of his handiwork.

Once, Macy had called the condo a money pit. Magda had told her that she thought the pictures looked lovely and that she and Jack were throwing around the idea of buying it from them, retiring in Campbell River. That had shut her up about the condo. Magda had only been half kidding.

She drove past the wood carvings that dotted the bike trail running along the Old Island Highway—a pelican with sunglasses reclining on a bench, an old man of the sea with a wild beard and fish that seemed to swim in and out of its tendrils, a totem of wolves, a giant eagle holding what she assumed was a salmon in its talons. Some she recognized from years past, their crevasses darkened with salt, wind, and rain. Some held the pale glow of having just been carved at that year's competition.

She passed Willow Point, where she used to ride with Nash to rent movies, and Stories Beach, where they all went swimming (or in her case, wading) one hot day and lit a fire to cook out over afterward.

In her head Magda knew Nash wasn't there, but she still felt her eyes scanning the beaches on her left, and the parking lots, yards, and garages on her right. She felt him here.

Magda had forgotten to map her route, but she seemed to be instinctively feeling her way along. Perhaps that was giving herself a little too much credit. After all, the two main roads in Campbell River—the Old Island Highway and the New Island Highway—routes 19 and 19A, respectively—were about the only way one could go south out of town. She had a fifty-fifty chance of getting it right.

By the time Magda turned onto Galley Road—a long, winding dirt road that eventually ended at Macy's modest ranch home, which seemed out of place next to the immense, immaculate barn that shared the property—the spotty radio signal she had picked up in town had faded, as had that day's sun.

Magda fiddled with the radio for a second too long and looked up to see a flash of blond curls and pink just off the driver's side. She veered sharply to the right, coming to rest just inches from a post-and-rail fence that contained four wild-eyed mother horses with babies that were running away from her car as fast as their spindly legs would take them, tails straight in the air like little flags.

Magda turned to find a girl with blond ringlets and jeans with dirt-stained knees standing right where she had veered off, waving her arms wildly.

"Jesus! Watch where you're going, you crazy ol' coot!" the girl yelled at her.

But by the time Magda had found the locks (they were manual—something she hadn't seen in quite some time), gotten the door open, and gotten herself out of the car, the girl was gone. A little flash of white and blond disappearing into the thick woods on the opposite side of the road.

Magda leaned herself up against the rental, still nose-down in the shallow ditch. The horses that had previously run in fear for their lives—and, more specifically, in fear of Magda coming straight through the fence at them (a distinct fear of hers in that split second as well, if she were to be honest)—had seemingly gained confidence and were walking en masse back toward her. Their put-on bravery was betrayed only by their loud snorting and halting steps.

Magda had never understood horses. In addition to their being dirty, she found them to be completely unreasonable. In the time she had spent in their company, mostly thanks to Macy, she had seen horses scared to bits over a blowing leaf, a running child, and a waving hand, respectively. Not to mention that their physical makeup itself unnerved her—all that weight and girth on little sticklike legs. It was unnatural at best. Like a sumo wrestler's body atop Paris Hilton's legs. Then God the Creator thought to supersize all those attributes and pair them with a brain the size of a walnut? Usually in awe of all God's creations and creativity, Magda thought that maybe, when it came to the horse, God might've just been having a really, really off day.

And so, it appeared, was she.

Upon inspection of her rental car, she found one long, deep gouge running alongside the passenger-side door, seemingly from a hearty bush located a few feet off the road. And then, when attempting to back out of the ditch, she perhaps used just a wee bit too much force on the gas and bottomed the little car out, snapping something near the rear. The muffler, perhaps? She had no real idea what else might be in danger of coming off on the back end of a car, but it was now too dark to stop and try to figure out what, exactly, that sound could be. So she just shifted into drive and continued up the road, albeit more slowly this time.

Macy and Nash's house was lit from within, and she could see a shadow moving back and forth past the windows. She could tell it was Macy. The shadow had her height and stature, with hair pulled back into a messy ponytail, as Macy was prone to do. And Magda caught herself, just a second too late, searching for another, bigger and beefier shadow floating beside Macy.

Magda hadn't thought this through very well. When she had told Jack she wanted to come and meet her granddaughter, she had imagined only how the girl might run up and throw her arms around Magda, or how much she might look like Nash, or even herself and Jack. She had looked forward to burying her nose in the girl's hair and knowing, intimately, what it smelled like, to buying her books and clothes and ice cream. To taking long walks and talks together on the beach, and to taking her for what would probably be her very first pedicure.

What she had not pictured was the rest of it. Having to greet Macy at the door after their last disastrous conversation, what she'd say—what they might both say. She hadn't pictured a scenario in which Jack wasn't there when she arrived, when she'd have to sit in awkward silence at Macy's kitchen table waiting for him to return from an errand or fishing trip. She hadn't pictured having to walk up a dark sidewalk with legs wobbling as they were now. She certainly hadn't pictured all of the ways in which this surprise visit could go horribly wrong.

But she was here, and she wasn't about to turn around and leave. So Magda raised her fist to the door, took a deep breath, and decided that it was all too late to worry about any of that now.

And there, standing in a slice of light from the now-open door, was the same little girl she had nearly run over. Her granddaughter.

She heard Macy's voice call out, "Who is it?"

"Worst driver in the entire *world*," the girl yelled back, leaving the door ajar as she turned and walked away from it.

Magda stood for a moment, contemplating whether she should follow the girl into the house, or knock again. But before she could decide, Macy stood cross-armed in front of her.

"Well, well," Macy said. "Welcome. We thought you'd be here tomorrow."

Magda couldn't have felt more unwelcome.

Macy was already on her way back toward the kitchen. Magda pulled herself up straight and followed.

Even though her eyes were slow to adjust after being thrust from near-darkness into the bright light of Macy's kitchen, she could clearly see that Jack was not there. Dishes were stacked near the sink. A Tupperware container filled with hunks of steak sat near the refrigerator. A bowl held a wilted-looking salad, half gone. And there was the little girl, sitting at a stool at the island and swinging one leg faster than necessary. But no Jack.

Magda could have kicked herself for catching that night's ferry instead of laying over in Vancouver, as she had planned. She wished she'd called ahead.

"So, Magda. Nice surprise, you coming to visit, too." It wasn't a question. It was a statement. One delivered with edge.

She had always wished that she could be in control with Macy. Be firm with her. And sometimes she could pull it off. Other times, like now, she'd be remiss for not admitting that Macy could be a little intimidating.

"I talked to Jack about it," Magda said. "I assumed he would fill you in."

"Oh, he did," Macy said.

Macy had been wiping dishes dry and tossed the towel onto the counter. She went to work putting the stacked dishes away, leaving Magda standing in a silence that was almost as uncomfortable as their conversation.

"And who is this lovely young lady?" Magda asked, bending at the waist with hands folded between her legs, even though the girl was on a stool and approximately on Magda's level, and even though Magda knew who she was. She didn't want to spook Glory by springing on her that she had yet another relative.

Glory rolled her eyes. "Glo-ry," she said, drawing her name out into two very distinct syllables, as if Magda were hard of hearing, or slow.

Magda fought the urge to roll her eyes in return. The girl needed to learn some manners.

A slow, smug smile crossed Macy's face. "Glory," she said, "meet your grandmother."

"This crazy ol' coot is my *grandma*?"

Magda fixed Macy with a steely look. She had allowed the girl to become practically feral, running in front of cars and talking that way to adults.

"She's Nash's daughter," Macy said. "Not mine. You can be mad at him." She laughed.

Magda didn't see what was so funny. But right then—in the way that the girl jumped down off the stool, wandered to the kitchen table, inspected a peach sitting in a bowl of fruit at the center, and put it back—she saw it. Or, rather, she saw Nash. Magda drew her fingertips to her lips, palm toward her face. Her mouth made the shape of an "O," but no sound escaped.

"Glory, why don't you show your grandmom to the back porch. I think she'd probably like to talk to Jack."

"Right this way," Glory said, a miniature maître d', motioning for Magda to follow her.

It wasn't Magda's first time in the house, and the house wasn't big enough to warrant a guide even if it had been. But she dutifully followed Glory.

As Glory slid aside the glass door and waved Magda through, things snapped into focus. In an instant she took it all in, even as her eyes were adjusting. The cigar. The laughter. The woman sitting precariously close to Jack. Her hand on his knee.

"Magda?"

Before Magda could take a closer look—make sure she really had seen what she thought she had—Jack stood up.

"Magda? You weren't supposed to be here until tomorrow."

Magda saw the woman, whose hand had been resting on Jack's knee, look from Jack to Magda and back to Jack. Then the woman put both hands on Glory's shoulders and pushed her toward the door. "Let's get you in a bath and to bed, little one," she said.

Glory protested, but the woman's hands were fast and firm on Magda's granddaughter's shoulders, and soon it was just Magda and Jack on the porch.

"My flight was early, of all things. I made the last ferry. I—I didn't want to bother anyone having to come and get me. Or . . . interrupt anything."

Jack motioned for Magda to sit across from him. It didn't escape her that there was plenty of room right next to him, where that other woman had been sitting moments before.

Magda stood where she was. "Maybe this wasn't such a great idea," she said. She felt on the verge of losing her composure.

Jack laughed. "Magda, you haven't 'interrupted' anything."

She let out a deep breath.

"Listen. It's just that . . . Look, I'm glad you're here. I am. And I'm glad we're going to have a chance to spend some time with Glory and to sit down and chat some. But"—he raised a nearly empty rocks glass in his hand and shook it—"I'm afraid I've probably had one too many of these tonight. And it's getting late and I'm tired. Tomorrow's just as good a time as any to say whatever needs saying, or do whatever needs doing."

She just nodded, staring down at her hands clasped tight in her lap.

"Where are you staying?"

"I—" She looked up at Jack, surprised. "I don't know."

"You don't have a reservation anywhere?"

"No. I was hoping that I—I mean, that we—that I could, you know, stay with you, maybe." She was talking to her husband of forty years, and felt as though she were propositioning a one-night stand. An intimacy that had taken decades to develop had disappeared so quickly.

"Sorry, sweet cheeks," Jack said. "That's not going to work."

Magda's face flushed red and hot in the dark. "Because of . . ." Magda looked in the direction the woman had gone. Jack followed her gaze.

"No, Magda. Because I'm living on a boat, and it's pretty tight quarters."

"A *boat*? But why? What kind of boat? Whose is it? Where?"

"It's a sailboat. It's mine. And right now, she's docked in a marina down the road from here."

"She?" Magda said. "Oh, my."

Jack mistook her befuddlement for wonder. "Wait till you see her. She's a real beauty. Be-a-u-ty!"

"Uh-huh," Magda said.

"How about this: There's a little B and B between here and the marina. They still had a vacancy sign out when I headed here for dinner. How about I drop you off there, we'll both get a good night's sleep, and then I'll pick you up for lunch tomorrow, just the two of us. Then we can pick up Glory and cart her around for the afternoon."

"But I have a car here," Magda said.

"Well, you can follow me to the B and B, then. We'll get you settled in, and the rest of the offer stands as is. Whaddaya say?"

Magda nodded and stood.

They said good night to Macy and started down the front walkway. Just before they reached their cars, Magda said, "So, Glory?"

"Oh, she's something, isn't she? Just wait until you get to know her, Magda. She is one amazing little girl."

"So it's for real? You're sure?"

"It's for real, all right. Didn't you see her? That little blond-haired spitfire is our flesh and blood. How do you like that?"

Magda fished the keys from her purse, unlocked the driver's-side door, and stopped.

"I'm still figuring it all out," she said.

"Do you have another location—one on the water?" Magda asked the man behind the counter.

"No."

He was counting change into the till and hadn't even looked up at her.

"Excuse me," Magda said, waving at him in an attempt to draw his gaze. "Excuse me, but are you certain?"

"Yes."

"Well, my husband asked me to meet him here—at Duke's, the fish place. But he said it was on the water."

"Lady," the man said, finally pausing to look up at her, "this is a fish place, but we're clearly not on the water. We're in a strip mall. Maybe you're looking for Dick's? That's a fish place, and it's on the water."

"No, he said Duke's," Magda said, as if she had something to prove to this man who had met her gaze only once.

Jack had called her earlier and said that something had come up. He'd asked her if she didn't mind just driving herself to lunch. She told him no, that she'd be happy to meet him. Truth was, she did mind. Not the driving itself. It was a straight shot down the Old Island Highway into town, after all. But she minded what it seemed to signify, having to drive herself. His not picking her up as he had said he would.

She could have sworn that Jack had said to meet him at Duke's. By the time Magda picked her way across the street and down the path leading toward Dick's, she was hopping mad. The little detour to Duke's had made her nearly ten minutes late. And she hated to be late. Even more, she hated to be wrong. And much more than that, she hated having to concede she was wrong even when she was clearly right, as she knew she was in this case.

Jack was already seated with a can of soda in front of him when she arrived.

"Nice of you to show," he said.

She scowled at him, but held her tongue.

"I'm kidding you, Magda. Go on, sit down." He got up from the table. "I ordered us each the halibut. You'll love it. What can I get you to drink?"

"Diet something or other."

"One diet something or other coming up."

Early in their marriage there was a time when Jack's little barely funny phrases, his puns that only he got a kick out of—or understood—endeared him to her. Eventually, they started to wear on her—right around the time when Nash began to find them endlessly amusing. In retrospect, Nash was probably just laughing at his dad laughing at his own jokes. But *she* was never the funny one. She could never get Nash to laugh like that.

In the days since he'd left, alone in her bed at night, it was the thought of Jack cracking himself up that would make her smile. That was how she remembered him. That was how she had pictured him.

And despite her annoyance with him now, she found herself smiling like a schoolgirl at his ribbing.

Jack hadn't been kidding about Dick's being on the water. It was literally a small shack atop a series of floating docks that bobbed on the ocean's surface. Magda let herself go with the motion, gazing out at the sailboats on the other side of the cove. She wondered which one might be Jack's. Wondered whether he'd invite her to go sailing with him. They could if they wanted to, wherever and for as long as they felt like. Jack had sold his business the week before, and she didn't work. All they had was time.

Magda didn't let the fact that neither of them sailed, or their pending divorce, stop her daydream. She imagined sunning herself on the deck of a little sailboat, Jack at the helm, the wind blowing through their hair. She imagined catching their own dinner, Jack fixing the fish just the way he always did, while she chopped and diced her way to a scrumptious salad. Then the two of them wrapped in a blanket on the deck, glasses of wine in hand, looking up at a night sky full of stars. They could make love right there, without another soul around. Or down below in the cramped sleeping quarters if the night grew too cold, the lack of room to move dictating their movements, keeping them close. Every day. Every night.

They could dock—if that was what one called it; she'd have to brush up on the language of sailing—in Mexico. Drink margaritas. Dance to a local mariachi band. Stroll the beach arm in arm with the squish of sand beneath their toes. It truly could be a great adventure. If only Jack were one who liked adventure, or margaritas, or even leaving the city limits.

Jack set a Diet Coke in front of her and then walked to the other side of the table, setting on it a traylike contraption with several doughnut-size holes in it, and in them, cone-rolled newspaper containing a mass of fried food—French fries and some sort of fish. Halibut, she believed he had said.

"This is rustic," Magda said.

"This is fish and chips the way it's supposed to be done."

Canada continually surprised Magda with just how British it often seemed, especially Vancouver Island. From the spellings and signage the locals used—*colour* instead of *color*, *flavour* instead of *flavor*—to how kids there called their mothers *Mum*, to Victoria itself, which looked like it had been picked up and transferred from one isle to another. She had never seen a fish fry—because that was what this was, a Wisconsin-style fish fry, just wrapped up differently—packaged so, but apparently this was how they did it overseas, and that apparently made Jack prone to liking it, despite his refusal to ever actually go to Europe.

"I didn't think you liked fish fries." A note of accusation had sneaked into her voice without her intending it to.

In Green Bay, there were two things people did with regularity—Friday fish fries and cheering on the Packers. These were activities so tightly woven into the local social fabric that you couldn't help but partake. If one didn't, it might be easier to move elsewhere. But Magda had rarely been able to get Jack out for a fish fry ("Fried fish?!" he would say, always. "Can you honestly think of anything more disgusting?"), yet here he was, happily sucking down breaded halibut like Long John Silver himself.

"There are a lot of things I didn't know I liked until lately," Jack said.

He tossed two fries into his mouth, brushed his hands together to rid them of salt, and rocked back, kicking his legs up on a spare chair. "So, what now?" he asked, though Magda wasn't sure he wanted an answer. He bit his lower lip, seemingly lost in thought.

She wanted to tell him that she took it back. All of it. "Are you sure we're doing the right thing?" she asked.

Jack nodded, but he didn't look at her. "I need to tell you something," he said. "I'm adopting Glory."

His words hit Magda like a punch. What about her? Why only him? Had he been planning this behind her back?

"Now, don't get all excited," Jack said. "Let me explain." And he did. Glory missed her mom, but after Jack had explained to Glory that because her mother was going to jail, she'd be placed in a foster home in California, she had solemnly agreed to let him adopt her instead.

"I'll still have a mom, though, right?" Glory had said to Jack, and he had told her that she'd have a mom forever and ever, that nothing could change that.

308   ERIN CELELLO

Across from Magda, Jack fiddled with his napkin, folding and unfolding it. Magda didn't like the looks of this. It meant that he didn't know what to say, or how to say it. It meant he was uncomfortable.

"Magda, I really do think we're doing the right thing—for a lot of reasons. But there's one other reason, too, that I haven't told you about."

Magda cocked an eyebrow at him.

"I don't want to leave here. And if we don't get divorced, Glory will end up in foster care."

"That's ridiculous, Jack. Where did you come up with that?"

"It's the law. If we're not divorced, then we *both* have to adopt her. And with us living in different countries, her case would be tied up in administrative international wrangling for years. And in the meantime, she'd be in California's custody."

Magda reeled from the unfairness of it all. Her son and now this. She had prayed hard her whole life. She had gone to church. She had read her Bible.

"It stinks, Magda. I know it does. But the legalities aren't going to change anything at all. It's only a piece of paper—a legal loophole we'll close. You'll be able to see Glory whenever you'd like. You have my word."

Jack's word might as well have been engraved in stone. He didn't make promises lightly. This she knew.

"Do you remember how Nash used to try to race the light?" he asked her.

She remembered it well. Magda had simply meant to share with a six-year-old Nash what she had learned in her astronomy class one night, and mentioned that light traveled at a certain speed. Every night after acquiring that newfound knowledge, when they'd turn on the light in his room at night Nash would try to race it to his bed, dismayed for a good part of his growing up as to why he never won.

Magda laughed. "What about his Superman year?" she asked, which got a big belly laugh from Jack.

"Who could forget!" he said. And he was right. Magda was certain that Nash's kindergarten teacher at Notre Dame as well as their postman and a whole slew of others remembered Nash's fixation with the Superman costume, since it had been the only thing he'd wear that entire year. It showed up in his school picture and their family portraits at both Christmas and Easter, although fortunately, by that last one, they had been able to convince him to at least take the mask off.

"Do you remember the night he wore it into our room?" Magda asked Jack, and they both smiled, thinking about the time when Nash had changed from his pajamas into his costume in the middle of the night, and, backlit by the hallway light, a miniature Superman appeared in their doorway, scaring them half to death. "I forget what a quirky kid he was sometimes. He turned into such a great young man."

"He sure did," Jack said. His face grew solemn. "You did that, Magda."

"We did it together," she answered.

Jack reached across the table and squeezed her hand. How different that simple gesture suddenly felt. It struck Magda as wrong, or at the very least surprisingly intimate. Even though they had shared a bed for the past thirty-plus years, it was as if they had been transformed into strangers with the help of a few legal documents.

"I want it back," Magda said, looking down at their intertwined hands.

"So do I," Jack whispered.

Magda wanted to throw herself at Jack's feet, circle her arms tight around his ankles, and beg him to stay. But she could finally see the Serengeti, the Dead Sea, the Arc de Triomphe, and Christ the Redeemer. She could still be a grandmother to Glory. So much promise had suddenly graced her life, though she couldn't help but mourn the loss of her partnership with Jack—the one person witness to almost her whole life's history.

"We just want different things, Magda," Jack said. "We have for a while now. Hell, maybe we always have. This life we made is too small for us. We hold each other back in all the wrong ways."

Magda nodded. She agreed. She agreed with it all, every last word. But it felt as if she were getting everything she had ever wished for and giving up everything she had ever asked for in one fell swoop. If someone were actually sawing her in two, the agony could not have felt more real.

As if on cue, the sky opened up, pelting them with drops that felt as big as gumballs. Magda reached for the windbreaker she had brought with her and started to tie it like a kerchief, to protect her hair, before thinking better of it. She let the jacket drop to the table. Jack smiled at her knowingly. He motioned for her to come with him toward shelter, but she stayed rooted in place. Magda smiled back at him. Then she closed her eyes, tilted her head back, and let the rain soak her straight through.

In the days that followed, Magda slowly, deliberately went about the business of leaving the island.

She couldn't do it all at once. It was something to be worked up to. And she worked up to it for weeks on end. She meandered the streets of Campbell River, imagining Nash here the whole time. Nash running to the post office. Nash leaving the house when Macy did morning chores to have coffee and perhaps a doughnut at Tim Hortons. Nash picking up milk and eggs and the generic white-cheddar macaroni and cheese from the Thrifty store that he loved so much.

She knew he did these things. But not when. Not how. This boy whom she had carried in her own body and known so well for so long—how he slept, how he ate his cereal, how he'd swing his right leg furiously and aimlessly all at once when he was still too short to reach the ground from her kitchen chairs—she could have given you a list of his idiosyncrasies and traits a mile long. Now? She knew that list would be much, much shorter.

It happened to every mother, she knew. Kids did what they were always supposed to do: They grew up. They grew up and moved out and became people in their own right whose histories you could recall so thoroughly, down to the day or minute, even though you weren't quite sure where they were yesterday or the day before that, or what they were planning to do next week or for their next vacation. She knew this. Yet the thought that she didn't know what Nash's routine had been here, where he went or how he ran errands, the fact that she didn't have a picture of him doing any of these things to recall, or the fact that she could only guess what he got at Tim Hortons and not know what it actually was—these things made it seem as if he had been taken from her all over again.

But trying to remember him here did her good. It connected her to him in a way she hadn't expected. As did the truce she seemed to have formed with Macy.

She hadn't been asked to come to Macy's for dinner. The day after her lunch with Jack at Dick's, she simply showed up early with some crab fresh off the boat that someone had been selling behind Discovery Pier, a bottle of white wine, and some bakery bread. Finding Magda on her front step with these items, Macy hadn't said anything to her. But that meant, too, that she hadn't said anything snide to her, and so she followed Macy inside, unloaded her groceries, and the two of them commenced cooking dinner in silence. Macy drank a bottle of Kokanee; Magda sipped some of the wine, using a splash here or there for the crab. Together their chopping, cracking, and sizzling formed a quiet, comfortable symphony to which they worked. And that evening, as conversation whirled around them at dinner, Macy raised her can of beer and nodded at Magda, who touched her own wineglass to it. *To the cooks*, Macy seemed to say. *To us*, Magda thought. No one else had even noticed, but it was a start.

The days that followed seemed to zoom by. She and Jack spent most waking moments with Glory, taking her to see a matinee, or Putt-Putt golfing, or for ice cream. Some afternoons they would head to the beach, sometimes Miracle Beach and sometimes Stories Beach, where they'd snack on the picnic lunch Magda packed and look for impossibly vibrant starfish in purples and blues, or for seashells. And in the midst of these activities, Magda found herself marveling at how all of it was real. That her life had taken such a turn.

Those moments ran together until Magda found herself counting the hours, not days, until she had to leave. She had woken too early, though. So here she was, driving aimlessly along the shoreline of a place where she didn't belong, where her husband did, and where their son no longer was. *Was*—such a strange word. *Was* and *when*. Every single moment of her life to that point could be attributed to one or the other. Now she was caught in the middle, waiting.

Magda had had Tim Hortons in hand by seven a.m., and as she approached Stories Beach, she slowed and pulled to the shoulder. She located a spot on the beach, now obscured by the tide that had come in, and thought of the previous night—her on one side of the fire that Jack had built and Glory and Jack on the other, singing "The Banana Boat Song," Glory punctuating many of the lines with giggles. And Magda knew then that as much as she might want to take them back to Wisconsin with her—and with all her heart she did—it was a selfish want. Jack and Glory needed to be here for their own separate reasons, but they still needed to be here, together. Eventually, she would find her own place with them. Of that Magda was confident.

Without thinking, Magda put the car into drive and turned up a road to the right, just past the stretch of rocky beach. She kept on driving, out into the country, which was where she came upon an unattended produce stand with a hand-painted sign advertising bell peppers, corn, and rhubarb.

She had plenty of time. And so she stopped, dropped four loonies in the wooden piggybank fixed to the signpost, and scooped up a handful of sorry-looking rhubarb stalks, even though she knew that they were likely the dregs of this year's crop.

As expected, the house sat empty. Even though there was a note taped to the door from Macy saying that she should let herself in, Magda knocked anyway.

She didn't have time to waste, so Magda immediately turned the oven to 425 degrees, even before she had set down the few groceries she had brought in with her—the rhubarb, butter, and a jar of cloves. She figured Macy wouldn't mind her borrowing a little flour, sugar, and salt.

Magda worked on the crust first, careful to cut the shortening into the flour as fast as she could. This was the key to a good crust: not taking so long to meld the flour and lard that the latter started to soften. When the mixture beaded into pea-size chunks, she dripped water into it a tablespoon at a time, adding just enough to bring it together. Usually, it was less than any recipe prescribed. Then she separated the batch into two pieces, wrapped each in waxed paper, and set both balls of dough in the freezer. She hadn't ever tried cooling her dough on the quick before, but she said a small prayer asking God to help her out, just this once, and that she'd follow the recipe as it was supposed to be followed from here on out whenever she made it again. If she made it again.

Next she set to chopping the rhubarb. She had always found chopping to be satisfying work, and as the family's main baker, she had never gotten to do enough of it. Jack, with his marinades and meats and grilling—he got the satisfying jobs: dicing onions, crushing garlic, slicing mushrooms. She wondered if he knew how lucky he was to have that much knifework to do. Like all things, though, Magda figured, you tended to appreciate those that came around less often.

Magda slid the squares of rhubarb from the cutting board into a waiting bowl. A door slammed. Magda jumped.

"I'm sorry. Didn't mean to frighten you." Sophie appeared in the doorway to the kitchen.

Magda smiled at her: thin, not toothy. "No bother," she said. Then she added, "No one's here."

"I figured. But Glory needed to run off some energy, and I'm so close to that dang water that I end up having to watch her every second. So we decided she could come play in the woods up here."

Magda nodded. She had met Sophie just once since their first encounter that night on the back porch, now glazed with sun.

"Want some help?"

"That's okay," Magda said. "It's pretty much a one-person job." This wasn't true—she had enlisted Nash for help with this very same process many, many times—but it could have been. And truth be told, today this needed to be her project—hers alone.

"Pie?" Sophie asked.

Again Magda nodded. She checked the dough in the freezer, called it good enough. She sprinkled a dusting of flour on the countertop, a little more on the dough, and ran a floury hand over the rolling pin. Then she set to work, rolling the pin first vertically, and then horizontally, until the crust flattened, evening out into a rough circle.

Sophie had wandered to the opposite side of the island from where Magda stood. She tipped the steel bowl toward her, took a whiff. "Rhubarb?" she asked, furrowing her brow. "Bit late in the season for that, no?"

"I suppose so," Magda said. She continued her rhythm without a hitch: Up one, down one. Across one, back one. Repeat. "The farm up the road had some dregs for sale. Figured I'd try, and see if it would work."

"I was always afraid of cooking with it, because of the poisonous leaves and all. Guess I should've given it a chance," Sophie said. "But maybe this is a good time to leave you to your cooking." She dismounted the stool that she had just hoisted herself up on not a minute before, pushing it back under the counter. "It's been nice meeting you, Magda. Really nice. I hope you have a safe trip back."

Magda remembered the night she had arrived, to Sophie's hand on Jack's knee. She had seen other gestures pass between them in the days that followed. She had seen the way Jack looked at Sophie. None of it had been obvious, and she could sense that nothing had happened between them, but she suspected things wouldn't continue that way. The thought of Jack falling for someone else pinched at Magda when it should have felt like being stabbed. She suspected it had something to do with the fact that Jack and Sophie themselves seemed oblivious to what was happening.

Sophie had nearly cleared the doorway leading from the kitchen to the living room and, beyond that, the back entryway, before Magda called out, "I guess I could use a little help."

Sophie poked her head back through the kitchen doorway like a question.

"I don't know if I'm going to finish in time," Magda said.

"No problem. Let me wash my hands, and then you can tell me what to do."

When Sophie returned from the sink, Magda instructed her on the proper combination of the sugar, spices, and cornstarch. She told her how to stir the mixture to best distribute the spices and cornstarch—in a folding motion, not a beating one. She explained to Sophie that if she were at home, she'd take one of those turkey-cooking bags and place the whole kit and caboodle right in there, and toss it as if it were Shake 'n Bake chicken, so as to get the best, most even coating on the pieces of rhubarb. Magda told her that she might want to add a little vanilla and brown sugar, too, if that was something Sophie thought she'd like. And she warned her about doing all that—the mixing of the pie innards—too early. She told Sophie her best-kept, most closely guarded secret: about how the sugar leached too much water out of the rhubarb if you didn't wait to combine the pie innards until right before the crust was ready.

Sophie did as Magda instructed. Meanwhile, Magda worked

at making the lattice topping for the pie. When she had all of the lattice strips cut, she cued Sophie to pour the filling into the waiting pie tin.

"This isn't just for show," Magda said, nodding at the strips of dough. "Rhubarb retains a lot of water, and when it cooks, all that liquid needs someplace to go. A full crust top won't allow that to happen, but a lattice crust will. Plus, if you do it right, it sure looks pretty. Not surprisingly, Macy doesn't have a pastry wheel, so it won't be as pretty as it could be."

Magda thought back. When they were first married, and Jack had suggested they plant rhubarb in their measly garden patch, Magda had been first surprised, and then unnerved, by its bounty. And so she had started experimenting, trying to find the very, very best rhubarb pie recipe she could. Because really, what choice did she have? But it became her thing. She even won a "County's Best" contest at the Brown County Fair, and she brought in top dollar with this very same recipe in the baked-goods auction at Nash's school. Magda's rhubarb pie recipe reputation preceded her.

And now, as she showed Sophie how to make the lattice topping, placing five strips of dough horizontally at even intervals across the pie, she wondered if this might be her last one.

"You fold the first, third, and fifth strips back to the edge and lay one strip of dough vertically across the horizontal strips. Then fold the first, third, and fifth horizontal strips back, then fold the second and fourth strips back to the first vertical strip. Really, you're just weaving these pieces," she said. "Then lay a second vertical strip an equal distance from the first one. Fold the second and fourth strips back. Do the same thing with the final strips." She talked to keep her thoughts corralled, to not let them go where they seemed so desperately to want to go. And despite her best efforts, a couple wayward tears escaped Magda's eye. They fell onto one of the lattice pieces yet to be assembled, and she brushed her thumb over the wet, hoping Sophie hadn't noticed.

With the pie in the oven and dishes washed and drying in the sink, Sophie excused herself for a second time that morning.

"Take care now," she said, having said most everything else once before.

"You too," Magda said.

They nodded at each other. Magda surveyed the distance between them. Usually, she tended toward hugging, but this didn't seem like the proper situation for that gesture.

"Well, then," Sophie said. She started around the kitchen table toward the back door, giving a little wave as she went.

"Sophie?" Magda called. Sophie hesitated and looked back. "Rhubarb is Jack's favorite. Only pie he likes. One small dollop of Cool Whip on top."

Sophie nodded, a faint smile playing at the corner of her mouth. "I'll remember that," she said.

Outside the security checkpoint at Campbell River's airport, Magda looked at Glory and bent to kiss her cheek. She straightened and looked at Jack, unsure what to do with him, what to say.

"So," she said.

"So," he replied.

It was like a bad movie script. But those seemed to be the only words they had left.

She thought of the pie cooling on Macy's kitchen counter, the simple note she had laid on top of it, and her breath knotted in her throat. "I should go," she said.

Magda placed her carry-on and purse in two separate bins and removed her sandals, placing those in another bin. She stole a glance at Jack, standing with Glory in front of him, a hand on each of her bony shoulders. He looked somber, and for that, Magda was grateful. No smile on his lips to suggest he was happy that she would be gone in a few minutes. No tears in his eyes that would surely set Magda off on the same path. Even, as always. Just-right Jack, she thought, conjuring up what she had privately, fondly called him for as long as she could remember.

But Glory was not so composed. Try as she might to prevent it, her whole body hiccuped and her face was slicked wet. Magda saw Jack bend down and whisper something in Glory's ear, saw Glory turn her face up to Jack in a question. And just as Magda handed her boarding documents to the security officer, she felt a pair of arms wrap tight around her hips.

Glory buried her head into Magda's waist. "Don't go," she said, and Magda felt her insides go straight to mush.

She extricated herself from Glory and knelt down in front of the girl. "What's wrong, honey?"

"I don't know," Glory croaked.

Magda brushed the back of her hand over her granddaughter's wet cheeks. Her granddaughter. She was still trying to get used to what that meant, to really believe it. "What's going on here?" she asked, fingering a single, rolling tear.

"My eyes are leaking," Glory said. The girl fixed her eyes on Magda. She chewed on her lower lip.

"I'm going to miss you," Magda said. She tapped a finger on Glory's nose for emphasis.

She thought of all the moments with Glory she wouldn't be there for, and that thought made her ache all over. It was, she realized, more painful than when she thought there would never be a Glory in her life at all. She hugged the girl's waif of a body tight against her chest.

"Then don't go."

"I have to go. I have a trip to take, you know. I'll send you a postcard from every place I stop. And then, when I get back, you can come see me in Green Bay. I'll take you to the zoo, and we'll go to a Packers game. How about that?"

"You can, though," Glory said. "You don't have to take your trip. I want you to stay here with us."

"My sweet Glory," Magda said, shaking her head. "I love you to pieces. You know that, don't you?"

"Ma'am, it's time." The security agent stood over Magda and tapped her on the shoulder. "Everyone's boarding."

"Can I please get a smile before I go?" Magda said. She hooked a finger under the girl's chin. "I want to remember this little face as a happy one."

Despite her cheeks still running slick, Glory fixed Magda with a brave, giant grin, her upper lip trembling. "It's time," Glory said.

Epilogue

FALL HAD SETTLED IN FOR GOOD. ALTHOUGH BY AFTERNOON on most days the dense morning fog baked off nicely, there was no mistaking the now-bony tree branches that crawled like veins against the inside of a brooding sky, or the scattering of leaves they planted in yards, ditches, and forest floors throughout the island.

On Martine's advice, Macy had put her show schedule on hold until the following summer, even though she and Gounda had both made a full recovery. "The Talent Squad will be there again next year, and the year after that," he had said. "It is more important that you start over on the right leg."

Martine had been completing a program in equine experiential learning, and the extra time that Macy's new schedule allowed him was put to good use in perfecting his coursework and approach. Martine still came every Wednesday, but often Macy wouldn't even saddle up. Sometimes she and Martine would just sit in the center of one of the paddocks for one hour, two hours at a time, and Martine would tell her to breathe and clear her mind and allow her inner self to connect with the horses.

"You have to give to them, listen to them. It is not always about taking, taking, taking," he told her, both of them sitting cross-legged on a knoll in the pasture's knee-high grass. "You must ask what message the horse would like to send to your heart," he said.

"This is hocus-pocus shit," Macy had complained to Martine during their first session. Lately, though, she had secretly come to enjoy their times together.

And she thought that maybe, just maybe, they might have actually begun to work a little bit of magic on her.

Glory and Macy had settled into a delicate dance of getting to know each other, and Glory seemed to somehow know all the steps. She didn't call Macy "Mom." She didn't tell Macy she loved her. She didn't try to hug Macy or clamor for her attention. She never tried to substitute this new life for her old one. Glory seemed to know that it was different. No better, no worse. Just different.

And the days of that dance were tightly choreographed. Each weekend morning, they would clean stalls, pick hooves, and rotate horses between the barn and the paddocks, Glory working right alongside Macy. The girl never complained. Even more impressive, she remembered everything Macy told her the very first time: how to put a halter on, which horses belonged in which stalls, which horses got a flake of hay at lunchtime and which didn't.

"You're a regular barn hand savant," Macy muttered one day.

"What's that?" Glory had asked.

"Never mind," Macy said.

"Is it a good thing, though?"

"Yeah." Macy nodded, smiling. "It's good."

Glory had beamed then, and every once in a while, when

they were cleaning stalls on opposite sides of the aisleway, Macy would look up and Glory would be staring at her, that dumb-happy smile creeping across her face, a pitchfork full of shit balanced unsteadily in her hands. And Macy would think then that she should really get to work on painting the spare room down the hall from hers a nice, pale shade of pink.

The deal, when Macy bought Moses, was that Glory had to work if Moses came to live with them. She had to learn how to take care of him all by herself. No one had ever saddled Macy's horses for her, Macy told Glory, no one had ever wrapped her horses' legs or picked out their feet for her, and Macy wouldn't do it for Glory, either. "That's the only way you learn," she told Glory.

So on the way to pick up Moses, Macy pulled into Riverbend Tack and Hay just outside of Nanaimo and bought an extra-tall mounting block for Glory—a pink one, at Glory's request. When Jack came the following weekend, as promised, he attached wheels to the mounting block—the kind that locked in place—and a short rope handle, so that Glory could haul it all by herself from one end of the barn to the other.

Macy had been skeptical about Moses. He was blind in one eye, he'd been half starved to death, and his front legs were a mess of proud flesh from when he had wrapped himself in a barbed-wire fence. But a friend of hers had rescued him and had spent the past year putting some weight on him, and she insisted that if he didn't work out for any reason, she'd happily take him back. In any case, it was worth a try. Glory couldn't ride Gounda because of the sheer size of him, compared to her, and she couldn't ride any of the others because they were just plain dangerous—not beginner horses by any means.

Besides, Glory was positively dying to learn to ride, badgering Macy over and over about how it might be time for her to learn. Macy had made the mistake once of saying that it was because Glory wasn't quite big enough yet, which resulted in daily updates from Glory on how she had grown an eighth of an inch or put on a half a pound. Macy had watched the girl down three and a half hamburgers only a few nights before in an attempt to "be bigger," and wondered how much an eight-year-old could put away before actually exploding—something she didn't care to be personally responsible for.

So Moses it was.

Macy was right to worry about Moses. He nearly jumped out of his skin whenever she opened the garage-style door at the end of the barn. He'd bolt to the back corner of his stall when she threw him a flake of hay. But with Glory around he turned into a kinder, gentler horse. For that little girl and her noisy, rolling, hot-pink mounting block, he'd stand rock solid, even though the whites of his eyes would show like crescent moons against his dapple-gray face. Even though he looked like he was crawling with fear on the inside.

"You get Moses ready," Macy told Glory, who had stacked brushes, her saddle, and a bridle atop her mounting block and was wheeling it down the aisle. "I'll meet you outside."

Sophie and Jack were already waiting by the outdoor arena. Sophie with her thermos of green tea, Jack with his supersize travel mug of coffee. They had each given up their respective Saturday-morning rituals to watch Glory ride Moses for the very first time.

Macy started out by leading Glory around the arena on Moses. She told her to stroke his neck right above his withers, right where mares nuzzled their foals, to calm him. She showed her how to sit up and sit back in the saddle, how to gently pressure his sides with her calves instead of digging her heels into his sides. Little by little, Macy let out the lounge line until Glory and Moses were nearly rounding the circumference of the riding arena.

"Ready to do a little more?" Macy asked. Glory nodded. Her hands gripped the pommel of the saddle, her eyes fixed straight ahead, right through Moses's ears, as Macy had told her; she was concentrating hard.

Then Macy gave a quiet, staccato series of clucks, and Moses eased himself into a gentle trot, seemingly well aware of the first-timer on his back.

Macy had never seen a girl so unafraid, almost reckless—hadn't ever seen one meld with a horse's back that easily, that naturally. It was as if her butt and legs had been glued to the saddle. Moses's legs moved in pairs with long, lithe sweeps. *Bamp—bamp—bamp—bamp.* His hooves struck the ground like a snare drum. He was in no hurry.

"You hear that?" Macy called to Glory. She slapped out a rhythm that matched Moses's trot with the palm of her right hand against her leg. Glory nodded. "Well, you can't just *hear* it," Macy said. "You have to *feel* it, with your body. With your whole body." Glory nodded again. "I've got Moses," Macy told her. "What I want you to do is close your eyes when you're ready, so you can feel it. I won't let Moses go anywhere." Before Macy had even finished speaking, Glory had squeezed her eyes shut and pointed her chin defiantly to the sky.

Macy saw Glory drop the reins then, and watched as the girl raised her skinny arms, bit by bit, like a fledgling taking off for the first time, until they were straight out to her sides. A pan-icked "Noooo!" rose from Macy's stomach up to her throat, but just before it found air to sail out on, she swallowed it back down. Glory was a long way from being experienced enough to do horseback ballet, but Moses hadn't even noticed. He kept up his one-two beat, wholly unconcerned about the little blond bird fixed to his back.

When Macy finally slowed Moses to a stop, Glory lowered her arms and opened her eyes, looking straight at Macy, that same dumb-happy smile splashed across her face.

And there was Jack, one arm slung loosely around Sophie's shoulders, the other clapping one-handed against his thigh. And there was Sophie with her hands clasped in front of her chin like a young child praying. There was Moses, contentedly licking his lips, and Glory on top of him, now bent over his thick neck and trying to stretch her arms clear around it.

Macy stood absolutely still, her breath catching in her throat.

And all around them the trees stood witness, as still as ghosts.

ACKNOWLEDGMENTS

I OWE SO MUCH TO SO MANY THAT IT'S HARD TO EVEN KNOW where to start. So I'll start at the beginning: To Kyoko Mori for fostering in me the very first sense that this writing thing might actually be something worth doing. To Northern Michigan University's MFA program and my cohorts there who saw the very first, rudimentary versions of this book and encouraged me to keep going with it anyway; but especially to Ron Johnson and Katie Myers Hanson, without whose encouragement the manuscript would have never seen a thesis committee, much less publication. To one of my best friends and former roommates, Stolze, who kept me plied during the writing of that very first draft with supportive words and cheap red wine and had faith in this story long before I did.

Much of this book was initially written where it is set—overlooking the gorgeous Strait of Georgia—and I'd be remiss not to thank the Cockburns and all the fantastic people of Campbell River for welcoming me to your beautiful part of the world, your homes, and your lives during the summers I spent on Vancouver Island.

A big thank you to fellow Inkwellians Marysa, Carrie, Nick, and Maggie; and a special thanks to Dean Bakopolous for your sage and always generous advice; and to Theresa Roetter for your expertise. To Angela James and to Sandy, Mel, and Anson Kaye for your valuable feedback—but moreover, just for being you. To Andrea Somberg and Ellen Edwards for your patience, time, patience, guidance, patience, and vision (and did I mention patience?) in making this a better book than I ever imagined possible.

To my family, whom there are not enough superlatives in the English language to describe: I love you all so very much, and this book is as much yours as it is mine. Your love and support mean everything to me. You mean everything to me.

And finally, to my Chief of Stuff, without whom any of this would hardly be possible. You are my sun, my rock, my North Star, my best cheerleader/friend/critic, my muse. (Cliché? Perhaps. But also so very true.) How did I get so lucky? To borrow your own words, "What a world." I'm so glad you decided to stick around.

Erin Celello was born in Michigan's Upper Peninsula, where she also earned an MFA in fiction from Northern Michigan University. She now lives in Madison, Wisconsin, with her husband and two unruly Vizslas who have somehow trained her to let them sleep under the covers. When not writing or spending time with her favorite boys, Erin can almost always be found at the barn or competing with her American Quarter Horse, Gino (a.k.a. the Ironman), training for triathlons and marathons, or cooking. *Miracle Beach* is her first novel. Please visit her at erincelello.com.

MIRACLE BEACH

· ERIN CELELLO ·

*This Conversation Guide is intended to enrich the
individual reading experience, as well as encourage us
to explore these topics together—because books,
and life, are meant for sharing.*

A CONVERSATION WITH ERIN CELELLO

Q. What inspired you to write Miracle Beach? *How did the novel evolve?*

A. This novel started as a writing exercise, as a nonfiction short-short, that I wrote while working toward my MFA. Around that time, both of my grandfathers had passed away, and I thought of the moments before each of my grandmothers had to put the key in the lock of houses that they now lived in alone. What a heartbreaking, surreal stretch of time that must have been for them. When I, and probably most people, think about loss, those aren't the moments that come to mind. I wanted to delve into them in an attempt to understand, even a little, the experience of loss more fully.

I hadn't written fiction before—unless you count a story about a horse and a girl that I wrote and illustrated when I was nine and one other truly awful short-story attempt in high school that, fortunately, I don't think anyone ever saw (and if anyone did I hope they just plead ignorance). Anyway, I found that I couldn't make the exercise work as nonfiction, and so I fictionalized it. And then I simply kept asking, "What next?" Incredibly, an entire novel evolved.

To this day, when I read the scene where Macy is going home

for the first time after Nash's funeral, in my mind the house I picture her entering is not hers, but my grandmother's.

Q. *You chose to write in revolving third-person points of view, giving chapters to Macy, Magda, and Jack. Why not just pick one of them? What do you think the revolving points of view add to the story?*

A. Pick one? If my agent and editor would have let me, every character who appeared would have had his or her own chapter. Okay, not really (although Glory and Sophie did each have their own points of view for a brief time), but I do think that the story is richer for having multiple points of view, because no one experiences loss in exactly the same way. In this novel, we see Nash through the eyes of the three people who loved him most, but they each deal with his death very differently, because each had very different relationships with Nash. Only through examining each of those relationships are we able to get a more complete picture of who he was, and who he was to those who loved him.

Q. *Which of the characters is most like you?*

A. I suppose I carry little parts of each of them in me. Like Macy, I love nothing more than spending time with my horse, because when I'm at the barn all the worries or stress I might have simply melts away. I'm laid-back like Jack. And I share Sophie's love of the outdoors and Magda's loathing of socks and shoes.

Some members of my family are convinced that the characters are modeled after specific people (namely, them), but that couldn't be further from the truth. In my mind, they are all very much their own people who have their own distinct features, likes, dislikes, and mannerisms. None of the characters are even composites of any real people I know. I got to know these characters slowly with each passing page and with each new draft, much like the development of a real-life friendship or relationship. They each told me who they were.

I've heard other authors say something similar, so I'll admit to this, too, even though it sounds crazy: Over the years, these characters have become so real to me that I often think of them existing outside of my imagination or this book. I picture them going about their lives in Green Bay or Campbell River, and would half expect to run into them on the street in either of those places.

Q. Which is your favorite character? Which was easiest to write about? Which was hardest?

A. Picking a favorite character is, I imagine, a lot like asking parents to pick a favorite child. I don't love each of them equally, but I am attached to each character in a different way. That said, I would have to single out Glory. The story takes on a new light, a new energy, when she appears. Without Glory, these characters would be muddling through this terrible loss, together yet alone. Glory is the glue that binds them together and gives them perspective. Plus I, for one, think she's an absolute hoot.

Because of Glory's childlike innocence and directness, she

was probably also the easiest character to write. Her voice came through loud and clear every time. The two hardest characters were Macy and Magda, because it seemed that even though I understood—and very much liked—them both, on the page their behavior could be off-putting. I had to really work at showing their full range of emotions and personality so that hopefully readers would come to see them as I do—as good, kind women who are struggling through a rough spot in their respective lives. I think all of us would likely not want the world to see our inner thoughts and private actions at the lowest points of our lives, yet this is how we see Magda and Macy. They're sad, angry, and raw, and dealing with a profound loss in very different, but very human, ways. Yet they both push through to the other side of that loss and emerge with new perspectives, better understandings, and a peace that neither had before. In that way, Magda and Macy were difficult to write, but the most rewarding characters to watch develop.

Q. *What kind of research did you have to do in writing* Miracle Beach?

A. The old adage "write what you know" definitely applies in this case. Like Macy, I have always been a girl in love with horses and have competed at the state and national levels since I was very young. I ride hunters, not jumpers, and I'm not even close to being as accomplished an equestrienne as Macy, but I've been immersed in horses for more years of my life than not, and I had a great deal of fun immersing myself in horses on the page as well.

Q. You were born and raised in the Midwest. How did you decide to set the majority of the novel on British Columbia's Vancouver Island?

A. I was fortunate enough to spend several summers living in Campbell River, which is a real, incredible, and hauntingly beautiful place. In fact, a good chunk of *Miracle Beach* was written there, from a porch that overlooked the Strait of Georgia and the mountains beyond.

While the book is fiction, and while I took certain liberties with locations and events, I've tried to capture the spirit of Vancouver Island and convey its uniqueness, though I doubt I've even scratched the surface. I always looked forward to traveling there, and was always sad to leave. I haven't been back in years, but a piece of my heart will always remain there. It is a truly spectacular corner of the world.

Q. This is your debut novel. Can you talk about how you came to be a writer?

A. Lorrie Moore starts her short story "How to Become a Writer" by saying, "First, try to be something, anything, else." I want Ms. Moore and her narrator to know that I attempted to heed that advice. I really did. I switched majors several times in college before settling on English, and even then I applied to law school, thinking that was the most rational route for an English major to take. But on a lark I checked out Northern Michigan University's MFA program and applied, and on an even bigger lark, they let me in.

When I look back, though, I've always been writing. I journaled growing up, wrote for the student newspaper in college, freelanced for a newspaper and small magazines throughout college and graduate school and beyond, and afterward was lucky enough to land a job writing speeches for a sitting governor.

Although I feel fortunate that my debut novel is also my first novel, it was preceded by a lot of fantastically bad poetry and took nearly a decade to finish. I'm happy to have both behind me.

Q. Do you have any writing rituals? What is your writing process?

A. I used to think of myself as a fraud, that I wasn't a "real writer" because I didn't write every day. I would think obsessively about what I needed to write and then do anything but—cook, run, read, run, and cook some more—until, after days or weeks or sometimes months had passed, I couldn't help but sit down at my computer and start typing. It was like a dam bursting.

Then at a conference one year, an author who used the same avoidance technique I did said she had gone to a therapist to figure out why she couldn't nail down a writing process. The therapist told her, "But that *is* your process." A lightbulb went off for me. I instantly felt better about myself as a writer. I started writing more, and more regularly.

These days I no longer wait for my muse to tap me on the shoulder like I once did. Instead, I've learned to sit down and work anyway, whether she shows up or not. And I've learned how much I can accomplish by stealing snippets of time—an hour here, a half hour there.

As for rituals, that word sounds so definite. So set in stone. And I'm not prone to any sort of rigidity or big decisions. This is probably why I write on a laptop that I can, and do, take anywhere when the mood strikes. I avoid writing at a desk, and opt instead for big, comfy, overstuffed places full of pillows and warmth. Preferably, especially in the cold months, there's a fireplace. And usually there will be a cup of coffee or tea nearby if it's early, or a glass of red wine if the day is marching toward evening, when I tend to do my best thinking and writing. And a dog. There's almost always at least one dog curled up next to me, fast asleep.

Q. You mention Lorrie Moore, a fellow Wisconsin author. What other authors do you like to read? Who has influenced you?

A. I've always been a voracious reader. On vacation when we were young, my sister took to calling me "the Mute," because she liked to talk almost as much as I liked to read, and as you might imagine, we didn't make very good travel companions. I used to read almost anything I could get my hands on, though in later years, I've gotten more selective. My husband recently pointed out that there is a finite amount of time that one has to read a seemingly infinite number of books, so I've started to make tough choices. A book has to really engage me or add something to my knowledge of craft or the world. If it doesn't do one of those things, I put it down.

With respect to fiction, I tend to gravitate toward quieter

books that explore the relationships between people and their choices, books that pose interesting "what if" questions and then go about answering them, books that deepen the understanding of what it means to be alive—to be human. I'm going to refrain from listing any specific books that I've loved or ones that have influenced me, because once I start, I'm honestly afraid that I wouldn't be able to stop.

When I'm writing (which is, if I'm being honest, a great majority of the time), I choose books that I wish I could have written, either for the language or the voice or the plotting, because there's always something to learn; there's always something that someone else does better. During the writing process, I also read a lot of contemporary poetry—poets such as Pablo Neruda, Thomas Lux, Billy Collins, and a new, recent discovery: Martín Espada (another Wisconsin connection!)—in order to jump-start my creative juices. Poetry never fails to dig me out of a writing rut and prod me into varying my language and trying new things. I also read a lot of Raymond Carver, because few, if any, authors are able to elicit such powerful emotion with such economy of words as Carver. And also because I tend in exactly the opposite direction if left to my own devices.

Q. After working on Miracle Beach *for so long, is it hard to let it go? Are you working on anything now? What is up next for you?*

A. Libba Bray wrote a fantastic blog post a couple years ago called "Writing a Novel, a Love Story," in which she parallels the arc of a romantic relationship with writing a novel. One of the last phases, "Final Draft," describes an "it's not you—it's me" sort of breakup an author often has with a novel by the end. I was stuck in that phase for a good long time, and after working on this novel on and off for nearly ten years, I thought I'd be overjoyed to have it "completed." I didn't understand authors who talked about grieving a bit through the publishing process. Suddenly, though, I do. It's all so final, and I'm going to miss the world of *Miracle Beach*. But, as Glory says at the end of the novel, "It's time."

I'm now hard at work on my second novel, which I've promised my editor won't take nearly as long to write as *Miracle Beach*. Which is good, because it's due out next year. I hope to follow that with a third, fourth, and fifth . . . and so on. Most people dream of winning the lottery; I get to sit down every day and write stories. I've already won.

QUESTIONS
FOR DISCUSSION

1. Discuss the novel's title, *Miracle Beach*, and the First Nations legend that Sophie tells Jack about how the beach got its name. What does the legend have to do with a miracle? Is the title fitting for this book, and the lives of Macy, Jack, Magda, and Glory?

2. Discuss the novel's setting. What role does it play in the story, and in each character's life? Is it significant? If so, why? If not, why not?

3. Have you ever witnessed a death, lived through the death of a person close to you, or watched a friend or relative cope with grief? How do your experiences compare to Macy's, Jack's, or Magda's? How does each of the characters handle grief? Is there a right or wrong way to grieve?

4. What would you do if you found yourself in Macy's, Jack's, or Magda's situation? Which of their choices do you think are good ones and which are not so wise?

5. Daughter-in-law/father-in-law/mother-in-law relationships weave through the novel. Which are the most complex? Which are the most comfortable?